PRAISE FOR

For One Night Only

"Jessica James bursts onto the stage with *For One Night Only*, a sensational debut about first love, heartbreak, and getting your second chance while the whole world's watching. Valerie and Caleb's journey back to their music—and back to each other—had me grinning and kicking my feet 'til the very last note."

—Jenna Levine, *USA Today* bestselling author of *Road Trip with a Vampire*

"Jessica James's rocking debut, *For One Night Only*, will have you in your happily-ever-after era. Exes and former bandmates Valerie and Caleb fake-date in perfect harmony, finally free to explore their old feelings and unspoken regrets. They light a spark on the page as much as they would if they were really onstage."

—Jennifer Hennessy, author of *Degrees of Engagement*

"Get ready for the Glitter Bats to rock your world! With sizzling chemistry and a gripping second-chance romance that hooks you from the very first note, Jessica James has that unmistakable electric touch."

—K. M. Enright, author of *Mistress of Lies*

"Move over Taylor Swift—Valerie Quinn's journey to reclaim her reputation and her true love is pitch-perfect! *For One Night Only* is an edgy, steamy romp right for anyone who likes a little backstage drama alongside their fizzy romance."

—Timothy Janovsky, author of *Once Upon You and Me*

"If you've ever wished for a rom-com version of *Daisy Jones & the Six*, Jessica James's sparkling debut, *For One Night Only*, is everything you're looking for! Set in the world of punk pop, the book's cool vibes, music industry intrigue, and its captivating look at the trials and tribulations of chasing your rising star will have you hooked from the first page. Valerie and Caleb steal the spotlight on and off the stage, and their swoony second-chance romance will have readers screaming for an encore."

—Jenny L. Howe, author of *How to Get a Life in Ten Dates*

"Fans of Ava Wilder and *Daisy Jones & the Six* will adore this sexy, starry-eyed thrill of a romance! Jessica James wields both the celebrity fake-dating and exes-to-lovers tropes with imagination and expertise, leaving readers breathless and cheering for Valerie and Caleb's immensely satisfying happily ever after. Nostalgic and heartfelt with all the rush of a stadium anthem, *For One Night Only* is a sparkling debut worthy of a world tour. I'm a Glitterbug for life!"

—Courtney Kae, author of *In the Case of Heartbreak*

"*Julie and the Phantoms* meets *Daisy Jones & the Six* in James's glittery, glorious debut."

—Paste

"*For One Night Only* is the ultimate romance for music lovers."

—Culturess

"This second-chance romance between exes who are also estranged former bandmates was so sexy and compelling."

—Smart Bitches, Trashy Books

"*For One Night Only* is clever, immersive, and tons of fun. James conveys the story through both Caleb's and Valerie's points of view, as well as through extracts from Glitter Bats fan forums, news articles, and tweets. Perfect for fans of second-chance romances or celebrity encounters, *For One Night Only* is a sneak peek into a glamorous world and a sexy, tumultuous relationship."

—Shelf Awareness

"A lyrical dual-POV romance debut that's perfect for readers who enjoy elements of oral and print storytelling devices, such as in *Daisy Jones & the Six* by Taylor Jenkins Reid, but crave a happily ever after too."

—*Library Journal*

"A steamy second-chance romance full of behind-the-scenes music drama."

—*Kirkus Reviews*

"James's passion for music shines in her cute second-chance romance debut."

—*Publishers Weekly*

✦ TITLES BY JESSICA JAMES ✦

GLITTER BATS

For One Night Only
For Our Next Song

Glitter
Bats

For Our Next Song

A *Glitter Bats* BOOK

JESSICA JAMES

Berkley Romance
NEW YORK

BERKLEY ROMANCE
Published by Berkley
An imprint of Penguin Random House LLC
1745 Broadway, New York, NY 10019
penguinrandomhouse.com

Book design by Daniel Brount
Interior art: Keyboard and drums © Lemon Workshop Design/Shutterstock.com

Library of Congress Cataloging-in-Publication Data

Names: James, Jessica, 1961- author
Title: For our next song / Jessica James.
Description: First edition. | New York : Berkley Romance, 2026. | Series: Glitter Bats
Identifiers: LCCN 2025015216 (print) | LCCN 2025015217 (ebook) |
ISBN 9780593817735 trade paperback | ISBN 9780593817742 ebook
Subjects: LCGFT: Fiction | Romance fiction | Lesbian fiction | Novels
Classification: LCC PS3610.A4425 F67 2025 (print) |
LCC PS3610.A4425 (ebook) | DDC 813/.6—dc23/eng/20250626
LC record available at https://lccn.loc.gov/2025015216
LC ebook record available at https://lccn.loc.gov/2025015217

First Edition: January 2026

Printed in the United States of America
1st Printing

The authorized representative in the EU for product safety and compliance is Penguin Random House Ireland, Morrison Chambers, 32 Nassau Street, Dublin D02 YH68, Ireland, https://eu-contact.penguin.ie.

To my dear writing group, the Guillotines—for making me a better writer, sticking by my side through every high and low of this journey, and becoming a found family through it all.

AUTHOR'S NOTE

For Our Next Song deals with emotionally difficult topics, including religious trauma, emotional and spiritual abuse, homophobia, biphobia, and forced public outing of a character, and contains a brief depiction of sexual harassment. Any readers who believe that such content may upset them or trigger traumatic memories are encouraged to consider their emotional well-being when deciding whether to continue reading this book.

For Our Next Song

1

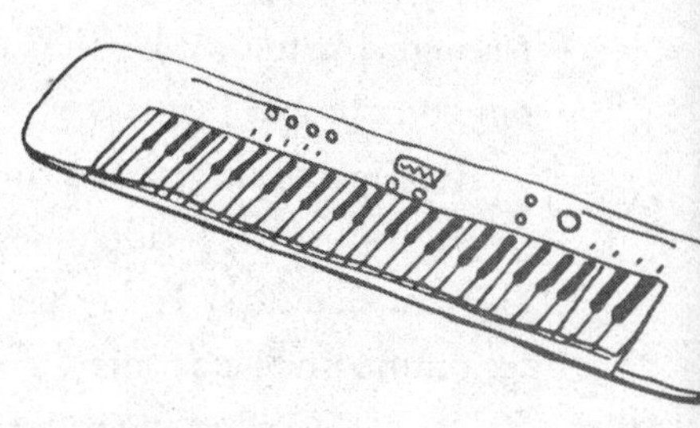

✦ Jane ✦

My parents said I'd go to hell for making rock music, but no eternal torment could be worse than today's session.

The thing I love about working in a recording studio is that it can be such a collaborative, transformative experience for all involved, the kind that challenges musicians to dig deep, perform at a higher level, and produce their best work. Watching those breakthroughs is the most rewarding part of my job. But on rare occasions . . . that doesn't happen, and the long hours in the studio are nothing more than pure torture. Unfortunately for my production schedule, Trevor Barnett is worse than fire and brimstone, and I'm not sure what I did to deserve the punishment.

Forget a great take—I'll be lucky to get something usable.

Trevor winks at me through the glass as we start yet again, and I cringe, wishing I wasn't alone with him. I told my sound engineer not to come in today, because we were supposed to be done by now and I thought *someone* should enjoy their Friday.

For the past three days, I've given Trevor more than a hundred chances to get this right, and it's ninety-nine more than any other producer would offer in this business. I bring an open mind into every session with a new musician, and usually, I'm proud of this approach. When people have issues or blocks, I recognize I don't know what's going on for them personally, so I help them work through whatever it is. The creative process is so easily affected by our complicated lives.

But Trevor has wasted three days I didn't have to spare.

Adjusting my headphones, I sigh, trying to figure out where it all went sideways. Trevor plays the exact opposite of what I asked for on the first verse this time, attempting a poor imitation of Neil Peart on "Tom Sawyer" for some reason I can't even begin to understand. As stoic as I try to be, my knee bounces impatiently under the heavy table holding the board, and all I want to do is scream.

This is ridiculous. I've never worked with Trevor before, but he came recommended by Kyle Harris—who both stars in and produces *Into the Dragon Realm*, the hit animated television series I compose and produce music for. This simple drum part should have been a breeze. But our doomed collaboration started on Wednesday with Trevor arriving four hours late with zero communication. Then, he forgot his "lucky stick bag" and we had to scrap the day's session entirely, because the wide selection of Vic Firths I'd ordered didn't *feel* right.

It should have been fine. I'd built extra time into the week on purpose, because I always pad my schedule to prepare for the unexpected. But this is beyond unexpected—it's impossible.

Trevor whoops on his way into the chorus, and I slump in my seat. *There's no chance the mics aren't going to pick that up.* Fanning myself with a spare piece of music, I try to stay focused despite the warmth of the studio, the wood-paneled walls that look straight out of the seventies now stuffy instead of strangely comforting.

When Trevor was almost on time yesterday, I let myself hope

that he'd pull it off. But from the first take, he kept trying to "mix it up," and we didn't get a single clean run-through. We were supposed to start fresh today, again, but we're no closer to making my deadline.

I groan under my breath. It's just one song. It's not supposed to be this hard.

When our director made major cuts to the first episode after test audiences hated a subplot, I knew it would mean working against the clock to write Sir Alec a number to fit his new emotional arc. Usually I write with a small team, so it was intimidating to work all on my own, but I had to do what I could to knock this song out in a few days. I'm proud of what I came up with under that kind of pressure. Now it's up to Trevor to get through this track without screwing it up.

When he spins around on the drum throne in the middle of the second verse like a kid in an office chair, I barely resist the urge to facepalm.

Because even being as generous as possible, I can safely say this whole experience has been a disaster. I've never heard of a drummer who refuses to use a click track in a recording session when asked by their producer. When I told him where to locate the metronome in his monitors, Trevor insisted, *Real drummers don't need a machine to tell them how to do their jobs*, but . . . it's not looking like he can do the job.

We're running out of time, and I need Trevor to do this. Just once.

So when Trevor loses three measures in the bridge because he's spinning on the stool again, I'm about ready to push him off the drum throne and sit on it myself. I'm no Aaron Sterling, but even I can manage to keep four-on-the-floor.

And again, the song ends. Again, the recording is useless.

"Let's take five," I say with the talkback mic that feeds into the booth, trying to keep my voice a steady dam against the tears that threaten to burst at any moment. We don't have time for a break, but at this point, I don't know what else to do. I grip the table in front of me, desperate to hold myself together, trying not to look at the clock that is getting way too close to lunch.

"I think that was the one!" Trevor says, his voice muffled through the glass. His sweaty, pale skin has put on a sallow tinge. Any last hope I have melts away when he pulls what must be a disgustingly warm PBR out of his backpack. The hiss and click of the can opening makes me want to hurl.

I cross my arms, glaring at Trevor's back from where he lounges in the booth. This was supposed to be a quick week in the studio: lay down one new track, produce it, and be home in time for Friday night dinner. And to think I was actually excited for the eighties-style power ballad I wrote last minute that will now inevitably haunt my dreams for the rest of my life.

Because power ballads need drums, and at this rate, I'll never get them.

Trevor takes a selfie from the booth, the beer sloshing over the rim of the can and onto the studio floor. *Perfect.*

For the millionth time, I wonder how this is the same guy who recorded "Gotta Give You More" for Hunter O'Brien. Then again, Hunter was super rude to my Glitter Bats bandmate Valerie Quinn the one time we played a festival together, so maybe he just bullied Trevor into being a better musician. I'm certainly not inspiring any greatness from him this week with my kindness approach.

"Sorry I'm late!" I whirl around to see another bandmate—and my best friend—barge into the studio. Riker Maddox, the Glitter Bats rhythm guitarist, is wheezing for air. I've known Riker for more than a decade, since we formed Glitter Bats as teenagers, and his presence instantly calms me.

He's quite a sight today: brown hair piled onto his head in a haphazard bun that's falling to one side, his hulking, Thor-like frame weighed down by the three guitar cases strung over one shoulder.

I blink. "Why are you out of breath?"

"Elevator was too slow. Ran up the stairs." He winces. "Shit, I'm sorry, I know we were supposed to do this an hour ago. There was construction right in front of my exit. Did you get any of my texts?"

Guilt twists my stomach. Riker is doing me a huge favor, squeezing this in on a Friday afternoon, and I haven't even checked my phone. Yesterday, Trevor took up the entire block of studio time I had scheduled for Riker to record the new electric guitar part on this same track. I forgot Riker was coming back in today to finish it out. "We're still behind schedule. You didn't have to rush and . . . I'm so sorry!" The tears I thought I was still carefully holding at bay sting the back of my eyes. Blinking, I swallow them back with a hasty sip from the trendy-but-ridiculously sized water bottle my sister sent me for my birthday.

Frowning, Riker sets his cases on the ground and joins me at the soundboard. "What's wrong, Janey?"

I nod at Trevor, who's now resorted to chugging the beer. Even though Trevor can't hear us through the booth's soundproofing, I lower my voice. "Haven't gotten a solid take on drums yet."

His eyes grow wide. "The fuck? Who even is this guy?"

Putting my elbows on the desk, I let my head fall into my hands. "Trevor Barnett. Kyle referred him."

The fantastic drummer we used for the rest of the season had a scheduling conflict this week, but Kyle promised everyone that Trevor was a "rock star." I know rock stars—technically, I'm one too, now that my band is back together—and Trevor doesn't fit the description.

"I don't know what to do to get him to play it right," I hiss.

Riker narrows his eyes. "That's not your responsibility. If he can't do the job he signed on for, just let him go. Doesn't matter who his friends are."

I look at Riker dubiously. Kyle is actually pretty great to work with, but he's a juggernaut . . . and he's been taking on a lot more responsibility as an executive producer. I don't think he's going to be happy with me if I fire his friend. He could fire *me*—but that's going to happen anyway if I can't finish this recording. I promised I could get one song done under the wire, because of course, the rewrite was in the first episode of the next season.

The first episode that's supposed to be surprise-dropped exclusively for the audience at our Royal Con panel two days from now. I have no idea how the animators pulled it off on their end, but if I don't do my part, it's going to be for nothing. They used my demo for the timing of the scene, and this song is the last piece of the puzzle. It has to happen. Today.

My jaw tightens. "I can't fire him."

Riker grumbles. "Is Kyle really that unreasonable? Just call him and tell him his friend can't hack it."

It's what I should do. If Trevor has done anything over the past three days, it's proven he can't deliver. But Kyle hired him, and he *is* Sir Alec. He's on a three-week wellness retreat in Iceland, and even *he* found a way to book a recording studio in Reykjavik and lay down vocals.

It'll all be for nothing if we don't have drums.

The unshed tears finally blur my vision. I should have done something about this sooner, but I was trying to avoid conflict. I never should have recorded without more of the music and sound department here, because then at least it wouldn't look like I was making personnel decisions unilaterally. "I don't know what to do."

"Just fire him and bring someone else in. Do you need me to do it?"

Despite that it makes me feel like a kid again, a part of me desperately wants to hide behind Riker and let him take care of this. When I was nineteen and my parents tried to cause a scene backstage at one of our "heathen concerts," Riker stepped in to run interference. They ignored my boundaries, tried to shove a bunch of Bible verses down my throat, and wouldn't leave when I asked—but for some reason (a reason that is probably the patriarchy) they listened to him.

But I'm not nineteen anymore, and I can't ask Riker to fix this. It's my responsibility.

"Who would we even bring in at this point?"

He cocks his head, a sly smirk creeping up his lips. "Hmm. Do you know any drummers who would drop everything at a moment's notice to help you out?"

I let out a long breath. "I didn't want to bug her about this." Keeley Cunningham, the brilliant Glitter Bats drummer, would show up for me in a heartbeat, but her schedule is just as busy as mine.

"*Janey*, come on."

"She has a gig!"

Knowing Keeley, she's diligently rehearsing for the show she's playing tomorrow with Bianca Martin. I don't envy her. Working with an ex sounds messy, but Keeley's always been good at navigating that kind of stuff. Besides, the whole situation is none of my business.

And if there's something going on with her and Bianca again, I don't want to be calling her to rescue me in the middle of *all of that*.

Riker narrows his eyes. "She'd figure it out. You need her."

Suddenly, I'm jarred from our hushed conversation by a belch over my shoulder. Trevor stands behind me, eyes already glassy somehow, his "lucky stick bag" in hand. "We're done, right?" he asks.

"Not yet," I say. "We still need to get through 'Never Your King' without losing measures."

He smiles placatingly at me, like *I'm* the one being unreasonable. "That last one was fire! I'm going to be late for a gig if I don't leave now."

It takes every last piece of restraint for me not to snap, but I plaster my own smile on. "We haven't recorded a clean take yet."

He shrugs, running a hand through his greasy hair. "Sorry, babe. I gotta get going. Remember—it's rock and roll! It doesn't have to be perfect."

Riker opens his mouth—no doubt to defend me against that *babe*—but I jab an elbow in his ribs. Riker coughs, and I jump in before he can say anything, plastering another saccharine smile on my face. "Well, thank you for coming in."

Trevor finishes his beer with another watery burp, then chucks it in the general direction of the trash can. He misses by a foot, and the can tumbles to the floor. "Yup. Anything for Kyle. You'll send me the check, right?"

I sigh. "That's all handled by accounting."

"Sweet. I already spent the money, but that's what credit cards are for, am I right?" He offers a fist to Riker, who just crosses his arms and uses every inch of his height to tower over Trevor. For the first time, Trevor actually looks chagrined.

"Okay, uh, bye." And then he's out of the studio.

I should be relieved, but my hands start to tremble. Now, I don't even have a *bad* drummer.

"Maybe I should just do it myself. I can count, at least. It doesn't have to be good," I hedge, as if that's any way to do this.

Riker raises a brow.

"You're right," I say with a groan. Of course it has to be good. The Network won't like it if the music for their hit animated series takes a dip in quality this season. They'll find any excuse to cancel musical shows, because original scores cost money.

Money that's paying me, the rest of the team, and all of the musicians we've hired. I have to figure something out.

Quietly, I bend down to pick up the empty beer can with two fingers, then toss it in the recycling bin, preparing myself to figure out a plan.

I run my hands over my long curls for the hundredth time today, which are no doubt frizzing from the familiar motion. Usually I try to look semiprofessional in the studio, but business casual went out the window when the air-conditioning stopped working. I'm down to a change of clothes I had in my car. "Can you get yourself set up in the other booth? I know we're behind, so once you give me a few solid takes, I'll let you go."

Riker puffs out his chest and salutes. "I'll do it in *one*."

I narrow my eyes at him. "Don't rush. I think I'd like to hear a few different riff options after that second chorus when I get back."

"Sure thing. Where are you going?"

I gesture to my phone, trying not to cringe. "I have to make a call."

Riker grins. "See? I bet she'll be on her way before you even hang up the phone."

Despite my reticence to bug Keeley, all of the anxiety of the past few days starts to fall from my shoulders as I pull up her name in my contacts. The call barely rings before she answers the FaceTime, grinning at the camera from somewhere out in the September sunshine.

That grin instantly calms me down.

"Jane Mercer! This is the best surprise I could have gotten today. I haven't seen you in ages!"

"I know, and I'm sorry. I've been booked." We haven't hung out since after the most recent Glitter Bats show in Vegas six weeks ago, which became quite the party when Valerie and our other lead singer and bassist, Caleb Sloane, eloped in a cowboy-themed chapel.

We spent the night with our friends and family, drinking way too much champagne and filling up my camera roll. It was one of the best nights I've had in a long time.

Keeley runs a hand through her blond bob, shorter than it was the last time I saw her, and I can't help but notice how much it suits her angular features. Her septum piercing glints in the light. "I totally get it—everyone wants a piece of you. I don't blame them." Obviously she's not trying to be suggestive, but my traitorous heart still races at that particular comment. "So what's up?"

I clear my throat. "You got a minute?"

Her lips twist. "I've got the whole fucking afternoon for you."

Okay, now that was suggestive. I swallow hard, reminding myself this is just how Keeley is. She flirts with everyone. It doesn't mean anything.

We're friends, and anything else is just my imagination running wild at the worst time.

"That's great to hear, actually. Long story short, I need a drummer. How do you feel about laying down a seven-minute track for *Into the Dragon Realm* this afternoon?"

Keeley pulls down her sunglasses, smirking in that way of hers that always makes my cheeks heat. "Sounds fun. When do we start?"

What's Next After *More to Say*?

BY MARY KATE HAMPTON, SENIOR STAFF WRITER FOR *BUZZWORD*

It's no secret that I'm a huge fan of Glitter Bats.

Longtime *Buzzword* readers know I got my start writing about the band for this very publication way back when I was a college intern. Joke's on everyone who didn't want to cover the random kids from Seattle who took over the internet with their homemade video for "Midnight Road Trip," because that song would become the lead single from *Wanderlust*, Glitter Bats' iconic debut album. I was in the right place at the right time. My first solo interview involved asking Valerie Quinn and Caleb Sloane about that viral moment (you know, *this* one), and I knew from that conversation that I would follow the Glitter Bats to the edge of the world.

Over the years, I've gotten to see this band grow as musicians as I became a full-time entertainment writer here at *Buzzword*. *Bittersweet*, their follow up to *Wanderlust*, was bigger, bolder, and took more risks, while still staying true to the Bats' pop-punk inspiration. Quinn and Sloane remained at the helm, and their songwriting only got better with each track as their confidence grew. After *More to Say*'s release earlier this year, everyone is saying the band has shown even wider range and potential . . . and they're correct.

Glitter Bats' sound has matured—to be expected after a six-year hiatus—and I think it's safe to say they've taken a departure from their roots while still honoring them. Of course there's still that vibrant punk sound on tracks like the angry "Used Up" or the rousing "Better Times," and the Bats show their softer side on tracks like "Daydreams Like This" (which we all got an incredible preview of at their reunion show last year) and "Found Family." But what's really great about this album—and keeping it on repeat in my car for the past six months—is the way it showcases the entire band.

Drummer Keeley Cunningham has her work cut out for her on the technical "Down this Road," but she doesn't miss a beat. Her percussion work is truly impressive.

Keyboardist Jane Mercer's wall of intricate sound makes "Light the Way" a standout track, especially with her tight vocal harmony with Quinn on the chorus.

In a rare moment outside of a live performance, we get to hear rhythm guitarist Riker Maddox on lead guitar *and* vocals on "Hollow," and the first time I heard the track, I got chills down my spine.

The unique thing about this band is that every single member has the talent to be the lead, and what makes them special is the way they work together to create the signature Glitter Bats sound. It begs the question: Following that all-too-short tour this summer, where will they go next?

After such a long hiatus, a new album felt like a miracle in and of itself, but now fans want more. And they have a good reason to hope, because what is truly miraculous here is the way this band keeps reinventing themselves for the better. With a maturing sound and an impressive range transcending genre, it's almost guaranteed *More to Say* will get an Album of the Year nomination. This third installment makes it clear that Glitter Bats have a place among fellows like Paramore and Lime Velvet as pop-punk bands that have crossed over into the rock space with ease—and they've been welcomed by rock royalty, as shown by two recent live covers of "Ghosts" by true legends of the genre. We broke it all down at this *link*.

Now that Glitter Bats are free from their fraught contract with Label Records, their next steps are unknown. Many fans were afraid that *More to Say* is a farewell album instead of a pivot point in the band's trajectory. However, a representative from Ortega Management promised, "This isn't the last you'll hear from Glitter Bats."

But no plans have been announced since their final show six weeks ago in Vegas, concluding their brief US tour. Most of the Glitter Bats tag has been devoted to that viral double onstage proposal between Sloane and Quinn, who reportedly eloped because, well, Vegas... Of course, most fans are over the moon for the happy couple.

That doesn't mean there aren't plenty of theories about what's next! While not impossible, it's highly unlikely the band would re-sign with Label. Rumors have circulated about the company's sharklike tactics, and it's no secret Glitter Bats were stuck for years in an incredibly controlling contract masterminded by CEO Landon Banks. (For those who didn't see the press release in 2014, Banks is responsible for rebranding his inherited Vitality Records empire into *Label Records*, because he wanted his company to be "the only Label that matters.")

That doesn't mean there aren't plenty of other possibilities on the horizon. No doubt there are countless rock labels who are willing to be in the Glitter Bats business. And with so much talent and range in the group, there truly could be anything in store for this band. Only time will tell.

After the sparkling achievement of *More to Say*, I can't wait to see what's next.

Rock and roll, please tell us Glitter Bats are here to stay.

2

✦ *Keeley* ✦

I was stretching the truth a little bit to Jane—I might have been chilling out on my patio when she called, but I really didn't have all afternoon.

One text to Bianca fixes that.

I try not to feel *too* bad about ditching practice as I head inside. Quickly, I change into linen shorts and a button-down to ward off the surprise late-September heat wave, then grab my stick bag and the keys to my Rivian before hurrying out the door.

As I drive out of my neighborhood, I push the guilt of cancelling on Bianca away, as much as I hate cancelling on *anyone*. But I can rationalize it easily. I played these songs with her band enough times during the three years we were dating, and we still have a sound check tomorrow before the event, so I'm not worried. Besides, what is she going to do, break up with me? She already did that after we got too busy for anything more than a quickie between gigs.

This industry will do that to you. We probably could have made it work, but while the sex was good, the romantic sparks between us were starting to fizzle out.

I tap my finger impatiently on the steering wheel as I brake for a pause in traffic. Driving a massive SUV is the worst, especially in So-Cal, but hauling drum gear requires cargo space. At least I was able to go electric when I had to replace my old rig.

A response from Bianca pops up on my nav screen, and I swipe it away to focus on the road. Hopefully she's not upset.

We've managed to stay friendly since our breakup. Bianca is famous enough that our split earned us a few headlines, but they weren't very inflammatory. The media has never really cared about my personal life—it's one of the perks of not being a frontperson.

Valerie, on the other hand, has inspired a true media circus ever since the first Glitter Bats single dropped. The internet is obsessed with who she dates, and every move she makes is analyzed for the worst possible motivation. Even now that she and Caleb are married, they make headlines whenever they go out, and people still speculate about if it's "real"—or even worse, if she was playing up her bisexuality for the attention.

Fucking pricks.

God, I'm so glad that my drum kit protects me from that life. Valerie and Caleb's relationship made it, eventually, but watching it all go down from the inside was brutal. Now, more than ever, I know I'll do anything for my fellow Glitter Bats.

And Jane needs help only I can give.

Okay, maybe not *only* me, but I'm a drummer and I can help her, and I always want to help Jane. Is there more to it that motivated me to drop everything? Sure. Have I had a crush on her since high school, when she was the dance team captain and I was playing with the pep band at every football game? Maybe. But I'm not going to act on it.

I'm just going to fucking help her, because she's my fucking friend, and I'm fucking good at what I do. Still, that doesn't stop me from fluffing up my bob and touching up my mascara at the next red light. I think I did okay for putting in almost no effort—it's wild how access to top-quality skin care and a kick-ass stylist can make it easy to look good. I know I'm lucky to have that . . . and so many other things.

A lot of people think I'm living a dream: because sure, at twenty-nine, I've already had one hell of a career. Glitter Bats are back and rocking again with our third album. That same album has received rave reviews thanks to the songwriting brilliance of Caleb and Valerie, our star-crossed lead singers who finally figured out their personal shit and got the band back together last year. Beyond that, I've drummed on chart-topping tracks for everyone from Pizza Dream to Daphne Rose, and I'm never wanting for gigs. Hell, my cowriter credit on Bianca's "Your Body and Mine" got me nominated for multiple awards two years ago.

But some days, it doesn't feel like enough. I was on track to go to Stanford before we got a record deal, and on the quieter days, my mind can't stop racing to think what might have happened if I'd chosen another path. It's especially bad when I'm talking to my twin brother, Oliver, who actually *went* to the prestigious university he got into and is now a hotshot attorney. On paper, he's a lot more successful than me.

I know that path would have burned me out eventually. Back in high school, I was at the top of my class, managing extracurriculars, *and* spending every free moment at Glitter Bats practices and gigs. But I wasn't happy. I had undiagnosed ADHD, and I was surviving on caffeine and my day planner and the sheer urgency of deadline stress. It's not that I couldn't have continued down that road, but I wouldn't thrive the way I do with the surprising amount of flexibility in the music industry.

Objectively, I know my career is impressive. Without it, I wouldn't have my best friends in the world. But I'm bored of drumming for other people, and I want to do more with Glitter Bats.

When I get to Jane's studio space in Culver City, I miraculously find quick parking and head inside. I forego the elevator in favor of the stairs, and it doesn't take long before I'm pushing my way into the cramped recording space. It's a little stuffy, but the place is otherwise immaculate: music is stacked neatly on one table in the corner, while guitars and basses are hung in a perfect row on the far wall. Even the vintage-inspired rug is tidy, save a few errant cords.

Jane is leaning over a laptop next to the soundboard, her wild red curls pulled back into a haphazard braid. She looks more casual than usual for work, wearing the hell out of an oversized *Shooting Stars* T-shirt and faded cutoff jeans that hug her ass. While I can't pretend I mind the view, I'm more concerned by the weary slump of her shoulders.

"Thank you for coming," she says faintly as she turns to me, sinking onto a stool. She looks fucking defeated, and it's hard to take in. I just want to fix it.

"Of course, Mercer. I'm always here when you need me."

She's silent for a beat, and the way she's staring makes me wonder if I've said too much.

"I know," she finally says, biting her lip. "You're the best."

My mouth goes dry at that.

"Keeley!" Riker says, emerging from the booth, toasting me with a watermelon Red Bull. I stiffen as I see him. I don't know why I'm surprised. These two are inseparable.

Still, I wasn't expecting him, and it throws me.

Quickly, I fix my face and roll my eyes at Riker. "Maddox! Do you still have shit to do, or are you just loitering?" There's a strange bite to my tone, and I try to fix it by casually leaning against the wall.

Riker shrugs, but something flickers in his gaze, like he can't figure out why I'm being weird. "I got done a little while ago, but I wanted to say hi before I left."

"I'm honored," I deadpan. I turn and look at Jane. "So, Mercer, what are we doing?"

Opening the binder next to her on the table, she hands it to me. I lean back against the wall again and start to read through the piece titled "Never Your King."

Normally, when we're doing Glitter Bats stuff, we don't bother with anything more formal than guitar tabs, but TV is a completely different arena. I took years of piano and percussion lessons and can actually read music, unlike some rock musicians I won't mention, and it's easy to follow along with Jane's melody.

It's fucking brilliant. Of course it is.

Jane bites her lip, like she's nervous for some reason. Maybe she's shy about sharing her work—neither of us ever really wrote anything for the band, so this is new. Still, it's not like I didn't already know she's amazing at this. Sometimes I listen to the *Shooting Stars* soundtrack even when I haven't played the game in months.

There's something comforting about it.

She picks up a loose cable off the ground and starts winding it. "I wrote this song when the showrunners decided to take episode two point one in a different direction. Think 'Total Eclipse of the Heart' meets 'Lost in the Woods.'"

Nodding, I run my hand over my hair. "I dig what you're doing with the vocal line. This is for Kyle Harris, right? It's perfect for his range."

Jane ducks her head. "Thanks. I, uh, just want to get this right. Trevor took my only hard copy of the drum part, but I can print it out again if you want."

Fucking Trevor Barnett. Over the phone, Jane gave me a quick rundown of what happened, and I honestly can't believe she was even in this position to begin with. If you're going to hire a rocker to do soundtrack work, they need to actually know what the fuck they're doing with a drum kit.

But I know *I* can handle it. It'll be a fun afternoon.

"It's fine. Can I just hear what you did in Sibelius?"

"Yeah, of course." Jane hurries over to the sound system and plugs her laptop into a jack.

"You should flip through more of her stuff for season two. It's all so good," Riker suggests.

"Of course it's good. Jane wrote it," I say as the track plays. The piano part starts off, the output tinny and robotic from the music-writing software. But even beneath the awkward sound, I can hear the genius of what Jane has put together.

It's going to be so fucking epic. A big, dramatic piece, perfect for this kind of show.

"So?" Jane asks after the song ends, in a voice that almost sounds shaky. "What do you think?"

"It's fantastic. That drum part you wrote is great."

Jane moves to grab her fancy water bottle and takes a long sip. I try not to laugh at the absurdity of it, because I know there's no way she bought that for herself. She's been reusing the same Hydro Flask for ten years. Still, I'm a little distracted when she licks a stray drop off her lips.

"Thanks," she says. "Feel free to play around if you think of something better. I was hoping to make it a little more intuitive, but drum parts aren't my strong suit."

I look sharply at her. There's something about this that is rattling her confidence, and I don't understand why. "You shouldn't say that. It's good. We can collaborate on it, though, if it would make you feel better."

"Do you have time?"

Probably not, I think. I really should go home and practice through Bianca's set list, even if I'm skipping out on rehearsal. Instead, I practically jump at the chance. It's nice to be around Jane again. "My schedule is clear for the rest of the day. I'm here for whatever you need."

This gig with Bianca is actually the last I have scheduled for a while. I decided to clear my calendar so we can focus on the future of Glitter Bats. Wade Ortega—who manages my drum career on top of his longtime work for Glitter Bats—suggested that move might be premature, but I felt good about my choice. All I can think about is focusing on Glitter Bats, anyways, so it's pointless to try to take on other projects.

We haven't talked much about our next steps as a band yet, despite all the speculation from our fans. But that last show was so strong and tight, and now that we're free of our garbage contract with Label Records, I'm confident there are good things in our future.

Hell, maybe we can talk a little about it tonight once we're done recording. Riker is here, so he might as well make himself useful, and we could probably get in touch with Caleb and Valerie for a late dinner or something.

"Well, *I* have to go," Riker drawls, ruining my unspoken plans in a way that makes it hard to hide my scowl.

"Oh . . ." Jane trails off. "I thought you were sticking around. I could use your ear."

Riker glances between the two of us.

"Sorry, I gotta pick up a new pedal I special-ordered before the store closes," he says, patting Jane's shoulder.

"You do that," I say. Again, my voice sounds too harsh, and I regret it right away.

Before the Glitter Bats got back together, I hadn't spoken much with Caleb or even Valerie. But Jane, Riker, and I stayed in touch as best we could.

It was fucking hard. Our careers took us in different directions over the six-year break. I was doing a lot of recording work, tracking drums for mostly pop, rock, and folk artists . . . anyone who needed to fill out an album, really. Meanwhile, Riker started working as a touring guitarist, and it meant he was on the road for months at a time. Jane took the biggest pivot, first assisting on music for a video game company, then getting hired on as the composer for *Shooting Stars*, a now-cult-favorite space fantasy RPG with a soundtrack so popular it launched her career into TV.

Even though we were all still based in the LA area, Jane and Riker saw a lot more of each other than they ever did of me during the Glitter Bats hiatus. I've started to wonder if there's something going on there. They've always been close. Still, it's none of my business. If he can make Jane happy, that's all that matters. Me being weird and cold to him is actually kind of embarrassing.

Riker raises an eyebrow. "You kids have fun." With that, he shoulders his guitars and shuffles out of the studio.

"What was that about? Are you two getting along?" Jane asks.

"It's Riker, who knows." I shrug dramatically for effect. "Let's just get started. If we have time, I can lay down some alternate takes and listen through them with you."

"I really just need the one clean run-through," Jane says. "I'll get you out of here as quickly as I can. You already had to drop everything today to help me."

I shrug, trying to keep it casual. "It's nothing."

"Well, I appreciate you. My goal was to get everything done by midnight," she says. "Multiple takes would be a huge help in case I need to shift things around once I relisten to Kyle's vocals."

The Network really got lucky with the cast. Kyle Harris—precocious-child-star-turned-classically-handsome-Broadway-heartthrob—is both hilarious with dialogue and an obscenely talented singer. The rest of the cast is stacked too, with industry legends like Rose Carrington and new up-and-comers like Josie Ramirez. But there's no way they'd have done as well as they have without Jane's brilliant songwriting. It's really made the show, and I'm so fucking proud of her.

I grin. "Then let's get started."

Despite the tension lingering on her shoulders, the furrow in Jane's brow softens at that.

"Sounds good. Why don't you set up while I adjust some things here?"

I nod. In my haste to get to the booth, I nearly collide with Jane on her way to cross the tiny space, and she glances up at me, eyes wide. Heat floods my cheeks.

"Sorry!" she squeaks. I swallow hard as I catch the scent of that goddamn vanilla perfume that lingers in the warmth between us.

"It's fine. This is a tiny space!" I laugh. A little too loud, but I hope she doesn't notice.

I'd give anything to pull her closer, to eliminate the inches between us, to feel those soft, generous curves under my hands . . .

"Right, I'll just—" She nods past me to the water station, where she must have been headed.

Fuck.

I step back, gesturing to it. "After you."

"Thanks." Jane hurries past me to fill her water, and I step into the sound booth, shaking my head.

I hate playing when I don't have a clear mind, but I'll just have to grit my teeth and focus on the work. For now, I can show up for Jane, and maybe it will be enough. It has to be. So I just settle myself in the space that, for some reason, smells like cheap beer.

Doesn't matter. I'm a professional. While Jane prepares to record, I look through the sheet music one last time. It's a great song, and even more impressive knowing Jane literally just wrote this on the fly.

I glance at her, jaw tightening as she leans over to adjust something on the board. Despite the hellish day she's had, Jane is still trying to get this done on time. Most people would have said no to rewriting a song in a week, even if it's for The Network. I'd have probably demanded an extension.

"Ready to run it?" Jane asks into the talkback, her voice a little rough. I startle, swallowing hard.

Instead of showing how much being this alone with her is rattling me, I place my hands on my hips and smirk at her through the plexiglass. "I was born ready, Mercer."

Jane cocks her head. "Prove it, Cunningham."

A thrill buzzes across my skin, but it has nothing to do with her words. It's just the thrill I get every time I play the drums . . . or so I'll keep telling myself to get through this session without melting onto the floor.

I nod at Jane, and she presses play on the digital sample. I listen to Past Jane count off the tune and begin playing what she asked.

It's an eighties-style power ballad, so I don't have to do much—the wailing guitar that Riker recorded will do the heavy lifting—but I listen carefully to Past Jane's cues, the click, and the instrumentation, doing my best to fill out the sound.

All of my nerves melt away as the serotonin rushes in with every thrum of the kick. Something deep in my soul just knows how to find the beat, and no matter what kind of music I'm playing, drumming just makes sense the way nothing else does. It settles my brain when everything else is loud. And it's why I'm so in demand in the studio, and why I love playing live with musicians across genres. The rhythm flows with the blood in my veins, pulses with my heartbeat.

The track ends quickly enough, and Jane doesn't say anything for a long moment. I peer over at her through the glass and see her shoulders shaking.

Shit, is she crying?

I rise to get out of the booth, but when Jane looks up at me, she's *laughing*.

"Fuck, Mercer, was it really that bad?" I ask through my relief, even though I know it wasn't. I played exactly what she asked. Her reaction is just confusing the hell out of me.

She shakes her head, then leans into the talkback mic.

"No, that was perfect . . ." She trails off, laughing again. "It's just . . . do you know how hard I tried to get Trevor to do that? Three days, Keeley. Three of the longest days of my life."

"I told you I was ready."

She sighs. "I should have called you two days ago."

My chest swells, and I soften my voice. "I wish you would have."

She clears her throat, running her hands over her braid. "Well, thank you for showing up now."

"Anytime, Jane. I'm always here for you," I say. Then, realizing what I could reveal with those words, I clear my own throat. "But that was just one take, and I want to make sure it's nice and clean. Let me run it a few more times and give you some options."

"Thank you, seriously," she says. I lean down and take a sip of my water, then resettle on the drum throne. It's not my own, and it's a little wobbly, but I do my best to keep my balance and stay focused. Soon enough, I hear the familiar, soothing tone of Past Jane in my ears counting me off again.

We spend the next two hours like that—Jane giving me notes, me trying different things. After the tenth take, she nods.

"I think that will do it."

"You sure?" I ask. The last thing I should do is linger, but I don't want to lose this moment with her, even though it's all business.

We've been so busy since our last show, and I've missed my friend. That's all.

"Yeah, you gave me more than enough great takes. I'm sure you have better things to do than sit in a sweaty studio."

I do have other things to do, but I wouldn't call them better. Even this short time with Jane is better than a night out with Bianca . . . which is what would inevitably happen after a long rehearsal like the one I'm supposed to be at right now. Maybe we'd hook up, maybe we wouldn't—it's been a toss-up ever since we broke up. But even though Bianca is gorgeous, she's the last thing on my mind.

No, my only thoughts are of the redhead hovering over a laptop like she can will it into submission. I pack up my stick bag and tidy the drum kit, then emerge from the booth. Still, I'm not ready to leave yet. Is Jane really going to be here all by herself? Who is going to make sure she takes breaks, eats dinner, doesn't fall asleep on the table?

Not me, I remind myself. *It can't be me.*

"You good?" is the best I can do.

"Yeah, I'm just exhausted. I wasn't supposed to come back to the studio for this season. Recording another song completely upended my schedule."

"I'm sure this has been stressful," I say. "But you're almost done, right?"

"Yeah, thank goodness."

I smile. "That must be a relief. Now we can focus on Glitter Bats."

Jane glances up at me, frowning. "What are you talking about?"

I run a hand over my hair, confused. "Well, I mean, we're finally free of Label! It's the perfect time to make another album."

"I don't know, Keeley . . ."

"How don't you know? We have momentum!" Okay, by the dubious look on her face, she might just need some convincing. That's fine. Jane's a reasonable person—I know she'll understand when I spell it out. "Our fans are desperate for more, so this is the time to make music! With how well our tour went, I'm positive there are labels lining up to work with us. We should strike while we're hot." We only did four stops for *More to Say*: LA, New York, Chicago, and Vegas. Tickets sold out within minutes. The band was trending for weeks. When "Daydreams Like This" started slipping on the charts, "Better Times" hit the top ten, and then "Used Up" joined when we released it as our third single. The end of our contract with Label can't be the end of the band—things are just getting good again. "You have to see this is the perfect timing."

Instead of her face clearing in understanding, the furrow between Jane's brows deepens. "I don't have time to make another album right now." She avoids my gaze. Almost . . . cagey. Like there's more to it.

Panic tightens my chest. "What do you mean?"

She blinks rapidly, more agitated than I've seen her in years. "I mean that I was supposed to consult with Defiant Games about writing something for their sequel to *Half Moon Ranch* this week, and I had to push that meeting back for these recording sessions. On top of all of this, I can't work this weekend because I have to go be on a Royal Con panel. Then our showrunners want to talk to me about their next project in development once *Dragon Realm* wraps, and I'm auditioning for a film that might turn into a franchise, and . . . I just can't add anything else to my plate."

I stiffen, my head swimming. Those are mostly maybes and mights, but she's certainly keeping herself busy. "So just fuck the band, is what you're saying?"

She flushes, eyes flashing. "No! I'm saying I'm booked and I'm not sure I can work on another album. I don't even know if that's what I want right now."

My mind reels. She doesn't know if that's what she wants?

"I can't believe what I'm hearing."

"I'm sorry, but I have so many other commitments to juggle," she says, exhaling. "The band can't take priority over all of that."

Her words feel like a slap in the face.

I shake my head as I move toward the door, fighting the wave of disappointment coursing through me. I thought we were all on the same page. We even talked about it in Vegas six weeks ago—how perfect it would be to make another album now that we don't have a bullshit contract hanging over our shoulders.

And suddenly, Jane doesn't care about that because she's too busy? Fuck that.

"Being scheduled at 100 percent is a *choice*, Jane."

Her eyes narrow. "Don't therapize me. It's condescending, even for you."

Even for *me*? My neck heats. "Wow."

Her face goes pale. Jane is never mean like this, and I'm honestly a little taken aback. She hurries to apologize. "Look, I'm sorry, that was out of line. I just have a lot going on!" She throws out her hands in frustration. "Give me time to take a breath."

It's too late. The damage is done—it's perfectly clear how she feels. "Come on, Jane. All of those things you listed sound like potential projects, not commitments. You could choose the band. You just don't want to."

"That's not true!" she says. "I need to make sure I have income coming in." I stiffen. God, she sounds like my parents. "And besides, I have *obligations*, Keeley. I can't just drop everything because the band wants to make music again. People are relying on me!"

I laugh dryly. "Oh, you mean how I dropped everything this afternoon for you?"

Her eyes widen. "I didn't ask you to do that!"

"No, but you literally did, and I came here to save your ass because we're *bandmates* and that's what we do. And your precious schedule might be in better shape if you hadn't let Trevor Barnett dick around in here for days and walk all over you."

I almost *feel* the barb as it lands, and I want to steal the words back immediately. But instead of cowering, Jane crosses her arms and sets her jaw, a challenge in her shining eyes. "That's not fair."

It's not, and I know it, but we're in it now. "You want to know what's not fair? Thinking your career is more important than the band."

She reddens even more. "Stop putting words in my mouth! I'm just saying I should think about my priorities before I jump into another project."

Another project. As if that's all we are. My shoulders tense. "Fine. Call me when you want to *prioritize* your friends."

"Keeley, please—"

But I shut the door on her words before she can finish the sentence.

3

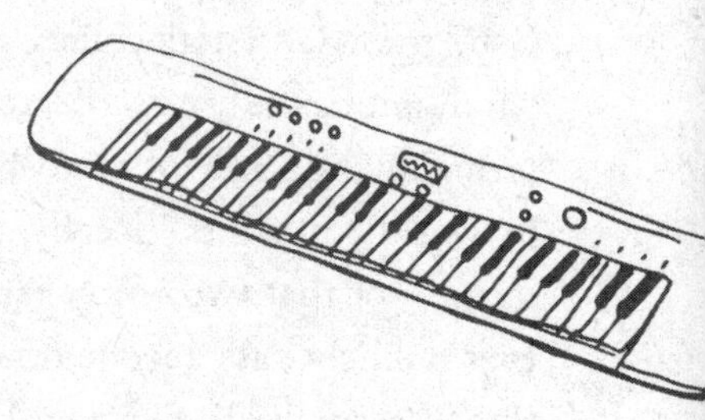

Jane

I fight back tears as the studio door slams.

Keeley doesn't understand the kind of pressure I'm under. Instead of telling her about any of that, though, I got defensive. It's just . . . I can't just clear my schedule to make music with the band. I love the Glitter Bats, but I spent our six-year hiatus building an entirely different career.

Sure, after Caleb and Valerie got married, we started talking about future plans. But that was the kind of after-midnight, champagne-soaked dreaming filtered by the neon lights of the strip. We weren't making actual decisions about our next steps.

Of course I want to pursue more music with the band, but I don't see how it can happen anytime soon. Once I know more about where my career is heading, then I'd be happy to reevaluate. I just can't drop everything now.

And I'm not the only one with other projects. Riker is probably heading on another tour any day, and Caleb is back to teaching for the school year. As far as I know, Valerie is booked for acting gigs too. So where is Keeley's urgency coming from?

Groaning, I set my elbows on the desk and lean my head into my hands.

I really am exhausted. I haven't stopped working since I decided to pursue a career in the music industry. When I chose the Glitter Bats over a Christian college (where I was expected to find a husband, not actually get a degree), my parents sat me down in their formal living room for a two-hour lecture about "not being seduced by worldly pursuits." Really, they didn't like the swearing in our music—or that two of my bandmates were very openly queer. If I ever publicly date anyone other than a straight, cis man, I'm sure they'll actually disown me. It's why I've been so quiet about my relationships . . . if you can even call them that. I've stuck to quiet hookups with clear boundaries from the outset, usually with other industry people who understand the consequences of the public knowing your business.

And so far, I've managed to keep my private life private—to avoid family conflict, if nothing else. I wish I didn't care about what my parents think. But a part of me, deep down, is still beyond terrified of what would happen if they ever learned all my truths.

Still, I escaped out from under the shadow of their expectations with that first Glitter Bats paycheck. I refuse to ever need their help again, and that's why I make sure to have multiple paying gigs lined up: so my financial security is never in question. That means saying yes to the opportunities in front of me.

I love Glitter Bats, but the reality of no longer having a label is that we have no security. Sure, our fans might be eager for more now, but the music industry is fickle. What if their excitement fades before we drop our next album? If we're going to move forward, all my composing work gives me the stability to take that risk.

With a sigh, I grab my laptop and headphones, carefully packing them into my workbag. I think about the stricken look on

Keeley's face, and I wonder if I'm being practical about my career or just clinging to security as a trauma response, like my therapist says.

I grew up in a structured home, but there was no safety there—at least, not the kind that allowed me to be myself. Safety was something I had to build on my own when I left. I hope my parents find some space to be proud of all of the things I've accomplished, but it feels more like they're watching every move to see if I'll slip up. Like they're waiting for me to confirm their fears were correct, and I sold my soul to the devil to work in this industry.

It's fine. I don't need my family's support or their money, because I've been taking care of myself for more than ten years. Heck, I have an amazing career. I have great friends who love me just the way I am. Now, I even have the Glitter Bats again . . . but that doesn't mean I can just abandon everything and pivot.

Dazed, I tug my bag onto my shoulder and head to my car. Inside the garage, I unlock my Prius and settle in the driver's seat, leaning back against the headrest with a groan.

Part of me regrets bringing in Keeley today. If we hadn't worked together, we never would have fought. I can't *ever* remember fighting with her.

But . . . I needed her help. She drummed fabulously, because she always does. While she was in the booth, I could only watch, mesmerized as she played with that charismatic, laser-sharp precision. Her forearm muscles flexing with concentration as she played a steady rhythm on the snare, her eyes sparkling as she tried something different with the crash during the third run.

Riker was right—I should have called Keeley for help hours before I did. Days, even. But being in a studio with her made me feel claustrophobic, like I couldn't get air in my lungs without breathing her in. She's got a big personality that always takes up space, but with all that tension focused on me, I felt so on edge.

And then we had to argue.

Maybe I should call her right now, apologize, and tell her what she wants to hear . . . but I can't. It wouldn't be honest. I don't know how to make her understand that I'm drowning and on the edge of burnout. I can't be all in on the Glitter Bats stuff the way she wants me to be.

Shaking my head, I order delivery from my favorite noodle place on my phone, then queue up *Waitress (Original Broadway Cast Recording)* as my soundtrack for the drive home in an attempt to self-soothe. Getting out of the neighborhood is easy enough, but by the time I hit the freeway, I'm accosted with Friday-night traffic. I turn Jessie Mueller up, trying to drown out my emotions in show-tunes of sugar and butter and flour, even as I can't stop thinking about how my friend left the studio.

I roll my shoulders and grip the steering wheel with determination. I can't think about Keeley right now. We got the track recorded, which is more progress than I would have had without her. I'll be able to sit down with some lo mein by eight o'clock, pour a glass of lemonade, and marathon my work on this track until it's done. It *has* to be done before my flight to the con tomorrow afternoon.

It's not the first time I've pulled an all-nighter for this show. All of those late nights were worth delivering a product I was really proud of back in season one, when we were on a shoestring budget and I was doing so many other jobs on top of composing. Kyle and the rest of the team offered to bring in a new music producer this season, but I wasn't ready to put my work in someone else's hands. I like working with the team, and I like seeing musicians take risks and find their best sound.

Trevor was an anomaly.

By the time the traffic thins, I'm just reaching my exit, itching to get home and start on the track. My phone rings on the Bluetooth, and I answer it without checking the screen for the identity of the caller.

"This is Jane Mercer," I say, trying to keep my voice polite and friendly despite my sour mood.

"Jane, I'm surprised I caught you." My mother's haughty tone fills the car, and I resist the urge to shrink behind the steering wheel.

She can't see you. Don't be ridiculous.

I really, really should have checked the caller ID first. Mom only calls me to give me updates on the family or tell me she's praying for my soul to be saved from the decisions I've made. She thinks it's a loving thing to say. This conversation is the last thing I need right now.

My jaw tightens, but I do my best to greet her. "Hi, Mom. How are you?" A loaded question, but I ask it anyway, because I know it's easier than going five rounds before she tells me why she called.

"Oh, I'm over the moon. I have the best news!"

I brace myself, gripping the wheel harder than necessary as I take one of my usual turns. Nothing my mom is excited about can be good. "What's your news?"

She sighs dreamily. "Nora is engaged!"

I feel the warmth drain from my face. My sister, Nora, is *twenty*, which, sure, is a year older than I was when I signed a record deal. But she's just a kid. How is getting married a good thing?

But I don't ask any of that, because my heart is sinking with a more pressing question . . . Why is Mom calling me, and not my own sister? We're not exactly close, between the ten-year age difference and the fact that I'm the black sheep of the family. The only family I really talk to regularly are my cousins from Portland, and even then, it's just when they're going to Disney and want to crash at my house.

But my sister and I do text. Sometimes. When I remember to

reach out, which hasn't been happening much with how busy I've been over the past year. Crap, maybe I've messed that relationship up all on my own.

"Wow," I say, trying to keep my tone light. "Who's the lucky guy?"

Because of course it's a guy. Mom wouldn't be excited if it wasn't a guy.

"Daniel Brady. You remember him, don't you?"

"Sure do," I say as I pull on to my street. Of course I remember Daniel Brady. I babysat the pastor's kids when I was in high school, and Daniel was a handful. Even at nine, he knew how to get away with just about anything.

I can only imagine what he's like now.

"Wow, that's really something," I say, because it's the only honest thing I can.

"And he's about to become the worship pastor. Can you imagine? My daughter, a pastor's wife! What more could a mother want for her child?"

I grit my teeth. The chances of me marrying a pastor died before I even turned eighteen, but Mom doesn't believe that. She thinks the Glitter Bats influenced me to leave the faith. The Shore, the trendy church my parents attend, looks progressive on the outside, but in reality, "all are welcome" really means "all are welcome if you live exactly the way our interpretation of the Bible says you should."

Once I started to fully comprehend how outsiders were treated, that "love your neighbor" had conditions, I was ready to leave and never look back.

My first instinct is to be worried about Nora. The way I see it, no one should be allowed to get married until their prefrontal cortex is done maturing. Marrying into the Bradys could be a nightmare that my baby sister still sees as a fantasy. If she'd been the one to call me, maybe I could have talked to her a little, just made sure she's okay. I can't shake the fear that something's not right about all this.

"You must be really happy," I say, pulling into my driveway. But I don't make any effort to get out of the car. Sometimes switching from Bluetooth to my cell disconnects the call, and hanging up on my mom isn't going to do our fractured relationship any favors.

Even if this conversation is making me want to toss my phone into the ocean.

"Like I said: I'm over the moon!" my mom says. "All of the other ladies in my Bible study group are so jealous!"

"That's nice," I say, and as much as I try to keep my tone placid, Mom doesn't buy it.

"Oh, you know I'm not really serious. It's all in good fun! Everyone wants to be a Brady, even if only by proxy."

"Right," I say, because everyone at The Shore practically worships Mike Brady as much as they claim to worship their god, and I'm sure his oldest son enjoys just as much adoration. If he's anything like his dad, Daniel is the last person I'd want my sister to end up with.

But I hope for Nora's sake that I'm wrong.

"So the wedding is going to be on New Year's Eve. You'll be home, right?"

My hand was already on the door handle, but I freeze. "That's less than four months away. How are you planning something that quickly?"

Mom laughs dismissively. "Oh, I've been planning your sister's wedding for years on Pinterest. We can come up with something quickly enough. And when you know the person God has put in your life is your future spouse, it's foolish to wait too long, isn't it?"

I clench my fists. Four months won't give Nora even a breath to make sure this is what she wants for her life. With Mom in control, it's going to be a nonstop marathon of decorations and cake tastings and who knows what else. And I've put so much distance between us that if I ask Nora what she really wants, I'm sure she'll just get defensive. I barely know my baby sister anymore, and that's my fault.

Still, she's getting *married*. I have to do something.

"I don't know what my schedule is yet, but I'll do my best to be there."

"That's ridiculous. Of course you'll be in the bridal party—what would everyone think if you weren't? Your family is more important than that secular music you're so proud of making, Jane Rebecca."

"I know," I say, because it's the only thing that will get her off the phone, even though I'm sure Nora doesn't want me in her retinue on what is hopefully a happy day for her. "I'll let Nora know once I figure out my plans."

"Don't bother, I'm handling everything. You'll come home before Christmas and stay with us—your sister is going to need all the help she can get before the big day."

I open my mouth to argue and close it again. It's bad enough that this is coming from Mom, and I don't want to fight. Not when I'm heading inside for a marathon producing session tonight. There's no way I'm going home for Christmas—I haven't in years—but it's no use arguing with Mom right now.

That can come later.

"Sure, Mom. Look, I just got home. I'll talk to you soon, okay?"

"I'm praying you'll soften your heart toward your sister. You should be celebrating her happiness! This apathy is from the devil," she says, and then she hangs up.

Because of course any rational thought is from the devil, but that's just how my mom sees the world. Overwhelmed, I lean my head on my steering wheel and let out a long-suffering groan.

Every call with my mother throws me into emotional turmoil for at least an hour.

I don't know how long I sit there, but finally the food delivery car pulls up behind my Prius. Blinking, I force a pleasant expression onto my face, step out of the car to greet the delivery person, and collect my noodles. They smell like garlic and soy sauce and every good thing in the world, and I hold the bag close as I walk over to my front porch.

I can't believe my baby sister is getting married. Mom calling me with the news instead of Nora doing it herself feels like the worst sort of commentary on our relationship. When I was still at home, she came to me for everything. Dad was always working and Mom was so busy with the church, so I was the one teaching her to read and making sure she brushed her teeth. But the age gap between us now feels like a ravine. She must think I'm horrible—some wayward, prodigal sister, a person she has to keep at arm's length to avoid being led astray by my *sins*.

When I get inside my house, I'm struck by just how empty it is. I've done everything I can to liven up the space: I've painted the walls and filled the rooms with furniture in bright colors, every available shelf and corner hosts a lively, well-maintained plant, and the whole place smells like vanilla, my favorite scent.

And none of it makes me feel less alone.

I want to call Keeley, ask her if she'll come over the way she's done countless times. We'd split the noodles, and I would apologize, and for a few precious hours, these lonely walls would be filled by her brash warmth. We'd both get a little tipsy on wine, and I'd rail about my family, and she'd tell me *fuck all of them* for making me feel this way.

But no matter how much I want to fix things and find comfort in her friendship, I have a track to finish. So I take my food over to the counter and light a couple of candles, trying to warm up the room.

Maybe my mom was right, and I doomed myself to a lonely life when I chose the music industry. I'm exhausted from the constant grind. Church taught me how to navigate the games people play when they want something from you, but that doesn't make dealing with Hollywood any easier. I might not get the brunt of the media's wrath the way Valerie does, but I still have to put on the perfect, people-pleasing persona that makes everyone say they *love* me if I want to keep it that way.

If I'm wearing a mask anyway, maybe it would have been easier to be the girl my parents wanted me to be. I know I'd never have been happy. I'd have found another kind of loneliness in that life.

But it doesn't make *this* loneliness hurt any less. Gosh, I should at least go adopt a cat one of these days.

I set the takeout bag down and rifle around in the cupboards for a wineglass. Drinking is usually off-limits when I'm working, but half a glass with my dinner won't hurt anything. At least it might take the edge off this ache in my soul.

I don't want the path my sister is taking, but I also don't want to be alone like this anymore either. I want . . . well, it doesn't matter what I want.

There's nothing to do about any of that tonight. Instead, I just pour myself a glass of white wine. Foregoing the time it would take to set my meal out on a plate, I open up the takeout box, load up my fork, and take a big bite of the steaming noodles.

Then I grab my laptop and get to work.

ROYAL CON PANEL LISTING: THE MAKING OF *INTO THE DRAGON REALM*

Location: Conference Room C
Schedule: Sunday, 1PM
Panelists: Kyle Harris, Finn Lewis, Josie Ramirez, Rose Carrington, Jane Mercer, Kate Taylor, Jordan Tyler
Moderator: Inez Thomas

Join us to get exclusive updates on all things *Into the Dragon Realm*! The panel will feature creators Kate Taylor and Jordan Tyler; composer Jane Mercer; stars Kyle Harris, Finn Lewis, Josie Ramirez; and special guest Rose Carrington. The panel will be moderated by Inez Thomas of *Twenty-Two*, who will ask a variety of questions about the making of the hit musical series and what fans can expect going into season two. We'll also get an in-depth look at how they create music for these beloved characters.

After the moderated panel, there will be fifteen minutes for audience questions, followed by an exclusive surprise for our Royal Con guests. The room will then be directed to a signing line. All guests will receive an exclusive *Into the Dragon Realm* art print, but the cast and crew will sign up to three items each. Photos must be purchased in advance.

Arrive early! This panel is expected to be full, and standing room will not be permitted.

Missed the door? Access the exclusive recording 24 hours after the event with your conference badge!

4

✦ *Keeley* ✦

By Sunday morning, I'm completely exhausted—not just from playing a gig with Bianca that went late, but from two near-sleepless nights worrying about my fight with Jane.

All I want to do is go back to bed and shut out the world.

Problem is, I promised Caleb I'd run with him on Sundays after school started. The daily runs we took all summer aren't possible with his teacher schedule, so he always likes to get out early on the weekends to maximize his time. I agreed.

Mostly because I want my SB fix. Sebastian Bark is the best dog in the entire world.

We meet at Runyon Canyon and take an easy route, keeping mostly to a jog for the dog's benefit. There are off-leash dog areas on some routes, but they trigger Caleb's anxiety, so we stick to specific trails and keep the pit bull on his harness.

Or not-so-pit-bull, as Caleb explains.

"The shelter said Sebastian Bark was pure pittie, but I've always thought he was a mix—his face is too narrow. Valerie encouraged me to do one of those doggie DNA kits after they messaged us on his Instagram account, and I finally went for it," Caleb says proudly as we pick up a trail.

Sebastian Bark is a social media star all on his own, and I think it's hilarious that Caleb became a dog-fluencer. No one but the other Glitter Bats knows who's behind the account, officially, but there are plenty of Glitterbugs speculating in the comments that the account belongs to Caleb, especially after a few paparazzi shots of SB, Caleb, and Valerie hit the internet. That dog now has half a million followers and more brand partnerships than any of us.

It's fucking hilarious. But it's also fun to watch people fawn over this dog we all love so much. "Big guy is like 50 percent Lab, then a roulette of Staffy, boxer, and a tiny bit of pointer."

We pause to let a family with a stroller cross in front of us, and I lean down. "But you're 100 percent handsome, aren't you, baby boy?"

SB licks my face for my effort. I laugh.

Caleb shrugs. "Who knew? I started a poll so his fans could guess his breed, but we're revealing the results next week."

I cock my head. "*We?* Is Valerie helping you run his account now?"

He laughs, his cheeks turning pink. "I mean, we do have joint custody. I'm pretty sure he likes her better than me, and I can't even blame him."

I nudge his shoulder as we pick back up into a jog. "Gross. You're in love."

Caleb flushes more, way redder than he should be for such a light workout. "Yeah, I am. Don't knock it until you try it."

"I'm perfectly happy on my own, thank you very much. Love is for suckers." I say it automatically, but there's no venom in my voice.

Caleb knows I'm happy for him. What he doesn't know is that I'm also a little jealous. Not specifically of *him*—Valerie is objectively hot and all, but the two of us together would be an absolute disaster. Even when we had that first *oh, you're queer too?* moment, it was all solidarity and platonic joy, zero attraction.

I've only ever been attracted to one Glitter Bat, and by the mischievous flash in Caleb's eye, he knows it.

Caleb runs a hand over his hair, ruffling his damp curls. "Speaking of which . . . have you talked to *Jane* recently?"

I take a swig from my water bottle to buy time, even though I know Caleb can see past the way I'm squirming. He'd clocked my crush on Jane way back when we were still touring with my first VW van. "Uh, yeah. I helped her with a track for *Dragon Realm* on Friday."

He raises his brows. "All alone in the studio?"

"Yeah, and?"

"How successful were you in keeping your hands off her?"

I gape at the accusation, as if I would try to seduce Jane like she's innocent Laura and I'm Carmilla, the irresistible vampire. "Nothing happened! Especially not after . . ."

I trail off, knowing I've doomed myself. Fuck me and my lack of filter.

"After *what*, Keeley?" Caleb stumbles to a stop, and SB whines as he tugs at the leash. "Sorry, buddy," he says. To ensure I can't escape the question, Caleb makes a show of taking the dog's collapsible water bottle out of his fanny pack and setting it up. At least SB can lap up a little hydration . . . while I get grilled. "Keeley, tell me what's going on."

And I'm so tired of replaying Friday in my head that I fold like a house of cards.

I wince. "Jane and I kind of had a massive blowout fight after we recorded."

Caleb's mouth drops open, like he's just heard the most salacious piece of news from *Gossip Daily*. "*What?* You, I believe, but Jane? *Jane Mercer* fought with you?"

I bring a hand to the back of my damp neck, and when I realize what I'm doing, I try to turn it into a stretch, feigning nonchalance. "Yeah."

By the look on his face, it doesn't work. Caleb is calculating the situation, trying to make sense of it and also figure out how to ask me his next question so I don't completely dodge it.

"That's unlike her."

I nod. "I'm very aware. But we'll work it out. Can we get back to our run now?"

Caleb shakes his head, and then he fucking sits on the ground along the side of the path next to the dog, so my only option is to wait for him to get up. And we both know he won't get up until I tell him the story.

From the moment I met Caleb Sloane, I knew I was gaining another brother, and that means this kind of bullshit. If Ollie were here, I'm sure the conversation would go the same way: me being forced to talk about my feelings to a nosy person I'm not paying for therapy.

"Tell me *exactly* what happened or I'm not going anywhere."

I shrug. "I don't know! I was exhausted and so was she, and well . . . I asked what she thought about making another Glitter Bats album. I started this, okay, it was kind of a rant? But I was talking about how it needed to be sooner than later to get something of our own that isn't connected to Label, and she started pushing back. She totally went off about her demanding schedule, and how she couldn't commit to anything because there are all these things up in the air, and . . . I panicked that she's thinking about leaving the band."

Caleb blinks. "Did you ask her if that's what's going on?"

Warmth floods my skin, and it has nothing to do with the sunshine. I scrub a hand over my face and clear my throat. "Not really? We just started sniping at each other." The shame of my words comes back at me in full force.

Still, it felt like she had more important things to do than think about the rest of us. And she *is* killing it. What if she doesn't have time for us anymore?

Caleb places his hands on his hips and gives me *a look*.

"What?" I demand.

Caleb gestures at me with the hand that isn't attached to Sebastian Bark's leash. "That sounds awfully familiar."

I stand up, waving dismissively at him. "Oh, hell no. This is totally different."

He chuckles. "This is different than Valerie forcing me into the Glitter Bats reunion, culminating in a big blowout argument about the future of the band, that was really all tied up in years of unresolved sexual tension?"

I gape at him as heat floods my face. "What sexual tension? No one said anything about sexual tension."

"Keeley. Are you really going to stand there and tell me you're not attracted to Jane?"

I throw my arms wide in frustration. "It doesn't fucking matter, because she's not into me!" And besides, I'm not going to do anything to risk the band after what Caleb and Valerie put us through. Then again, that worked out for them. But this is different. I know better than to hope for a happily ever after. "I don't understand why we're talking about this again. We've had this bullshit conversation a hundred times!"

Caleb raises a placating palm, and I glance around, realizing I'm making a scene. Fortunately, Runyon is quiet today. "The point is that there are four other members of this band, but you're only putting this amount of pressure on one of us. I think you picked that fight because somewhere, deep down, you've tangled your feelings about her with your feelings about the band, and it's why you tried to strong-arm her into committing to an album as she was emerging from a marathon recording session for another project."

I close my eyes and open them again. He's right, and I kind of hate him for it. "Like I said, it doesn't matter. Nothing is ever going to happen between us. But it still really fucking hurt when she said she didn't want to prioritize the band." It was like she didn't want to prioritize *me*.

I'm not even sure how to unpack that, but it made me feel like absolute trash. Jane is amazing and I always look at everything she's done with starry eyes, but I'm terrified that she'll keep moving on to bigger and better things until she leaves this family we've built together.

And then I'll lose her completely.

My phone buzzes then, and I yank it out of my running shorts as an escape from this conversation.

When I read the screen, I immediately regret it.

MOM: Are you picking up another gig soon?

I groan and shove my phone away.

Caleb raises a brow as he folds the water dish back up, stuffs it in his fanny pack, and pops up to meet me. "What's wrong now?"

I huff. "My mom thinks clearing my schedule to focus on the band was a bad financial move. She keeps saying, *You're an adult, but I'm concerned about your choices*, as if that's helpful. She's been hounding me to get back to work." I shrug my shoulders. We video chat every Sunday afternoon, and I'm not looking forward to today's conversation. The last one turned into a lecture. "When we talk today, I'm going to tell my parents about the gig with Bianca to get them off my back."

Caleb frowns. Instead of picking up a jog again, he starts walking. "I didn't know you'd taken a step back from gigs. Wait, are you and Sasha not getting along? That's weird."

Don't I know it. I've always been super close to my parents.

They're careful about money, sure, but they've never done anything to make me feel unsafe or unloved. When I came out to them as pansexual at fifteen, they bought a ton of rainbow flags and invited the whole family to Pride. Hell, even when I told them I was rejecting my acceptance from Stanford for our record deal, they supported me following my dreams.

The only thing they asked is that I manage my money well and become financially independent, and I've done so. When my bandmates went on spending sprees after that first check (well, except for Jane, who threw it all in savings), I opened up a tiny investment portfolio and started planning ahead.

And because of that, I'm comfortable now. Even now that I've rented a condo in Southern California and bought a new vehicle, I *can* afford time to focus on the band . . . as long as the band is participating too.

But I don't say all this to Caleb. "Mom and I aren't fighting, we're just . . . not seeing eye to eye at the moment," I say.

He sighs. "God, if you can't get along with *your* parents, what hope is there for the rest of us?"

"Thank you," I drawl. "That's very comforting."

"I try," he grins. "But really, are you okay? Do you want to talk about it?"

"No, I want to fucking run until I hit my Strava goal," I say.

"Okay, let's fucking go."

Caleb bolts into a run, SB bounding happily alongside him. He tries to leave me in the dust, but since my legs are longer than his, it doesn't take long for me to catch up. I've got at least six inches on him.

But I'm still distracted. My pulse pounds in time with my shoes on the trail, and the beat *almost* drowns out the worry buzzing around my brain.

It would be easy to explain this desperation to make more music as neurodivergent hyperfocus, but I owe myself more than that. There are a lot of good reasons to move forward with the band now that we're free of our last contract. I'm terrified that I'm the only Glitter Bat willing to go all in this time. What if we lose all the momentum we had from *More to Say*, and we fade into obscurity before we can decide our next move?

And what if I lose my best friends again?

What if, in my desperation to hold on to her, I've already lost one?

5

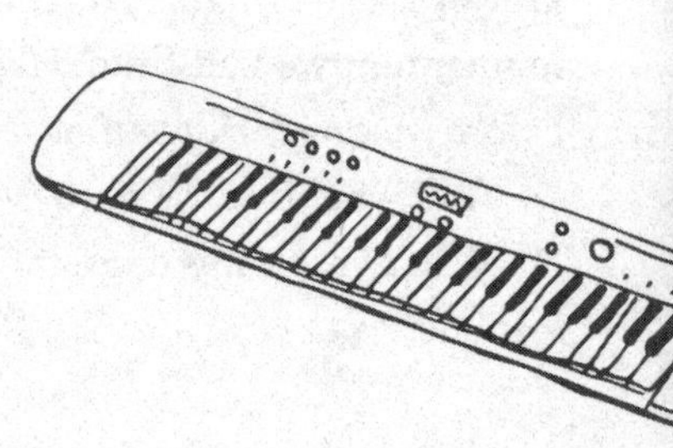

✦ Jane ✦

The Wednesday after my recording session with Keeley, the Glitter Bats gather for what was supposed to be a jam session at Valerie and Caleb's town house. Jamming hasn't actually happened yet, because we've all been catching up, and then Caleb got food going.

It's nice, though, to just talk to them all. It's been too long since we were together as a band.

After they eloped in Vegas seven weeks ago, our lead singers upgraded from Valerie's tiny one-bedroom to a quaint place in Long Beach close to the ocean. This is the first time we've all been over, and it's fun to see how they've put the space together. It's a cute home, with terra-cotta-colored walls and vintage-looking brass furnishings and plenty of windows to let in sunlight. They've even got pre-hiatus Glitter Bats memorabilia mounted all over the living room, and Riker keeps standing up to examine each frame and statuette, as if he doesn't have the same keepsakes in his own music room.

It's good to see them up, because our early days were a sore spot for Caleb during the time he was away from the industry. He wasn't even sure he wanted to come back at all, and I'm thankful every day that he did.

My heart aches knowing *I* might be the holdout this time.

Keeley and I haven't cleared the air yet, and it's beyond awkward. She's sitting on one of the green velvet sofas next to me, but I think that's more because it was the only free seat and not because she actually wants to be close. And I'm all too aware of her presence. Today, Keeley's wearing a yellow crop top that shows off her toned stomach in the gap of skin above her high-waisted jeans, tied effortlessly together with an open short-sleeve button-down in a bright, abstract pattern.

It's not much skin, but it's distracting enough, especially when she shifts again and I catch the herbal scent of her shampoo.

Pathetically, I tried to look pretty today, because I knew Keeley would be here . . . even though she's seen me at my most unkempt hundreds of times, so there's no reason I should feel embarrassed by how casual I was at the studio last week. But I couldn't help it. Instead of putting my hair up, I styled my curls with water and my diffuser and let them hang around my shoulders. I'm wearing a vintage blue long-sleeved minidress that's casual enough for a group hang but makes me feel a Stevie Nicks kind of cool.

I almost thought I caught Keeley checking out my legs when I walked in, but it had to have been my imagination. I shake my head, willing myself to think of literally anything else other than how much I want Keeley Cunningham to pay attention to me.

So we can clear the air. Obviously.

Sebastian Bark takes turns leaning his head in each of our laps as we lounge around the living room, snacking on cheese and crackers and passing around a bottle of wine while the oven preheats for Caleb's homemade pizza.

When the dog comes over to me with happy snuffles, I make him sit and offer him a tiny piece of cheddar. He takes it gently before bounding proudly over to his parents.

"Hey, no human food! It makes him gassy," Caleb says from his spot on the other side of Valerie. He's chopped off his shaggy curls from the summer, his dark hair now trimmed closer to his head so only the top is longer. Teacher Caleb is back now that school is in session.

Valerie leans down to press a kiss on Sebastian Bark's head, and he wags his tail as her freshly platinum hair tickles his nose, any last trace of her turquoise dye from our tour long gone.

"Don't listen to your daddy, he's mean. You can have whatever you want," Valerie says in a baby voice I've never heard before.

"You're going to spoil him," Caleb warns, but there's more fondness than frustration in his tone. Valerie reaches for her wineglass and takes a sip. He opens up his arm as an offering, and she snuggles in close to his side, nursing her drink. She's so much softer than the Valerie I saw last summer—relaxed, smiling, unworried. It doesn't hurt that her acting career is booming on top of *More to Say*. After her musical TV series, *Epic Theme Song*, got cancelled by The Network, Sunset Streaming+ picked it up for multiple seasons, and Valerie is in the middle of promo.

Stability is rare in this industry, and it makes it easier to relax. It's the thing I'm clinging to.

But Caleb is obviously the true reason for Valerie's change, and it's good to see them happy together. The two rarely separate, and if you didn't know them before they got hitched, you'd think it was just a newlywed thing. They've always been tactile like this. Even when they were pretending they weren't together, they couldn't stop holding hands, leaning shoulders, stealing kisses when they thought no one was watching.

I'm glad they found their happily ever after.

"You two are disgusting," Keeley says, gesturing at the happy couple.

Valerie rolls her eyes as Caleb kisses her temple.

"Deal with it," Caleb says, but he seems to take the hint. "So, uh, should we discuss the elephant in the room?" Heat floods my cheeks, and I wonder, for a moment, if Keeley told him about our fight. "Do we want to talk about band stuff, or just hang out?"

A year ago, he didn't want the band to have a future at all, so it's strange to see he's even open to more conversations. Despite my busy schedule, I'm not opposed to talking about things.

I'm just worried about where they might lead.

My agent, Lacey Sampson, has been wrangling my schedule into submission, but it doesn't look pretty. I also have to factor in my sister's wedding. Nora still hasn't called me, even after I sent her a flower arrangement with a carefully crafted congratulatory message, and I wonder if I taught her that.

Maybe it's no different than me avoiding confrontation instead of calling Keeley to clear the air.

Riker's brows raise as he stares at his phone in his hand, jaw dropping open. "I think we should talk about *this*. Check your fucking emails."

I grab my phone out of my bag and start to read the most recent message, forwarded from Wade, with an apology that he's heading onto a flight and won't be available to discuss this directly for a few hours.

NOTICE TO CEASE AND DESIST

> On behalf of Label Records, the lawful owner of the copyright to the albums ***Wanderlust***, ***Bittersweet***, and ***More to Say***, it has come to our attention that Glitter Bats have been using copyrighted work without permission.

> This letter serves as formal notice for Glitter Bats to cease and desist all use of these recordings immediately. The unauthorized use of this intellectual property, as observed in Glitter Bats social media accounts, is clear infringement that goes beyond fair use . . .

It drags on into more pretentious legalese. From her perch next to me, Keeley hisses. "Those motherfucking cunts."

My jaw sets. I don't get angry very often, but I'm furious.

All we did was take over our own social media accounts after separating from Label Records. We created a few videos with the recorded versions of "Ghosts," and "Light the Way," and "Better Times," compiling footage from the summer tour. It was harmless. The fans loved it.

And now we have to take it down.

Of course I know how copyright works, but they're talking about *our* music. I hate that they have total control of where and how it's used.

"It's so ridiculous—this would never hold up in court," Riker says from his spot on the armchair across from us.

"It just fucking might," Keeley says ruefully. She starts typing furiously, pursing her lips in a way that is just too distracting given the gravity of this conversation. "Caleb and Valerie wrote the lyrics, but Label owns all of our masters. This has Landon written all over it."

Landon Banks is the current CEO of Label, but he was also a high-profile producer when we first got into the industry, with experience actually playing in bands that influenced us. When we were offered a chance to work with him, we were all starry-eyed. That lasted until we realized Landon wasn't on our side. He was demanding and had a huge ego. We wrote all of our songs, but he always wanted to take credit for our success, and for a while, we let him. He was out of the country last summer when we came together for that fated Glitter Bats reunion, so we almost thought we were in the clear. We should have known better. When we finished *More to Say* six months ago, he threw a bit of a tantrum when we were finally walking away from that last recording session.

It's really awkward when a man in his fifties throws a tantrum.

I'm so glad Label no longer owns *us*, but they still own our music, so they can do whatever they want. This is . . . so much worse than I was expecting, and I feel like a fool.

I nod. "Keeley is right." She startles, like she forgot I was here, and her face flushes. "If Label is saying we can't play the song, we can't play the song. Live shows are different, but they own the recordings, and there's no disputing that."

It's such a weird position. We've never had control of our own music. That's what we got for signing a contract we didn't understand as teenagers, and it doesn't help that our first manager, Valerie's mom, Tonya, didn't look out for our best interests. In fact, I think she might have sided with the label on this one. She was always a little too cozy with Landon and his VP, Gina Choi, for my liking. It never felt like she had our backs.

"What should we do in the meantime?" Valerie asks. "I know we're all busy, but this is so important. Do any of us have the capacity to fight this?"

Keeley stiffens next to me, and I know she's remembering our argument just as vividly as I am.

Riker laughs dryly. "Regardless of our schedules, we can't just sit here and let them steamroll us. We need to figure out if and how we can legally still use our own music."

"For now, I think we have to play Label's game and figure out what our options are," I say.

"I'll connect with Wade once he lands and get his thoughts," Keeley says. "My schedule is open, and I have plenty of energy to do some fighting. I know Ortega has a legal team, but I might even call my brother." Keeley's twin brother, Oliver, is *almost* as smart as she is, and he's got an impressive corporate law résumé already.

Not the worst contact to have in a bind like this.

"Should we . . . try to fight them for the rights to our music?" Valerie asks, biting her lip.

I have no idea how to do that—if that's even a financial possibility—but for now, it feels like we're stuck. In this moment, I face the horrifying possibility that *I* cursed us by not being willing to drop everything to make more music. Maybe this is the universe's way of punishing me for choosing my career over the band.

Now we're not even allowed to play our own albums.

"Goddamn it," Keeley groans, shifting on the seat next to me in agitation. Even upset like this, I try to ignore the way warmth radiates off her skin. "I'm so proud of *More to Say*, and we don't even get to celebrate that. It's just more of the same fuckery with the same label."

"We'll figure it out," Valerie says. "I know we're all busy, but I hate to just let Landon get away with this. Let's fight."

"Is there really anything to fight?" I ask quietly, unable to shake the feeling of defeat. "They own our music."

"Fuck that. We can't let them get away with this!" Keeley says, and I nearly want to cower at the fury in her tone. The sting from our fight lingers like a bad hangover, and everything unresolved between us makes me feel like that fierce anger is directed right at me.

"Whatever it is, we have to figure this out," Caleb says. "The school year is brutal, but I'm happy to do whatever I can. I'm worried that if we don't fight this now, we'll lose our chance to do something about it."

"Please," Riker says. "I've been playing shows here and there, but I definitely don't want to commit to any tours until we know what we're doing with Glitter Bats. It was nice of Jane to call me for *Into the Dragon Realm* because at least it got me off my ass."

When Riker's not playing guitar for me and everyone else in this town, he's either baking or hiking, so it's not like he was truly doing nothing, but I laugh. "You're welcome, I think?"

He chuckles. "Yeah, she kept both me and Keeley busy."

Keeley shifts again on the couch, uncomfortably this time.

Valerie straightens. "What? I didn't know Keeley was helping too. Now I feel left out, Jane. You all got to play music together and I wasn't a part of it. Those opportunities are in short supply these days." Her voice is playfully whiny despite the true undertones there, and I try to laugh.

"Keeley was just doing me a favor."

"It wasn't a big deal," Keeley murmurs.

"It was *huge*," I say, trying to catch her eye. But she doesn't look at me. So instead, I tell Valerie and Caleb the short version of what happened with Trevor Barnett while Riker gasps in all the right places, even though he's already heard my rant.

"Wow," Caleb says. "That sounds like a nightmare."

"Jane handled it, though," Riker says. He mock-bows to me from his seat, as if he's not worthy, and I can't help but laugh. "Just wait until you hear what she put together for this season, it's so good. If we're not careful, she's going to get too busy to clown around with us making our silly little rock songs."

Keeley huffs beside me, and I try to make eye contact again, but she stares at her aquamarine nails.

"Never," I say, and I mean it. Even if I'm not ready to make another album, I'm not walking away from Glitter Bats. Next to me, I can feel the tension rolling off Keeley like a heat wave.

"I can't wait," Caleb says.

"Of course it's amazing—it's Jane!" Valerie says, and I smile a little at her unrestrained faith in me, despite the awful news we just got. The oven timer beeps, and we all transition into the kitchen, where Caleb serves us up homemade chicken pesto pizza and mixed greens. We don't talk much as we settle around their dining room table and eat. The food is delicious, but the mood in the room is decidedly somber.

And when our plates are clear, we all just stare at one another, the late-September sunset streaming in through the windows illuminating the awful new reality we're facing together.

Suddenly, Valerie claps her hands together with faux enthusiasm. "Now who wants to go out to LuLu and celebrate that we're a band with no music!"

Her voice is light, but I don't miss the tightness in her eyes. This is what Valerie does when she's hurting: she finds a way to blow off steam, usually out in public. Sometimes it gets a little destructive, but she's gotten more subdued over the years. And with how much frustration we're all feeling right now, I, well . . . I don't blame her one bit.

Caleb squeezes her closer. "Do we really have to go out? It's a school night."

Valerie laughs tightly. "I just want to dance a little, let off some steam! I promise we'll be home before you turn into a pumpkin." LuLu is a club that's hard to get into unless you know someone, and Valerie *is* someone. It's really not my scene, but the bonus is that there are no phones allowed. They'll literally kick you out if they see one, so there's no risk of images making it out on the internet.

If we want to let off steam, it's a good place to go.

"Home by *nine*," Caleb says emphatically.

"Yay, I'm in!" Riker says, eyes bright with interest. Maybe it's the energy drinks, but he has endless stamina to go dancing after a long week of work. I'm not like that—I have to have the right headspace to go out and surround myself with strangers. Dancing doesn't sound fun tonight. It just sounds exhausting. Even with *Dragon Realm* wrapped up, I still have a ton of things going on.

I need to sleep for twelve hours from the comfort of my own bed. "Sorry, I'm out," I say.

Riker turns to Keeley with a puppy dog expression mirroring Sebastian Bark's.

"Please, Cunningham?"

She shakes her head, staring at the carpet. "Nope. I have a headache."

And that's that. The other three make plans, and the tone in the place is all forced lightness to soothe the sting of that letter. Riker volunteers to do the dishes so Caleb can take Sebastian Bark on a short walk. Valerie frantically tries to decide between two lipsticks before shoving both in her bag. But since we're not going, Keeley and I both say our goodbyes and head out. The salty breeze coming off the ocean is cool with a bit of a bite, and I close my eyes and breathe in the air.

My Prius is parked behind Keeley's Rivian, but we don't talk as we head down to our respective cars. I know I started it, but this is getting ridiculous. We have to talk sometime.

"Keeley?" I ask, my heart racing as I try to decide what to even *say*.

She turns to me like it pains her, and I can't tell if she really has a headache or if she's just tired of me. "Yeah, Mercer?"

My keys shake in my hand, and I ball it into a fist. "Uh, have a good night. I hope you feel better."

I'm such a disaster. Keeley is my *friend*. Why can't I just apologize to her?

She sighs, running a hand through her hair. "You too."

I can't get into my car fast enough. Traffic is pretty light, and I make it home in record time, cringing at my awkwardness. When

I get to my doorstep, I'm more than ready to change into my favorite silky PJs and crash with a romance novel and another glass of wine.

But when I open my front door, a gush of water soaks my Rainbows. I jump back, trying to figure out what's happening, my mind whirring in disbelief.

Because I'm pretty sure my house is . . . flooded?

It's in that moment that all of the emotions I've been suppressing come crashing in, and I burst into tears.

The Glitter Bats' Night Out!

BY RYAN TATE FOR *GOSSIP DAILY*

Besties! I regret to inform you all that I still can't get into LuLu. The bouncer is mean.

However, that doesn't stop me from hanging at the door. And who did I see but Valerie Quinn, Caleb Sloane, and Riker Maddox heading into the exclusive club tonight! Notably, Jane Mercer and Keeley Cunningham were missing from their group, and I can't help but wonder what the story is there. Is trouble ahead for the Glitter Bats?

Or was this night out a way to soothe the sting of a salacious cease-and-desist letter from Label Records? You can view our exclusive on that HERE, because of course I figured out how to get my hands on it. Wonder who Valerie pissed off to elicit *that* reaction from the company!

Alas, while I couldn't get inside, there was no one stopping me from waiting by the door. The three emerged an hour later, all looking a little worse for wear. Valerie even had bright red lipstick smeared on her mouth that didn't match the nude lip she was rocking on the way in. Check the photos below!

Did our favorite bad girl cheat on her husband right in front of him? It wouldn't be the wildest thing she's gotten up to.

Too bad Caleb Sloane didn't ask me for advice before he put a ring on it—I would have told him to run like hell. If you ask me, Jane Mercer is the only Glitter Bat who is stable enough for a long-term relationship. (And yes, I'm considering the *entire* band with that statement, fully aware of the recent nuptials. I said what I said.) Maddox gives too much himbo energy, and Cunningham, while she may have made it three years with Bianca Martin, is far too volatile for anything that lasts.

Follow our Glitter Bats tag for more updates!

6

✦ *Keeley* ✦

As I drive home, I try to ignore this weirdness between me and Jane and focus on what I can control—and that is how hard we fight Label.

Before he was a CEO, before he even started producing, Landon Banks was the first drummer I obsessed over as a kid. He was one of those musicians who was just fun to watch and also incredibly good at what he did. When we got the deal with Label, having a chance to work with him as a producer felt like a dream come true.

And then I got to know him. Landon knows his shit when it comes to music, but he's also slimy and entitled, and no one calls him on it because he's talented. It doesn't hurt that he's produced some of the biggest names in the industry, and he inherited his position as CEO from his millionaire father. He absolutely took advantage of our naivete as starry-eyed teens to lock us into a horrible contract that gave him total control over us.

Never meet your heroes. Mine sucks ass.

Maybe my decision to clear my schedule wasn't so foolish.

Because now, I have nothing but time to fight for the band. I'm no lawyer, but that's what twin brothers with law degrees are for. I'm just about to ask Siri to call Oliver when the Jacob Collier album I'm playing suddenly pauses and Jane's name comes up on my console.

So much for focusing on something else.

"Hello?" I ask, pulse pounding despite myself. I don't know why she startled me.

"Keeley? I'm sor-sorry to bug you, but everyone else is going out and . . . and I didn't know who else to call . . ." Her voice is frantic, tearful, and it makes me sit up straighter. I grip the wheel tighter, trying to focus on the road and the conversation at the same time.

"Jane? What's wrong?"

She gasps, letting out a sob. "I think my house is flooded? What do I do?"

Oh no. That sucks, but I still let out a breath at the knowledge that she's not in immediate danger. Still, even in a catastrophe, this type of emotional reaction is so unlike Jane—she really must be exhausted. Maybe our friendship is strained right now, but I can take some of this weariness off her shoulders.

Because the universe is feeling extra ironic today, my brother isn't the only useful Cunningham family connection. My dad is an insurance claims adjuster, and I was a star at Take Your Child to Work Day five years in a row. I know exactly what she needs to do.

My mind scrambles as I think through the scenario. "You need to try to shut off your water main if you can access it safely. Do you know where it is?"

She hiccups, trying to contain herself. "Yeah, it's outside under the back porch steps."

My shoulders relax a little. It's a lot safer if she doesn't have to wade through the water. "Okay, so go shut that off." I hear her walking around on the sand around her home, and she lets out the cutest little huff as she turns off the water.

"Okay, that's done."

"Good job. Now you need to call your homeowner's insurance right away. They should have a twenty-four-hour claims line, and they can help you get a restoration company out there to address the immediate damage."

She gulps, her voice steadying. "I'll call them when we hang up."

Good. She's focusing. "Can you get to the second level without walking in the water?"

She makes a humming sound. Now that I've given her some actionable steps, Jane is sounding a bit more like herself. Even her tone is more measured, and I feel myself relaxing with her. "Yeah, I can get in through my upper deck," she says.

"Okay, go pack some bags. Once a restoration company is out there, you might not be able to get into the house, so try to get anything you might need for a while." But if her ground floor is flooded, she won't have access to her kitchen or her living room or . . . shit, her basement music room full of instruments and priceless mementos.

I don't bring that up right now.

"Right. So I'll call insurance, then book a hotel," she says.

That sounds so wrong. I know Jane likes to be independent, especially after what she went through with her family, but a last-minute hotel room in her part of LA is an unnecessary expense. She doesn't need to waste the money. And, well . . . with how distressed she sounds, I don't want her to be alone.

I blurt the words before I can regret them. "Don't be silly. You'll stay with me."

"I couldn't possibly . . ."

"Jane. Stay with me. There's no reason to pay for a hotel."

"Okay . . ." She trails off. "If you're sure?"

"As soon as I get home, I'm getting the guest room ready, so don't waste my time." I try to keep my tone teasing even as I clench the steering wheel, and her responding laugh makes it feel like things could be normal between us again despite our fight. I just wish it were under better circumstances.

"Fine, I'll stay with you. But promise you'll kick me out as soon as it gets to be an imposition."

"I promise," I say, but we both know I won't. I can't imagine a world where Jane Mercer would be an imposition. Despite all this weird, fresh tension between us, she's still one of my favorite people in the world.

As soon as I get home, I get to work.

Over the next couple of hours, while I wait for Jane to show up, I scramble to clean my condo. It's not dirty, but with my ADHD, things tend to end up in the wrong places. So I tidy the laundry from the kitchen chairs, then throw all of the piles of unsorted junk mail into the recycle bin. Once that's done, I vacuum the carpets and sweep the floors and put fresh sheets on the guest bed.

The bed where Jane Mercer will be sleeping for the foreseeable future. God, help me.

I put unopened bottles of shampoo, conditioner, body soap, and face wash in the shower of my guest bath. I place clean, thick towels on the bar fresh out of the dryer. I light a couple of vanilla candles: one in the kitchen, and one in the bathroom. For a moment, I wonder if I'm too obvious, keeping that scent around me at all times.

But before I can snuff them, the bell rings, and I hurry to let Jane in. She squeezes through the door, overloaded with canvas tote bags and two giant rolling suitcases.

"How did you get those down your steps?" I ask, in lieu of a greeting. Jane's face is a little tearstained, but there's a grim determination in the set of her jaw that tells me everything I need to know. She called insurance. They're taking care of it.

And now she's here.

Jane moves one bag with her hip. "I got down very carefully." Then she laughs. "I know this is a lot more than a week's worth of clothes, but I was so nervous to leave anything that I packed up as much as I could. I just thought it would be easier, instead of the possibility of having to go back, or worse, go buy stuff. I don't own very much anyways."

Jane's a careful spender. She's probably got most of her wardrobe in those two suitcases, including her shoes.

"I totally get it. You can do laundry whenever—I have one of those tiny stack sets in the hall closet, but it does the trick."

She swallows. "Thank you. Where should I . . ."

And then I realize: Jane hasn't been in my new place yet. We always go to her house. Maybe it's because of her proximity to the ocean, or just the beauty of how well decorated her home is, but it's a lot cozier than the stark minimalism I adopted when I got this place last year. I never felt the urge to do much with it, so other than a few odds and ends my mom always brings whenever she visits, it's completely impersonal—except for the third bedroom I set up as a soundproof practice space.

And as I'm looking at the starkness of it all, hyperconscious of what she's thinking about it, I realize Jane is just waiting for an answer.

"Uh, sorry, guest room is down the hall," I say, gesturing in the general direction. Jane doesn't hesitate to wander down there, and I just stand, awkward, in the entry.

"It smells great in here!" she says, and I flush, grateful she can't see me. I'm sure if she saw the look on my face, she'd know at once that it's all because of her.

Desperate to do something with my hands, I hurry over to the kitchen and pour her a glass of water, then one for myself. I down the drink, trying to calm my nerves. When that doesn't work, I start to fiddle with one of my fidget rings.

It's not weird. A woman is just staying in my apartment. Not a woman, a *friend. Jane.* This is fine.

When she emerges from the spare room, I hand her the water.

"Oh my gosh, thank you! I couldn't get to my kitchen," she says, taking a long sip. Her throat bobs distractingly as she swallows, and I grip the edge of my kitchen counter to steady myself.

"I figured as much," I say.

"How are you feeling?" Jane asks.

"What?" I blink, confused. I'm not the one who just dealt with a house flood.

"Your headache?"

"Right," I say. Because that was the only lie I could come up with. After making no progress at the band meeting, I just didn't want to see Jane dancing at LuLu with Riker, which was a silly worry, given that she also declined the invite before I even had a chance to do so. But I'd already decided how I was going to respond at that point. "I totally forgot—guess it went away."

"That's good," she says. She sets down the water glass and crosses her arms, awkward. "Look, I know this is a major imposition, and things have been tense between us, and—"

"Jane—" I interrupt, but I stop when she gives me a look.

"Can we just talk about our argument?"

I swallow thickly. The last thing I want to do is add stress to her night by rehashing that conversation. "You had a rough night. We can talk about it later."

She rounds on me. "Please, Keeley. These last few days have been killing me."

I resist the urge to rub my temples. I don't have a headache yet, but having this conversation might just give me one. I don't respond.

Jane stares at her soaked Rainbows. "I'm sorry I yelled at you. It was out of line."

My hand goes to the back of my neck almost automatically. Resigned, I settle myself onto one of my barstools backward, so I can face her. "I was out of line too. I'm sorry I picked a fight with you."

She frowns, opens her mouth, then shuts it again. Finally, she decides to continue. "What started all of that?"

"I don't know . . . you were just so cagey about recording something new that . . ." And then I finally speak my fears out loud. "I was afraid you were thinking about quitting the band."

She gapes, genuine hurt flashing across her face. I want to do nothing but soothe that pain. "What?" Her voice is quiet, disbelieving.

I hurry to continue before I lose my nerve. "We . . . we wouldn't be Glitter Bats without you, and I couldn't bear the thought of losing this thing I love again."

My eyes sting. I couldn't bear the thought of losing *her*.

Jane sighs, leaning against the counter. "I get it, and I'm sorry if I made you feel that way. Of course, I want to make more music with you all—but I also need to be true to myself."

I blink, because whatever I expected her to say, it wasn't that. "What do you mean?"

She takes a sip of water as if to steady herself, closes her eyes, then looks back at me.

"Well . . . I've done a really good job at letting other people define my life. First, it was my parents—"

"That wasn't your fault," I say, and she puts up a hand. "Sorry," I say. I didn't mean to interrupt her. Jane is just so hard on herself for the life she was forced into growing up, and it always breaks my heart.

"I know you want to defend me, and I appreciate that. But when

I escaped my childhood home, this band became my identity." Jane must sense the hurt that tears through me at that, because she hurries to continue. "No one did it on purpose, and I don't think anyone actually did anything *wrong*, but I clung so hard to you all when really, I should've taken space to figure out who I was for myself. When the band broke up, I thought I lost everything. So I hustled nonstop, panicked that if I didn't find another steady job in the music business, I'd have to move back in with my parents and lose myself again. But I figured out how to stand on my own two feet, and I'm really proud of the career I've built all on my own in the years since."

I run a hand through my hair. I know Jane has been through literal hell with her family, and instead of cowering to their demands, she's become this incredibly brave, independent person. Someone weaker would be bitter and jaded, but she sees the best in everyone, and she really tries to pour herself into her work and help the people working with her to thrive.

And she's damn good at what she does. "I'm proud of you too," I say, then hurry to add, "We all are."

Her eyes gleam. "Thank you, I appreciate that. I just felt like if I passively went along with everything you were saying like last time, I would lose myself again. That I would stop growing and just stay stagnant, back to playing piano and smiling for the cameras and being so *nice*."

I think about what she's saying, and then I purse my lips. "You know, the cool thing about being free of Label Records is that we can grow together . . . no matter how much time it takes. The possibilities are whatever we want them to be. Fuck it, we could pivot and make a country album. We can do whatever we want, and we can grow creatively as a group. We make each other better."

She nods, biting her full bottom lip. "Yeah, I've started thinking about that too. Not the country album—I think folk is about as close as I would ever get." She laughs. "But just so it's abundantly clear, I have no intention of leaving the band. I just need us to take our time and give everyone space to work on their own projects. Another album will come, but I don't want to rush it."

It's not what I want to hear. Last year was hell trying to coordinate everyone's schedules, and we definitely powered through *More to Say* to finish out our contract with caffeine, late nights, and sheer will. With more freedom, I don't think we'll make another album that quickly. But . . . I understand. "I respect that. And for the record, I'm really sorry I stormed out."

Jane's mouth quirks up, but the smile is a little sad. "It was weird, not talking to you this week. There were so many times I wanted to text you, and then realized I couldn't."

"You could. You *always* can." I wish she would text me more.

"I know. Thank you."

"Anytime, Mercer."

Something lingers in the kitchen then, weighing the air, and I don't know what to do with it. I look at Jane, who is staring back at me with tired eyes. Her curls are frizzing out, her clothes are rumpled, and her skin looks alarmingly pale—not that any of it makes her look less beautiful.

But god, she really is exhausted. All I want is to ease some of that tension. So I deflect, which is something I don't usually do, but I can tell she needs it. This conversation was heavy enough.

"So . . . how was your week?"

She laughs, sinking onto one of my barstools. "I had to go to Royal Con, which was a little stressful. I don't like being on panels. But it was okay, and it felt good to share the song with the audience. The fans were so excited! Now that the work on *Dragon Realm* is done for now, I finally feel like I can breathe and focus on my other projects."

"That's fair. Were you planning to work tonight?"

Grabbing her phone, she grimaces. “No, it’s way too late, and I’m frazzled. But I’m not ready to sleep yet either. I just want to try to relax and clear my head a bit.”

“I could use that too, after the bomb of that cease and desist.” I’m so mad at Landon Banks I could scream, which isn’t a new feeling, but there’s nothing we can do about it tonight. “Have you watched the newest season of *Epic Theme Song*?” I ask. The latest installment of Valerie’s show dropped just last week, after they fought for a renewal for nearly a year, got cancelled, then eventually found a home at a new streamer who put them right back into production.

Jane’s shoulders slump. “No! I feel like a terrible friend too, but I’ve just been so busy.”

I grin, moving over to the pantry. “What if I make popcorn and pour us some wine, and we catch up on as many episodes as we can until we crash? Then we can roast Valerie the next time we see her by knowing the words to the songs.”

Her tired eyes brighten with mischief, and it’s the first time I’ve seen the *old* Jane looking back at me. I want to memorize this moment.

“She’ll hate that,” she says. “Let’s do it.”

@WanderlustMemes

Poll: Glitterbugs! What's your favorite track from More to Say?

Results: (Used Up 17%) (Daydreams Like This 31%) (Better Times 23%) (Light the Way 29%)

@MakeMeMrsSloane

@WanderlustMemes Used Up was ROBBED. Daydreams Like This is trash.

@ValerieQuinnSuperFan

@MakeMeMrsSloane you just hate Valerie, which is so weird. Are you even a real Glitterbug?

@MakeMeMrsSloane

@ValerieQuinnSuperFan no one asked you. And besides, literally everyone else in the band is more talented than her. Jane or Keeley would be way better on lead vocals, but everyone likes Valerie because they think she's the hottest. Which she's not? It's such bullshit.

@ValerieQuinnSuperFan

@MakeMeMrsSloane It's really weird to pit the band against each other, because they're all incredibly talented. Jane and Keeley are both wonderful singers and musicians, but that doesn't make Valerie bad. The special thing about this band is that everyone is so versatile. But, uh, have fun hating Valerie on your own.

@MakeMeMrsSloane

@ValerieQuinnSuperFan you started this. I'm blocking you.

@GlitterbugsUnofficial

When are we getting new Glitter Bats content? It's been silence from the band since that concert in Vegas, and that was almost two months ago. Any theories?

@BatsThatGlitter

OMG **@GlitterbugsUnofficial** what do you know??? 👀

@GlitterbugsUnofficial

@BatsThatGlitter I know nothing. I just hope.

@BitterSweetGlitterati

Sure **@GlitterbugsUnofficial**
[Frodo: keep your secrets GIF]

@GlitterbugsUnofficial

Hey **@BatsThatGlitter** and **@BitterSweetGlitterati** you know my account is UNOFFICIAL, right?

@BitterSweetGlitterati

Yeah but **@GlitterbugsUnofficial** I've always suspected you know more than you let on.

@GlitterbugsUnofficial

@BitterSweetGlitterati **@BatsThatGlitter** I just want more music like everyone else. But in the meantime, did anyone see the Into the Dragon Realm drop at Royal Con? OBSESSED with Jane's songwriting.

@BitterSweetGlitterati

@GlitterbugsUnofficial I wasn't there but I caught a recording of it. AMAZING! I would love to see Jane write for Broadway.

@BatsThatGlitter

@GlitterbugsUnofficial @BitterSweetGlitterati OMG CAN YOU IMAGINE??? TBH I'd love to see Valerie on Broadway . . . or OMG CALEB!!!

@BitterSweetGlitterati

@BatsThatGlitter @GlitterbugsUnofficial I WOULD PASS OUT FROM EXCITEMENT IF CALEB STARRED IN A MUSICAL WRITTEN BY JANE

@BatsThatGlitter

@BitterSweetGlitterati @GlitterbugsUnofficial BRB going to write a Broadway AU about the entire band, give me a day and it'll be up on FanficDream Archive

7

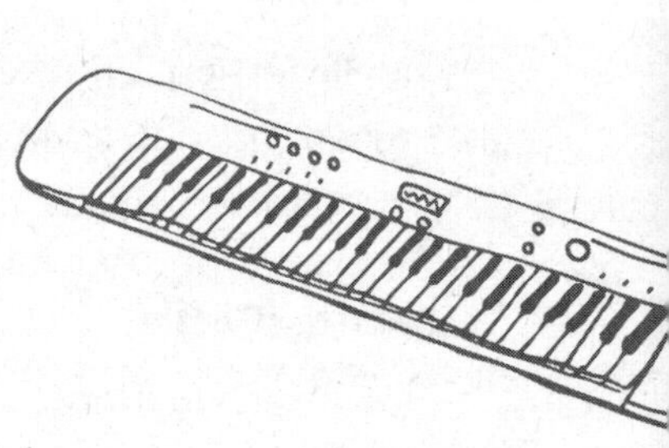

✦ *Jane* ✦

I don't *do* lazy mornings, but I sleep two hours past my usual alarm the first morning at Keeley's, a dull ache in my head throbbing from the lack of caffeine.

Instead of getting out of bed the way I should, I lean against the padded headboard and wrap the soft down gray comforter around me like a cocoon. This apartment might be a little stark, but the linens are nice and cozy and have the faintest lavender scent, and it's tempting to linger in bed knowing my schedule for the day is clear.

Hanging out with Keeley last night almost felt . . . normal, as we watched three episodes of *Epic Theme Song*. I'll never get over seeing talented friends do well, and Valerie was as charming as ever as Wendy the Wonder. It's a fun show, and I'm so happy for her that it got renewed after such a long hiatus.

Even though Keeley and I cleared the air, it still feels like there's something unsaid between us. It makes my stomach drop every time I see something that reminds me of her in this space. The guest bedroom is nearly as stark as the rest of the condo, and you wouldn't know at first glance that anything is personalized at all. But there are a couple of touches that scream Keeley.

Beneath all of that snark she wears like a mask is one of the most considerate people I know. She'd never admit it, but hospitality is kind of Keeley's thing. I see it in the tray with soaps and mini toiletries she's set out on the dresser, in the homemade crocheted blanket in a basket in the corner, even in the cozy vanilla candles and lighter on the bedside table.

She wants this place to be welcoming to guests, and I smile a little as I hug the quilt even tighter around my shoulders, realizing that's going to be me for a while. Warmth seeps to my toes.

Still, my to-do list is a mile long, and the thoughts of everything on it banish any desire to stay in bed. Because the problem is, Keeley wasn't wrong about my schedule. I *know* I'm too busy. I just don't know how to stop.

I've talked to my therapist about this a dozen times. Apparently, I try to produce at unsustainable levels because staying busy kept me a little insulated from my parents' scrutiny as a kid. It's a textbook coping mechanism. Every time I thought I was a pretty good person, I read a Bible verse I didn't measure up to, and then I would get so sick with worry that I was going to hell for not being good enough. So I padded my schedule with hobbies they approved of to avoid being forced into extra Bible studies.

Because *How can you be bored when you could spend time with the Lord?* was my dad's favorite saying.

Now . . . I don't know how to stop. My therapist says I'm "allowed to rest," but it doesn't feel like it when hustling keeps you afloat in this business. I prefer knowing when my next paycheck is coming in.

When the self-loathing—and the coffee craving—becomes too strong to ignore, I change into leggings and an oversized T-shirt and pad out into the hall. A keyboard catches my eye through the cracked door of the room across from mine on the way to the empty kitchen.

I perk up at the Chemex sitting on the counter. There's a bag of fresh coffee beans from my favorite place, a box of filters, and a burr grinder sitting next to it on the counter, along with a key and a little pink sticky note.

Jane,

I think this is all the right stuff? I remember seeing these beans at your apartment, and I thought you might like something normal after the stress of last night. If it's not right, I'm so sorry! Blame the damn hipster barista who helped me pick it out.

Help yourself to everything, obviously. We can get groceries later, but there should be some options in the pantry for your breakfast (I hope!).

I'm heading out for a long-ass run, but I should be back by 11. Here's a key if you need to leave. My entry code for the gate is 1725.

Keeley

A delighted giggle escapes my lips.

Keeley Cunningham took an extra trip across the city to my favorite coffee shop and bought, not just my favorite beans, but *all* the supplies to make coffee just the way I like it. She has a machine that takes coffee pods, so that would have been fine. I'm already inconveniencing her by staying here.

And then she went out of her way to do something special for me.

I'm struck by the gesture, and my chest warms. Maybe it's a sign that she's . . .

No. It's just a peace offering after last night, or her way of being a good friend. Keeley is like this—she'll do anything for the people she cares about, just like making her guest room cozy, and that even means going halfway across town to get coffee. It doesn't make me special.

It's like she wrote—she's trying to make things a little easier for me.

I search through the cupboards until I find her mug collection. Compared to the starkness of the apartment, these are a lot more personalized: there's one with a llama in the pan pride colors; one with supercool fan art of the entire band as vampires; a few from brands like Zildjian and Gretsch; and one with the Rebel Alliance symbol from Star Wars painted in a rainbow.

But I grab the one covered in simple doodles of breasts, because it makes me laugh.

For the next fifteen minutes, I lose myself in the routine of making coffee, feeling oddly soothed by the motions. I find a food scale deep in the back of the pantry and weigh the beans for two cups of coffee, then grind them while I put on a kettle to boil the water. The scent of the fresh grounds fills my lungs, and my brain perks up at the incoming boost of caffeine. Once the pot begins to boil, I stick a filter in the Chemex and add a little hot water to ensure the filter is set into place. Then I scoop the ground coffee in the filter and begin my slow, careful pour.

And I nearly swoon as the aroma of my favorite coffee in the world permeates throughout Keeley's kitchen, adding just a little bit of *me* to this space. I lean my elbows on the kitchen counter as I wait for the pour-over to percolate, then prepare a cup. I take a slow, careful sip, and it fills me with warmth from head to toe.

Fine, I'm addicted to caffeine, but it's not the worst vice I could have. In this industry, it practically makes me a saint.

My stomach rumbles, and my eyes land on the fruit basket next to the fridge. I grab a perfectly green-yellow banana from the bunch and eat while I scroll through my notifications.

The most urgent is a message from my insurance company. When I call them back, I learn the restoration company is already hard at work. Unfortunately, I have rusted-out pipes that finally burst from corrosion, and they'll all need to be replaced before any other repairs can begin, which is going to extend the time I'm away from my house. The agent asks if they can put me up in a hotel, and I hesitate for a moment before assuring them I have that figured out for the time being.

The last thing I want to do is crash here for weeks on end, but Keeley's offering of the pour-over coffee supplies makes me think she *wants* me to stay. After our argument, it's an olive branch, and I don't want to overlook it. I'll talk to her before I make other plans.

After I hang up with my insurance agent, I return my *other* agent's call.

"Jane! Good to hear from you." Lacey's voice is chipper but no-nonsense, as always. With her on the East Coast, I know she's been working for hours, and she emailed me asking for a check-in this morning. But Lacey knows I'm normally on top of things.

Still, I should explain why it took me so long.

She gasps dramatically after my story about the house flood, and I'm a little vindicated by the horror in her tone. "Oh my god, are you okay? Do you need a hotel? I can have an assistant from the LA office jump in to help."

Lacey is located in New York, but the agency also has a location here. Still, they're not my personal assistants, and I have everything under control.

"I appreciate that, but I'm staying with a friend, and my home-owner's insurance is already taking care of everything."

"Good, good. Well, I called you because we already heard back from Defiant Games. They *loved* you after the meeting, and of course they already adored what you did for *Shooting Stars*. They want to know if you can come up with a theme song for *Half Moon Ranch 2* as a formal audition, but I think the job is yours if you want it."

I sigh. After recording "Never Your King," going to the Royal Con panel, and throwing myself into meetings this week, I haven't had a break in . . . ten days.

"Umm . . . how long do I have?"

"They want it by Monday. I know it's tight, but you've pulled off worse deadlines. Are you still wanting to go for it with everything you have going on?"

My shoulders tense. Between dealing with insurance and my scheduled meetings for other potential projects, it's going to be another marathon writing week. I guess I will be taking advantage of Keeley's keyboard.

Out of all of the things on my radar, this video game gig is probably the least stressful. Still, my creative well is nearly dry. I don't know how I'm supposed to fill it again.

But that's not Lacey's problem.

"I can make that work. Thanks for the update."

She lets out a *hmm* that feels like judgment. "Please let me know if anything changes. If this is too much, we can try to push that deadline."

"No, I can make it happen."

"Are you sure? We can reevaluate priorities if it's too much."

"It's fine," I say quickly. We've had this conversation before. One of the things I appreciate about Lacey is that she's a great advocate for her clients, but she's not a shark—she's gone far because she's savvy and kind. She even checks in about my workload capacity before we sign any new contract.

But I can handle this.

She lets out a long breath. "I wouldn't dream of slowing you down, but I need you to tell me when it's too much. Deal?"

"Deal," I say, and I hope it's not a lie.

"Before I go, I wanted to let you know I'm in touch with Ortega about that cease and desist. I know I don't technically manage you for Glitter Bats stuff, but I'm in your corner. We're prepared to combine resources on this."

"Thank you," I say, my shoulders tensing as I think about all the trouble Label Records has put us through already. We can use all the help we can get.

"Sure thing. Let me know when you have an update on the video game track."

"Will do."

And then Lacey hangs up.

There's nothing to do now but the work. Sighing, I pour myself a second cup of coffee and start listening to the opening themes of other farming sims: *Stardew Valley*, *Ranch of Secrets*, even the old *Harvest Moon* games. These games definitely have a sound, but I don't know which direction I want to take yet.

Suddenly, Keeley bursts into the apartment, practically slamming the door in her pursuit of the refrigerator, dressed in lime-green running tights and a black sports bra. She tugs open the door, cracks open a Gatorade, and takes a long swig. It's hard *not* to notice the sweat trailing down the taut skin of her throat . . .

I take a sip of my coffee just to do something with my hands.

"Hi, sorry for being scarce when you woke up," Keeley says, a little breathless, leaning in my direction from the other side of the counter. "Usually I get out earlier, even this late in the year. It can feel really fucking hot out there." She runs a hand through her damp hair.

"I bet." I try not to notice the flex of her forearm, but my cheeks heat anyway. "Um, you didn't have to delay your run just to get me all this." I gesture at the coffee setup that I haven't cleaned up yet.

She sets down the Gatorade bottle and puts her hands on her hips, panting. "Was it the right stuff?"

My cheeks heat. "Yes, thank you."

"Then it was worth it." She pulls the bottle to her mouth and takes another long sip, then licks her lips.

"I can make another batch of coffee if you want that too." I gesture as if to stand, but she waves me off.

"Nah, I'm good," she says. "Thanks, though. What are you working on?"

I wave my phone. "Listening to some inspiration for *Half Moon Ranch 2*. They want me to audition with an opening theme."

I brace myself for her reaction, still nervous about our new tentative peace, but Keeley doesn't criticize. "Of course they do, if they know what's best for them." She clears her throat. "I'm going to go shower, but let me know if you need anything."

"I'm good," I say. "I might go use your keyboard?"

"Yeah, go for it. You know you can make yourself at home," she says, her voice softening.

My neck warms at her tone, but she disappears before I can think too hard about it. Instead, I grab my laptop, head into her spare room, and try to get to work.

She's converted the third bedroom into a music room, and it's the most personalized spot in the house. One of her drum kits is set up in a corner, surrounded by foam soundproofing on the ceiling and walls. The rest of the walls are dotted with images of famous drummers: John Bonham, Meg White, Carter Beauford, Sheila E., and so many others I don't recognize on sight. In another corner, there's that keyboard I spotted. Not as nice as my Korg, but it has a MIDI feature to plug into a laptop for writing music.

I go to sit down on the padded bench, flip the on switch, and start noodling.

My songwriting process is a lot of trial and error. I play through chords until I find a progression I like, then I toy with a melody until I hit the mood I'm looking for. I wonder if I can take a different approach than other games in the genre. My first thought when it comes to *farm* is *country*, and I head down that path for what feels like an hour.

None of it sounds right. Even on piano, I feel like I'm writing Nashville's next flop.

"*Ugh!*" Defeated, I rest my elbows on my knees and my head in my hands. I know there are huge fans of these games, and I don't want them to be turned off by the music. Maybe I don't have any business auditioning for this.

"You okay in here?" Keeley drawls. I glance over, and she's leaning casually against the doorframe of the music room, grinning at me.

"No. How am I supposed to write for a farming sim? I know nothing about farms!"

She laughs, stepping over to the keyboard. "You've never been to space either, but you absolutely rocked *Shooting Stars*. This self-doubt isn't like you."

I sigh, glancing up at her. "Normally I have ideas, but it's like I've completely forgotten how to write. Everything sounds like garbage."

Even I cringe at how petulant I sound. Keeley gestures at the bench, and I take the cue to scoot over, making as much room as I can. There's not quite enough room for two people on it, and the heat of her freshly showered body radiates in waves. Our thighs just barely touch, and I try to ignore the way the warmth of her seeps into my skin.

"Doubt is a natural part of the writing process. Play what you have for me," she says.

"I don't want to! It's awful," I say.

She nudges me gently with her shoulder. "I'm sure it's not awful, Mercer. Just play."

"Fine." I roll my eyes and play the chorus of the world's worst country song, my neck heating with embarrassment more and more with each line.

When I finish, Keeley laughs.

"See! It's bad!" I say.

"It's not that bad," she says, eyes dancing. She nods at the keys. "Here, can I try something?"

"By all means," I say.

Keeley's brow furrows, and she starts to play the simple melody that I wrote, but at about half the tempo and in a lower key. On its own, I can hear that it's not all that bad. It's lilting and lyrical, and with each time the melody restarts, she layers some inversions of chords under the line, and the result is much more pastoral than the honkey-tonk I came up with. Her arm brushes mine as she plays the last bit, and instead of leaning away, I welcome her invasion into my space, too mesmerized by her to do much of anything.

"Oh my gosh, that's so much better," I say.

She grins. "The pieces were all there. You just had to adjust the vibes."

I hurry to transcribe what she just did into my laptop. "Gosh, I don't think I would have gotten here on my own."

She bites her lip, the almost-shy expression surprising me. "Sure you would have. I just helped you along."

"No, I'm giving you cowriter credit."

Keeley crosses her arms. "Don't you dare. I did practically nothing."

"You saved me. I can actually work with this. Seriously, thank you."

"Don't mention it," she says, rising from the piano bench. "I'll let you get back to work."

And then she leaves without another word. Shaking my head, I try to ignore her absence as I move to the next part of the song.

But the room feels colder without her.

8

✦ *Keeley* ✦

I can't think straight with Jane in the house.

(And there's nothing *straight* about it.)

Fuck, I need to focus. Jane is hard at work, that determined set to her shoulders just visible through the crack in my music room door as she works out the next lines of her song. Now that I've helped her remember what a musical genius she is, it's time to turn to my own project.

I step into my kitchen and grab a notepad off the counter. Last night, I told the band that I would look into our legal options, now that Label is playing games with our masters. I intend to do just that.

Once Wade confirms his availability, I give him a call.

"Hey, Keeley. I'm glad we were able to connect."

There's already a restless energy in my feet, and without a kick drum to occupy me, I begin pacing around my dining area so I can think. ADHD is a bitch.

"Me too."

He sighs. "That cease and desist is unexpected, but our lawyers took a look: it's binding."

My heart falls, even though Oliver told me as much while we were texting about it this morning. Label Records has always played games with us, but they're always frustratingly legal about it. "Fucking hell."

"Social media rights are interesting, because they're often treated like fair use, but @GlitterBatsMusic is a business marketing channel. They have the legal right to ask you to take the music down, even if they allow it elsewhere on the platform."

I pick at the nail polish on my middle finger, still aquamarine from playing that gig last weekend. It starts to chip away with the last dregs of my self-restraint.

"Ugh, that's such bullshit. Like I get that, but do we have any room to negotiate about our rights now that our contract is up?" I already know the answer, but I have to ask, if only for the edification.

"Your ten-year contract was about recording new work, but the masters are a separate conversation. As you're aware, Label owns the original recordings in perpetuity. A limited term would have had to be negotiated at signing."

"I guessed as much, but *fuck*," I say. Valerie's mom was our manager when we first signed with Label, and the contract was absolute garbage. Landon Banks basically owned us. Tonya Quinn wouldn't have known to fight for something like the rights to our masters, if she even would have cared—she was just in it for her. The only negotiating she did was to ensure she got more than her fair share of our royalties.

"You should also know that they're using 'Daydreams Like This' on the new season of *Love, Unscripted*."

"Well that's just perfect. I'm so glad Landon asked us before he sold that song," I say dryly, as I chip away at the rest of my nails. Valerie and Caleb will be *overjoyed* to know their personal, intimate love song six years in the making is being used on the trashiest reality dating show of the year. No shade to folks who enjoy reality shows, but when the entire premise is structured around cheating, well . . . the Glitter Bats struggle enough with reputation.

"Can we get a meeting with them to discuss *our* use of our songs?" I ask.

Wade hums. "I can ask. I'm not sure how much they'll be willing to negotiate, but it's worth a conversation."

I let out a resigned breath. "What do you think the likelihood is of getting rights to our masters?"

Wade pauses. I know that pause: he's trying to figure out the kindest way to deliver disappointing news. "Well, masters are guaranteed income as long as people are buying or streaming albums. Most labels aren't willing to give that capital up if they don't have to. And if they are willing to entertain the conversation . . . it won't be cheap."

Of course it won't. I can't imagine Landon would let us go that quietly.

I grab my pen and start scribbling on the notepad, trying to make sense of our situation. Our record deal was so bad that we hardly see any royalties anymore, and since the band has only recently reunited, we don't really have much money to speak of in our joint band account. And that's going to mean putting personal capital on the line.

Which could be a problem.

I'd gladly contribute as much funding as I could into getting our masters. My financial situation is solid, but I know the same can't be said for the others. Caleb had a really hard time managing money from the start, and his teacher salary isn't exactly putting a lot of extra money on the table. While Valerie and Riker both work in the industry, they also have expensive taste, so I have no idea what their savings look like.

And then there's Jane. Like me, Jane is also financially cautious, but to an extreme that I'm not sure how to navigate. My jaw tenses as I think back to our argument. If she's got so many other projects on her plate, is she really going to want to *invest* in Glitter Bats?

We may have cleared the air, but things still don't feel quite right.

"I have no idea if that's an option for us," I finally say. "First, I just want to know how far they plan to take this cease and desist."

"I'll reach out about Label's meeting availability."

"Sounds good. You know my schedule is wide open."

"Label may not bring your masters up, or they could throw a wild price tag out there—you know what games they play. But do you want to put your energy into this, or do you want to focus on new music?"

"Hell if I know," I mutter. "But thank you for talking me through this. I really appreciate you."

"Of course, Keeley. I'll ask for a meeting and keep you informed. Call me if you have any questions."

"I will," I say.

When we hang up, I sink onto my couch in defeat. I don't *want* to think about what buying our masters would require, but I don't want to give up on the Glitter Bats either.

Owning all of our masters would be life-changing. We would get royalties, and we'd get to choose when and where our music is used. Unable to sit still, I go to the kitchen and unload the dishwasher, then scrub down the counter. In my frustration, I realize I'm scrubbing a bit *too* hard, my shoulder aching from the effort.

Defeated, I head to the living room, settling onto the floor to stretch. I should have done this after my run anyways, but I was too distracted by the presence of Jane Mercer in my house to linger long enough to take care of my muscles. I go through my usual routine, starting with a side-body stretch, trying to focus on a strong mindset for the Label meeting instead of thinking about the redhead in the other room.

Even when she's stressed beyond what most reasonable people can handle, she's stunning. It's almost too much to bear. As though my thoughts summon her, Jane emerges from the music room, looking exhausted but smiling.

"How'd it go?" I ask.

She shrugs. "Better, after you helped. I appreciate it."

"Of course," I say.

Jane settles down on the floor across from me and mirrors my stretches. "What have you been up to?" she asks.

"Just talked to Wade. We're going to try to meet with Label to discuss this mess with the cease and desist. I'll take the meetings so you all don't have to worry about your schedules."

I brace for more reluctance, but Jane just nods. "Makes sense. We have to start somewhere."

Finally, I admit my fear out loud. "I think they did this because Landon wants something from us."

Jane lets out a labored breath. "I'm worried about that too."

I purse my lips. "I'm just . . . I'm not sure what that is."

"We'll just have to go in with our eyes open."

"You're right," I say. I want to ask about the masters, but I'm afraid of what she'll say when it's just the two of us, and the band isn't here to keep the peace if we start arguing again. So instead, I change the subject. "I'm getting hungry. Did you have lunch today?"

"No," she says. "But I could eat. Sometimes when I'm working, I forget to feed myself."

"I can relate to that." And then I realize I have nearly no groceries in the house. "Want to run to the store or order in?"

Jane purses her lips. "Why don't we order in? It's on me."

I flush. "You really don't have to do that."

She smiles ruefully. "I know, but I want to. The last day has been a bit of an ordeal, and I'm craving pizza again. Is that weird?"

I blink. If I wasn't already a little in love with her, I might be at this moment. "Pizza is always a good idea."

"I'll order the spiciest thing on the menu."

"You're an angel, Mercer."

She beams, and I try not to think anything of it. While Jane grabs her phone and orders, I run into my bedroom and put together a load of laundry to calm my nervous energy. By the time I've put darks in the washer, folded the rest of the towels that were sitting forgotten in my dryer, and gone to rejoin Jane in my living room, she's got the next episode of *Epic Theme Song* cued up.

"Want to keep watching?" she asks.

"Ooh, yes please." I sit next to her on the sofa. "I'm pretty sure this is a big Lola Martinez episode. *Jesus Christ*, she's hot in this."

Immediately I want to take the words back. The last thing I want to do is make Jane uncomfortable. It's bad enough that I'm creepily pining after her and she doesn't even know it. She doesn't need me talking about other girls on top of it all.

But then she says something that would make me fall on the floor if I hadn't just joined her on the couch. "She really is. That Shadowgirl costume is . . . distracting."

Holyfuckingshit.

My pulse picks up, and I clear my throat. "It definitely is."

We watch the next episode while we wait for pizza. It is indeed a big Shadowgirl episode. Even though Valerie gets a nice verse on one of the songs, it's Lola's time to shine in a big dance number on top of one of the buildings of the college campus where the ragtag superheroes go to school.

I pause at the end of the episode.

"Do you need anything? Something to drink?" I ask. "I'm going to get myself a glass of water."

"That sounds great," she says. "I'm thirsty."

We lock eyes for a moment, and I feel frozen. Was talking about Shadowgirl Jane's way of telling me she's into girls? Or is she doing the thing straight girls do when they talk about other women as if they find them attractive, but are really just admiring them and being ridiculously confusing?

No, that's not like Jane. Suddenly, I *have* to know. I can't stop thinking about what it would mean if she *was* into girls. If she was . . . fuck, I'm scared to even go there.

And we're not in high school anymore. I can't pass her a note like:

Hey Jane,

Do you like girls? *Check* ☐ *Yes* *or* ☐ *No*
Do you like me? *Check* ☐ *Yes* *or* ☐ *No*

Love, Keeley

God, that would make it so fucking easy. But we're not teenagers the way we were before, strangers sitting in the same Pre-Calc class, only interacting to compare answers on homework before that fateful summer at music camp when the Glitter Bats were born. If only I'd have had the nerve to tell her I was into her *then*. When you're in high school, everything feels so important—but looking back, the stakes were so damn *low*. I could have said something.

Maybe our story would have turned out differently if I had. Now, I'm too afraid of exploding our relationship—or hurting the band—to say anything. Not when I can't gauge her interest because I'm overanalyzing everything.

Before I can figure out what I even want to say, the buzzer sounds. "I'll go get the pizza!" I say quickly.

We watch another episode of *Epic Theme Song* while we eat, and I do my best to focus on the screen and not the girl next to me. When I finally manage to follow the plot, I'm once again struck by what an incredible show this is. I know Valerie isn't happy with how she and the rest of the cast were treated by the previous streamer—The Network, who also happens to own Jane's show. They basically shamed Valerie for her sexuality and tried to force her to "clean up her act" to get the show renewed, then cancelled it anyway.

But next time I see Valerie, I'll tell her how proud I am of her hard work.

After I give her shit for the song about the subway, though. The episode ends on a cliffhanger, with Valerie's character kissing Lola's before jumping off a roof to see if her powers are back, which would cement their rekindled romance . . . if she's not pancaked on the city street below. God, this show is fun.

"I think I love this show," Jane says when I pause the TV. "Like when we were teens, there wasn't anything like this, where characters were so casually queer and it was never a plot point, you know? They just get to be who they are. I'm shipping Wendy and Madison so hard."

I nod, even as blood rushes in my ears. "It's kind of amazing."

She stares at her empty plate. "I can't help but think it would have made things easier to figure stuff out if there were characters I could relate to on TV. Instead, it took me way too long to realize a lot of things about myself."

My breath tightens. This conversation feels important once again, and I don't want to scare her off. I try to keep my voice as casual as I can when I respond with nothing more than "Oh?"

She flushes, folding her hands in her lap. "I'm, um, bisexual."

I blink, completely frozen. I guess I didn't need to pass a note. "Cool. Thank you for telling me," I say, because it's what I've said to so many other people, when all I want to do is pump my fist and scream, *Jane Mercer is into girls!*

She laughs nervously. "I know I don't talk about my personal life with everyone, not the way the rest of you do. I never told you if I was seeing someone, or even about the kinds of *someones* I'm into. Because I've been in a few relationships. I just keep them quiet, because I don't trust the press not to catch something my parents will see, and I'm not ready for them to . . ." She trails off.

"I get that," I say, even though all I want to do is ask her a million questions. I know how fragile it can feel, coming out to someone, even if you know they'll be chill about it. You're still revealing a part of yourself that is personal and intimate and entirely up to you to navigate.

Keep it together, Cunningham.

"I'm honored you shared that with me," I say.

She laughs ruefully, playing with an errant curl. "I don't know why I never told you before. It's not like I thought you, or anyone else in the band, wouldn't be cool about it. Obviously."

I smirk. "Obviously."

She looks at me, biting her lip. "Well, actually . . . Riker knows."

I clench a fist to fight back the jealousy that barrels in. They're just so fucking *close*, and it's hard not to wonder how far that goes.

"Naturally," I say. I try to keep my tone light, but I can't hide part of the bite in it.

Her eyes widen. "Oh. Not like that. It's only because he caught me kissing Savannah Jude in the greenroom on that last Glitter Bats tour before hiatus."

My jaw drops. "You hooked up with Savannah Jude? Actually how dare you." Jude—Savannah's family folk band—opened for us on one leg of our last tour before the hiatus. They're these incredibly talented sisters, and they're all superhot.

She giggles, tossing her hair playfully like she's proud of herself, even though I know she's only doing it to mess with me. Jane isn't the type of person with *conquests*. "Only during the tour. We agreed it was casual."

"How did I not know this?" I ask. I pride myself on being observant, and I'm kind of shocked I never put it together. Jane is not only queer, but she's known for a long time. That tour was seven years ago. Maybe I never saw it because I was scared to see it, but looking back, those two *were* pretty inseparable as the tour stretched on.

She shrugs. "I'm discreet."

"Who else did you hook up with?" I blurt, and then my neck warms. "I'm sorry, that's none of my fucking business. Like at all. Shit, sorry."

"No, it's fine." Her cheeks somehow turn an even deeper shade of pink, more like magenta. Redheads, I guess. "Uh, so being involved with musicians we toured with was kind of a habit? I might have slept with Charlie from Lime Velvet back in Denver."

We played exactly one show at Red Rocks, and it was opening for them years ago. A lot of years. "Oh my god, wasn't he like thirty-five?"

"He was twenty-nine!"

"And you were twenty!"

"Yeah," she says, biting her lip. "Not my best decision ever, but he was actually pretty sweet and really respectful with me, which wasn't bad for my first time. We're still in touch—I went to his wedding, and his wife invited me to her baby shower."

"Wow." I laugh. "What else don't I know about Jane Mercer?" Something darkens in her eyes, and I wonder where her mind went just then. Instead, she laughs.

"You know everything. I'm a workaholic with religious trauma who doesn't even know how to have fun anymore."

My mind snaps onto the new direction of this conversation, because thinking about everything Jane just revealed is too much. So I put on the smirk I love to hide behind. "I can help you with that. I'm good at fun."

She rolls her eyes. "Wow, you must think I'm pathetic."

"You know I don't," I say seriously. And maybe I can give Jane a little honesty too. "I should tell you the reason I got so panicked in the studio last week," I say. It's only one reason, but it's still important.

Jane nods. "You can tell me anything, Keeley."

Fuck, I wish that were true. "I haven't felt happy with my studio work in a long time." She opens her mouth to protest, but I put up a finger. "No, I know I'm really good at it. I'm just getting really bored and *restless*. I don't know—until Glitter Bats got back together, I wasn't feeling very fulfilled creatively. I don't mind playing on other people's albums, but the work never felt like *mine*. Now that we're making music again, I just remember how it feels to be so invested in our work. I'm so proud of *More to Say*."

"Me too," Jane says quietly.

I clear my throat, leaning back against the pillows. "I don't want to lose that feeling, but I'm worried that without Glitter Bats, I've peaked. There's nothing more impressive for me to accomplish."

She nods. "I understand that, the need to feel like you're achieving something—but it's not like you're a slouch, Keeley. I mean, look at 'Your Body and Mine,' or that work you did on the Pizza Dream album. That was super technical, and you made it sound effortless. You're so good at what you do." She stacks the plates but doesn't move to get up. "I saw your wall of drummers in your studio. You belong up there too."

The fact the most talented person I know thinks I belong on my own inspiration wall might just make me do something reckless, like closing the distance between us. I blink, trying to banish the thought. "Uh, I don't, but I appreciate that." I swallow.

"No, Keeley, truly. You're the best drummer I've ever worked with. I'm proud of you—and proud to be your friend."

God. The earnestness in her tone just might destroy me.

I wish there could be more to it than *friends*, but I'll take what I can get.

ONE WEEK LATER

Group Text Chain: The Supersecret Official Glitter Bats Chat

KEELEY: Just got out of the meeting with Label. I fucking hate these assholes.

RIKER: Oh god. What did they want?

CALEB: Do we even want to know???

VALERIE: ugh, tell me my mom wasn't there

KEELEY: Oh yes, Tonya was there. I didn't know she had a Birkin bag.

VALERIE: PROBABLY FROM THE ROYALTIES SHE FUCKING STOLE

VALERIE: I HATE IT HERE

KEELEY: She "accidentally" smacked me with it on her way out the door. Tonya's a peach.

RIKER: 😬😬😬

CALEB: . . . what did she want?

KEELEY: She wanted to "make sure we understood the scope of our original contract." The Label execs really didn't like when Wade brought up fair use of our music. They offered to draw up a contract, but then they threw out that we would have to SIGN WITH THEM FOR TEN MORE YEARS before they would entertain that kind of agreement.

JANE: I'm so sorry I'm late, but . . . excuse me?

KEELEY: I know! I'm so fucking pissed. I knew they wanted something, but I wasn't prepared.

CALEB: We were very clear that was never on the table.

VALERIE: Did you tell them to go fuck themselves?

KEELEY: Believe me, I wanted to, but I let Wade do the talking. Every time I wanted to say something, I just shoved another one of those Trader Joe's mints in my mouth. By the time the meeting was over, I went through a whole tin, but it was better than telling them what I really thought.

RIKER: So . . . no go on the masters.

KEELEY: Not exactly. Once Tonya left, Wade went into Gina Choi's office and spent a good hour in there. I know she's only one VP, but he seemed hopeful they might be open to letting us purchase some rights. He said he'll send us all an email as soon as he hears something.

KEELEY: Oh fuck, Landon's on his way over. I'll let you know what he says.

9

✦ Keeley ✦

I recoil as Landon Banks approaches my car with way too much confidence.

Despite the fact that he's in his fifties, he dresses like he's trying to look younger: a bomber jacket, ball cap, designer jeans, and the kind of Jordans people pay $15,000 for on eBay. The characteristic that oozes off him isn't charisma, though; it's ambition. The kind of ambition that makes me nervous.

And he was eerily quiet in our meeting, letting his employees do the talking. Something feels off, and I can't put my finger on it. Whatever it is, I don't like this feeling in my gut.

Every instinct tells me to throw my vehicle into drive and get the hell out of the parking garage, but I know this is the game, and I have to play it. So I force the scowl off my face and roll down my window. The cologne he doused himself in almost makes me gag as he leans on the door, and his pale skin is a little sallow and puffy in this light, no doubt from a drinking habit.

"Hey, Keeley, I'm so glad I caught you. We didn't have a chance to catch up."

I blink. "I wasn't aware there was anything we needed to talk about."

His eyes flash, but that too-perfect smile doesn't leave his face. "Oh, come on now, KeeKee, we're old friends."

My jaw tenses. "I'm not a kid anymore. Please call me Keeley."

His eyes rove over my body, lingering a little too long on my cleavage. I knew I should have buttoned a few more buttons under my blazer. "That's for sure."

Ew. "What do you want, Landon?" I clench my fists to try to ground myself, and it's all I can do not to shove him away from my car. Part of me wants to get out just so I can tower over him, because that's a thing men like him hate, but I don't want to lose my getaway options.

It's not that I feel exactly unsafe around Landon—he's never physically threatened me, or any of my bandmates. But he's a sleazebag who plays games. He takes credit for *our* work.

I don't trust him at all.

He cocks his head. "I want what you want. I want to see my Glitter Bats succeed."

I glance around the garage, hoping against hope that I'm not alone, and someone will interrupt before I say something that will get me in trouble. But I'm not that lucky.

"We're not *your* anything anymore."

Landon tenses. "I still own all of your music, in case you forgot."

I want to snarl at him. Instead, I plaster on a smile that's all teeth. "Tell me something I don't know. Wasn't discussing that the whole point of this meeting?"

He leans into my car, lowering his voice. "Indeed it was. I'm glad you haven't forgotten. We *own* you, and we have the power here."

God, does he think he's a Batman villain or something?

"How nice for you."

"Gina might be meeting with Wade out of professional respect, but I make the final decision, and I'm not giving an inch unless *I* want to. There's a lot on the line here. I could take all of your music down, from every platform, and call it a write-off."

"You wouldn't." My hands tighten on the wheel. There's too much demand for our music right now. If they wrote it off, they'd look like idiots. But he does have that kind of power, and it makes me sick.

"Want to bet on that?" He shrugs. "You really should be nicer to me."

I purse my lips, not liking where this is heading. "What do you mean?"

Landon's eyes rove back down my body, then leer up at me. "Come up to my office. We can work something out."

Literally gag me. I always knew Landon was a womanizer, and he's fresh off his third very public divorce. Before, when we first made music at this label, I was practically a kid. Now, I'm twenty-nine, finally old enough to not make him look like a creep if he went for it.

As if he'd ever be my type. So gross.

Just then, the door to the garage creaks open, and relief melts over my shoulders. I smirk at him, refusing to be cowed.

Then I raise my voice so it's loud enough for whoever has just joined us to overhear me crystal clear. "Are you propositioning me, Landon Banks?"

He splutters, going red-faced. "Of course not! I want to *talk*. God, you women are so paranoid these days. No one is here to threaten you."

We're paranoid because we have to be. I know that. He knows that. But he gets to say shit like this, because he's a rich cishet white man in a rich cishet white man's world. Fuck, I can't believe we ever worked with this asshole. I can't believe I ever had his drumming photos on my walls. Forget me, I don't want him anywhere near my friends.

I shrug my shoulders back. "No, you're just threatening my livelihood. And for the record, there is no scenario in which I would *ever* consider what you just implied. Now get the fuck away from my car."

Landon straightens and steps away, a little stunned. Clearly, he's not used to people standing up to him.

The clack of heels gets louder, and over Landon's shoulder, I see Gina Choi in her Louboutins making a beeline for us, Wade close at hand.

Our manager is wearing a sharp-as-hell suit and a thunderous expression. Gina also looks all business in her pencil skirt, silk blouse, and those fuck-me heels.

Normally, Gina is serene and presents a united front with Landon. But now, she's fuming.

"Mr. Banks, it's time to go inside. You're late for your next meeting," Gina says stonily.

And just like that, Landon's calm facade returns. "You're absolutely right, Gina. We'll be in touch soon, I'm sure."

He turns on his heel and leaves. Gina looks at me, frowning. "What did he say to you?"

"It was nothing," I say, even though, by the way she's looking at me, we both know it's not nothing. Still, I can handle assholes like Landon Banks. And when I can't, well, that's what the Taser in my glove box is for.

Gina pales, tucking a shiny lock of her bob behind her ear. "If you say so."

"So we'll be hearing from you, right?" Wade asks.

Gina nods sharply. "Absolutely. As we discussed."

At that, she hurries back inside, leaving me alone with my manager.

"Are you okay, Keeley?" Wade asks quietly.

I cross my arms, laughing dryly. "Fucking great. Guess Landon doesn't see me as a 'kid' anymore."

Wade's eyes darken. "That's it. You're not coming to any more of these meetings."

Then, I really laugh. "Like hell I'm not! I'm not going to cower from Landon Banks just because he hit on me. I'm skeeved out, sure, but he can't scare me."

Wade sighs, running a hand over his fade. "Yeah, okay. But next time I'm walking you to your car."

I nod, more determined than ever to fight back. "Sounds good, boss."

He rolls his eyes. "Get out of here, Keeley. We'll talk once I hear something."

So I do. But my hands start to shake as I get on the highway—not because I'm scared, but because I'm pissed.

I pull over at the nearest exit and drive around aimlessly for a bit, until I find a place to get a green juice at a little hole-in-the-wall next to an art studio. Beverage in hand, I decide to walk around a nearby park, trying to get my bearings and shake out all this weirdness. What right does Landon think he has to not just our music, but my body?

Fuck that shit. Fuck it all the way to hell.

Glowering, I pull up our group text.

ME: For the record, Landon Banks is still a fucking creep.

RIKER: WHAT DID HE DO?

ME: Nothing I can't handle.

VALERIE: Umm, hold on. That's not an answer.

It's not, but I don't know how I'm supposed to tell them what just happened. Somehow, I feel embarrassed about it, which is bullshit. Fuck the patriarchy.

JANE: Keeley? Is everything okay?

And, well, that breaks me. Now that Jane is worried, I want to reassure her.

ME: He just hit on me. Big fucking surprise.

CALEB: EXCUSE ME?

VALERIE: [April Kepner knife gif]

RIKER: The next time I see that tiny man, I swear to god . . .

JANE: Oh my god, are you okay?

ME: It's fine. Nothing happened, and he was dumb enough to do it in public so Gina Choi knows about it now. I've never seen her angry before.

JANE: Are you really fine, Keeley?

ME: Yeah, I'm okay. If anything, I just want to fight back harder, because I'm more pissed about what he said *before* he tried to hit on me.

ME: He reminded me just how much power they have over our music right now. As if I wasn't already aware. He threatened to take our albums down from all platforms and write them off.

CALEB: He's not going to do that. He's making too much money off of us.

God, I hope Caleb is right. I agree with him, but Landon might pull some shit just because he wants to mess with us. I don't trust him. Trying to steady myself, I take another sip of my juice and sink onto a nearby bench.

RIKER: I'm sure that wasn't the point. It's a power play. He's trying to remind Keeley that he *could*, which is absolutely ridiculous, but unfortunately true.

VALERIE: So what do we want to do now? Do we want to *start* working on GB4?

Maybe we should. Despite what Gina said, I can't forget the viciousness in Landon's eyes. If Label comes to the negotiation table at all, it's not going to be pretty. For a moment, I finally pause to consider: Is fighting for our masters worth my energy? Or are we destined to lose? Another album is the safer route—Landon Banks can't touch it.

My mouth goes dry as I think about the look on his face back in the garage. We used to be so afraid of him, and maybe we were right to be.

But I don't *want* to be afraid anymore. I lean back against the bench and glance around at my surroundings, at the toddlers playing on the playground, the people playing fetch with their dog, others playing a pickup game of ultimate Frisbee.

Something about the normality of it all gives me perspective.

Life goes on, even when I'm hyperfocused on the one thing I think I need. Yeah, I want to get the rights to our albums, but making something new is what we can control.

If we make the damn time for it.

ME: God, I would love to make another album, but I know you're all slammed.

I brace myself for the comments, but then the band surprises me.

CALEB: We're busy, but if we could at least start writing, I think it wouldn't hurt.

VALERIE: I'm in 😘

RIKER: Me too. Can't wait to release something Landon Banks can't touch.

I hold my breath until Jane responds.

JANE: I agree. Let's get a little momentum going, at the very least.

I'm so relieved I could cry.

RIKER: What if we plan a retreat in a few weeks? My uncles own that resort in Montana, and they made an open offer for us to stay there anytime, in exchange for a few tags on social media.

CALEB: Why don't you all compare calendars? I can probably take a long weekend from work. They gave me a few personal days, and it's a good time to get away, now that our fall concert is done.

ME: I'm in.

JANE: Sounds perfect.

VALERIE: I'm actually pretty free for the next month, so let's go for it.

RIKER: Perfect. I'll text you all the details. In the meantime, let's try to get a little writing done on the side so we're not starting from scratch.

VALERIE: We . . . may have a few things we didn't share with Label for More to Say . . .

ME: OH HELL YES

CALEB: You all should write stuff too! It's always better when we're all bringing stuff to the table.

JANE: I'd love to try! It'll be a nice change after all the epic fantasy.

RIKER: It's decided then! Let's make the best fucking album we've ever made. If we're lucky, we might even make Landon cry.

10

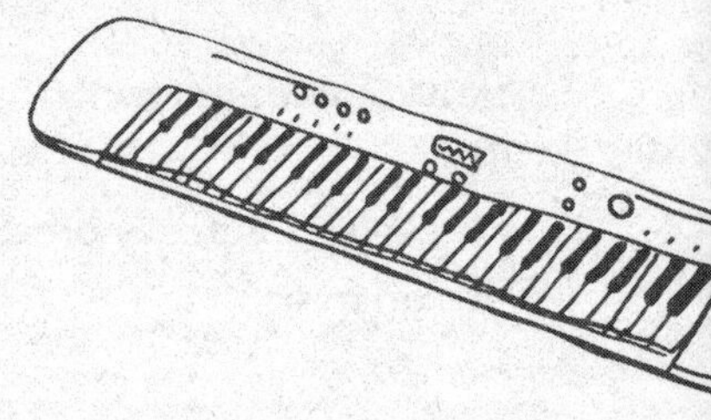

✦ Jane ✦

When the email comes in from Defiant Games the following week to offer me the *Half Moon Ranch 2* job, I almost laugh when I see the deadline.

They're giving me a full *six months* to work on the rest of the score, and my entire body relaxes at the luxury. For once, I can set a reasonable schedule that gives me time to breathe and work on other projects.

So, after I've spent a morning carefully mapping out a writing schedule, I decide to take the next week to try my hand at Glitter Bats music. And there's no time to start like the present. I settle myself behind Keeley's keyboard and open one of the oldest entries in my Notes app, where a few random ideas I never did anything with are typed in haphazard formatting. There's a reason I never saw these through.

While I've spent a lot of time playing in a rock band and writing music for different genres, I don't have a ton of experience writing actual rock songs. Valerie and Caleb wrote most of our stuff for the band, and while Riker and even Keeley sometimes helped with lyrics, the most I really ever did was write my own piano parts.

I've never been sure where to start.

The thing about composing music is that it requires a creative spark, and with what little downtime I've had over the past year, I feel like I'm hitting a wall before I've even begun. There's not much I can do with that. For about an hour, I just listen to a playlist of old Glitter Bats influences: Paramore, Lime Velvet, My Chemical Romance, Dirty Crayons, Blink-182, and Swerve In 2 Sunset, hoping for guidance.

I hate sitting in front of a keyboard that's not being played. When the inspiration doesn't come, I start playing a Chopin piece to get my hands moving, hoping that will inspire . . . something.

My parents allowed nothing but Christian radio and classical music in the house growing up, and Chopin was a highlight of my early piano education. I was only allowed to take lessons if I would *use my talents for the Lord*, so when I wasn't practicing études, I was playing the keyboard in Sunday services. I plastered a serene look on my face, secretly ignoring the religion of it all and getting lost in the structure of the songs, in the dancing of my fingers on the smooth piano keys. Manipulating my parents to find little wins among all their restrictions was an art, and along the way, my pursuit of music ended up being more than a diversion.

They wanted their god to save me, but music was my true salvation.

Playing piano was the only good thing about those days, and even then, it gave me only a fraction of the joy I get with Glitter Bats. That's what's frustrating about living under strict control: you have to take your joy in tiny snatches of goodness among the stifling expectations.

If my parents ever knew the real me, they would believe I was going to hell. Even that wouldn't shake their faith. They'd just say I was a lost soul they were praying for, claim it's my responsibility to change who I am at my very core to be worthy of redemption, instead of letting my truth challenge their narrow worldview.

It makes me sick.

But it's why I'll never tell them about my sexuality. They'd never accept me, and it's easier to pretend. Besides, it's not like I'm going to have a partner any time soon. The one I want is definitely not interested, even if she was super chill about me coming out to her. I knew she would be, but it still felt like my heart was in my throat for that entire conversation, like she'd see right through me to the crush I've spent years trying to hide.

As if summoned by my thoughts, Keeley appears in the doorframe of her music room. "Any luck writing something for the band?"

I groan. "No. I'm creatively fried."

"Me too, and I'm still feeling super weird about the Label Records stuff, so I really want to write new Glitter Bats material."

"Same," I say. It's wild how we argued about this just a few weeks ago, and now we're on the same team. But truly, I get Keeley's need to reclaim our music. She hasn't said more about it, but I feel weird about the Landon situation too. I know Keeley says she's okay—and I trust that's true—but it still doesn't sit right. He's old enough to be her *dad*.

It's absolutely disgusting. After growing up in a community built on patriarchy, I'm not surprised Landon went there. I'm just disappointed and indignant on Keeley's behalf. She hasn't been upset since it happened, though. If anything, she's more determined to take back what's ours.

And if that's a new album, that's a new album. I'm with her on that, finally. But my creative well is dry.

Keeley leans across the doorframe, one arm above her head,

filling it with her height. It's . . . distracting. "All that being said . . . I did something kind of silly, if you're up for it."

I perk up, unable to stop the smile from tugging up my mouth. "I like silly."

She smirks. "Do you want to go to a pottery class tonight?"

"Pottery? That's new." I fold my hands in my lap, considering.

"Yeah, I saw this place last week and decided to check it out. Sometimes doing something completely out of my wheelhouse helps me get creative, and it reconnects my wandering brain to my body when that task is tactile. Are you in?"

My mouth goes dry, as I'm momentarily distracted by things that could involve her being *tactile.*

"Jane?" Keeley asks.

I blink, my face heating, and stare back at the keyboard, refocusing on her question. I could sit here and play keys until my fingers ache, and it's not going to help me write a rock hit.

Or I could spend a night hanging out with Keeley. It's no contest.

"Sounds like it could be fun. I'm in."

She flashes me a finger gun. "Great. I'm going to go change. You okay to leave in half an hour?"

"Sure."

The class is in a random storefront in West Hollywood, wedged between a furniture store and a juice bar. It's all industrial floors and white walls inside, with shelves of vases and pots lining the walls of the entry.

An easel that reads FALL IN LOVE WITH CLAY greets us as we step into the main area of the store, which has been cleared of any merchandise. Stations with wheels, two stools, and a bag of clay each are scattered around the room, and "L-O-V-E" recorded by Nat King Cole plays through the speaker system. The space is dimly lit, with low lamps and white candles casting a warm, inviting glow that causes Keeley's ear covered in piercings to glitter. More vases, these full of bouquets of flowers, decorate the space, and there's an assistant handing out glasses of champagne to two men in front of us who are holding hands.

And they're not the only patrons in the room who are getting cozy.

"Keeley," I hiss, as I glance around.

"Yeah?"

"Is this a *couples'* pottery class?"

She glances over at me, paling. "Uh, the reservation defaulted for two. I assumed this was one of those stereotypical paint-and-sip girls' night things, but for pottery."

I swallow. "I don't think it's a typical girls' night thing."

She laughs nervously, bringing her hand to her neck, and I try not to notice the way the lean muscle in her forearm flexes with the movement. "We can totally leave."

I shake my head. "It's fine. We're next, anyways."

The assistant turns to us, brandishing a clipboard. "Name on the reservation?"

"Keeley Cunningham," Keeley says.

The assistant brightens, turning to me. "And you must be Keeley's partner."

My mind reels at the suggestion, even though I should have seen it coming. "I, uh—"

The assistant doesn't let me finish. "Go ahead and grab a name tag and write down your name and pronouns, then help yourselves to champagne and choose a station. We'll get things going shortly."

I open my mouth to argue, but Keeley is already filling out her name tag. I do the same, then stick it on the faded T-shirt I picked specifically because I knew it might get stained. Then Keeley is placing a hand on my elbow and ushering me away, somehow handling two glasses of champagne in one hand.

"We could have corrected them," I murmur as we grab the nearest station. I settle onto one of the hard wooden stools, and Keeley grabs the one next to me. She hands me my champagne, and I down half the glass in one go.

Liquid courage, I guess.

"Hey, I didn't want them to kick us out in case they're strict about the couple thing. It's fine. We can pretend to be together for one night, right?"

I laugh, and it comes out high and unnatural. The men from the next station over raise their brows at me. "Yeah, it's fine," I say, but I know it's not convincing.

Keeley lowers her voice. "Are you sure? We can go."

"I want to learn pottery," I say determinedly, desperately taking another sip of champagne to wet my suddenly dry throat. "And it's just a couple hours, right?"

I fold my feet under me on the stool and try to relax, desperate to convince myself I can pull this off. I can pretend to be Keeley's girlfriend for one night without catching fire, right?

"Whatever you say, *baby*," Keeley says, and I think I might ignite right in my seat from the amount of warmth that floods my cheeks. "It's not like it's going to be hard to pretend. You're a catch, Mercer."

Holy crap. I'm done for. The way she eyes me up and down makes my mouth go dry. "I, um . . ."

Fortunately, my splutter of an attempted, incoherent response is interrupted by the instructor, who turns down the music and begins her introduction.

"Good evening, romantics! Welcome to night one of our Fall in Love with Clay sessions. Tonight, you will work with your partner to make two guided projects over the next two hours. The projects will take two to three weeks to dry in our studio, after which they will be fired. Next month, you may return for night two to glaze your projects."

Keeley lowers her voice. "I guess it's two nights of pretending, if you want to make it pretty."

I thrust my shoulders back. "That's fine. We should definitely paint them."

The instructor continues. "Now, how many of you have thrown clay before?" To my surprise, Keeley is among the few hands raised. The instructor points to her. "What was that experience like for you?"

Keeley flashes her trademark smirk at the room. "It was hard, but super rewarding to learn how to get it right. I actually took the AP Art exam back in high school."

I whirl on her, gaping. "You took AP Art?" We went to the same high school, and we were *friends* . . . after camp at least. How did I not know this?

She shrugs. "The counselor told me to take an elective that wasn't music to diversify my résumé, and I liked it a lot."

"What else don't I know about you?" I ask. The words are innocuous enough, but they feel . . . weighted, in this context.

The instructor beams. "One of the things I love about art is how it reveals us to ourselves and the people around us. Your partner has learned something about you already. Beautiful."

She leads the room in snaps, not claps, and I watch in bewilderment as everyone joins in.

"Is this a class or couples' counseling?" Keeley mutters.

I elbow her and lower my voice. "You're going to get us kicked out."

She rolls her eyes but leans over and kisses my cheek. My breath catches at the softness of her lips on my skin, and I resist the urge to press my hand to my face as she pulls away, as if I could capture the feeling before it disappears. "Better?" she asks, eyes lighting in mischief.

Oh. So she wants to play it like that, does she? "Much," I rasp out.

I guess we're leaning in.

The instructor is already calling on the next hand-raiser, and we listen politely as the other participants discuss their experience with ceramics. There are seven other couples, so there's an intimate, casual vibe in the room.

This is not a real date, I have to tell myself, but a part of me wishes I were wrong. That's the problem with living with Keeley, with the way our friendship has been teetering like a seesaw after our fight in that studio. Things don't feel right between us, because there are things left unresolved.

Feelings left unspoken.

Even when I told Keeley about my sexuality last week, I held back. I certainly don't know how to talk about my deeper feelings, or if they'd be welcome, but tonight is not helping. At all.

I will myself to focus on the person speaking about their college pottery seminar. Once everyone has had a chance to talk, the instructor moves on to the directions. We're starting with a flower vase, and the instructor advises us to split the clay into two pieces. The first, we're to work together with our partner to soften and prepare for throwing.

Keeley scoots her stool closer to mine as I lean over the work surface. Her hands cover mine on the clay. "This okay?" she asks, breaking off a piece.

"Of course," I say, hoping she can't sense the rapid beat of my heart with that drummer's intuition. We knead the clay in tandem, our fingers tangling against the warming material as we trade clay between us, and soon it feels almost soft, like sticky dough under our hands. The instructor goes around to each station to confirm we're ready for throwing, then they explain how to start the wheel.

"Do you want to try throwing, since you've never done it before?" Keeley asks.

I nod, trying to remember why we're here. "Sure."

I wet my hands in the provided water bowl, then use my foot to turn the wheel. The motion feels so familiar, like playing keyboard, and I almost laugh. Trying something new could be just the inspiration I need.

My wandering mind misses the rest of the directions, and I realize I'm forming a shapeless ball of clay, achieving nothing but getting pieces stuck under my fingernails. But then an idea sparks to get Keeley back for that "innocent" kiss *and* get back on track.

Even if that spark is playing with fire.

I glance over my shoulder at Keeley. "Can you help?"

She blinks. "You want me to take over?"

I wink at her. "No, but you can get in here and guide my hands."

Her brows shoot up, but then she's scooting her stool behind mine, wrapping her arms around me, and placing those strong, lean hands on top of my own. She's so close, I can feel the warmth radiating off her skin. "It's all about balance. You have to be delicate without being tentative, really get your hands in there and coax the clay to yield to your touch. You're not wrangling it into submission . . ." She lowers her voice. "You're seducing it."

I swallow. Maybe this wasn't the best idea. She rests her chin on my shoulder, and I can't help it; I lean into her touch. *Is she doing this on purpose?*

Because if I'm not completely mistaken, she leans back. I set my jaw, trying to focus. Together, we shape the clay into a simple, tall vase, and I'm struck by just how good this feels—her long, calloused fingers wrapping around my own with a purpose. I thought being in Keeley's arms would be good, but this is beyond good. It feels perfect.

Like coming home.

And it feels like it's 120 degrees in the studio. I can't even blame the excessive candlelight for what I know must be a brilliant red flush on my cheeks. I have to remind myself a hundred times that this romance act is only for the class, because god, it feels real, and I can't let myself get used to this sparkling feeling. The instructor pauses at our table and smiles serenely.

"This is excellent. What a wonderful example of trusting your partner to help you build something beautiful together. Bravo."

She snaps again, and the room follows in agreement. I try not to blush at the attention. For a moment, I think Keeley is going to lean away at all the eyes on us, but she doesn't.

If my pulse was rushing before, now it's galloping like a racehorse.

The instructor guides me through releasing the pot, and we separate to clean the space and prep the next ball of clay. But before I can do anything, Keeley boops my nose with a wet finger.

The cool clay lingers on my face from her touch, but my hands are too wet to wipe it away. "Hey!"

She raises her own clay-covered hands in surrender. "I'm sorry, I couldn't resist. You look cute, though, like you have sunscreen you didn't rub in."

I purse my lips and lean forward, drawing a single line on her cheekbone with my own wet forefinger. Keeley gapes. "Excuse me?"

"You started it!" I say, shrugging out of her reach on my way to the wash station as she lunges to get me back.

The men next to us laugh.

"While we're not here for facials, I'm happy to discuss the benefits of clay for the skin," the instructor says with a chuckle. Once the whole room is ready to move on, she instructs us on making a bowl.

Without me even asking, Keeley wraps her arms around me again as we get started, even though I got the hang of it and no longer need her help to guide my hands.

But I just . . . give in. I let myself pretend, for the last quiet half hour of the class, that this could be real, and she could be mine. I know better than to get my hopes up. But every rogue beat of my heart yearns for it to be true.

After the class, we leave the studio champagne tipsy. Everything shimmers under the streetlights, and a flicker of anticipation burns through my mind as we step forward into the rest of the night. Keeley smiles softly at me as she hails a rideshare back to her condo, and I want to bask in the beauty of it—no snark, no smirk, just pure happiness radiating off of her like neon. When the car arrives, she jumps into the back seat first, then gives me a hand up into the lifted SUV. She closes her eyes and leans back against the headrest as we slip into the lull of traffic, and when her hand falls next to mine on the seat, I don't pull it away. I hook my pinky around hers, and her fingers curl back.

Maybe it's not conscious, but the touch is harmless enough that I let it linger for the rest of the ride as I stare out the window. Between the glittering lights and the innocent contact, I'm mesmerized into silence, trying to savor every moment.

When we pull into Keeley's driveway, I turn, thinking she's totally out. But she's wide awake and looking at me, her fingers still wrapped in mine. We just stare at each other for one breath. Then two. Something unmistakable passes between us . . . and suddenly I wonder how much of tonight was pretend, and how much was inevitable.

"Shall we?" she asks. I nod and follow her out of the car and to her apartment steps. We're quiet as she unlocks the door, but something still remains in the air between us, something I don't dare name.

I'm afraid if I speak, it'll disappear, like a birthday wish that will never come true.

But I want Keeley Cunningham, and I'm starting to think she

wants me too. I never would have thought that possible before. I clench my fists, banishing the thought as we walk through the door.

In the darkness of her kitchen, my eyes fall on a bright bouquet of sunflowers, resting casually on the counter.

"What are these?" I ask. They weren't there when we left.

She shrugs. "I got you flowers to put in your vase. Snuck them in when you weren't paying attention."

My mouth falls open. "Keeley, you didn't have to . . ."

"I wanted to," she says. "Vases should always have flowers. But these are going to die before your piece is ready, so I kind of failed epically. Just had the idea and ran with it."

Warmth swells in my chest. "We can put them in water. They'll still be pretty."

"You like sunflowers, right?"

I bite my lip. "They're my favorite."

She grins. "Good. I'll get you more when we pick up the pottery."

It's such a date-like thing that my throat tightens. This isn't something you do for just a friend, right? I want to do something to thank her, but I don't even know where to begin. As I rummage in her cupboards for a suitable flower container, I sense Keeley come up behind me. I whirl around, glass in hand.

"Find what you're looking for?" she murmurs.

I raise the large Mason jar. "This will do," I say shakily, trying to catch my breath. She's closer than I expected, and I'm drawn to the heat of her for so many more reasons than the harsh air-conditioning.

"Good," she says, but she doesn't step away. Instead, she cages me in, arms on either side of the counter behind me. There's barely a foot between us, and I catch the scent of her minty bodywash and the champagne on her breath. Before I can stop myself, I lean closer, almost imperceptibly, just to see if this is going where I hope it is.

Keeley moves even closer. She glances down at my mouth, then back up at my eyes. I lick my lips.

"*Jane*," she murmurs. "Was tonight . . . inspiring for you?"

"Yeah," I rasp. "It was."

"Good." I'm pretty sure neither of us is talking about the pottery.

Suddenly, a blaring car alarm sounds from outside.

"Oh!" I gasp as we spring apart.

"*Fuck*," she mutters.

"Was that mine?" I ask, and even though I know my Prius doesn't have a gross aftermarket alarm, I run to the window just to check.

But I'm pretty sure before we were interrupted, Keeley Cunningham was about to kiss me, and I had every intention of letting her.

Once we've determined the alarm doesn't belong to either of us, though, the moment is shattered. Keeley sighs. "I had fun tonight. Good night, Mercer."

I nod, resigning myself to another night alone in her guest bed, knowing she's just on the other side of the wall. "Me too. Good night, Keeley."

11

Keeley

The day after the pottery class, Jane texts me that she's moving back into her house.

I almost drop my phone. But I'm helping Paulino from Lime Velvet run a drum clinic for local high school students for most of the day, so I don't even get to say goodbye in person . . . as if it's that big of a deal.

Still, it's hard to focus on rudiments when I already feel the absence of her so strongly.

I try to tell myself she's only leaving because the place was ready, and not because I almost threw myself at her in my kitchen last night.

Letting Jane stay was supposed to be about *helping* her, not coming on to her. For the rest of the afternoon, I'm distracted by worry, wondering if I pushed too much.

This is all my fault for booking that stupid couples' class. I really did make a mistake on the registration—I thought it was ceramics for *two* as in two people, not ceramics *for two* as in a romance extravaganza. Sometimes the ADHD tax is an impulsive purchase that skips the fine print, because I get an idea I'm excited about and just need to make it happen. I just *needed* to try something creative. I wasn't trying to force Jane on a date, even if those sunflowers might have been a little overkill.

Still, all those feelings from last night felt real.

When I get home from the clinic, I find a plate full of cookies on my counter along with a note:

Keeley,

Thank you for everything. I hope these are still your favorite.

♥ *Jane*

I grin, my pulse picking up at the little heart she drew next to her name, but I remind myself it's just a sign-off. Jane doesn't actually mean anything by it. The snickerdoodles are, in fact, my favorite, and I devour three as I ponder what I want to do with the emptiness of my condo.

Who am I kidding? I'm grinning like the Cheshire cat through every bite. *Jane Mercer, I'd follow you through any looking glass.*

I want to go see her, but I know she's busy moving back into her house. She's probably already deciding which items she's going to clean and repair, and which are simply lost causes. But I'm fighting the urge to go visit.

Because a simple text isn't going to cut it. Now that we're both sober, I need to know if last night was as real as I wanted it to be.

As if on cue, my phone lights up in the Glitter Bats + Wade text thread:

WADE: I have an update. Does everyone have time to discuss it over dinner?

RIKER: I'm around!

VALERIE: Caleb is at an after-school function, but he should be home by 6:30. Can we do 7:30?

JANE: 7:30 works for me.

ME: 7:30 is good for me too.

WADE: Perfect. I'll get reservations and send the details soon.

A few minutes later, Wade passes along the directions, and I decide to tidy my spotless apartment. I haven't dusted in a while, so I do that, even though Jane left the place cleaner than it was when I went to teach this morning.

Last night, it felt like something really was happening between us. Sure, we were playing along for the fucking pottery class, but she leaned into my touch like it was genuine. And after, in my kitchen, she looked like she wanted to kiss me as much as I wanted to kiss her.

I don't think it was just my imagination. But . . . shit. Now that I know Jane is into girls, I'm getting ahead of myself, and that's the worst thing I could do.

Cue Stockard Channing.

God, I don't know how to process this. I've never felt this unmoored by the possibility of a relationship before . . . because it's never been *Jane.* I should talk to someone, but I don't have the kind of "call during an emergency" relationship with my therapist, and it's not like I'm going to call one of the other Glitter Bats. The last thing I need is a reminder that a relationship I desperately want could hurt the band. We've all fought so hard to get where we are.

Why did it have to be someone in the Glitter Bats I was attracted to like this? I've tried so hard to rationalize these feelings away, but now that they might be mutual, I don't have the strength to ignore them.

What I really need is a distraction. I usually FaceTime with my family once a week, but we missed last Sunday. My parents should both be home from work, so I send a quick text to check their availability, and then I settle onto my couch to take the call.

My parents are huddled around the same phone screen, smiling at me.

"We've missed you!" Mom says. I can tell she's changed out of her work clothes, but her silvery blond hair is still pulled back in a no-nonsense bun.

"I wish you came home more," Dad says gruffly, but there's an easygoing smile softening the wrinkles on his face. He's growing out his facial hair into a neatly trimmed beard, and it's a good look.

"I know, I'll come home soon," I say, because I should. Los Angeles to Seattle isn't *that* bad of a flight, and I do really love my parents. I'm lucky that coming home feels like a soft place to land, not a place for tension and trauma.

"What have you been up to?" Mom asks.

"Well, Jane is no longer staying with me," I say.

"I'm glad she was able to move back into her home. That whole situation sounded stressful," Dad says, frowning. Because of course, I gave them the whole rundown when Jane moved in.

I swallow. "Yeah, I, uh, I'm glad her insurance was able to take care of everything."

"What else is new?" Mom asks.

My stomach clenches. They've always supported me—whether that was in my queerness or deciding to pursue music. But things have been a little tense since I told my parents I was clearing my schedule to work on the Glitter Bats.

"I helped Paulino Diaz with a drum clinic today," I say, eager to have something to report. "And, well, we have a meeting tonight to talk about the band's future."

Mom pulls a face. "You're not going to try to buy the masters, are you?"

I shrug. We talked about that too, briefly, and I know she's worried about the cost. "I don't know if we can, but we have to do something. That music is ours."

She hums. "Just be careful, honey."

I stiffen. "What do you mean?"

"Well, I was talking to your brother about entertainment law the other day . . ." Oh, here we go. I'm going to have a word with Ollie later. "He said these fights can be expensive. Shouldn't you all focus on moving forward and releasing more music instead?"

I purse my lips, sinking back against the couch. "We can do both. Like sure, buying our masters will be expensive, but then we'd be making profits off of them instead of most of the money going to the label."

"That's a good point," my dad says, ever the reasonable one. "But could going up against the label hurt you professionally? It seems like they have a lot of power."

"This is my concern," Mom says. "The last artist who went up against Label Records—who was it, Nick Evans? I did some research. He hasn't been able to get another contract since."

Nick also doesn't have an original bone in his body, so I'm not surprised. Still, it makes me nervous, thinking about all the ways Label could ruin our future. What if we fight them and lose? Will that wreck our future as a band? Maybe this isn't worth all the effort.

A part of me wonders if I should listen to my parents this time. I've always trusted their guidance. And maybe, just maybe, I'm pushing too hard because I'm being stubborn and not calculating every move the way I should be. This battle could be for nothing.

But then I remember the smirk on Landon's face when he said he could take our music down. I have to believe we can win—even if it scares the shit out of me.

I try to defend it. "Wade won't steer us wrong. That's what Ortega Management's lawyers are for." I'm not used to arguing with my parents, and it leaves something leaden behind. Still, I won't back down.

"Just . . . don't sink all of your money into this."

"Isn't that what my savings and investments are for? To use for things I care about?" I don't know if I'm trying to convince myself, or her.

Mom sighs. "You know it's to make sure your future is secure, especially since there's no Glitter Bats money coming in right now. Are you sure you don't want to take some other drumming jobs? I'm assuming that clinic today didn't pay very well."

It didn't pay *anything*, but I'm not going to tell Mom that I worked for free. If I want to make quality drum instruction available to teens, I'm not going to let her shame me for that.

"I've got it under control," I say bitterly.

Mom puts up her hands. "Okay, I'm sorry. I'll drop it."

Dad nudges Mom's shoulder. "We taught our kids to take care of themselves, Sasha. Keeley is going to be fine."

I hope he's right.

"So . . . what's new with you guys?" I ask, desperate for a change in topic. My parents tell me all about the renovations they're finishing up on the house. Even though they're changing all the things that made my childhood home so familiar, I actually can't wait to see the new cabinets and wooden floors.

But when we end the call, I'm feeling anxious about dinner, and not just because I'm concerned about our fight for our music.

I'm nervous to see *Jane*. We've only been apart for a day, but after the past month, I don't like not having her around. And I'm starting to hope she might feel the same, especially thinking about all that heady tension last night. I've never seen Jane blush as stunningly rose pink as she did in my kitchen before that damn alarm went off.

My heart races with nerves, but more than that, it races with possibility. If I didn't have the last few weeks to prove it, I'd tell myself I'm a sucker and I need to stay away and pine in peace. But I have hope, now, that I never had before. Maybe this isn't unrequited at all.

Still, I'm going to stay professional when I see her at dinner tonight, because it's not like I'm going to put Jane on the spot in front of the rest of the band. After dinner, though, all bets are off. Maybe I can ask if she wants to go get a drink, or dessert, or skip all the pleasantries and come back to my place for more than just TV and chill . . .

No. With Jane, that doesn't feel right. Of course I'd be thrilled to be with her like that, but our relationship is too important for it to be just sex. No, with her I'll take it slow, even if I want to go full speed ahead.

If I come on too strong, it could ruin everything.

I got dangerously close to finding out if that was true last night. So I decide I'll be the consummate professional. I even grab an oversized blazer to throw over my vintage Levi's and striped crop top, pairing it all with white Jordans and a fresh coat of my lucky aquamarine nail polish before I head out the door.

Blessedly, traffic is light, and I get there a good half hour before we're supposed to meet.

We're gathering at a trendy restaurant, an old-Hollywood tribute place that used to attract climbers until Valerie was seen here with her piece-of-trash ex Theo last year. The buzz from his big fantasy movie and the general cacophony surrounding her love life was enough to get the place photographed, and now it has a wait list as long as any other hot spot in this city.

I never understood the whole crooner thing, but even I can admit Sinatra had pipes. "Fly Me to the Moon" plays over the loudspeakers, and there's a jazz band setting up over on the stage. It's definitely a vibe.

It's a strange place for a working dinner, but we've had stranger. When we first got into the industry, Wade knew we were on a tight budget, so he turned as many meetings as possible into meals someone could write off for tax purposes. The tradition stuck, and now nearly every Glitter Bats business decision is made over food, whether one of us chooses to cook or we go out.

I catch a whiff of something warm and buttery, and I decide this was a good pick on Wade's part. The maître d' leads me through the glamorous dining area to a private room reserved just for us.

But I'm not the first person to show. Jane is sitting alone with a glass of white wine, the menu forgotten on the table while she scrolls on her phone. She's dressed in one of those tantalizingly short Stevie Nicks–esque minidresses she loves, this one in a green cotton that makes her hair glow copper in the contrast. Her curls are down, for once, soft and flowing past her shoulders.

"Hi," I say.

"Hi!" she says, and it's almost a little too perky.

I bite my lip. "Thanks for the cookies."

She ducks her head shyly. "Of course. It's the least I could do, given how much you've saved my butt recently."

I laugh and change the subject to keep my mind from lingering on her butt for much longer. "So . . . how's the house?" I ask.

She grimaces. "It's cleaned up, but I'm starting to determine what to replace. Once I got back, I spent the afternoon trying to figure out which plants I can salvage. Most of them seem like they'll bounce back, but I'm afraid a few are lost causes. And, well . . . my music room is ruined. A lot of the Glitter Bats stuff is framed, so it should be okay . . ." Her face falls. "But my Korg was down there, and it wasn't in a case."

Jane played the same Korg keyboard at every Glitter Bats show. Instruments, even electric ones, can last for decades if you take care of them properly. Jane takes so much care she should be studied. I can tell by the shadow in her gaze that she's feeling guilt about all of this. Still, this wasn't her fault. "Is insurance taking care of it?"

She nods, folding her shaking hands together on top of the table. "Yeah, but it was sentimental, you know? They don't make that model of my keyboard anymore, and I know I'll be able to track one down if I look long enough, but I can't believe it's gone."

I reach my hand across the table to place it on hers. "I'm sorry, Jane," I say.

Our gazes lock. "Keeley, I—"

"Hello, friends!" Riker's voice announces him before he fully enters the room, and we snatch our hands away in unison. He pokes his grinning face inside once the server opens the door, and Wade follows, with Valerie and Caleb slipping in after.

"Whatcha talking about?" Riker asks, his light brown hair pulled back in a bun that rivals every hipster in the valley.

He glances from Jane to me, no doubt seeing the flush on my cheeks.

"Jane's poor house."

Riker frowns, moving over to give Jane a tight squeeze, whispering something in her ear. My jaw tightens at the soft smile she flashes at him. Maybe I was wrong.

Maybe this was all in my head. Riker is, well, *Riker Maddox*. He's charming and kind and whoever he ends up partnering with—if he decides he wants that—is going to be super lucky. If I were Jane, I'd pick him over me any day.

Resigned, I grab a menu as the small talk starts up. When our server stops in to get drink orders, I ask for a whiskey sour and hide myself behind the heavy menu. After the drink orders arrive, Wade clears his throat and folds his hands on the table. Today, like all days, he's wearing one of his trademark suits—this one in a fun, brighter-than-navy blue pinstripe. The rest of us are more casual in comparison, but that's just Wade. After he quit playing major league ball, he transitioned to talent management, and he said he started with suits so everyone would take him seriously.

Now I just think he wears them because his wife, Michelle, loves them. But who am I to judge?

"I have some news about your back catalog," Wade says. "I didn't want to send this over text or email, just in case anything could leak. I know none of you would share the information, but with the recent hacks of Holly Harper's cloud storage, we're taking extra precautions with sensitive details."

Valerie's jaw drops as she bolts upright in the lavish dining chair. "Is it really that serious?" She's had her fair share of private information sold to the media, so I know her phone and computer are locked down to an almost governmental degree.

It's not like the rest of us are careless either. Caleb grabs Valerie's hand, threading their fingers together. Valerie sags a little, but her eyes don't leave Wade.

He nods. "Label is officially opening up negotiations about purchasing your masters."

It's the news we've been waiting for, but my shoulders rise. After Landon's power trip the other day, something isn't right about this. There's no way he just changed his mind out of generosity.

But determination flashes in Riker's eyes. "That's good, right? We can pool our money together and get our music back."

Caleb's face tightens. "Hang on, we haven't talked numbers yet." He's always struggled with money in a way the rest of us never had to think about because of his family situation. We still get a few royalty checks, but we're not seeing the returns we should thanks to that impressively shady language Valerie's mom slipped into our contract. Caleb's teaching just part-time now that he's down in California, and I know it makes him happy, but it doesn't bring in the same kind of money the rest of us get from working in the industry. The contrast certainly can't help his financial anxiety or trauma, that's for sure.

"Caleb's on the right track. There's at least one other interested party, and Label is proposing an auction. They want to know our best and highest bid," Wade says.

And there it fucking is.

Is one of Landon's buddies trying to break into the industry, and so he thinks he can just sell our entire catalog to them? It's got to be something like that. Whatever it is, I don't like it.

Fuck it. It doesn't matter. I'm not about to go down without a fight. We all glance around at one another, and I try not to think about my earlier conversation with my parents, my fear that we're playing a rigged game.

There's so much at stake. We're so close to getting our music back, but I wish we had more time to figure out what we can afford.

What if we bid too low and lose?

"So what do we do? How do we come up with a number?" I ask.

Wade folds his hands, a resigned look passing over his face. "I've been in touch with your accountant, and he gave me the exact figure in your band account. It's not nearly enough to bring to the table. That being said, how you move forward is up to you."

"Hell, I can put up some personal cash," Riker says. "I've been thinking about it a lot."

Caleb and Valerie exchange a glance. "We can come up with a

number to contribute," Valerie says hesitantly, and Caleb just nods, jaw twitching.

"I can add to the pot," I say. Despite my mom's misgivings about my financial situation, I'm more than solid. I hired a badass financial advisor after I got my second Glitter Bats check, and I've been having him manage my funds ever since. Even with my monthly expenses, I can contribute a big chunk of my savings and investments for this fight.

"I have some money set aside I could move for this," Jane says softly, but her expression doesn't betray more.

Wade nods, glancing around at each of us with a determined expression. "Okay, well, would you rather all just say out loud how much you're willing to put up, or would you prefer to do it privately?"

"Out loud," Riker and I say in unison, just as Jane and Caleb answer, "Privately."

Riker laughs. Jane and I exchange a smile. Caleb clears his throat, and I don't miss Valerie squeezing his hand under the table. She was noticeably quiet just now.

Wade nods. "Privately then. Why don't you all text me the amounts, and we'll get to eating. I'll send the total to our contracts department so they can draw up an initial offer. They'll put in overtime tonight to get this on the table first thing tomorrow."

"And then we wait," Valerie says, staring at her hand intertwined with Caleb's.

"And then we wait," Wade agrees. We all fire off our texts, and Wade sends an email as the server comes in to get our dinner orders. Soon enough, we're laughing again.

Wade steps out to make a call.

Riker stands, raising his glass of rosé, which has become a bit of a Glitter Bats joke, but I think he genuinely likes his juice. "So we've got solid dates for the band retreat, and it's not going to cost us much. I think the best thing we can do now is focus on what we can control, and that's making new music . . . eventually, I know," he says before anyone can protest. "I say we move forward with this retreat to distract us from the fight for our masters, and keep hoping for the best when it comes to that. We'd just have to travel there."

"I can cover that," Jane says. "I have a ton of air miles because I never pay for my own flights for work, so it wouldn't cost us anything to get there. I could use a break."

I wink at her. "I might have to get you to try horseback riding, if we're in Montana," I say.

She flushes, but her voice is light and breezy. "I just might let you convince me, to get in the spirit of things."

My neck warms, and I glance away, my gaze bouncing across the table to Valerie. She's smirking at me.

Don't say it, I mouth at her.

I didn't say anything, Valerie mouths back.

"I have a four-day weekend for staff training I can get out of, so if we can still make it happen in two weeks, I'm in," Caleb says.

"Yeah, at least we can all cry together if we don't get the contract," Valerie says sarcastically. "But I'm in. I like horses."

"Yes!" Riker says. "Now, if we lose our masters, at least we get a fun trip."

It doesn't feel as lighthearted as Riker's tone implies, but I guess we can only hope it's a celebration and not a wake. And four days in the Montana wilderness with Jane, well . . . at least we'll have the buffer of the rest of the band.

Glitter Bats Masters Up for Sale

RYAN TATE FOR *GOSSIP DAILY*

HOT GOSS: The rights to all three Glitter Bats albums are up for the highest bid.

It's an open secret in this industry that Label Records offers wild contracts to clueless new musicians, and Glitter Bats were one of their victims. After the successful release of *More to Say*, the long-awaited follow up to *Bittersweet* and *Wanderlust*, Glitter Bats were free of their contract with Label Records, but Label issued a ceast-and-desist order to the Bats for trying to use their own songs on their social media platform.

And so we suspect the Bats took matters in their own hands and are attempting to purchase their masters, following in the footsteps of some of the biggest artists in the industry: Jay-Z, U2, Holly Harper, Metallica, and Jude. But with all the rumors of the Glitter Bats' financial instability flying, I can only wonder if they'll be able to put up enough capital to win.

In this business, you've got to be willing to be a big spender . . . on the right things. And yes, I am looking at Keeley Cunningham's shiny new EV, Riker Maddox's guitar habit, and the fact that Caleb Sloane allegedly works an actual day job. [*shudder.*]

It's safe to say I'm skeptical the band will come out on top. With news of the sale going public, it will be interesting to see who else puts their hat in the ring for ownership of these tracks. Anything could happen, and we'll be following the news eagerly.

Keep your eyes on the *Gossip Daily* Glitter Bats tag for updates!

12

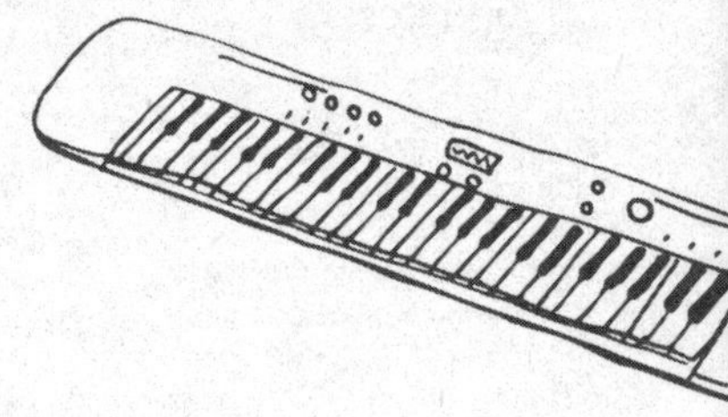

Jane

We weren't expecting things to go public.

Now that everyone knows our masters are up for grabs—thanks to Ryan Tate, naturally—anything *could* happen. Our strategy was to keep the fight quiet, and now, I don't know how this will change things. After dinner, Keeley confided in me that she thinks something doesn't add up, with Label suddenly being willing to negotiate, and I agree.

Either Landon Banks is desperate for capital, or he's playing a game here.

Wade has been keeping us updated, but at this point, the future of the band really is unknown. All we know is there are multiple parties who have expressed interest since the article a couple weeks ago, and it's turning into a drawn-out bidding war, tied up in lawyers and red tape. And then last week, Landon said he's going on vacation, and he'll review the bids with "a fresh mind" once he returns from a month in Fiji.

Whatever that means.

It's why going on the retreat is starting to feel so important—

making more art is the one thing we can control in this whole situation. On the flight to Montana, I've used extra miles to tuck myself into a first-class seat with a warm blanket and a soft pillow.

Usually, I bring a new romance novel on a flight, but instead, I've spent today staring at the same page of *Emma* for more than an hour. I've read Austen dozens of times, and not just because I was named after Jane Bennet and my sister was named after Elinor Dashwood—the one thing I don't resent my parents for. I hoped a reread of my favorite would give me some comfort. But I just don't have the focus for anything. My anxiety is on high alert. I'm terrified we'll lose the control of our music that felt just within reach. I'm hoping this retreat is magical, and somehow helps me feel better about the future.

After all my blustering about not having time for a new album, making more music is all I can think about these days. If we can just have *something* of our own, then I'll be able to believe the band will survive, even if we lose the auction.

I just want to know how Ryan Tate found out. Did Landon Banks leak the news on purpose, so more people might participate? There's no way to know.

But for now, I just keep staring at the ink on page three of my book.

I manage to get through a chapter when the flight attendant announces it's time to prepare for landing at Bozeman-Yellowstone. I stare out the window and watch as the plane descends, the landscape getting closer and closer, like a camera zooming in.

It makes me feel small and grateful to live in the world.

We come to a bouncing landing. As soon as we've slowed to taxiing, I sigh, taking a sip from my water bottle before slipping it into my backpack.

I don't mind flying alone. Originally, we'd all planned to arrive together, but the timing didn't work out. Keeley is coming from a quick visit out to see her parents in Seattle, and Riker, Valerie, and Caleb had to grab a later flight.

So because we're landing at similar times, it'll just be me and Keeley splitting a ride on the way to the resort. We haven't been alone since that last night in her apartment, when I thought we were about to, well . . . nothing happened, right? Besides, our entire focus should be on the band right now.

Once we've stopped at the gate, I step out of my seat, swing my backpack over my shoulders, and grab my carry-on from the overhead compartment. I always try to pack light, but fall in Montana is a lot different than fall in Los Angeles. I had to bring lots of layers to stave off the cold.

As we deplane, I mentally plan my rush to the bathroom to freshen my makeup, fix my doubtlessly flattened hair, and make myself presentable before I see Keeley. But all of those plans go out the window when I see her casually leaning against the wall by my gate, her blond hair swooping across her smiling eyes as she runs a hand through it.

My mouth goes dry. Keeley has gone for casual, in a gray sweatsuit that hangs perfectly on her long, lithe frame. The pants are slung low on her hips, exposing the tiniest strip of taut bare skin that makes me wonder how soft it might feel.

I hurry over to her, clearing my throat.

"Hey, I hope you didn't have to wait long," I say.

She shakes her head. "No, I landed about twenty minutes ago. Thought you might want this." She hands me an iced coffee in a to-go cup, and I reach for it with my free hand. "It's not going to be as good as you're used to, but I avoided the big chain."

I take it from her gratefully, pulling a big sip from the straw. After a three-hour flight, my body craves the shock of caffeine to my system, and I don't care where it's from. Involuntarily, I let out a moan of pleasure.

Keeley brings her hand to her neck. "Good to see you too, Mercer."

I laugh, my cheeks warming. "I didn't realize how much I needed this."

"Happy to be of service," she says. I still, our eyes locking in this crowded, stuffy airport. It's like the innuendo has made me short-circuit, because my tired, sad mind can only think of all of the ways we could *service* each other. Keeley laughs, hopefully coming to her own conclusion about her words and not reading my reaction. "You know what I mean."

"Yeah." I thrust the coffee back at her, suddenly desperate for just a moment to collect myself. "Do you mind holding this for a minute?"

"Of course," she says, blinking.

"Thank you." I leave my bag with her but keep my backpack on my shoulders as I hurry to the restroom. Inside, I forego all plans to primp with the exception of splashing cold water on my face and swiping on some lip balm.

Not because I'm thinking about lips or anything, just because it makes me feel a semblance of polish. We just have to get through the couple of hours alone before the band gets here, and then we'll have buffers for the next four days.

Buffers are good.

When I've exhausted the amount of acceptable time I can spend in an airport bathroom, I head over to meet Keeley again. She hasn't left her spot by the gate, and instead of her face being buried in her phone the way it usually is, she's staring out the windows at the planes landing and departing.

"Ready to go?" I ask.

"Of course," Keeley says. We pick up her guitar at baggage claim, then head out of the airport together.

"Should we order a rideshare?" Keeley asks, pulling out her

phone. We really should have planned this part sooner, but I just assumed we'd figure out rides when we got here.

"Sounds good," I say.

"Holy fuck, that's expensive," Keeley says, tilting her phone at me. I blanch at the cost.

"That's just to get us to the resort?" I ask.

She nods. "It's like an hour away."

"Wow."

"Maybe we should just . . . rent a car," she says. "It might be cheaper in the long run, if we want to go anywhere."

I shrug. "Sure, that's not a problem. Should we wait for everyone else to land before heading to the resort?"

Keeley frowns. "You want to hang out here for three hours?"

That's the last thing I want to do. "No, you're right. Let's go see what rentals are available."

"I'm on it. Do you want to call the resort and see if we can do an early check-in?"

I nod and head away from the crowded area to make the call while Keeley waits in line. It doesn't take long to reach them and confirm we can check in early, so I spend a few minutes downing the rest of my coffee, then recycle the cup and head over to check in with Keeley on her progress.

Over by the counter, she's beaming at me like she's just gotten something she really wants, and it's hard to look away.

"What is it?" I ask.

Keeley swings the key fob around her finger, and the unmistakable glint of the lion crest hits the light.

I laugh, shaking my head. "You didn't."

She raises her hands. "I *had to*, okay? The guy recognized me—which never happens to me, by the way—and asked if I wanted a free upgrade to a luxury car. It's a *Porsche*, Jane. I like fast cars."

I roll my eyes. "You have no self-control."

"Hey, I would never own one, but we're on retreat and I'm anxious about the masters, okay? Shiny cars make me feel better."

I laugh, shaking my head as she leads the way out of the airport. "You are ridiculous."

"At least this way, we couldn't all fit anyways, so there's no use waiting for the others. Can you imagine Riker squeezing into the back seat?"

I laugh. "No, not at all. I could sit back there, though!"

"I'll just text Riker and suggest he gets another car. This way, if we want to head back into the city to go out to eat or anything, we won't be stuck in the middle of nowhere."

She has a point. As soon as we get through the glass doors, I shiver at the wind whipping through the air. I'm wearing a cardigan over jeans, but that isn't enough to keep out the Montana chill.

"Fuck, it's cold," Keeley says. "I have a North Face packed up in my carry-on, but it's buried.

"I've got a jacket too," I say, already regretting using it to line the bottom of my suitcase. "Should we make a run for it?"

Keeley nods, and before I can register what's happening, she grabs my free hand with hers and bolts for the rental lot. My carry-on rolls and bounces reluctantly along the asphalt, and I'm nearly out of breath trying to keep up with her long strides. By the time we get to the car lot, we're both breathless and grinning despite the cold air.

Her cheeks are flushed pink.

It doesn't take long to find the Porsche—it's the only fancy car out in the lot. Keeley opens up the trunk and puts my suitcase inside, followed by hers. Then she unlocks the car, and I hurry over to the passenger seat, shivering.

Inside, Keeley starts the car. The engine purrs to life, and we both scramble to switch on the heated seats. Even for a rental, the Porsche is luxurious, and I momentarily ponder ordering one of the electric ones before deciding I'm perfectly fine with my Prius.

Keeley, though, looks like she's in heaven.

"God, I want one of these," she sighs, running her hands along the steering wheel, then gripping it gently with those long, strong fingers. I swallow thickly.

"Why don't you buy one?"

She shrugs. "It seems silly to have two cars with how little I drive, and it's not like I'm going to ever get rid of my Rivian." With all the equipment she has to haul, it makes sense that she'd keep the electric SUV. I think she'd love a car like this, though. I smile as she inspects all the bells and whistles, before pairing her phone and plugging the resort's address into the GPS. She catches me looking at her.

"Don't worry, I won't go too fast," she says with a smirk, mistaking my pensive admiration for worry.

I laugh. "I'm not too worried. I know you'll keep me safe."

"Always," she says, her expression sobering.

I swallow. "Shall we?"

She clears her throat. "Right."

Keeley cues up music on her phone before heading out onto the road. It's an old-school pop-punk playlist, all Good Charlotte and Green Day and Lime Velvet and The Used, which we listen to in silence. But I laugh when "Sadie Hawkins Dance" pops up.

"Seriously?" I ask.

She laughs. "I remember hearing it in your car when we were kids, and the chorus is catchy."

I groan. "Relient K and Switchfoot were the only *good* bands I was allowed to listen to. Sometimes I could sneak in secular bands if they sounded similar enough, which is how I got into emo."

Keeley looks over at me, then refocuses on the road. "You got around all those rules pretty impressively."

I lean my head against the seat. "It was exhausting. The best thing about getting that record deal was the freedom it gave me to be myself."

"I'm so glad that happened for you," she says quietly. She takes her right hand off the steering wheel and laces her fingers through mine. This touch is different than the "accidental" brush of fingers in the back of the cab after our pottery class. Different, even, than the casual way she grabbed my hand to run to the car.

It's intentional.

There's no way to explain away the contact now, and yet, neither of us pulls away. I just squeeze her fingers, leave my hand in hers for the rest of the drive, reveling in silent awe of just how *right* this feels. We're just on the edge of something, and exhilaration blooms across my skin at the possibility of taking the leap.

Like listening to my favorite song, I don't want the moment to end.

But soon enough, the resort comes into view. It's on the banks of the Yellowstone River, set in sprawling fields surrounded by mountains. A herd of horses grazes in a paddock by a beautiful wooden barn, and in the center of it all sits a giant lodge with floor-to-ceiling windows and a rock exterior. Other matching buildings surround the main lodge, probably the spa and who knows what other amenities.

"Damn, Riker's uncles must be loaded," Keeley says with a whistle as we find a parking spot.

"It's nice of them to let us stay, but this place looks pretty packed for the off-season," I observe, staring at the line of vehicles.

She nods, biting her lip. "This is not what I expected."

Me neither. I pictured a ranch house with maybe a dozen

rooms, not a full-blown vacation resort. Together, we head to the main building, and we're immediately greeted by someone in khakis and flannel. He directs us to the front desk, and I give the receptionist our names.

"Welcome! One king room, yes?"

I blanch, glancing at Keeley in alarm. "I'm sorry, that doesn't sound right. Riker Maddox should have booked four rooms for us."

The receptionist raises her brows as she types something into the computer. "I'm sorry, this says the other rooms in that reservation were cancelled this morning."

"What?" I ask. "I'm going to try to call Riker, hang on."

Keeley shrugs at the receptionist and asks her about the facilities, and the woman visibly relaxes at the change in subject as I step to the side. While I wait for him to pick up, I stare out at the river shining under the afternoon sun.

"Janey!" Riker says, sounding relaxed and happy to hear from me and not at all like he's racing to the airport last minute, the way he always does. Suspicion prickles my mind immediately.

"Don't *Janey* me! We're at the resort. Why did the receptionist tell me the reservation was cancelled?"

Riker laughs nervously. "It shouldn't be the whole reservation, just let go of a couple of rooms. I tried to call you, but your phone was off."

"Because I was on an airplane? What do you mean, you cancelled a couple of rooms?"

"I, uh, have to back out of the retreat. Jared had a family emergency and Lime Velvet needs me to cover this weekend." We opened for Lime Velvet back in the day, and they're old friends, but I can't imagine it's really that dire. Not when this was already planned. Normally, I'd let Riker give me an excuse and take it at face value, but not today.

Because I suspect he has some kind of ulterior motive.

"And you're the only guitarist they know in LA?" I demand.

"Sorry," he says breezily. "I couldn't say no."

"And what about Valerie and Caleb?" I ask.

"They, uh, had to stay behind because of Caleb's work. Yeah! His principal denied his request to be off on Monday because a bunch of teachers have the flu. It's, uh, really bad this year. You should really go get your flu shot if you haven't already."

"I'm all covered, actually," I say, as even more suspicion begins whirring through my mind. "So why are we only finding this out now that we're at the resort?"

"Like I said, it was all last minute," Riker says. "But you and Keeley should stay and enjoy your weekend. Relax. See the, uh, pretty sights. Eat good food."

I huff. "In one room? What's that about?"

He lets out a humming noise. "I don't know what you're talking about. I only cancelled two of the rooms."

"Sure," I say, because I don't believe him for a minute. When Riker is lying, his voice gets higher, and he's speaking a full octave above his usual baritone. "This is absurd."

"Don't say I never did anything for you."

"Riker!" I snap.

"Make good choices!" he says before he disconnects the call.

I try to mask my annoyance as I go to meet Keeley back at the desk. She's scrubbing a hand over her face.

"What is it?" I ask.

"They don't have any more rooms available, since a family just booked them for a last-minute vacation. So unless we all want to squeeze into the king, we're going to have to find somewhere else to stay."

I laugh nervously. "Well, turns out the rest of the band isn't coming."

Keeley's mouth drops open. "What?"

I relay Riker's message, and she sighs, apparently more convinced by his excuse than I was. "Well this blows. I thought we were going to have a creative retreat."

I nod. "Me too. I guess we could just head back, then."

Keeley freezes. "Is that what you want?"

"Not really, but what are we supposed to do now?"

A spark lights in her eyes, and she glances at the concierge. "I think we should stay."

"In one room?" I rasp out.

She shrugs. "Why not? You and I could still try to write something together, right?"

"Sure," I say, even though I'm anything but. Four days alone with Keeley Cunningham in one hotel room just might break me.

13

✦ *Keeley* ✦

I didn't think this through. When we get to the hotel room, I'm alarmed by just how *intimate* the whole thing is.

It's a stunning space, with shining plank floors and neutral walls and rustic-chic wooden fixtures. Afternoon sunlight shines through large windows that overlook the mountains and pastures. An electric fireplace with stone accents sits under the TV in the first room, with a large white couch and oversized chair facing it. We set down our bags and head into the bedroom, where there's even more windows, and a soft green quilt folded over a plush white comforter on that all-too-cozy king-sized bed.

A bottle of champagne and a tray of chocolate-covered strawberries sit on the vanity. I walk over to check it out. Over in the nearest corner, I shit you not, there's a jetted tub. Did Riker book us the fucking honeymoon suite or something?

We both stare at it for a moment, taking in the reality of our accommodations for the next four days. I clear my throat.

"I can, uh, crash on the couch," I say quickly.

Jane's ears go pink. "Don't be ridiculous. We can share. It's not a big deal."

Isn't it? I want to scream, but I'm not about to argue with her. Sleeping on couches inevitably leaves my back sore and my legs cramped, and my tall body is less forgiving as I near thirty.

"Okay," I say, and other than that, I'm at a loss for words. Usually, I can't shut up, even when I wish I could, but staring at her looking so beautiful, in nothing fancier than the loose jeans and oversized cardigan she traveled in, leaves me tongue-tied.

So how the hell am I supposed to survive sharing a soft, inviting bed with her for four days? It wouldn't be easy to lay inches away from her even if we hadn't almost kissed in my kitchen a few weeks ago. When I held her hand in the car, it was like I couldn't help myself. I *needed* to touch her.

I feel like I'm on the edge of losing my self-control. All my reasons to keep my distance feel flimsy, and I just don't care about them anymore. I want her so much that I can hardly breathe. And if any of the glances we've shared are as loaded as they've felt, I'm starting to hope she just might feel the same way.

But what if I'm wrong? I'm terrified to find out. Time for a distraction.

"So, uh, do we want to check out the amenities?" I hand Jane one of the activity menus sitting on the vanity and grab one for myself as I perch on the foot of the bed.

Jane leans against the wall, and her face pales as she reads. "I thought you were kidding about the horseback riding."

I laugh. "What do you think the herd of horses is out there for?"

"The aesthetic?" she squeaks. "I don't know! Horses are scary!"

Her expression tightens, and I'm desperate to reassure her. "Hey, we don't have to go." I drop my menu on the bed and bring a hand to the back of my neck. "There are a lot of other great things to do here. We can hike, or check out the heated indoor pool, or book a day at the spa, or ooh, there's even a day trip to visit the hot springs if we want to make a day of it?"

"I don't know. Honestly, I was looking forward to relaxing, so I don't want to do a bunch of traveling while we're here. But . . ." She trails off, biting her lip. "*Maybe* I could be persuaded to try some horseback riding. As long as they can get me a really gentle horse."

"I'll ask," I say, and I mean it.

"I, uh, have been noodling on some music. Do you want to hear it?" she says, almost shyly. I've listened to so many of Jane's compositions that the tentativeness in her voice is new, but I understand. We didn't do much of the Glitter Bats writing. That was all Caleb and Valerie, and occasionally Riker on certain songs. I maybe wrote a lyric or two, but I left most of the songwriting to them.

It's cool to have the opportunity to contribute to the band in a way we haven't before. Still, the stakes feel impossibly high when we don't know what's going on with our masters. She must feel vulnerable, but I have no doubt that whatever she has is going to be brilliant.

I grin. "That sounds great. You can use my guitar."

"Perfect," she says. She heads over to my acoustic case and pulls out the shiny Martin I brought on the trip. I know I don't play guitar for Glitter Bats, but a guitar is the most portable instrument for writing on the go, and in my defense, we were supposed to write.

Even if bringing the damn thing was a pain in the ass.

Jane bites her lip as she starts to play through the progression, humming a melody. "I like what I have so far, but I haven't landed on any lyrics yet."

I nearly scream with excitement as I listen, because I have some lines on my phone that I think might be perfect. Even if I wrote them in the middle of the night after she left my apartment and sharing them is . . . scary. But now that I've imagined them fitting on top of what she's written, I can't help it.

"Can I try to sing something over it?" I ask, gesturing at my phone.

"Of course," she says.

I pull up my lyrics document and start to sing, trying to hold on to my composure, even as my voice shakes.

Oh, you fill my head with possibilities
Oh, when you smile I forget how to breathe

I shrug, my cheeks warming. "That's all I've got."

Jane grins, her hand pausing on the strings. "That's something. Did you just come up with it?"

"Uh, it's been in my Notes app awhile." *Awhile* being open to interpretation.

"Oh!" She gapes, her eyes lighting up. "I, uh, think I have an idea. May I?" She gestures for my phone.

I hand it to her, ignoring the thrill of her fingers brushing mine as she takes it, pretending the sensation dancing across my skin is just in my head. She furrows her brow, typing furiously before handing the phone back.

My mouth goes dry, but when Jane plays back through the chorus, I sing the full thing:

Oh, you fill my head with possibilities
Oh, your hand in mine makes me want to believe
Oh, when you smile I forget how to breathe
Oh, if you say yes I'll give you everything

As the final chords reverberate through the hotel room, you could cut the tension with a knife.

Jane grins at me. "Keeley, I think we've got something."

My breath catches at that, but I somehow manage to speak. "I think you're right."

Again, I'm not sure either of us is talking about the song. But then she blinks as her phone starts buzzing. She stares at the screen, confusion muddling her features.

"Oh! It's my agent. I'm so sorry—I know we're writing, but can I take this?"

I laugh. "Not much of a retreat anymore. Have at it, Mercer."

She flashes me a grateful look and steps out into the hall. I feel bad, like maybe I made her think she can't take the call in here, but I know it's just Jane being as conscientious as ever. She doesn't like to be a bother to anyone.

I'd let her bother me any day.

God, Keeley, get a grip.

I stare out the window at the valley. The sky is turning orange with an impending sunset on the horizon, and as much as I'd like to plan one of the guided adventures for the rest of the afternoon, I think our best bet is to just keep writing. Jane hates to have plans change last minute, and this shift from band retreat to one-on-one is definitely not what she signed up for. The closest we can get to sticking to the plan, the better.

First, I call down to the restaurant and get us dinner reservations for tonight. Then, I change into jeans and am just shrugging into a sweater when the door opens.

"Oh! Sorry!" Jane squeaks. I hurriedly tug the sweater over my bra and peek my head out, where Jane is staring at me from the door of our room. She hastens to shut it.

I laugh nervously. "It's fine. I should have changed in the bathroom."

"No, you don't have to. I don't mind seeing you change." Her eyes widen. "I mean . . . you can do whatever you're comfortable with! A body is just a body, right? I'm all for breaking down the stigma. Free the nipple!"

I bark out a laugh, because *really*? "Are you done?"

"Sorry, I babble when I'm nervous."

I swallow, stepping over to her where she's frozen, standing against the entry. Resting an arm above her head, I lean over her and lower my voice. "What's making you nervous, Mercer?"

She blinks rapidly, shaking her head, then meets my gaze with a disbelieving smile. "I just found out I . . . somehow . . . got nominated for a RECORD award for *Into the Dragon Realm*? I didn't even realize the first episode was out before the deadline!"

I stand back and gape at her, joy and pride flooding my chest. "Oh my god, you did? Mercer, that's fucking *incredible*!"

Before I can stop myself, I sweep her into a hug. She sinks into me, warm and soft and *perfect*, and I resist the urge to bury my nose in her curls as I squeeze her tight. That familiar vanilla scent envelops me.

I wish I didn't have to let go.

She pulls away, and I try to ignore the way her phantom touch lingers on my skin.

"Thank you," she says. "The awards were announced an hour ago, and I didn't even think to check. Lacey was stuck in a meeting and just got a chance to call me. I still can't believe it."

"I can. You're amazing, Jane Mercer. We should absolutely crack that champagne before dinner. I hope it's okay I got us a reservation?" She just gapes at me, so I continue. "We don't have to head down for another half hour or so, but I figured we could eat early and then not have to leave for the rest of the night. We can always bring dessert back and watch some TV or something if we don't want to keep writing." Now I'm the one babbling.

Jane brings her hands to her heart. "That sounds perfect, thank you." She lets out a breath. "Sorry, I'm still processing the news."

"Of course you are!" I proclaim, as if we're not the only two people in the room. I hurry over to grab the bottle and glasses, then pop the cork over the bathroom sink. Jane follows me, and she pours a generous amount in each glass.

It's hard not to stare at her like this. She's proud of herself, as she should be, and it makes her glow like a ray of sunshine. She worked incredibly hard to make this happen. I always knew she was a superstar.

Now the world is finally noticing.

"Cheers, Mercer," I say. "You fucking earned it, and I'm so proud of you." Beaming, she clinks her glass against mine, then takes a long sip. I follow her lead. The champagne is dry and fizzy, just how I like it, and I head back into the living room and settle back on one of the couches.

"Do you mind?" Jane asks, gesturing at her phone.

"Not at all," I say, and I mean it. Of course she should respond to what I can only imagine are hundreds of notifications. The *Into the Dragon Realm* soundtrack has been critically acclaimed for a reason, because it's fresh and unique and inspiring. Getting nominated for a RECORD is the height of achievement in this industry.

But Jane Mercer is the real deal. I have no doubt in my mind this will be one of many accolades for her hard work and dedication to her craft. Even as we sip more celebratory champagne, my stomach twists as I think about our argument in the studio, despite the magic of our writing session just minutes ago.

The more work she does in the TV space, the more—very well-deserved—recognition she's going to get, and then where will that leave us? She certainly shouldn't fuck around with Glitter Bats when the other path will bring her statuettes and fancy parties and name recognition. I was terrified she was leaving the band, but now I'm scared if she doesn't, we'll hold her back.

Jane deserves the world, and I don't want to be the reason she doesn't get it. Maybe if I can stop being so wounded about keeping her in the band, it'll give her the freedom to make the right choice for her. Even if that choice means leaving us behind. It's not too late—we can reassess whether we want to keep making music.

I've loved this girl from afar practically since the moment I met her, and even if I got my feelings hurt back in that studio, that doesn't mean I want to hold her back. Of course I want what's best for her. I won't stop her from following her dreams, even if they take her away from us. So tonight, I'll just celebrate with her and help her relax and let her enjoy the hell out of this moment.

She's worth it.

@DragonRealmLoverrr

CONGRATS TO JANE MERCER ON HER RECORD AWARD NOMINATION

@UnicornRidingIsCool

This is so rad. With something like the RECORDs, maybe our little show will get all the attention it deserves.

@WeAreTheDragonRealmers

#DragonRealmers assemble! Not only did Jane Mercer get nominated for a Record, but our show is back in the top ten! Keep streaming Season 2 so they get that renewal news out!

@GlitterbugsUnofficial

Celebrating Jane Mercer tonight! 

@BuzzWordCeleb

Visit our RECORD nominations roundup at the link in our bio! We're excited to celebrate all of the nominees!

@RyanTaterTotz

The RECORD nominations are out! Check out my article for the biggest snubs and flubs of the day!

14

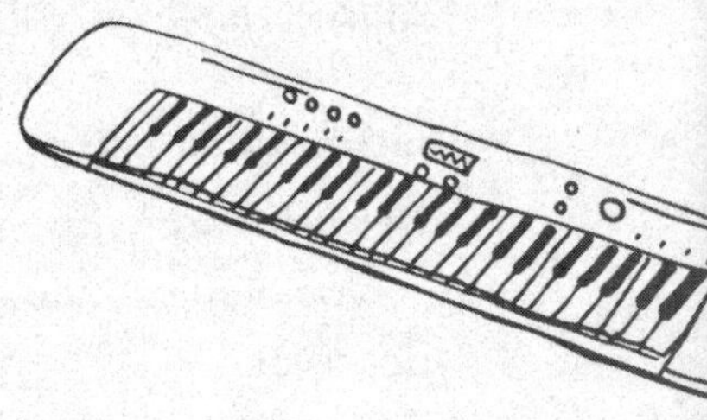

✦ *Jane* ✦

My phone has been blowing up all night, and I'm beyond grateful for all of the congratulatory texts rolling in:

> **RIKER MADDOX:** JANEY! I am so fucking happy for you. You deserve this and I hope you get to celebrate tonight 😉
>
> **VALERIE QUINN:** 👑👑👑 YES BABE LOOK AT YOU FINALLY GETTING THE RECOGNITION YOU DESERVE
>
> **CALEB SLOANE:** So proud of you, Jane. You're rocking it. Let's celebrate when you get back!
>
> **ANGEL CRUZ:** WAY TO GO BOSS! The whole music team is having drinks tonight in your honor.
>
> **WADE ORTEGA:** Congratulations, Jane. You deserve this moment.

CARRIE SLOANE: (Caleb gave me your number for emergencies and I know as my older brother he's going to yell at me later for abusing it but) CONGRATULATIONS YOU STAR!

KATE TAYLOR: I knew that song was special. Congratulations, Ms. Mercer.

FINN LEWIS: JANE MERCER! Putting us on the map!

KYLE HARRIS: Congratulations! It's so rare that nominations go to the truly deserving in this industry. You earned this.

JOSIE RAMIREZ: OUR SHOW GOT A RECORD NOM???? YOU ARE AMAZING! 😍

It's all been a blur. After Keeley and I enjoy a glass of champagne, my head is buzzing with adrenaline, and I slip into the bathroom to change into a long silk dress before dinner. It's black, not my usual color, but I managed to find a vintage one that doesn't wash me out. To dress it down, I pair it with my favorite denim jacket. When I emerge, Keeley is touching up her mascara in the bedroom mirror.

She turns to me, her jaw dropping.

"Holy shit, Mercer. You look incredible."

My neck warms. "Thank you. You look nice too." And she does. She's still wearing those dark jeans and a green sweater that skims over her long lines and makes her hair shine gold in the lamplight. That short blond hair is tousled in a deep side part that makes me desperate to tangle my fingers in it, and her bangs fall dreamily over her eyes.

Eyes she proceeds to roll at me. "You are too kind to me."

Before I can swallow back my champagne boldness, I stare openly at her, hoping I don't sound too breathless. "I mean it. That green is . . . really your color."

She tugs at her sweater, cheeks flushing. The moment feels electric, but I don't know how to cross the last few inches to get where I want to be. Before either of us can make a move, her phone alarm goes off with the strum of a factory-installed harp.

"That's dinner!" Keeley says. "Move your ass!"

I blink. "Right. Okay."

We hustle out of the room and down a flight of stairs to the main lodge, through a corridor, and into the rustically elegant dining room. It really is a sight to behold this evening. Strategically placed lamps cast an inviting glow throughout the space. Soft folk music plays through the sound system. The scents of garlic and butter and cedar smoke waft in the air. Keeley checks us in, and a host escorts us to an intimate table in the back of the room.

"Is this okay?" the host asks.

Keeley turns to me. "Jane?"

I nod as I take a seat, and she sits across from me.

"Your server will be here shortly to take your drink order."

In the quaint space, our fingers brush as we both reach for the drink menu at the same time. We spring apart.

"Go ahead," we say in unison.

I laugh, and Keeley smirks.

"You take longer to decide. You go," she says.

I gape. "As if. You're the one who spends ages looking at menus."

She raises a brow, challenging me. "Fine then, prove me wrong. Clock's ticking."

I grab the menu and skim it rapidly, noticing a variety of classic cocktails with a twist. The first drink I know I'll like catches my eye, and I shove the menu at Keeley before I can get a chance to second-guess myself.

"Really?" she asks.

"I'm getting the blackberry bramble."

"God, you are doing this just to fuck with me," she says, glancing at the menu. "Wouldn't you rather have a 75?"

I bite my lip, because I am partial to anything that adds champagne, but now we're in a battle, and I'm not about to lose.

"I'm good with my choice," I say breezily.

She runs a hand through her hair, and I'm sure my gulp is audible as I watch it fall across her face again. I have to clench my fists to avoid reaching over and tucking a stray lock behind her piercing-covered ear.

I bet her skin is soft there.

Dang it, I've got to keep it together. Fortunately, I'm saved by the server, who asks for our drink order.

"I'll have the bramble," I say, not looking away from Keeley even though I know it's rude. I'm pretty sure we're playing the staring game, but I don't know the prize if I win.

"Good choice," they reply. "And for you?" they ask, turning to Keeley.

She doesn't look away either. "I'll do the French 75."

"Excellent. I'll give you two a few minutes to peruse the menu, and be back to check in with your drinks shortly."

The server leaves, and Keeley sticks out her tongue at me.

I laugh, and blink. "Dang it!"

She flashes finger guns at me. "I win."

I shake my head, but I can't stop smiling. No matter how it happened, I'm alone with Keeley away from our real lives, smiling and laughing and basking in the delight of what turned out to be an incredible day. The outside world is falling away, and I'm not mad about it at all.

Just then, a buzzing noise sounds from my bag.

"Sorry, I forgot to silence it," I say, wincing as I scramble to pull out my small travel purse and dig out my phone.

"It's fine," Keeley says. "I don't expect you to ignore your calls just because we're having a meal."

But doesn't this feel like we're on a date? I want to scream. Instead, I grab my vibrating phone and feel my stomach fall as I check the screen.

"It's, uh, my mom," I say.

Her face sobers. "Do you need to answer it?"

"No, I can call her back later." I want to hold on to this joy as long as I can.

Keeley cocks her head at me. "Our drinks aren't even here yet. Would you feel better to get it over with now, so you can enjoy the rest of the trip?"

Wow, she really does know me well. The task of calling my mom back would only hang over my evening, inevitably souring my mood. And . . . well, I got a nomination for a RECORD today. Maybe Mom is calling to congratulate me for once.

I hate myself for it, but a tiny glimmer of hope sparks in my chest.

With Keeley's encouragement, I swipe to answer the call and step away from the table, down a hallway that leads to a secluded bathroom area. There's no one here, just a big mirror that I turn my back to as I answer.

"Hi, Mom!"

"Jane! It rang so long I thought you were pushing me to voicemail. I'm glad I caught you."

I bite back my retort, because at least she's reaching out. For once. "Thank you so much for calling! It's been a big day."

She scoffs. "I'm sure all of your days in that horrid city feel like big days, Jane, but that's neither here nor there. I'm calling about your sister."

I practically stumble back against the lacquered mahogany wall. "Oh. I just thought—"

"Yes?"

"Never mind."

She huffs. "Spit it out, Jane, I don't have all night."

Even as I gather my words, they make me feel small, like a mouse cowering in front of a cat. "I thought you were calling about my RECORD nomination."

"Really, Jane? We taught you better than to take any stock in worldly accomplishments. Really, if anything, this kind of nomination just proves your God-given talents are being wasted in that filthy industry. You should be using them for the Lord."

Tears sting my eyes, hot and unrelenting. Usually, I can keep a brave face when Mom gets like this, but maybe it's the fact that she can't see me, or the importance of this moment she's belittling. My therapist calls it spiritual bypassing, when people use their faith to ignore the emotions or reality of another person.

And maybe I'm just tired of Mom choosing her religion over me.

When I'm on a phone call like this, I can admit to myself that I'm envious of Keeley. If Sasha Cunningham learned Keeley was nominated for an award, she wouldn't just call her to congratulate her, she'd send flowers and cupcakes and maybe even show up on her doorstep. Keeley said her parents did that when she got nominated for cowriting "Your Body and Mine" with Bianca.

When she visits them, she always comes back happy and refreshed. I'd do anything to have family like that.

Mom is rattling on, and I blink, trying to refocus. Time for a little white lie. "Sorry, Mom, I lost you there for a moment. What was it you were calling about?"

The sooner I can get her on topic, the sooner I can end this call.

"Oh, Jane, Nora simply cannot find a wedding dress in Seattle that will be ready in time. There's just not enough selection to appease her." If I know Nora, she doesn't have that picky of taste—just give her a few pretty options and she'll pick something out. No, I'm sure this is all Mom.

But if they weren't scrambling for a *December* wedding, they'd have more options.

"I'm sorry to hear that."

"Do you have a stylist you can get me in touch with in Los Angeles? Nothing too . . . worldly, I just want to be sure Nora looks perfect on her big day."

God forbid it be *worldly*, but Mom has no compunction about finding a way to show off demurely to her friends. Guess LA isn't so *horrid* that she won't go there if it suits her.

I clench my jaw. "Sorry, Mom. There are a lot of great boutiques in the LA area, but I'm sure the Seattle ones sell a lot of the same dresses. I don't know a stylist who would be able to help you with bridal." And I'm pretty sure most boutiques take months for alterations.

"Hmm, okay then. I'll just make some inquiries. But call me if you think of anyone!"

"Right," I say. "Anything else?"

The line goes quiet. For one awful moment, I hope she's going to change her mind and congratulate me on the award. "No. But I'm praying for you, Jane. I just know the Lord will reward me for my faithfulness and you'll return to the church someday. Jesus will give you more fulfillment than any of these meaningless earthly achievements."

I don't even dignify that with a response. Instead, I hang up, seething.

With a sigh, I lean against the wall, trying to get my bearings. I bring my hand to my face and realize it's wet.

Whirling around, I step over to the mirror to inspect the damage. It's really not that bad, just a tiny smudge of mascara, and I use my pinkie to dab at the excess makeup. I could step into the bathroom to splash water on my face, but I've left Keeley alone enough already.

Instead, I throw my shoulders back and head to the table.

Fortunately, my drink has arrived. I reach for it without sitting down and take a long sip.

"You okay?" Keeley asks.

I blink hard. "Mom was calling me about Nora's wedding? I don't know what's wrong with me, I thought . . ."

Keeley straightens. "Of course you did." She sets her drink down, then rises to face me. She peers at my face and brings her thumbs to my still-damp cheeks. I close my eyes, leaning into her gentle touch. I want nothing more than to fall apart in this moment.

Because I'm here with Keeley, and I know she'll catch me.

"Jane," she murmurs.

Usually, I try to be stoic when it comes to my mom, but I'm so tired of this and can't hold my feelings back any longer. "I know, it's ridiculous to think she was calling to, I don't know, congratulate me? Mom never does that. But this is a RECORD, you know? It's kind of a big deal." I sniff, trying to keep a new wave of tears at bay.

"It's a huge fucking deal. The hugest. You *made it*, Jane."

Her hand falls to my elbow, and I press my arm into her fingers, taking the comfort where I can get it, my traitorous pulse racing despite my tears. "I just hoped . . . she'd be proud, for once. Isn't that pathetic?"

"You're not pathetic, Jane," Keeley says. She steps closer, lowering her voice as she tucks one of my curls behind my ear. "You're

Jane fucking Mercer. You took this industry by storm. You're working on a hit show and you got nominated for a RECORD and even if none of that were true, you would still have so much to be proud of, because you're *you*."

I sniff, letting out a sound that is part laugh and part sob. "You're just saying that because I'm crying."

"No, I'm not." Her gaze locks on to mine, and I'm powerless to look away. "Jane, you impressed me the day we first met at camp, and you've been doing it ever since. You're smart and talented and gorgeous as hell, and you work your ass off to persistently get better and make even more incredible art. Anyone who doesn't see all of the ways you shine is a fucking fool." She shakes her head, a small smile tugging at her mouth. "I'm constantly in awe of you."

My breath catches at her words, and it hits me just how lucky I am to know this woman. She cares fiercely and deeply and sees the best in me despite all the ways I fall short. Keeley is just so *good*. She makes me want to believe anything can happen, and I know deep in my soul that I'll never get over how remarkable it feels just to be close to her.

And I'm tired of hiding what I want.

So, even though I'm terrified that I'm crossing a point of no return, I step into her space. She doesn't step away. She just licks her lips, glancing down at mine before staring back into my eyes.

Oh.

At the hunger in her gaze, my pounding heart throws my self-control out the window.

"There's something going on here, right? It's felt like we've been dancing around each other for . . . ever." My mouth goes dry, but based on the way she's looking at me, I feel like I won't be able to breathe until I get this out. "*God*, Keeley. Is this in my head? I don't even know what to think anymore."

"*Jane*." Keeley leans closer, impossibly close, so I can feel the warmth radiating off her skin. She lowers her voice so it's only the softest, sweetest whisper. "It's not in your head."

My world spins, and it's not from the bourbon. I know I want Keeley, and yet I'm still terrified of what might happen if we open ourselves to the possibility of us. But there's no use resisting anymore. My desire for her is undeniable, and there's only one response I have left:

"Please."

Her chest heaves as she stares at me, the heat of her gaze setting me aflame. It feels like this moment is frozen in time, on the edge of something. All we have to do is jump.

It's a race, a game, a dance. Like we're both waiting to see who will step off the ledge first.

"Fuck it," she says.

And then, before either of us can second-guess it, she reaches her hand to my jaw and pulls my mouth to hers.

15

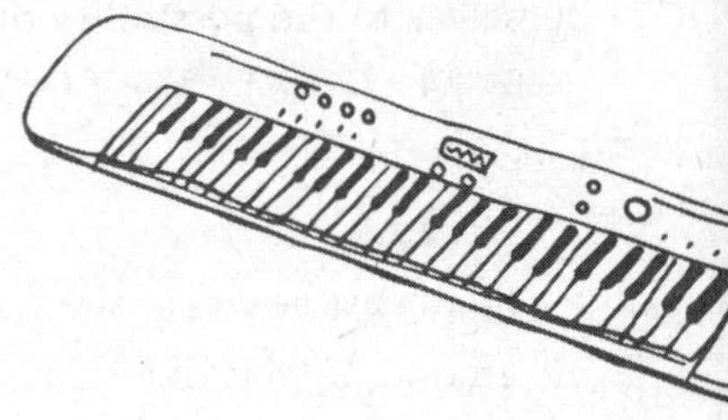

✦ *Jane* ✦

My heart nearly explodes as Keeley Cunningham's lips fall on mine.

Kissing her like this, without pause or restraint, is something I dreamed about for years. How it could happen. When we could steal a moment. Just the thought of what it might feel like to be wrapped up in her gave me butterflies. Ever since the first time we played music together, I've longed for this woman. Those inescapable *what-ifs* lingering between us have haunted my every fantasy.

But *damn*, the reality is so much better than I imagined.

She kisses me like she's been running a marathon and I'm the one waiting at the finish line. My pulse is rushing, my hands are shaking, and still, I press into the kiss with everything I have. The brush of lips is soft, but I'm not tentative. I lean in, determined to make sure, finally, she knows I mean it.

"Oops, sorry to interrupt. Are you two ready to order, or do you need a minute?"

We spring apart, heat flooding my cheeks as the server stares at us. She's keeping her face carefully neutral, but I know it must have been a surprise. I forgot we were in *public*.

Crap.

Keeley grins. "Actually, can you just bill the drinks to our room?"

"Of course," the server says, completely unfazed.

And then Keeley grabs my hand and leads me from the restaurant. As soon as we turn a corner and find ourselves alone, she pulls me in for another kiss, crowding me up against the stone wall with so much tenderness I nearly fall apart.

I find her rhythm in every heartbeat, the way I do onstage, moving in time with her steady pulse. My hands slide into hers, and I feel that same pulse beneath the soft skin of her wrists. It's as fast as mine, locked into the same desperate, frantic tempo.

I'm lost in the softness of her lips. The warmth of her hands in mine. The shadowy quiet of the alcove as we fall into each other.

This moment is perfect.

I hope she feels the perfection too. But I pull back, just to be sure. The tiniest whimper escapes her lips, and she looks at me with wide, wanting eyes.

"Was that okay?" Keeley asks. "I thought we could just head back because food is the last thing on my mind right now, but *fuck*, if that's not where your head is at, I'm so goddamn sorry, and—"

I press my fingers to her lips, charmed by just how *nervous* I've made the most confident person I know. "Keeley Cunningham, stop freaking out and take me somewhere we can be alone already."

The panic on her face is replaced with a wolfish smirk, and she gently bats my hand away, twining our fingers together and leading me back to the room in a daze.

As soon as the lock clicks behind us, the charge ignites.

Keeley grins at me, and I revel in that grin falling on my mouth as she draws me back to her. I've always felt small and unimpressive around Keeley, who has a good ten inches on me and fills every room she walks into with her bold snark and incredibly sharp mind.

But in this moment, as her hands slip around my waist and gently tug me closer, I don't feel small.

I feel like the only person in her world.

Every inch of me aches for more, but I draw back, leaning my forehead against hers to savor the moment. "Wow."

"Yeah?"

"I've wanted this since camp," I blurt, because it's the only thing I *can* say, with her this close to me.

Keeley laughs, the sound warming me to my core. "Thank fuck I wasn't the only one." I reach a hand to her face, and she leans into my touch, closing her eyes. "Shit, Jane."

I slide my fingers into her hair and pull her close again.

In nothing but a heartbeat, our next kiss turns wild and ravenous. Fireworks burst through me at the brush of her tongue, and I open my mouth to her with a sigh. She tugs my jacket off my shoulders and tosses it on the floor, and that steady touch skating across my bare shoulders nearly undoes me.

Keeley bites my lip in between deep kisses. I can't help it; I let out a little moan at the tiny spark of pain that fills me with wanting, the shock it sends straight between my thighs.

"Fuck, I love that sound," Keeley says, chest heaving as she draws back to look at me. Her eyes are dilated, her cheeks flushed, and she already looks debauched even though we've barely started. "But . . . shit . . . do you want to slow down?"

I blink. "Absolutely not." Then I clear my throat, suddenly feeling a little self-conscious. "But if you do, I can . . ."

"No. God no. I just wanted to check." Keeley lets out a long breath. "I've wanted you for longer than you can possibly imagine, and I know we should, like, talk about our feelings for five minutes, but . . ."

"We can talk later," I say, pulse pounding in my ears. "But I need you. Right. Fucking. Now."

I feel, rather than hear, Keeley's sharp intake of breath. "I've never heard you curse before and I think I love it."

Grinning, I settle my hands on her waist. "If I'd known you were into this, I'd have fucking done it before," I breathe.

"I'm into everything you do," she murmurs.

And then we're kissing again. She spins us around, walking me backward to the bed until I sink onto it. And then she's crouching over me, hovering with the steadiest care as our momentum carries me onto the downy soft pillows. She presses hot kisses down my jaw, the column of my neck, the place where my dress strap grazes my collarbone, and I sigh at the decadence of each one.

"Fuck, this dress is killing me," she says, toying with the hem until she finds the skin of my calf, the careful touch sending a tingling sensation down to my toes. "This okay?"

"More than okay, it's perfect. You're perfect," I say, catching her lips with mine. She kisses me again, deep and exploring, her tongue swiping mine with the grace of an artist.

Her hand slides up my skin, splaying against my thigh. I whine when she pauses.

"What are you waiting for?" I demand.

"Someone is impatient," she says, laughing softly. To prove the point home, I rise, just enough to shrug my dress over my shoulders. I had to go braless, and by the look on her face, I know taking it all off has the impact I intended.

Her jaw drops. "Oh my fucking god," she says under her breath as her pupils dilate. "I think I'm dead."

"You'd better not be, because I have plans for you," I say, pulling her back to me for another kiss. But she pauses. For one excruciating moment, her eyes rove across my skin, drinking me in like I'm an oasis in the middle of a desert.

And then her gaze falls to my hips.

"What's this?" she asks. I glance down and look at it with her.

It's the only tattoo I have, a melody on a lightly sketched music staff. It's the lead line to "Midnight Road Trip," the song that started it all for us. I practically swoon as her fingers brush across the tattoo, setting my skin on fire all over again. My mouth goes dry, and I try to remember what words are.

"It's . . ."

Her eyes sober with understanding. "It's perfect," she says. "But . . . I have one too." She pulls her sweater up just enough for me to see her rib cage, where five tiny bats are silhouetted. I missed them when she was changing before. "I got them the winter after Vegas . . . well, the first Vegas," she says. She's alluding to the concert after which Caleb and Valerie broke up more than seven years ago, causing the original Glitter Bats split.

I gape. "Mine was around then too." It's unbelievably perfect, the way we were on the same wavelength even at a time we were hardly speaking. I wonder if that's what made this take so long, if we were *both* so scared of ruining things, the way the relationship between two of our friends put the band at risk. But that worked out in the end.

Maybe we can work this out too.

"I wanted you all to be close to my heart," she says. Something warm spreads through my body, and I have to resist the urge to giggle. This is one of the things I adore about Keeley—when she decides you're her family, you're hers for life.

If I say that, though, she'll just tell me I'm being sappy. "You're so sentimental, Cunningham."

"There's nothing sentimental about what I want to do with you. Can I touch you? Kiss you?" she asks.

"Yes," I breathe, even as my mind screams *finally*. "God, please, literally wherever you want." She tugs her sweater back down, and I open my mouth to protest the disappearing skin, reaching for her top, but then her hands are cupping my breasts, and I think *I* might be the one dying, and I can't do anything but close my eyes at the sensation of her touch.

"Holy fuck, your tits are perfect," she says. I reach for her again, desperate to touch her too, but she pushes my hands away. "Nope. This requires focus, and if your hands are on me I won't be able to think straight," she says.

"I hope you're not thinking straight," I say, winking at her.

Her eyes light up with mischief. "Oh, you've got jokes? That means I'm not doing enough to shut you up."

And then her mouth is on me, kissing the swell of a breast, moving closer and closer to my nipple. When she grazes it with her tongue, a jolt surges to my center.

"*Oh my god*," I murmur.

"You like that?" Keeley asks.

"More," I say, practically begging. Then she sucks my nipple into her mouth and I don't know how long I'm going to survive this before I combust. I'm already writhing beneath her, chasing the crest of something sweet and delicious and impossible to define. It's not quite enough, though, despite the marvel of her mouth as she moves to my other breast, palming the one she abandoned, pinching one nipple into a point as she licks over the other.

"Keeley, I—" I lose my train of thought as one of her thighs presses between my legs, giving me some delicious friction despite the layers of fabric between my skin and hers. It's *so close*, but not enough. Not to get me where I'm chasing.

I've never needed to get off more desperately in my life.

"God, Jane, I want to make you feel even better. Tell me how to make you come."

My mouth goes dry, and I stare at her hovering above me. I've never been great at asking for things in bed, but I somehow know it's safe to do that with Keeley. I feel wanton and worshipped and empowered as hell.

I prop myself up on my elbows, leveling at her. "I want your fingers in my cunt."

Her jaw drops open. "Fuck yes, I can do that for you."

And then her hands are on the waistband of my underwear, dragging them down my thighs with a flick of the wrist. Almost instinctively, my knees fall together, and I don't know if it's the slight chill in the room or just the overwhelming significance of this moment.

She presses her forehead into my shoulder, groaning. "Oh my god, I have Jane Mercer naked underneath me. Give me a minute."

Guess I'm not the only one who's undone. I laugh, but it turns into a gasp as her fingers find the bare skin of my ankle. She caresses up my calf again, to my knee, and finally my thigh, her grip gentle but firm as her hand traces the curves of my skin.

Keeley leans in even closer, whispering in my ear. "You're so damn soft, Jane. Fucking *perfect*." My breath catches at the reverence in her tone. "I honestly can't believe that I'm finally here, seeing so much of you like this. You look so damn pretty splayed out on these sheets, your skin flushed, your hair wild. God, I've never seen anything more beautiful than you in this moment." Her chest heaves as she pulls back to stare at me, so obviously hot and bothered, and I can't help but whimper at the look in her eyes.

"Keeley?"

She lets out a sharp breath. "Yeah, Jane?"

"Will you please make me come now?"

With a soft exhale, she presses her lips to mine as her fingers press just as intently into my skin.

Her touch is slow at first, palm ghosting between my thighs, until I arch my back into her hand and she increases the pressure. Even the *lightest* pressure is almost too much as I process the reality of her touching me for the first time, and I'm afraid I'm going to come before she does anything else. I kiss her wildly, seeking more and more of *her* and willing to take anything I can get.

She starts to circle my clit with one of those long, perfect fingers, moving with a practiced ease that makes me lose my mind. It's a brilliant, steady rhythm that brings me almost to the brink again.

Almost.

"Can you take more?" she breathes against my ear. "Do you want my fingers in your cunt, like you asked?"

"Please," I whisper.

And then she slides a finger inside of me and I let out a moan. "Oh my god."

"*Fuck*, Jane. God, touching you is better than I imagined."

One finger becomes two, and she begins working me up with slow, driven purpose, expertly using her palm to make sure my clit still gets attention. She trails kisses down my neck and then sucks a breast into her mouth again, palming the other with her free hand, my pussy unbelievably wet as I begin to clench around her fingers.

And then she curls them into a spot that makes me gasp. Noticing my reaction, she repeats the movement, finding the sweetest, most perfect rhythm to bring me to the brink.

"Let go, Jane. Let me see you come," she murmurs into my ear.

And that's all it takes. I shatter.

I cry out as I ride the wave that Keeley works relentlessly from me, and my entire body trembles with pleasure as she gives me exactly what I need.

But the wave doesn't stop. If anything, it crests, bigger and brighter, and sweat drips down my skin, and I don't even care because this is the best I've ever felt in my entire life. And I think I have more in me.

"Harder," I gasp, and she gives me what I ask for, taking me even higher. My mind can barely form a coherent thought other than *Keeley, Keeley, Keeley*, and I think I'm sighing her name but I'm not even sure if my voice works. I've never orgasmed this hard in my life.

With one last sob, I crash out of the free fall. Gasping, I reach up and pull Keeley to me again, kissing her with breathless abandon. Her hand slips out of me and rests on my thigh, carefully raising the two fingers that are drenched so she doesn't make my skin slick, and I marvel at the tenderness of that gesture.

I was taught this was a sin, but there's nothing sinful about this moment. If anything, the way she just touched me feels holy . . . and I think that, if there is a heaven, it couldn't top this.

She pulls back. "How was that? You good?"

I laugh. "Clearly."

She laughs too. "Holy fuck, Jane. That was the single hottest thing I've ever experienced."

I reach out to her for a third time, trying to finally touch her the way she's just touched me. She presses a playful finger to my sternum.

"Someone is handsy," she says.

I beam. "I just want to make you feel as good as you made me feel."

Keeley swears under her breath. "Fuck, I want that too, but I'm not in any rush. We have all night. Right this moment, I just want to lie here with you and take it all in." She rolls onto her back in invitation, and I nestle into the crook of her neck, not caring that I'm naked and sweating and she's still wearing a sweater and jeans. I fall into place like a puzzle piece, knowing exactly where to put my hand, my thigh, my head. "God, you feel so perfect right here."

"I know," I murmur. "I feel it too."

Tears prick at the back of my throat, because even though we're miles away from Los Angeles, being right here, in this bed, with Keeley's arms around me?

It feels like home.

16

✦ *Keeley* ✦

I wake up from what feels like the most incredible dream.

But Jane Mercer, sprawled out on white sheets like an angel, gorgeously writhing beneath my touch? That was all real, and I can't believe I got this lucky. Literally. My skin tingles just thinking about it as I pull her closer, inhaling that delicious vanilla scent that has plagued me for years.

After I got her off, fucking stunningly I might add, we both fell asleep, twined together in this perfectly soft hotel bed. Still dozing, she nestles herself deeper into my side, and I press my face into her curls, breathing her in.

For so long, Jane has been my biggest what-if, and here she is, folded against me, all warm skin and lovely freckles and soft, perfect curves. If this is a dream, I never want to wake up.

I never want to lose this.

You love her, I think, and I know it's too much, too soon. No one falls in love in an hour. Then again, it's not like we slept together as strangers. I've known Jane for years, since she was the pretty dance team captain shaking pom-poms at every home game, and I was the gawky kid with her first (bad) queer haircut playing my snare drum on the bleachers.

I didn't fall in love with Jane over a matter of hours. I've been falling in love with her for more than a decade, and I swore I'd never do anything about it because it could threaten the band—which was really just an excuse, because I was petrified that she wouldn't feel the same. It never occurred to me that my feelings could be reciprocated.

I hoped, but . . . this feels like everything I've ever wanted, and I'm almost scared to believe it's real.

She shifts on top of me, turning to look at me with sleepy, soft eyes. "Hi," she murmurs.

"Hello yourself," I say, my chest warming as it hits me again how lucky I am to be here with her. "How are you?"

She lets out a little sigh, snuggling in closer. "Amazing."

"That's good," I say.

Her stomach rumbles, and we both laugh. Our dinner plans were long forgotten, but the chocolate-covered strawberries might still be edible. Jane rolls off me and slips out of the sheets, pulling a shirt on before grabbing the plate from the fridge and setting it carefully on top of the covers. I cross my legs and lean against the headboard, reaching for a berry.

She takes a bite, considering as she chews and swallows. And then she blurts it all out. "Look, I wanted you so badly that I basically threw myself at you, but I'm not messing around." She stares down at the comforter, toying with a thread as she takes a bite of her strawberry. After she's done eating it, she continues. "Actually I'm pretty sure I've been falling for you since I was a teenager, which I know is completely pathetic and I probably shouldn't be admitting it out loud, but I just really needed you to know, because I can't pretend anymore . . ."

I almost launch myself at her, narrowly avoiding sending the plate of fruit cascading across the room. But I place a hand on her cheek, and she leans into my touch, her expression so tender and fucking beautiful I don't even know how to handle it.

"Jane," I say, unable to hide the grin on my face. "This isn't casual for me, and I can't imagine a world where it could be."

Her eyes brighten. "Yeah?"

I shove the fruit aside and pull her closer. "You'd better believe it. Like if you want me, I am so fucking *in* this, it's not even funny."

She beams up at me, then pulls me in for a kiss that tastes like berries. "Me too." But then she pulls back, letting out a long breath. "It's just . . ."

My heart stops, but I wait for her to continue.

She bites her lip, and I resist the urge to soothe it. "My parents don't know I'm bi. You know they wouldn't be cool with it—they're hardly cool with me even being in the music industry, much less doing anything . . . like this. And it's not like I care about their approval, but I just . . . all eyes are on the band with that press release, and my sister is getting married, and I don't want to disturb the peace, and . . ."

I thread her fingers in mine, and her babbling trails off. "Jane, it's okay. We don't have to tell anyone anything is happening. We can just figure out what this is between the two of us first, and then decide the *next* step when it comes."

Her brow furrows. "Are you sure? I know you're out and proud and I love that about you. I want to be that brave, but—"

"Jane, I'm sure," I say, pressing a kiss to the back of her hand. She has no idea how brave she already is. "I'll follow your lead." And I mean it. I'll take Jane however I can have her, even if that means keeping things quiet.

Besides, we've both seen how vicious the media was to Valerie about her sexuality. I'm sure they'd have a field day if Jane were to come out. She deserves to do that on her own terms, not anyone else's, if she wants to at all.

She deserves to do this for her, not me.

"Thank you," she says, wrapping her arms around my shoulders. I pull her closer, and her gorgeous, generous tits press up against me in the most distracting of ways.

I clear my throat, pulling back. "We should . . . probably talk about some stuff." Normally I would have said something sooner, but in the heat of the moment, neither of us were thinking clearly. But it's important. "I get checked for STIs regularly, and my most recent tests came back clear."

"I'm all clear too," she says. "Thank you for bringing that up. I meant to, but . . ."

"Of course," I say.

Then, she grins wickedly. "Is that your way of asking me to go down on you?"

My throat goes dry. "No! I mean . . ." I trail off as she leans over me, looking like a cat that's just got the cream.

"Because I'd love to, if you're up for it."

I let out a shaky breath. "Are you kidding me? Of course I'd be up for it."

Her eyes light with mischief. "Good. Because I've gotten off so many times fantasizing about burying my face between your legs."

"Holy fucking hell, Jane," I murmur, leaning my head back into the pillows. That dirty mouth of hers is going to make me swoon like a Victorian heroine.

She pulls away from me then, and I practically whine at her absence as she places the strawberry tray in the minifridge, then goes into the bathroom to wash her hands. Finally, she returns to the bed, still gloriously naked except for that thin T-shirt.

And I'm just lying there, stunned.

"Why are you still wearing clothes?" she asks breezily, as she gets back on the bed and shrugs out of her shirt. I gape at those perfect breasts, round and full, and my eyes trail down that lovely expanse of soft belly.

I hurry to yank off my sweater, and my jeans are down my hips in a matter of seconds. This time Jane's eyes are widening as she drinks her fill of me. My breath catches as her eyes rove over my small breasts, my stomach, the apex of my thighs.

"Fuck, you're bare," she murmurs. "I wasn't expecting . . ." she licks her lips, and I can't help but smirk a little.

"Like what you see?" I ask. I have some sensory issues on top of my ADHD, and I can't stand the feeling of hair against my underwear, but waxing has a few other perks. Like the way she's looking at me like I'm dessert.

"I'd like you no matter what," she says, stalking closer toward me. Once she's within reach, I pull her closer, relishing in the feel of her skin pressed up against mine. Our lips brush, and I open to her, taking her tongue deep inside my mouth, overwhelmed by all of the contact between us. Her body is warm and soft and it makes my mind spin, feeling her this close. I know we were talking about oral, but fuck, she feels good like this too. When her thigh slides between my legs, I gasp at the contact.

"Don't stop."

"I thought you wanted me to eat you out," she murmurs.

I want that too, but this is already almost too much. "Later. This friction is perfect. Can you just . . . touch me?" I ask, closing my eyes, savoring the sensation of her skin.

"Yeah, I can do that for you."

Her hand cups my cheek then. She trails her fingers down my neck, skating the edge of my breast and down the curve of my waist.

"Jane," I beg, because I was already worked up and this teasing is too much.

"How bad do you want it?"

"*So bad,*" I breathe.

Then, one of her hands is on me, sliding between my thighs to my already wet pussy. I shudder at the efficient pleasure of her fingers, so lithe and confident.

She's going to play me like a melody, and I'm going to love every fucking minute.

My breath catches as she grips my chin with her free hand, pulling me in for another kiss as she grazes my clit with her fingertips. I gasp. Something about being in bed with a very naked Jane, about remembering the cries of pleasure she made *all for me* before our little nap . . .

I'd be embarrassed if the whole thing weren't so hot. "Oh *god*, Jane."

"I can't believe I finally get to touch you," she murmurs.

Holy shit.

She leans her forehead against mine, pressing our bodies so close that our skin connects in nearly all the right places, legs tangling together. My eyes flutter closed as she holds on to me, just like she said she would.

I reach to touch her again, but she puts her hand on my wrist. "No, let me concentrate on you this time." And then she's sliding a finger inside my cunt and *fuck*, it's good.

"So fucking good," I say, widening my thighs, hooking a leg around her hip to give her better access. It's wildly intimate, feeling her so close to me, kissing her as she fucks me with the hand between us, taking me right to the edge within minutes.

Every nerve in my body is on fire at all the delicious ways our bodies are connected. Then she brings her free hand to my breast and squeezes. Not hard, just firm. I groan, and she takes that as a cue to bring her mouth to press a wet kiss to my collarbone before dragging her lips down to my cleavage. I'm already so keyed up that the moment she sucks a nipple into her mouth, I'm nearly there. When she replaces her mouth with the pinch of her fingers, it sends me right over the edge.

"*Fuck.*" And then I'm crying out as fireworks fill my vision. The sensation is warm and buoyant and vibrating through my body, and all I can think is *Jane*, like meditating on her has taken me to a higher plane of existence.

"God, Keeley, you're perfect," she says, whispering into my ear before pressing a kiss beneath it. "You sound so pretty like this."

"*Jane*," I practically sob as I lose all coherent speech, unable to do anything but moan as I keep chasing the high. Even though the room is spinning, I manage to catch her lips in an indecent, searing kiss, and she sighs into my mouth as she draws the last bit of pleasure out of me.

And then the kiss turns impossibly sweet, soft and languid, like we've kissed a thousand times. Maybe we haven't yet, but I hope we will someday. Because now that I've had Jane Mercer, I have no intention of letting her go.

Finally, we break apart, breathless and panting as we both fall onto our backs.

"That was fucking incredible," I murmur.

"It really was," Jane says. She twines her fingers through mine, and the innocent gesture feels so sweet and tender despite everything that just happened. Even holding her hand threatens to undo me. I've never wanted anyone more in my life.

"I can't believe this is real," I say, turning my head to look at her. It feels like admitting a secret. And as she smiles softly at me, I'm sure I'm not the only one keeping it.

"Me either," she says, grinning cheekily. "I mean, I just had sex with critically acclaimed drummer Keeley Cunningham."

I laugh. "And I just had sex with RECORD-award-nominated Jane Mercer."

She lets out a giggle and pulls me closer, our bodies sliding together again, slick with sweat. We don't do anything more than kiss, but it feels so precious to be entwined like this now that we've been brave enough to take this leap. I thought my feelings for Jane were nothing more than foolish hopes kept locked away where they could never hurt anyone, where my heart could never break.

But I've never been happier to be wrong.

Lime Velvet Takes the Stage in Los Angeles

BY MARY KATE HAMPTON, SENIOR STAFF WRITER FOR *BUZZWORD*

One of my favorite things about this era of nostalgia is getting to relive moments from my past. Music was a soundtrack to so many important memories: my first kiss, my first time driving a car, my first weekend at college, my first . . . well, you know.

So I'll always jump at the chance to see one of my *first* favorite bands of all time, emo/punk sensation Lime Velvet. They played a small, intimate showcase at The Orpheum last weekend to preview their new album—which I'm still not allowed to talk about, but that review is coming—and I volunteered as tribute for the press pass.

Frontman Charlie Yeoh was as charismatic as ever, crooning into the mic and taking up every inch of that stage. It called to mind his persona fifteen years ago, and although he seems to have leveled out a bit now that he and his wife have started their family, he still knows how to leave it all on stage. Bassist Lake Streeter and drummer Paulino Diaz were as locked in as ever, and the energy was incredible from start to finish.

Guitarist Jared King was missed—but not bitterly, as Yeoh announced King was in the hospital after the successful delivery of his first child. None other than Glitter Bats' rhythm guitarist, Riker Maddox, replaced him onstage. Maddox is no stranger to Lime Velvet sets, having toured with them just a couple of years ago when King was recuperating from a broken arm. Unexpectedly, Maddox kept the quality as high as we expect from LV.

Rumor has it that Maddox was originally unavailable for this show, but fans know he's the type of guy who is always there for people. Maddox has a not-so-secret habit of spreading his wealth as much as his charm, quietly paying for fans' meals at restaurants, or "anonymously" dropping $10K on random GoFundMe campaigns. (Those aren't so anonymous, friends!) But his talent on the guitar is equally as impressive.

Side note: I had the luck of sitting next to his fellow Glitter Bats Valerie Quinn and Caleb Sloane that night. Newlywed bliss looked good on the couple, and I enjoyed talking rock and roll with the two legends in the making. To be entirely transparent, I've known this band for so long that they feel more like friends than subjects. They've been in the news recently due to negotiations for the rights to their masters, but the two were tight-lipped on the subject, so I let it be.

It started to feel like the groupie table when Streeter's husband and Diaz's fiancée also joined us for a round, but I didn't mind. They were both gracious and welcoming. Attending concerts solo for these articles can sometimes be lonely, and no one made me feel any less for being a member of the press.

After the show, Maddox came over to say hello. When I asked if Jane Mercer or Keeley Cunningham were in attendance, Maddox told me they were both otherwise engaged.

[continued below break]

Comments:

@LIMEVELVETFAN5EVER: This took a weird detour into a Glitter Bats piece. I thought this was an LV showcase?

@PUNKROCKISNEVERDEADDD: Yeah **@LimeVelvetFan5Ever** I was thinking the same thing. Biased much?

@ALLMYFRIENDSAREVAMPIRES: so curious what has Jane and Keeley "otherwise engaged." 👀 Secret album????

@BATSTHATGLITTER: yesssss **@AllMyFriendsAreVampires** I hope you're right! So excited for more LV in the meantime though. Two more weeks!

@WANDERLUSTING: Here for all the Riker Maddox coverage 🤤 and I hope the Glitter Bats are back in the studio too. I need more music!

17

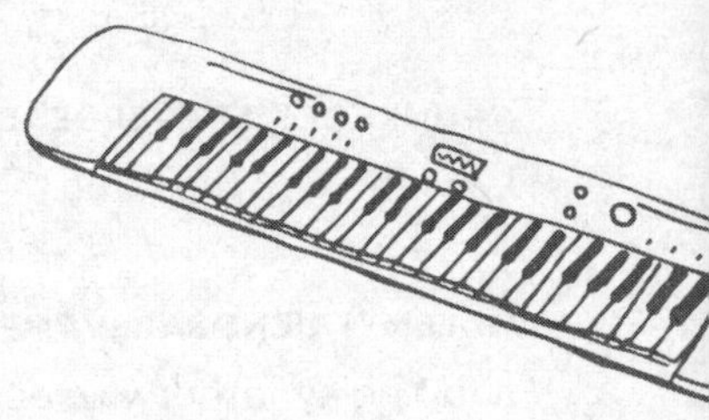

✦ Jane ✦

While Keeley slips out after breakfast . . . in bed . . . to check in with Wade about the masters situation, I step onto the balcony and FaceTime Riker.

He grins as he picks up the video. “How’s it going? You look happy.”

I roll my eyes but feel my cheeks heating. “I think I am.”

Riker’s face lights up in the biggest of grins. “Fuck yeah you are. I knew it!”

I groan. “Are you going to be this obnoxious for the rest of our lives?”

He laughs. “It must be serious if you’re talking the rest of your lives.”

Heat flushes my cheeks. “You know what I mean.”

“I don’t, exactly. Now, I don’t want any details because I think of you both as sisters so it’s creepy as fuck, but are you good?”

I nod. “I’m more than good.”

“You’re welcome.”

“You are way too excited about this, Emma Woodhouse,” I

say. More and more, it feels like I brought the correct book on this trip.

He grins again. "You don't know the half of it." I suspect this isn't the first time he's meddled.

"Was there ever really going to be a retreat?" I demand.

He raises up a hand in surrender. "Yes, okay! When I got the call that Jared's wife was going into labor, I decided this was a perfect opportunity to, I don't know, push you in the right direction. But for the record, I'm also responsible for getting Valerie and Caleb together last summer. Or at least, a tiny bit."

I roll my eyes, because of course he is. "Sure you did." Those two are meant for each other, and I don't think any external influence could have kept them apart . . . or pushed them together.

But he's not deterred. "I maaaaaay have called the hotel we stayed at before the reunion concert and asked for adjoining rooms for our lead singers. Thank god I never got any details, but you can't tell me that didn't nudge things along."

I roll my eyes. "You're incorrigible."

"But you love me!"

"Despite my better judgment," I say. "So how was the show, anyways?"

He shrugs. "It was playing with Lime Velvet. I have fun with those guys, but I still always feel like the little kid who is tagging along with the grown-ups. Did you know they *all* have kids now? Lake and his husband have the twins, and even Paulino and his fiancée had a baby last year. It's weird to see everyone settling down."

I nod. "I get that. Nora is getting married and I still don't know how I feel about it."

"That's still so wild to me," he says, as if I didn't have a full-on panic with him about it after I first got the news. "She's like . . . what, nineteen?"

I sigh. "She's twenty. I've been wanting to make sure she's okay, but I don't know if she wants to hear from me. She didn't even tell me about the engagement *or* ask me to be in the wedding. That was all Mom."

Riker groans. "I'm sorry, that fucking sucks. Have you tried calling her at all? Maybe she's nervous about your reaction and waiting for you to reach out?"

I blink, because I can't believe I didn't think of that. "Oh my gosh, you're right. I sent flowers, but I should probably at least try to text her too."

He nods. "You should. So . . ."

"Yeah?"

"You taking Keeley as your plus-one?"

I blink at him, shocked by the suggestion. Even just the thought makes my heart race. In a different world, maybe . . . "Riker, we just got together last night. I'm not going to ask her to do that. And besides . . ."

His face grows solemn. "You can't take her as your date to a Mercer family function. It would be a bloodbath."

I nod. "Or they just wouldn't acknowledge her. Either way, it'd be terrible."

"God. I'm so fucking sorry your family is a mess. I wish you had more support from them."

"Right back at you," I say, because while Riker may not have the religious trauma, his home life was no less complicated. I think it's why we've bonded so much. We both needed family at the same time, so family we became. "At least we always have each other."

"Fuck yeah we do." He laughs. "Did you know Caleb and Valerie came to my show last night and tried to embarrass the hell out of me? Like proud parents and everything. They sat with MK and made a sign and shouted my name a hundred times."

I raise a brow. "Mary Kate was there?" Mary Kate Hampton is the *Buzzword* reporter who has been following the Glitter Bats since we first went viral. She's my age, and she and Riker have carried on an obvious flirtation for the past decade.

It's supercute, actually.

Riker raises his brows. "I can hear you thinking it, but there's nothing going on there."

"That's a lot of protesting for someone who wasn't asked an actual question."

He flips me off. "You're impossible. Just because you're all coupled up now doesn't mean I have to be. I've known for years I'm destined to be the fifth wheel in this band. It's almost a relief now that it's finally happening."

"Whatever you say," I say.

"I mean it!" he says.

"Okay. I should go, though. Keeley and I have a spa day planned."

He grins. "Let me guess: facials, couples' massages, followed by . . . more couples' massages?"

I gape at him. "You said you wanted no details! You're being gross."

"I'm not being gross. I just want to make sure you're having a good time. If that means finally banging it out multiple times with the girl you've been in love with for more than ten years, more power to you. Honestly, I'm in awe of your manifestation skills."

My eyebrows raise. "This conversation is getting weird."

"Go get some!" he calls, like he's across the room. I just laugh and hang up.

When I step back into the suite, Keeley is already back, sitting cross-legged on the sofa while sipping a fresh cup of coffee. She raises the other one for me.

"Got you another cup," she says.

"Bless you," I say, walking over to her and eagerly taking a sip. "It's chilly out there."

"I was wondering where you disappeared off to," she says.

I chuckle. "Riker is taking full credit for whatever is going on here."

Her jaw falls open. "You told him about us?"

And . . . oh. I guess I didn't even hesitate. "Not exactly, but I didn't really have to? It's like he knew, somehow . . ." I trail off at the look of shock on her face. "Is that okay? I know I said we should keep things quiet, but I assumed the band is an exception. But I'm really sorry, I should have asked you first, and—"

She shuts me up with a hand over mine on my coffee cup. Carefully, I set the mug down and lock my gaze onto hers. Keeley is *smiling*, so wide and brilliant that I couldn't look away if I tried. "Jane, I love that you told someone about this. That makes it feel . . . real, you know."

I nod, chest warming. "Yeah, I know what you mean. I've been so afraid that once we get back to LA, it's not going to feel like this is actually happening, but I *want* it to."

"Me too," she says, leaning in for a kiss. I press my lips to hers, and she tastes like the faintest hint of coffee, and it somehow turns me on even more. Before I can stop myself, I'm moaning into the kiss, pressing up against her, desperate to get back to where we were last night. Maybe it's time to make good on my promise to go down on her. I want to know how all of her skin tastes.

She laughs into the kiss, pulling back. "God, Jane, you have no idea how much I want you right now, but we need to leave soon if we're going to make it for our reservation. We're booked for most of the day."

I pout. "But I can think of ways to relax right here."

She chuckles, then nudges me to turn around. Confused, I follow her lead, but then I soften as she tugs my sweater off my shoulders and those long, capable fingers dig into the knots in my muscles. "We can do plenty of that after we get mud wraps," she kisses my neck, "manicures and pedicures," she kisses lower, "facials," she presses one to my cheek, "and a two-hour long aromatherapy and massage session for two, followed by champagne, chocolates, and an uninterrupted hour to enjoy them together."

I sigh as she continues to trail kisses down my spine. "Who knew you were such a romantic?" I murmur.

She hums gently, whispering into my skin. "I can be romantic as fuck, but only for you."

18

✦ *Keeley* ✦

The spa day really is magical.

In the industry, we spend so much time being prepared for *something*—this awards event, that photo shoot, a big concert, and now, a legal fight—that it's easy to forget how nice it is to just relax in the chair without a destination or a time crunch.

And there was something so intimate about sharing this kind of day together—the champagne, the plush robes, the rose-petal soaking tubs for two. And even more than just being together, I really enjoyed seeing months of tension roll off of Jane.

"We should get massages more often," she says, collapsing onto our bed as soon as we return to the suite.

"We can get massages every week if that's what you want," I say.

She gasps, feigning outrage. "We can't! That's so expensive!"

I shrug. "You're worth it—but I could also invest in some good oil and give you massages at home," I say, lowering my voice suggestively.

Jane's eyes widen, a pretty flush creeping up her neck. "I think I'd like that."

"Me too," I say. "You know . . . it was weird having you leave a few weeks ago. I liked it when you stayed at my place."

She beams, tugging me down on the bed next to her. "I liked it too." I pull her close, and she snuggles into me. It's wild how quickly we've figured this out, all the ways we fit together. Like she was my missing piece.

"We can take things at whatever pace makes sense, though. I know this weekend has been fast."

Jane hums, snuggling closer. "Fast, but also not. It feels like all the time we've known each other was leading to this moment."

I laugh. "You're right." And thank god she feels it too.

"As much as I want to keep going fast, I'm exhausted from all the nothing we did all day. I could use a nap before dinner."

"Sounds perfect," I say. We strip down to our underwear and slip into bed, her heat folding so easily back into mine. I set an alarm for an hour and start to doze off, succumbing to the comfort of *us*.

All too quickly, the alarm goes off, and we reluctantly get ready for dinner. The resort is hosting a bonfire sing-along. We weren't going to go at first—it felt too dude-ranchy for us—but when I heard the host was taking suggestions, and they got excited when I mentioned Phoebe Bridgers, I knew we had to show.

I was picturing burgers on the fire, but the host quickly cleared up that the main courses will be grilled on wood planks and everything else will come from that delightful kitchen. I'm no food snob, but after eating Valerie's burned grilled-cheese sandwiches night after night on our first tour, then getting food poisoning the one time I tried to venture out with a gas station hot dog, I'm very suspicious of anything cooked without proper equipment.

Jane and I bundle up and head out, through the maze of the resort and out the back doors, where a small bonfire is set up against a sparkling starry sky. There are well-cushioned chairs spread out in a small circle, and we find a couple of free ones and take a seat. A few outdoor heaters are set up further back to cut against the chill, but we eagerly take the blankets offered by the staff greeting everyone. The stars glitter on the still surface of the river winding past the outbuildings.

But none of it compares to the radiance of the girl at my side.

"It's beautiful, isn't it?" Jane asks.

I smile, looking at her as she gazes up in wonder. "Yeah, it is."

She glances over at me, and even in the firelight, I can tell she's blushing. "You're ridiculous. You can't compare me to *the wonders of the universe*."

"Why not?" I ask, nudging her foot with my own.

"Just look at the stars with me," she says. And even though it's too soon to admit, I know I'll go anywhere, do anything as long as it's with her, even if that's just looking up at the sky. "Oh hey, there's Cassiopeia. It's my favorite."

"The vain queen who got hung upside down in the sky?" I ask.

"Only for half the year!" she chuckles. "But it was the first constellation I learned to spot, and I was in the middle of my Greek mythology phase—which my parents *hated*, by the way, because it was 'heretical nonsense,'" she says, even using the air quotes. "So I claimed my seventh-grade English teacher offered extra credit during our mythology unit and used it as an excuse to check out a bunch of books from the library and memorize the pantheon."

I laugh, despite the twinge in my chest as I think about all the backflips she had to do to cope with her demanding family. "You would rebel by doing homework."

She rolls her eyes. "Says the woman who graduated valedictorian of her class! I remember you bringing your SAT flash cards to band practice and making Riker and I quiz you while Valerie and Caleb were arguing over song lyrics."

I shrug. "I had a tight study schedule to keep, and it wasn't my fault practice kept running long because they were too busy dancing around their attraction to each other."

"I kind of miss those days," Jane says. I'm surprised by the admission. I reach for her hand, and she threads her fingers into mine, squeezing them tight. "I know I pushed back when we first talked about making more music, but it had nothing to do with the band. I loved it when we were really getting into the mess of writing songs together, and yesterday was so fun, it's just . . ."

"You have a growing career. I get it," I say. "Besides, I think I want to branch out, the way . . ." And then, I decide to take another chance. "I want to branch out the way my *girlfriend* has."

Jane's eyes sparkle, and she turns in her chair to face me better. "Girlfriend?"

God, that word sounds so good from her mouth. I try to ignore the pulse racing in my ears, because something about the way she looks at me makes me feel like I'm a teenager again. But I try to be cool. "I mean . . . if that's okay with you?"

"Obviously!" she says, squeezing my hand. "And as your girlfriend, I want to support you by hearing about your goals."

I laugh, resisting the urge to pull her closer for a kiss. We're together, but I don't know if she's comfortable kissing in public. Even a public that's only about a dozen other people who can barely see us in the firelight, more than a thousand miles from home.

"I just thought I'd have everything figured out before thirty," I say. "I've thought about producing, or writing, but it's just . . ." I trail off, trying to figure out how to articulate the hesitation she can so clearly see in my eyes, despite the dim light. "I don't know . . . I think it's why I've been holding on so tightly to the band. It's just scary, to try something new at this age."

Jane laughs. "You're twenty-nine, Keeley, that's hardly old."

I roll my eyes. "I know. But I really hoped we'd get a win with those masters. Now that there's a bunch of interest, I'm terrified that we're going to lose them." What I don't say is that I'm terrified I'll have wasted all this time and energy for nothing. Is this a foolish fight?

She frowns. "Can I ask you something?"

I swallow thickly. "Of course."

"It seems like fighting Label is personal to you. Like I get it—it's our music, of course it's personal—but for you, there's more to it. Help me understand where you're coming from. I care about you, and I want to be able to support you."

My heart aches for how earnest she is, how much care she's showing me as she poses the question. I squeeze her hand. "It is personal. God, Landon was the reason I wanted to be a drummer."

Jane winces. "Did I know that?"

I shrug. "I'm not sure I ever told anyone. But I saw an old Our Toxic Dream video when I was thirteen, and he was so goddamn carefree and powerful. I wanted to feel the way that looked. So I asked my parents for drum lessons, and they did me one better—bought me that old Yamaha kit I used to use for gigs for my birthday . . ."

"Your parents are the best," Jane says.

A lump forms in my throat, and I swallow it away. I may not always agree with my parents lately, but they really are incredible humans, and I know how fucking lucky I am. Before my mind goes too far down that path, I continue.

"From the first moment I sat on a drum throne, I felt like my whole life made sense. I was gawky and feeling so weird in my skin and starting to think I maybe liked girls as much—if not more—than the few boys I thought were cute, and I couldn't stand being in my head to process all that. Fuck, it probably helped my ADHD too, since always having drumsticks in my bag gave me natural fidgets. Drumming just . . . changed my life. It was all because of Landon Banks."

Jane nods. "And then we got a record deal and learned just how awful he was."

I snort in agreement. "Exactly. So I'm fighting like hell for our masters, because I already had my asshole of a hero let me down—I'm scared to let him take anything else from me."

"You know, he can't take the Glitter Bats. We're not going anywhere."

My eyes sting. "I know." But it was good to hear her say it, just once.

"And, well, you may have started drumming because of Landon, but he doesn't define your career. You have these incredible credits because you're *you*, Keeley. You're such a gifted percussionist. You have a good ear and laser-focused attention to detail. You're incredible to collaborate with." She smiles ruefully, the firelight dancing across her face. "You're opinionated, but it's always because you know how to make everyone better. And you care so much, not just about the music, but about the people you're making it with. You're extraordinary, Keeley Cunningham."

"Thank you," I say. And this attention, for some reason, makes my cheeks heat faster than anything we did back at the hotel room. Her opinion matters so much more to me than anyone else's. And if Jane thinks I'm doing okay, well, maybe I'll be able to believe it.

We sit there in contented silence for a few minutes, until I blurt out my own deep question. "How did you do it? Move on from the Glitter Bats that first time and completely change course?"

"I mean, I didn't exactly move on. I was just desperate," Jane says, self-deprecatingly. "Because honestly? When the band broke up, I was faced with the terrifying reality that our royalties couldn't sustain my life in Los Angeles. The only other option was moving somewhere else on my own, and I didn't know what the heck I'd do for work if I did . . . or if I'd crash and burn and have to move back in with my parents."

I freeze. I never realized that's where she was coming from. I wish I'd asked her sooner. "Oh god, that would have been . . ."

"Yeah," she says quickly, running a hand over her curls. "I could never go back to that house. After all those years finally having the freedom to be myself, I couldn't live under their scrutiny and expectations again . . . or face the alternative. Lying to fit into a life that was never right for me."

"I get it," I say. "You're a lot braver than me." I'm talking about more than just producing, and we both know it. She faces her fears head-on. I might have been an overachieving kid, but even the ways I've found to challenge myself these days aren't very risky. "I suppose the stakes for our masters are pretty low, considering," I say.

"Fighting for what you believe in is always scary," Jane says gently. "But if we didn't fight for this band, for our family, we'd always wonder what would have happened if we *had*. Even if we lose, we'll know we did everything we could to reclaim our music. No one can take that away from us."

I nod. "My girlfriend is smart."

"And don't you forget it," she says playfully. Just then, we're interrupted by a server, who takes our dinner orders before reporting back to the grills.

The conversation turns lighter after that. We talk about our plans for the last day at the resort, movies we both want to see but haven't had time to watch, restaurants we want to take each other to when we return to LA.

What we don't talk about is what things will look like when we get back to reality. I want to believe this feeling, the joy and contentment and safety I have with Jane next to me smiling under the stars, will last.

I just hope I'm that lucky.

Post by @ThisIsKeeley (Keeley Cunningham's private account)

[image description: photo of the starlit view of the river from the balcony of the Skybound Lodge, a hand holding a glass of champagne in the foreground]

Caption: Never thought I'd say this, but I don't want to leave Montana.

30 LIKES, 9 COMMENTS

> **@JANEASINAUSTEN** 🖤
>
> **@OLIVERCUNNINGHAM** holy shit that looks so much better than grading papers 😍
>
> **@BIANCAMARTINOFFICIAL** that view is gorgeous! Wish I were there 😘 !
>
> **@THELAKESTREETER** umm, how have I never heard of this place? Looks amazing! Send me details?
>
> **@IAMSEBASTIANBARK** looks like an awesome time! (Sorry this is literally my only account and Valerie won't let me use her phone; SB hasn't suddenly mastered the iPhone.)
>
> **@VALERIEQUINN @IAmSebastianBark** I LOVE YOU BUT GET YOUR OWN ACCOUNT
>
> **@NOTTHATRIKER** glad you had a good time
>
> **@THISISKEELEY @NotThatRiker** you're the worst
>
> **@NOTTHATRIKER @ThisIsKeeley** who, me??? 😉

19

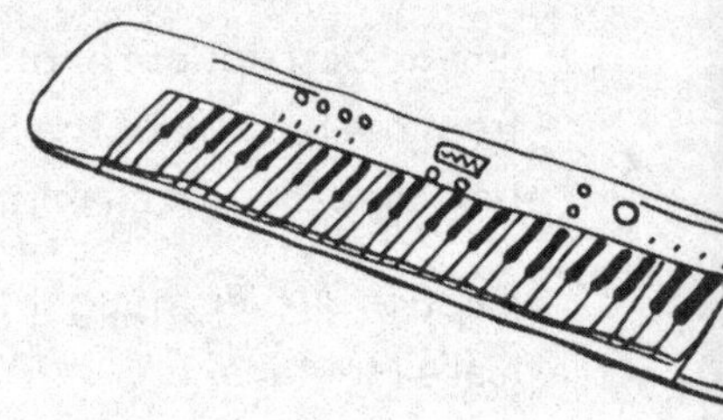

✦ *Jane* ✦

When our return flight lands two days later, my first notification out of airplane mode nearly makes me drop my phone.

> MOM: Your sister and I are in Los Angeles. We're on our way to your home. I don't know why you're not answering my calls, but I'm sending you a schedule of our bridal boutique appointments so you can meet us there.

My neck prickles with foreboding. Wordlessly, I tilt the phone so Keeley can see it.

"Fuck! Did she even tell you she was coming?"

I shake my head. "She hinted she wanted to come to LA, but she works fast." I can only take my mom in small doses. When I see the marathon of bridal gown appointments that starts in . . . less than two hours, I want to be sick.

Keeley nudges me to deplane, and I follow her out to the gate, then step to a quiet area and try to return my mom's calls. No answer.

I leave a message but keep trying every ten minutes with my heart in my throat. Keeley took a rideshare to the airport, so the plan was for me to drop her at her place, maybe *linger* for a few hours before I had to head home. I toss Keeley my keys so I can keep trying to make contact with my mom, but there's no answer throughout the drizzly gray October ride through traffic.

Just as we're pulling into Keeley's driveway, Nora calls me. My heart lifts. I might have to see my mom without advance notice, but I also get to see my baby sister. I still don't know how she feels about me being in her wedding, but the apprehension in my chest doesn't stop my excitement at hearing from her.

And . . . well, Riker's right. I probably should have tried calling her too.

"Nora!" I answer.

Her relieved sigh is audible over the phone. "Jane! Mom and I are at your house, but you're not here?" Her tone is apologetic. At least Nora's self-aware enough to realize Mom is pushing my boundaries, and we haven't even seen each other yet.

"I'm at Keeley's," I say. The moment the words escape, I want to snatch them back up. Will my family be able to sense that something is going on? But no, that's ridiculous. Mom would never assume one of her daughters is queer. That fact is so outside the reality she's constructed for herself.

I haven't even spoken to her yet and I already feel so small. Because I don't want to see my mom. Not so soon after, finally, discovering this wonderful thing with Keeley. I just can't shake the fear being around Mom will ruin it, somehow. I can't let that happen.

My parents have taken too many things from me already. I'm thirty years old, damn it, and I won't let them take this happiness.

And today is about my sister.

"Hi, Keeley!" Nora says, oblivious to my spiral.

I tilt the phone away as Keeley pulls into park. "Nora says hi," I whisper.

Keeley grins softly. "Tell her hi back."

"Can Keeley come shopping?" Nora asks. I hear my mom protest in the background, but Nora, expertly, cuts her off. "She has great style. I'd love her perspective."

"I'll ask Keeley if she wants to come shopping, but she might be busy."

Keeley's eyes widen, and I shrug. "I can," she whispers.

Our eyes lock. "You don't have to do that," I murmur.

"Hang on, Mom, Jane said something about a key back here. You don't have to walk on the sand in your shoes—I'll do it!" Nora lies, so effortlessly it takes me aback. All I hear for a couple minutes is shuffling and the crunching of sand. "Okay, it's windy enough that I'm out of earshot. I didn't want to make all of this fuss or fly down at all, but I tried to order a dress online because I couldn't find one in Seattle, and that really upset Mom. She's determined to give me the 'full bridal experience,' so I don't think we'll get to leave until we find a dress. We went to something called a sample sale this morning."

I blink. "You went to a sample sale?"

How did my mom even learn what a sample sale is? What a disaster.

"It felt like the Hunger Games! I gave up on finding anything, because dress shopping is stressful enough without fighting other people, and I wanted something low-key anyway. I'm so sorry she strong-armed you into this," Nora murmurs.

"It's fine," I say. "I want to be here for you."

She groans. "I would love that. I just can't . . . she's always around, you know?"

A warning bell goes off in my head. I know all too well what that's like, but I didn't know Nora felt that way. "What's wrong, Nora?"

"Nothing, nothing at all. I just . . . really miss you."

"I miss you too." I'm the worst sister ever, leaving her all alone like this. We may not be close, but I could try harder. I know I could.

"She wants to go to this place that I'm positive we can't afford, and I don't know how to stop her. I don't *want* a superexpensive wedding dress. Do you know anywhere we can go that isn't going to be totally awful?"

I frown, glancing over at Keeley as I draw a blank. "Sorry. I don't know much about the wedding dress scene here."

Keeley's eyes brighten with that spark that tells me she has a brilliant idea. "I do! Put me on speaker."

I have no idea where this is going, but I do as she asks.

"Hi, Nora, it's Keeley. How do you feel about a superchill boutique that specializes in secondhand designer and vintage gowns? They have a huge bridal section, and my stylist knows the owner. I bet they can totally get us some private shopping time. There's also a huge variety of price points."

We both hear Nora's audible exhale. "That sounds amazing. I just don't know how to sell Mom on a thrifted gown. Normally she's all about using restraint, but it's like she has something to prove with this wedding. I don't get it."

I glance at Keeley, but she's already texting Rowan, her stylist friend who helped Glitter Bats with a few shoots last summer. If anyone has the connections to hook us up with a last-minute appointment, it's them.

And I *do* know how to get Mom on board.

"Just remind her that you want to be a good steward of the financial resources you've been *blessed* with."

For a moment, I wonder if I sounded too sarcastic on that last bit, but Nora just laughs softly. "Oh my gosh, that's brilliant. Text me the details?"

"As soon as we hang up. And I'll meet you there."

"Thank you! It's going to be so much better with you there," Nora says, her voice strained before she hangs up. I wonder if she was on the verge of tears.

I don't like the sound. I've been worried about this wedding from the start, and now I'm more desperate than ever to see my baby sister and make sure she's okay. Part of me wants to try to talk Keeley out of coming—the whole afternoon promises to be painful—but I'm glad I won't have to face Mom on my own.

"So . . ." Keeley trails off, her hand falling to my knee. She gives me a light squeeze, and I want to tug her inside, sink into her warmth, let the real world fall away again.

Instead, I raise my chin. "So we're going to hang out with my *family* . . ." I trail off, realizing that I have to make an unfair request of Keeley. "Today, we can't . . ."

"I know," Keeley says. "God, I know. I can control myself for one afternoon."

She looks at me so earnestly that I can't help but pull her into a soft, sweet kiss, even though I'm gross from the plane and sitting uncomfortably in the passenger seat. After we break the kiss, I lean my forehead against hers. "I'm not sure *I* can."

Her cheeks flush. "And I adore that about you, but I'll try to keep you in line."

I let my gaze linger down the column of her throat, to where her hoodie is falling off her shoulder, revealing just a bit of skin. "And what do I get if I'm good?" I murmur.

Keeley's eyes flash. "Whatever you want."

My heart races at that. But there's no time to follow through. After I send Nora the details, we barely have time to go inside to change before we have to leave again. We avoid traffic and make it there in record time, which feels like a miracle itself. For a moment, I think it's all going to be fine.

It's a cute little shop. The place is bright and airy, with spacious windows letting in plenty of natural light, and rich wood floors polished to shine. One side of the space is clearly devoted to bridal, with gowns in every shade of white—and some not so white—stuffed together on racks. On the other side, there's a rainbow of jewel tones, pastels, and metallics, all of the pieces meant for other occasions. Toward the back, there's an elevated platform facing a three-way mirror, with a few dressing rooms on either side, and a smattering of overstuffed, mismatched armchairs.

I'm stunned out of my observation by a happy shriek.

"Keeley!" Nora barrels past me into Keeley's arms.

"Hey, kiddo," Keeley says, squeezing her tight with only the slightest surprise on her face. Unlike Caleb's little sister, Carrie, Nora never really hung around the band much, because our parents would rarely let her. But she's still known Keeley for a long time.

Nora releases Keeley and pulls me in for just as tight of a hug. My little sister is a bit taller than me now, but I still hug her back as fiercely as I did when she was a toddler. I squeeze her tightly, and if I'm not mistaken, I hear her sniffle quietly into my shoulder.

"Are you okay?" I murmur.

"Fine, fine!" Nora says. She pulls back, blinking rapidly, and I'm blown away by just how mature she looks. Her hair is lighter than mine, closer to strawberry blond, and today it's pulled into a neat bun at the base of her neck. She's wearing a modest enough blue jersey dress with cap sleeves, but it's on the short side of acceptable for a church girl.

Just then, Mom inserts herself between us and pulls me into a stiff, perfunctory hug. I squeeze once just to signal her to let go, and she does without complaint. Like the hug was just for show anyhow, and she didn't actually want to hold on to me.

"Jane, dear, you look tired," Mom says, giving me a critical once-over. "It's not becoming to work so much." I hate it when she talks like this, as if she's the mother of petulant debutantes. The only coming out I'm interested in is something that might make her faint, though.

I try not to smirk at the thought, even though it terrifies me. What would Mom say if I just dropped the bomb right here and declared that Keeley is my girlfriend?

She'd probably disown me for good. I clench my fists. "I'm fine, Mom, just got off a flight."

"Ooh, your life always sounds so glamorous. Where were you?" Nora asks.

Keeley clears her throat. Mom has barely acknowledged her, which is unsurprising, but it still ticks me off. "We were on a band retreat in Montana. I'm so sorry for inserting myself into your family time, but . . ."

"But I insisted she come when I talked to Jane on the phone! Keeley has such a great sense of fashion, and she's the one who got us this appointment," Nora says.

Mom's jaw ticks, but she doesn't protest. "Fine, fine. It's . . . nice of you to join us, Keeley. Nora was just about to start trying things on."

Nora's eyes widen as Mom shoos her off to a dressing room and scrolls through the nearest rack, pausing every so often to pull a gown off the hook and shove it at an attendant, a wisp of a brunette in a pale pink pantsuit who is hastening to follow.

After Mom darts across the room in search of something more *purely white*, I turn to the woman. "I am so sorry for her," I whisper.

The woman shrugs. "This is nothing. It's my job to help find the perfect look. We also have a lovely selection of vintage gowns that might be to your taste for your next red carpet, Ms. Mercer."

I'm actually pretty tempted by that, and my eyes wander in the direction of the other racks even as Mom shoves the first dress into Nora's dressing room. Most of what we wear on the red carpet is provided by the designer on loan, but I really hate wearing something that is meant to be used for one person on one occasion. Vintage is definitely appealing.

Before I can get too distracted, Nora steps out of the fitting room in a princess gown. Its layers and layers of tulle make her look like she's going to a cotillion instead of her wedding. Probably because she's just stopped being a teenager. The gown is a stark white that washes Nora out, because she shares my painfully pale Irish complexion. Nora wrinkles her nose as she steps up to the platform.

Mom gasps dramatically. "Look at you!"

"I don't think this is it," Nora says, frowning as she smooths her hands down the fabric. "It makes me look like a ghost."

Mom puts her hands on her hips. "Well, Nora, you have to wear white. It symbolizes your purity."

Nora flinches. "Right, but there are a lot of shades of white. Can I try something a little creamier? Maybe ivory or champagne?"

Mom audibly sighs. "You can try it, but I don't think it's going to look as nice as the starker white. Danny is going to want to see you look like a proper bride! You don't want to let him down."

And there she goes, making my sister's idea sound immoral, as if the shade matters to anyone but her. By the way Nora's shoulders hunch on her way back to the fitting room, I know she's already feeling defeated. Glancing around, I stride over to the nearest bridal rack, determined to locate something that fits my sister's request that Mom won't totally hate. I find a creamy ivory lace gown that looks to be close to Nora's size and take it off the rack. Keeley hums in agreement.

"Worth a try?" I ask.

Keeley's always had such a good eye for these things, so I really value her opinion. "Yeah, that one looks promising." She eyes my mom, who is still ordering the attendant around as Nora slips back into the dressing room to change into the next one. "I forgot how intense your mom is."

My jaw clenches, but I smile toothily across the room in Mom's direction. "And this is her on her best behavior, can you imagine?"

"I know I'm the lucky one in the band, but still, this is something to behold." Keeley really is lucky, with parents who not only love and accept every piece of her, but the Cunninghams have stuck together over the years and seem to still actually *like* each other. I know Keeley and Oliver are close too, even if they don't talk as often as they would like. She's never rubbed it in the Glitter Bats' faces, but I've always been a little jealous on my bad days. I can't imagine what it's like to have a family who doesn't expect you to fit into such a tiny mold of acceptable behavior.

Shaking my head, I take the gown and stride across the room, hanging it on the rack adjacent to Nora's fitting room.

"That's not white enough," Mom mutters as she puts another two frilly white monstrosities next to my more understated selection.

"It doesn't hurt to have her try on a lot of options," I say. "This is Nora's day, right?"

Mom blinks. "Of course it's Nora's day. But she's young and doesn't know what she wants. When she's looking back at wedding photos thirty years from now, I don't want her regretting going the *trendy* route instead of the timeless one." Mom says *trendy* like it's a four-letter word, voice lowered into a harsh whisper.

Before I can retort, Nora steps out of the room in another white dress, this one almost brighter than the last, with glittering appliques and a band of lace that looks more early-aughts fashion *don'ts* than upscale designer. She grimaces at me in the big mirror as Mom gestures for her to show it off.

"I want to try something in a different direction," Nora says, jaw set.

Mom opens her mouth to protest, but I cut her off. "Keeley and I found another option for you. It's on the rack."

Nora beams and steps carefully over the rack, avoiding stepping on the too-long gown. She picks up the lace and hurries excitedly into the fitting room, the attendant following to help her out of the dress.

"So, Mrs. Mercer, how have you been?" Keeley asks, as we move to stand over by my mom.

Mom almost glowers, as if she can't be bothered by Keeley's question. "Just fine, thank you. My beautiful daughter is getting married, and I couldn't be prouder. The Lord has blessed our family."

Keeley crosses her arms, leaning against the wall. There's no smirk on her face, but I see the spark of mischief in her eyes. "Yeah, you have *two* girls you should be really proud of. Jane has been working so hard, and she has a lot to show for it. She got nominated for a RECORD award for her first big streaming project."

I flash Keeley a grateful glance, and every part of me wishes I could squeeze her hand in this moment. I appreciate that she's trying, even if it's not going to work.

Sure enough, Mom huffs. "I suppose that's . . . something."

"It really is!" Keeley says, pretending not to notice the disdain. "Did you know Jane is in such high demand that she hasn't had a break in months? Everyone wants to work with your daughter, because she is brilliant and talented at everything she does."

Mom's brows furrow. "She should be using those gifts to serve God."

I want to shout, *Stop trying to bring me back to church!* but there's a part of me that still wants to keep the peace, despite how she treats me. Fortunately, we're saved by Nora stepping out in the lace gown, looking absolutely beautiful and not like a little girl at all. It has a sweetheart neckline that isn't too revealing, and the bodice fits like a sheath until it subtly flares from her hips into a slightly fuller skirt with a small train. The attendant spreads it out carefully as Nora ascends the platform.

"I like this silhouette a lot better," Nora says, biting her lip as she looks in the mirror. I can tell she's trying to keep a straight face, but Nora is practically beaming. "I feel pretty."

Mom frowns. "It's very different than what we talked about. I want to see the last one again. You looked like a *vision*."

Nora clenches her fists, trying to hide them in the lace. "But this one is perfect. I think . . . no, I know, it's the one I want."

I hate the look on Mom's face, like she wants to fight Nora on this. Before I can stop myself, I stride over to the rack. Maybe I don't need to stand up for myself today, but I can do it for Nora.

"Why don't I try that one on, and you can look at them side by side?" I ask.

Keeley snickers and hides it quickly with a cough when I glance her way. She knows exactly what I'm doing. I raise a brow, because I know it's going to *work*. Before Mom can protest, I stride over to the rack, grab the white monstrosity, and dart into the fitting room. The attendant hurries behind me.

And then I'm faced with the reality that I'm at least two sizes bigger than Nora.

"Is this even going to fit me?" I mutter.

She hums. "It's going to be snug, but I had to clip your sister in, so there should be some space to make up for your curves."

Curves is a nice way to say I have a butt, thighs, and a generous C cup compared to my sister's lithe frame. I strip quickly—years of fittings and photo shoots have made me pretty comfortable with my body, which was definitely a journey after being raised in purity culture—and the attendant makes quick work of getting me secured into the dress. The glittering embroidery is scratchy, and I'm careful to avoid resting my arms too casually as she tugs on the zipper.

I can't help but laugh, because the cleavage the thing gives me as soon as I'm all cinched up is evoking *pinup*. Still, the dress isn't that bad. It's kind of *A Cinderella Story* chic, which was great for Hilary Duff in 2004 but definitely isn't something you'd expect to see at a wedding more than twenty years later.

Grabbing the white tulle, I step out of the dressing room. Mom has made it over to Nora, where she's picking at the gown and grumbling in disapproval. I glance over at Keeley, bracing myself for a snarky comment, but her jaw is just open in shock.

I raise a brow but resist the urge to tease her for the reaction. This isn't the time. Instead, I step up onto the platform next to Nora, glancing at myself in the mirror.

"Hmm," Mom says, staring at me. "I'm not sure how I feel about this dress now."

Even though I'd never wear it, and even though this was *exactly* my plan, I wince at the dismissal in her voice. The only reason she doesn't like this dress now is because it's on me, but I catch Nora's eye in the mirror, where she mouths a *thank you* to me as Mom slowly moves around me in a circle, making disapproving faces.

"Too much cleavage," Mom says. Then she turns to Nora. "You really look so beautiful, honey. Now that I see them side by side, I think that might be the dress."

"Thank you!" Nora squeals, and she pulls Mom in for a careful hug. As they embrace, I can visibly see the moment Nora relaxes, her shoulders softening. She must have been stressed all day.

"If you want to come back one at a time, I can help you both change," the attendant says. "My associate can get the transaction started for you, Mrs. Mercer."

"That sounds fine," Mom says, heading over to the register.

"Don't worry about it—I'll help Jane!" Keeley says eagerly, and I let her lead the way back to the second dressing room. Once we're both inside, the space feels intimate, close, and I tug the curtain closed as quickly as possible.

"Holy shit, Mercer," Keeley breathes, grabbing my hands, then stepping back to look at me. "I was not prepared to see you in a white dress today. Like I don't want to freak you out or anything, but even though this dress is atrocious, it's also . . . a good look, you in white. I'm into it."

I roll my eyes, trying to pretend that's *not* making my heart race. "Just help me out of the thing."

"It would be my pleasure," she says huskily. Keeley motions for me to turn around, and slowly, gently, she tugs the zipper down, her fingers leaving a trail of heat down my back. She presses a kiss to my neck, then between my shoulder blades, and again at the dimple of my hip. I gasp.

"Not here," I breathe, stepping out of the gown as quickly as I can. But despite my protest, I whirl around and tug Keeley in for a kiss. She moans softly in reply, instantly deepening the kiss, pulling me closer.

"Oh!" a voice says with a surprised gasp.

Keeley and I snap apart at the unwelcome intrusion, glancing at the two-inch gap in the curtain.

Where Nora stares at us, mouth agape.

"Sorry! I just wanted to check on your plans. Mom is asking about dinner? I'll, uh, give you a minute."

I just blink, stunned, as Keeley tugs the curtain the rest of the way closed. Heart racing for all the wrong reasons, I hurry to dress and calm my nerves. I have no idea how Nora is going to react to this, and if it's what I fear, she just might tell Mom.

I glance at Keeley, whose face has gone white as a sheet. "Jane, I'm sorry, I—"

"No, don't be sorry!" I say, trying to make sense of what just happened as my pulse roars in my ears. "I started it . . . but . . ."

"But fuck," Keeley says, her eyes wide in alarm.

I glance up at her, at a loss for better words to describe the situation I've just found myself in because of my own carelessness.

"Fuck indeed."

Text Conversation Between Jane Mercer and Riker Maddox

JANE: I messed up, and I'm freaking out. You around?

RIKER: YES. What's happening?

JANE: Nora is in town with Mom to shop for dresses (long story) and she just caught me and Keeley in a . . . compromising position.

RIKER: Oh. Oh no. How compromising?

JANE: We were in a dressing room (another long story that involved helping my sister model wedding dresses for my mom) and we were . . . making out. And . . . I was topless . . .

RIKER: SHIT.

RIKER: That's not great.

RIKER: Are you okay?

JANE: . . . as well as can be expected.

RIKER: and again I say: SHIT.

JANE: Yeah I just . . . I knew they'd find out someday, I just wasn't prepared for it to be today. We only just got together, and . . . I wasn't careful enough. I know I need to talk to my sister . . . I just don't know what to say. Is she going to understand? God, I'm scared.

RIKER: I'm here for you. Do you want backup? I can get my ass over there.

JANE: As tempting as that is, no. I'll handle this one on my own.

RIKER: Okay, Janey. Whatever happens, please remember I love you and I support you.

JANE: I appreciate it ♥ Mom's calling me over to pick a restaurant now—wish me luck.

RIKER: LUCK! (and give me a location and I'll send you some recommendations.)

RIKER: and also . . . fuck the patriarchy

20

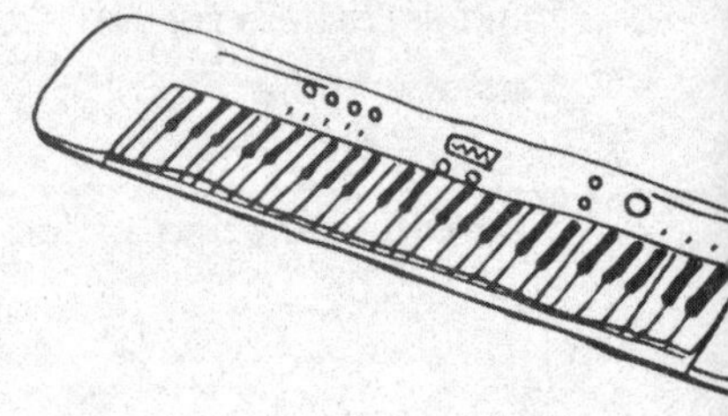

✦ *Jane* ✦

My mom and sister have a morning flight, so Mom decided we would eat an early dinner *as a family* before they head back to their hotel for the evening. I could have invited Keeley as a buffer, but it's better if I can try to catch Nora alone.

To, well, figure out if she's about to out me to the rest of my family, uninvite me to the wedding, and/or stop talking to me forever.

A desperate part of me hopes it's none of the above, but I can't wrap my head around what that looks like, because the ringing in my ears has been drowning out all rational thought ever since we left the boutique with a giant garment bag.

We pick a little bistro close to their hotel, thanks to a suggestion from Riker. He prides himself on being better than Yelp, always finding the best food wherever we go, having decided to become a foodie in the absence of attending culinary school himself. The bistro's also not too terribly expensive, which is a huge relief knowing I'll be expected to pay for the entire meal. Probably the least I can do, considering I haven't been a part of many of the pre-wedding activities, and I never made it out for the engagement party.

And my sexuality might ruin any chance of fixing my relationship with Nora. She hasn't really looked at me since we left the boutique, and I try not to take that as a bad sign.

It doesn't feel like a *good* one, though.

When we get to the small restaurant, all candlelight and greenery and high-top tables with barstools, I'm so tempted to get a drink, but I know I should be sober when dealing with my family. (Not to mention the fact that Mom would side-eye me for drinking alcohol.) Still, it would be nice to take the edge off this raw, ragged feeling.

My practically perfect church-girl sister saw me kissing a woman. Not just any woman either. She saw me kissing *Keeley*. This isn't just about me; it's about a person who matters to me. Deeply.

I . . . don't know how to handle this. It's why I've never bothered coming out. Why do I owe people an explanation for how I experience attraction? Why is it anyone's business, at all, about who I want to be with? Sexuality is personal.

And if the world *weren't* built to cater to heterosexuality, I could just live my life in peace.

My eyes swim as I read the menu, and I try to keep it together. The anxiety is largely under control these days after the lifestyle changes I've made. But an old, familiar feeling creeps in, like I'm so nervous I might vibrate out of my skin, and my eyes can't focus on the words on the crisp white page in front of me. My appetite is gone.

Mom orders an appetizer for the table, then disappears out to the terrace to call Dad, firing off her entrée order with several substitutions for Nora to remember in her absence. When it's just me and my sister, I take a long, cold sip of sparkling water.

Nora frowns down at her menu. We sit in silence for a full minute, ignoring the massive elephant in the room.

Finally, I clear my throat, trying to dislodge the words that are stuck there. It doesn't start well.

"I understand what you saw might have shocked you, but—"

"Stop." Nora snaps her eyes to mine, giving me the fiercest look I've ever seen on the face that still looks so much like the ten-year-old I left behind. "I literally don't care if you're a lesbian."

I blink, stunned. "I'm bisexual, actually."

She shrugs, folding her hands on the table. "That's cool too."

My head spins as I try to wrap my head around what she's saying. This feels too easy. "Really?"

"Yes, really! Are you serious? You're my sister, and I love you, and nothing is going to change that."

I swallow the lump in my throat. This is not going how I thought it would, and I'm too thrown to react. My sister is being . . . fine, about all of this? Great even. "Oh."

"You deserve to be happy and with someone you care about, no matter what that looks like."

Moisture pricks my eyes, but I squeeze them shut for a heartbeat, trying to get myself together before looking at her again. "I know you're saying that, but I also know you really care about the church, and—"

Again, she interrupts me. "I'm not Mom and Dad, okay?" she practically snaps.

I gape, trying to navigate the sharp turn this conversation has taken. "I never said that . . ."

But she continues, as if now that she's started, she can't stop. "And honestly, if God didn't want people to be gay or bi or however else they identify, why would he let you feel this way? It seems pretty cruel, and that's not the loving God I want to believe in. People should be able to love who they love without apologizing for it. That just makes sense." It's clear Nora has put a lot of thought into this, and that didn't suddenly happen today. I can tell she means it.

A massive weight lifts off my shoulders at the unwavering acceptance in her words, and I let out a shuddering breath. "Thank you," I say, still a little stunned. I never prepared myself for the reality that Nora would be an ally. *My* ally.

For my first real coming-out experience, this isn't so bad.

I know I didn't choose it to happen the way it did, but somehow my twenty-year-old sister has made me feel safe and loved. It was different when Riker caught me with Savannah all those years ago. I knew he wouldn't see me any differently. In fact, I think it made us closer friends, not having to hide this piece of myself. And coming out to Keeley was . . . inevitable.

With Nora, though, I had no idea how she would react. This moment in this funny little bistro with top-forty radio playing softly through the sound speaker is radically changing how I see the world, and the ways my full self might fit into it.

Maybe I'll be ready for more of the world to see me someday, if someone like my baby sister can accept me without a second thought. All my worry flutters away at the soft, wry smile on her face.

But then I'm worried for a different reason when she sighs, toying with the napkin on her place setting. "I'm not even sure what else I believe anymore."

I frown, wanting to be cautious—but also wanting, desperately, to understand her entire situation a little bit more. "That's okay if you're figuring things out. It just, with you marrying Danny, it seemed like . . ."

"Like I can't think for myself? I know my own mind, Jane."

"Why are you so angry, then?" She's looking at me like she's been betrayed, and I'm so confused.

Nora shakes her head rapidly, glancing over my shoulder. "We're still clear. And I'm not mad at you, even though it does kind of hurt that you haven't called me since I got engaged." I wince at that, but let her continue. "I'm pissed at Mom and Dad, that they created this environment where you can't be yourself, just because of all of these *truths* they claim come from the Bible that I'm not even convinced are in there after reading it so many times myself. It's maddening—and the cost doesn't seem worth it. Like, you're not around, ever, and I get why more than ever after today, but it still sucks! If they could just be better parents, maybe we'd be closer, you know?"

My eyes well up in earnest now, and I reach across the table to grab her hand. She squeezes mine. "Look, I'm sorry I haven't reached out. That wasn't okay," I say, trying to keep my voice steady. My sister deserved so much better, and here she is, showing me love anyway. "And thank you for being so accepting of me."

"I forgive you," she says. "And of course I'm accepting. I love you, Jane." Not everyone understands that love means accepting who people are, though, and that's the whole problem. I'm grateful my sister has figured things out for herself.

"I love you too. I'd really like to be closer, baby sister."

"Me too," she says. "And I *like* Keeley. She's a good person, and I think it's awesome that she's your girlfriend. How long have you been together?"

Despite the emotions threatening to overcome me, I can't help but smile at her question. The overwhelming happiness from the weekend hasn't faded—I'm not sure it ever will. Getting to be honest with my sister is such a welcome relief; it feels like sunshine on this gray October day. Neatly tucking my napkin on my lap, I fold my hands on the table.

"It's really, really new. But, Nora, I've been in love with Keeley for years. She's just . . . she's not just a good person, she's one of the best people I know. Not everyone sees it because Keeley is snarky and brash, but she cares deeply for the people in her life, and she works so hard. She makes me better just by being around her. And . . . she sees the real me."

"That's amazing," Nora says, beaming. "Because you're one of the best people *I* know, and you deserve to be happy."

"So do you," I say, steeling myself for this next bit, because I'm not sure we'll have another chance to talk without Mom, and this is important. "I have to admit . . ." I don't know how to get the next words out, but my sister takes care of that for me too.

"You're worried I'm getting married at twenty?" Nora says with a raised brow. "I thought you might be. That's why I was too nervous to tell you myself."

I straighten. *I* know I'm worried, but this isn't the starry-eyed, swept-up Nora I was expecting. She seems so . . . resolute. "I'm sorry you felt that way, but I can't pretend I'm not concerned. It all just feels a little fast, and you're so young. I just want you to be okay, you know?"

Nora glances over my shoulder again, but nods. "We're still good. They're probably arguing over how much this trip cost. But please trust me when I say I know what I'm doing."

That's easy enough to say, but I'm still not convinced she's not being influenced by our parents . . . or Danny's. She's *so* young. She has her entire life to make these kinds of choices. "Okay, but . . . what's the rush?"

She leans back, folding her hands on the table. "Did you know Mom and Dad practically shipped me off to that one-year Christian college? I didn't have a choice. They wanted me to find a husband there, but I didn't. They were disappointed I came home with a certificate of completion instead of a *ring by spring*." She says the stereotype ruefully, rolling her eyes. "But I came back and started going to U-dub Tacoma because I didn't know what else to do with myself. Danny was . . . in one of my electives. I wasn't even excited to see him, but he surprised me." She smiles down at her hand, where a modest ring sits. Finally, she looks back up at me. "He decided against Bible college to get a business degree, and I was still figuring out what I want to major in, so I guess we were both in this holding pattern when we found each other. That class was a Psychology class, and we discovered a shared interest in our study group . . . and that eventually evolved into something more."

"That sounds nice," I say.

She nods. "It was. After the class, I started seeing a therapist—it's someone the school counseling center connected me with, so Mom and Dad don't know about it—but I'm getting really interested in learning about religious trauma. Because I realized I have it."

"You're not alone," I say, shifting in my seat. "And therapy is great. I'm really proud of you for going."

"Thank you," she says. "Danny is the first person from church who actually sees me. He knows I'm questioning things, and he's not trying to discourage that. Heck, he's been really unhappy with how his dad handles things, like pretending the real issues with the church don't exist."

"Oh," I say. "I'm just surprised." I was so wrapped up in being as far away from my family as possible that I never considered Nora was anything like me. Now I'm realizing we have more in common than I ever thought.

I still don't love that she's getting married so young—I think young couples in the church make rash decisions because of the purity culture they're raised in—but I understand my sister a little better. And she's right—she seems to be going into this with her eyes open.

"Just because I didn't run away to LA doesn't mean I'm the perfect church girl. But after the wedding, Danny and I will have more freedom to figure things out together. He's set to come into a little money once he gets married, so we're not going to be completely broke, and we're just going to take things one day at a time."

"That sounds really sensible. Just . . . Mom made it sound like you're going to be the next pastors of The Shore."

Nora smirks. "Oh, that worship pastor thing? That's all Mike. He still hasn't *asked* Danny if that's what he wants to do, and we're just playing along until the wedding. Neither of us has any interest in being in ministry. We're actually thinking of moving out to Spokane or Pullman to finish our degrees and figure life out."

There are good state schools near both of those cities, so it makes a lot of sense. But still, I have to check that she's really okay.

"And you're sure this is what you want?"

"I'm really sure," she says.

"Okay, but . . . if you change your mind, you can call me. Any time. I will literally come get you and bring you down here to LA myself, and I don't care if I have to leave in the middle of a show or the dang RECORD awards."

Nora laughs. "Don't you dare! I'm fine, I promise. But if it will make you feel better, I also promise to call you if that ever changes."

"Okay," I say. "That works for me."

And then she waggles her perfect eyebrows. "But how can I move in with you if you're shacking up with your pretty girlfriend? I don't want to cramp your style."

Now I'm the one who rolls her eyes. "We're not living together. We literally just started dating."

She cocks her head. "Isn't there a joke about women who love women and U-Hauls?"

I gape at her, more stunned by this than any of the other revelations from the past few minutes. "How do you know about U-Hauling?"

Nora cackles. "I read romance novels! Not just the ones about straight people."

I shake my head, in awe of my little sister. I don't know how I missed that she's this full *person* who is thinking for herself and not letting our parents dictate her entire life. Gosh, she even has them convinced she's doing what they want her to do.

It's kind of masterful, if I can admit that to myself. I've never been able to handle my parents this way. I just gave up and left the first second I could.

I lower my voice. "I'm really glad we had a chance to talk."

"Me too," Nora says. "Because I love you, and I think you're amazing. You've accomplished so many things, and now you're finding real happiness too. I could not be prouder to be your sister."

I pat her hand, then release it as Mom comes around the corner. "I'm proud to be your sister too."

Save the Date

Nora Mercer & Daniel Brady

are getting married!

Please mark your calendar for our celebration

NEW YEAR'S EVE

MAPLE VALLEY, WA

Formal Invitation to Follow

21

Keeley

A few days after dress shopping, the Glitter Bats meet at my house to jam. We don't have any upcoming gigs, but we try to play together at least a couple of times per month to stay sharp and keep the creative flow going. It's been a while, though, between coming off tour and juggling our schedules.

And the retreat that never was.

We still don't have an update on the masters. I've spent my days in meetings with Wade and our accountant and even Label Records again, but they are being incredibly cagey about the asking price and who else is interested. They've said they're reviewing *all serious bids*, and will have an update when one is available, whatever the fuck that means. Landon sent me an email out of the blue with just a few lines that have haunted me for days:

KeeKee,

If you want this, make sure you put all your cards on the table. Truly, I hope it goes

your way. After all, this is your music,
like you said.

Landon

Cryptic as fuck. But I was terrified he was saying our bid was too low. So, quietly, I've met with my personal accountant too. After reviewing what's available, I told Wade how much more of my savings I can contribute. Maybe it's too risky to put up this much capital.

But despite my fear that this is all for nothing, I had to try.

So Wade increased our bid, even though Landon is still gallivanting across the world, if his recent social media posts are any indication. I've been using my burner account to keep tabs on him, because something still doesn't feel right. I don't love that one of his frat buddies from Dartmouth—who I only had to internet stalk for five minutes to learn is a venture capitalist who owns a small stake in a few different media companies—is traveling with him and included in a photo on a casino floor captioned, "To business and pleasure."

Nice to know Landon's out high-rolling while everything is on the line for us.

I'm terrified we're going to lose.

And it doesn't help that I haven't seen Jane since we parted ways at the boutique, and nervous excitement radiates through me like the fucking Energizer bunny. It takes all my effort to focus on being a good bandmate and preparing the place for everyone. I spend the afternoon vacuuming and wiping down surfaces, but my brain is so scattered that it takes twice as long as it should as I keep remembering shit I want to do.

I barely remember to take my Adderall, which isn't like me at all.

By the time the band has arrived, I'm still working on our after-practice snack in the kitchen, slicing up gouda and smoked cheddar for the charcuterie I decided to assemble at the last minute.

Unfortunately, Jane arrives after Caleb and Valerie, so we don't get a chance to talk about what happened in that dressing room. Ever since we were last together, we've tried to connect for dinner or at least *dessert* . . . but we've had to reschedule every plan.

Jane was supposed to be off this week, but she keeps getting pulled into meetings for *Into the Dragon Realm* that go for hours on end. It's not like I'm going to stop her from that. The last thing I'm going to do is pressure her to go out when she's exhausted from a long day.

It's fine. We knew, going into this, that our schedules would be challenging. The problem is, the absence is making me lose my mind. Not only am I craving her touch, but I have no idea how she's *doing*. We've been texting, but she just said talking to Nora was *good*, whatever that means. I have to trust that Jane knows her sister, and if she feels good about this, then it has to be alright. Still, it's weird going from our marathon weekend together to spending days apart.

And it's given me a little perspective.

I'm already out. In the first interview I did for Glitter Bats, I proudly declared to the world I was pansexual. Being seen together doesn't affect me the way it affects Jane.

Still, I'm nervous about what happened. Jane might have kissed me in that dressing room, but I did the seducing before the kiss . . . It's all my fault, really. It never should have happened like that. My heart races each time I think about what this could mean for her. I want her to be safe. I want her to be okay. I've tossed and turned every night, trying to figure out how to fix this.

Because Jane deserves to decide for herself what she wants the world to know.

The others set up their instruments while I hang back in the kitchen, restlessly moving between the fridge and my counter a dozen more times until I manage to put together a cheese board resembling the one in my head. We don't usually drink alcohol while we're rehearsing—we like to stay clearheaded—so I grab water and Lemon Spindrift from my fridge, and I'm just starting to put a tray of drinks together when Jane comes into the kitchen.

Even at her most casual, in old Levi's that hug her curves and a soft, striped baby tee, her hair down in soft curls, she looks so fucking lovely it takes my breath away. She makes a beeline for me, placing a gentle palm against my cheek and drawing me in for a sweet, soft kiss.

"Hi," she beams.

"Hi," I say, unable to look away from her. There's something about this girl that always draws me under her spell, and I never want to be released from the magic.

"I didn't get to do that when I got here, so I just wanted to fix that. I'm good now." Her words are light, flirty, but they don't erase the tightness in my jaw that's been lingering for days, the worry that I've put her in a compromising position.

"Are you?" I ask, pulling her closer.

She lets out a shaky breath, but the happiness doesn't fade from her cheeks. "I really, really am. Nora was . . . cool, about everything? We got to talk about her wedding too, which was good, but she made it very clear that she supports me. There's something about receiving acceptance from someone you thought would never be able to give it that just . . ." She clears her throat, stepping back, pressing her fingers to the corners of her welling eyes. "It's kind of remarkable."

"Yeah, it is," I say, because I know exactly what she means. My Aunt Daisy is super churchy, but when I came out at fifteen, she didn't tell me I was going to hell . . . she went with my family to

Seattle Pride and bought one of those Free Hugs T-shirts. Aunt Daisy never looked back. She has always been my fiercest supporter, whether it was replacing the American flag on her Little Free Library for a rainbow one, or coming to my marching band competitions, or inviting the Glitter Bats to play at a craft fair hosted by her knitting club back when we were just kids, desperate for places to play.

So I know exactly what Jane means. She bites her lip, looking up at me with an even more radiant smile. "It gave me a lot of hope. I might not be ready to come out today, but maybe someday it would make things easier for us, to, you know . . . not have to hide."

I pull her closer to me, my grip firm on her elbows. "Jane, I don't need that. Coming out is complicated enough for anyone, even without throwing public opinion in the mix. If, when, how—that's all up to you."

Jane nods. "I know, but I also think I could get there, you know? It might be nice to get to be fully myself all the time, even if there are a few consequences."

"I understand," I say.

"Thank you." And then she's reaching up and pulling me in for another kiss. My heart swells as I revel in the softness of her lips, the warmth of her body in my arms. I don't think I could ever get sick of being with this incredible woman. The craving for more burns through me, and *fuck it*, I don't care that we're not exactly alone. I deepen the kiss.

A throat clears, interrupting us. Caught again.

We snap apart, and I whirl around to where Valerie stands outside my music room, smirking.

"Um . . ." I begin, not even sure how to explain this. Valerie and I have had our differences, but I trust her with my life—and even more with something like this—but again, I keep risking Jane's privacy because I can't keep my hands off her.

I don't like putting her in these positions.

"Took you two long enough," Valerie says, flouncing over to my island, her now-orange hair swishing as she makes her way to the purse she left on a stool. Fishing inside, she pulls out a fresh pack of guitar strings. "Okay. Carry on."

With a cackle, she disappears inside the music room. Wincing, I turn to look at Jane, who just shrugs.

"They were going to find out eventually," she says, just as my door opens.

"Find what out?" Riker asks, barging in late like he owns the place. He's shouldering two guitars—a record low for him—and his thick brown hair is tied up in a bun on the top of his head. He's grown his facial hair out since I last saw him, and it's trimmed into a neat, short beard.

"Knock much?" I snap at him, but there's no real venom in it.

Riker raises a brow. "Since when do we knock at each other's houses?"

"Some of us like our privacy, dude," I say, rolling my eyes as he stalks past me into my music room.

Jane's cheeks are pink, but she thrusts her shoulders back, as if deciding something. "We should say something. Besides, we agreed the Glitter Bats were an exception."

She's not wrong, and technically Caleb is the only one in the dark now, but I'm still worried I'm forcing this on her. "If that's what you want," I say.

Jane threads her fingers through mine and leads the way into the music room, and I can do nothing but follow her lead, like a moth to a lantern.

Inside the bedroom I've converted into a practice space, warmth fills me at the familiar sight. The Glitter Bats are making music again, and this is what it looks like: Valerie is cross-legged in the middle of the area rug, restringing her electric guitar. Caleb is setting up his bass and amp in the corner opposite my drum kit, meticulously tidying the cords, and Riker is fiddling with his pedal board with a furrowed brow.

Caleb is the first to look up, and he glances at Jane and me, standing in the doorway with our fingers entwined, then gives me a look that says, *I told you so.*

I use my free hand to flip him off, and he just grins widely and goes back to his equipment.

"Keeley and I are dating," Jane blurts. Everyone freezes and looks at us. "I know you've probably all figured it out or whatever, but I wanted to make sure to say it for transparency. I'm not out, or anything, so we're keeping things subtle, but I wanted you all to know. Because us dating affects the band."

I try not to wince at that, like she's just telling them as a disclosure and not because she wants to, but I have to trust Jane is genuine. Especially when I spent so long keeping my distance from her *because* of the band.

"I'm really happy for you two," Caleb says, smiling that sunshine smile at us.

"Of course we're all happy. Honestly, I'm surprised you lasted this long," Valerie says, going back to her guitar. "You've wanted to fuck each other for years."

Jane gapes, and I just roll my eyes. "That's very presumptuous of you," I say.

Valerie cocks her head. "But am I wrong?"

"Nope," Jane says, her already-pink cheeks flushing crimson. "Now, should we talk about our masters, or just make some music?"

Valerie groans, setting her guitar down. "I'm so tired of dealing with Label's bullshit when we were supposed to be free of them. They're stringing us along because they know they have all the power, and I just want to know who *else* has bid on our music.

Shouldn't we get priority? Like why the fuck does Landon's vacation schedule have anything to do with stalling the auction?"

Riker groans, moving to sit next to her. "It's not ideal."

"Talking about business it is," Caleb says with a sigh. He leaves the room for a moment and comes back with my trays, like he somehow knew I forgot them amidst all the things competing for my focus. We each grab something and gather on the floor in a circle, and while I release Jane's hand, our knees are touching. Something about her presence grounds me despite the seriousness of this discussion.

"What are our options if we lose?" Riker asks. "We just have to accept that we have no control over our entire discography?"

Jane bites her lip, considering. "We technically still have control over the first recording of 'Midnight Road Trip,' and the other songs on our old EP. They're still on multiple platforms. I don't know if we could get people to play those versions, but that's a start."

"What if . . ." Caleb lets out a long breath, like he's bracing himself. He was the most reluctant to return to the industry last year. Even now, with his day job down to part-time, I know the balance can't be easy. "What if we made a backup plan to rerecord?"

"Like Taylor Swift?" Valerie asks, eyes wide.

"Well, Taylor Swift did it, but she's not the only one. I've, uh, done some research," I admit. Because that's what I've been doing in my off time—trying to figure out what our next steps could be if we lose this fight, knowing Landon Banks doesn't fight fair. "Bob Dylan, Bowie, Joni Mitchell, Prince, even Sinatra did it."

Riker nods. "Yeah, I've done a little research too. It would be a huge undertaking, but we could record on our own time line."

"I don't know . . . if I can commit to any kind of time line right now," Jane says softly. "I hoped it wouldn't happen this quickly, but

I'm already getting booked up for *Dragon Realm* stuff." I reach out a hand and squeeze her knee. After the RECORD awards nomination, she's gotten pulled into more press, and the team is already starting to discuss season three.

"That's okay," I say, and I try to mean it. "We don't have to decide anything tonight. Should we mix it up for warm-ups?"

It's a bit of a band tradition, picking a song to cover and swapping instruments as an exercise. It keeps our brains fresh . . . and it makes us laugh.

Jane pops up. "Dibs on the drum kit!"

"Damn it, Janey, I wanted to play," Riker says. "Keeley, please keep your girlfriend in line."

I grin. "My girlfriend gets dibs on whatever she wants." And then I press a kiss to Jane's lips. Jane melts in my arms, just a little. Caleb wolf-whistles in my periphery, but I hardly notice until Jane and I separate, breathless.

"Is this PDA going to be a thing now?" Valerie asks.

I roll my eyes at her as I saunter over to her guitar. "Like you have room to talk."

"Fair point." Valerie shrugs, taking up Riker's spot to play rhythm.

Caleb goes over to the keys, while Riker grabs bass.

I smirk at Riker. "I should make you sing Chappell Roan."

He shrugs. "I know all the words to *The Rise and Fall of a Midwest Princess*."

Riker Maddox is an enigma, that's for sure. Valerie cackles. "I'd pay money to see you sing 'Pink Pony Club,' but maybe something a little more on-brand?"

Jane seats herself on my drum throne, looking like a fucking queen as she grabs a pair of Vic Firths out of my bag. And it gives me an idea I know she'll love.

"On that note, I think we should play the most romantic song of all time," I say. Without preamble, I begin strumming the opening to "All The Small Things." Jane beams, quickly catching the iconic, frantic beat.

I have a hard time looking away from her as Riker begins singing the first verse. Jane is radiant and free, her muscles flexing as she does her best to learn the pattern on the fly. She laughs as she stumbles through a couple of measures and catches my eye, grinning with the kind of joy I want to bask in.

There's technically no keys part, but Caleb with his brilliant musical brain figures one out quickly enough. Valerie fills out the guitar part like a pro, and Riker hops on the balls of his feet as he plays the bass and focuses on singing. On the second verse, I jump in and double his melody, and I still don't look away from Jane. She winks as we launch into the chorus.

This is what I love about being in this band. The collaboration, the fun, the trust. Even on different instruments, we sense what the others will do before they do it. It really feels like we can do anything together, and I believe with my whole fucking heart that the possibilities are truly endless.

Optimism floods my veins, and I want to bottle this moment so I can inject it again the next time life feels uncertain.

22

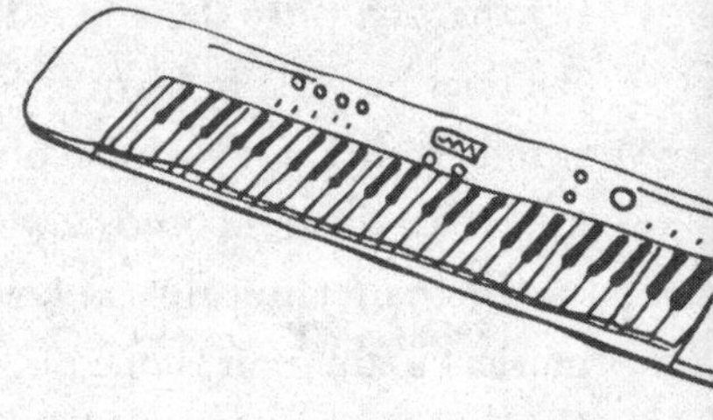

Jane

There's something so freeing about trusting people who love you with the most intimate parts of your identity and knowing they'll be held with care. I feel so much lighter after talking to Nora and the band.

And maybe I've been holding on to this secret for far too long. I get what Keeley said about coming out in my own timing—and I adore her for it—but part of me wonders if I just got so used to hiding parts of myself when I was a kid that I never learned how to reveal them, even when it was safe.

After the RECORD nominations, season three of *Into the Dragon Realm* was announced, so I keep getting pulled into stuff for that. Whether it's press or hours-long meetings about our production time line, my days are busier than I'd ever want. I'm exhausted. It's hard to stay focused on the show and also steal pockets of time to work on other things.

But I spend my nights with Keeley. As October crashes into November, we fall into a routine, trading off whose house we're sleeping at with only a rare, occasional night apart. It's so natural, the way our relationship has fallen into place.

The future of the Glitter Bats feels uncertain, but I know Keeley and I are headed somewhere exciting.

Which is why I'm an absolute jerk, because I'm at yet another meeting for *Into the Dragon Realm* that's going impossibly late, and Keeley and I were supposed to try a new recipe together tonight instead of going out. We're trying to save money in case we drain our savings to buy the masters, and cooking has been a fun challenge. I text her, repeatedly, whenever I get the chance, and all of her responses are understanding.

ME: I'm so, so, so sorry.

KEELEY: You already said that. It's fine.

ME: I know. I promise, I'll be there as soon as I can. We can still cook, right?

KEELEY: It's okay! I know you're busy.

It's not okay, though, and I'm tired of this pattern of blowing her off when I'd rather be with her than anyone else. When I finally get out of the conference room, I race home as quickly as I possibly can. Keeley's Rivian is parked on the street in front of my place, and it fills me with hope that the night isn't completely ruined. I recently gave her a key, for the sake of practicality more than anything else. Still, the guilt churns, deep and overwhelming, at the thought that she's been waiting for me.

Mouth dry, I hasten up my walkway and head inside. Keeley is sitting on my sofa, cross-legged, her phone rotated sideways as she watches a video.

"Keeley," I say, breathless. She glances over at me, a little ruefully, and my heart breaks at the disappointment she's masking.

"There are leftovers in the fridge. Want me to heat them up for you?" she asks.

I gape. "You cooked it without me?"

She shrugs. "I was hungry. Plus, I had everything for the eggplant parmesan, and I've been wanting to practice making Italian ever since Valerie wooed us with that pasta last summer. Can't have her being better than me at something."

The words sound like Keeley, but the tone doesn't. I rush over to her to press a kiss to her forehead. Normally I can't reach with our height difference, but with the way she's sitting, I can easily lean over. "I'm sorry," I say, murmuring into her hair.

She sighs, leaning in so her head is resting against my sternum. "I missed you today."

"I missed you too," I say. "The meeting was long and exhausting."

They're already talking through season three . . . and four and five. Because the songwriting is so integral to the show, my team got pulled into the writers' room so we can prepare for the big emotional points. If we wait until the whole season is written to start working on the music, the way we've done in the past, it's going to delay production. Today's meeting proved we have to work at a breakneck pace if we want to speed *Dragon Realm* up to a two-seasons-per-year schedule.

So much for getting any rest. Now I really will have to worry about finishing my work on *Half Moon Ranch 2* in my limited downtime.

The *Dragon Realm* writers are still hammering out some of the overall plot details, but once they have those, I'll be able to grab my team and map out some songs. We have a few new characters coming in, so I'll be writing for different voices and arcs.

It's a good challenge. I *enjoy* a challenge.

But I'm also just so tired, and worried about sustaining this kind of pace. I don't know if I can do it, especially if we start to rerecord Glitter Bats material. I love the idea in theory, I really do, but I'm not sure if I'm going to be able to work band stuff in with my demanding schedule over the next six months if rerecording is on the table.

We just have to hope we get those masters, so we can take a moment to breathe.

Keeley peers up at me. "Where'd you go?"

I sigh, sinking down on the couch next to her as she sits up. All of these things—whether they're the band or the show or any other projects I get pulled into—will take me away from my time with her. "I'm sorry. My brain just won't shut off."

"If anyone can understand that, it's me," she says. "And it's been a long day for you."

She's trying to minimize it, but I can tell she's still bummed about tonight.

"I'm really sorry I missed our date," I say, turning on the sofa so I'm facing her more fully. I press a kiss to her neck, just below her ear, then lower my voice to a whisper. "Can I make it up to you?"

Her eyes flutter closed. "God, yes."

I catch her mouth in a long, lingering kiss that tastes like desire and peppermint toothpaste. My hands start wandering almost immediately, and Keeley places a hand on the one making its way to her breast.

She pulls back, pupils blown, but she manages a stern expression. "Nope. Upstairs is more comfortable. Last time you had me on my knees on this wooden floor, I was sore for two days."

Laughing, I pull her in for another kiss. "I'm not going to argue with that, but I think it was worth it," I murmur against her mouth. And then Keeley is standing, reaching her hands to my hips and yanking me up her body, so she's cradling me against her. Relishing the contact, I grind my hips against hers.

Keeley groans. "You are *wicked*, Jane Mercer." She tugs me closer, stilling my movement.

"Are you going to let me fuck you or not?" I gasp.

Her breath hitches. "Let's go." With purpose, she walks in the direction of my stairs, not pausing to let me down. For a moment, I wonder if I'm too heavy, but Keeley doesn't relent. She just keeps kissing me and holding me until we make it to the bottom of the stairs.

"Probably not the smartest idea to walk up the stairs like this," she says, laughing a little. But it comes out breathy, and I can't get over the idea that I affect Keeley Cunningham in this way.

"Come on," I say, sliding down her body. She groans, but laces her fingers in mine, striding up the stairs two at a time. With my shorter legs, I practically have to run to keep up.

I don't mind, though. I always want to follow her.

At the top of the landing, Keeley whirls around to kiss me again. Through the open window, my favorite one that looks out over the water, the cold, salty breeze whips around us, and I shiver a little as she holds me tighter. But I don't dare let go.

Keeley pulls back at me, smiling. "I really, really like you."

I beam up at her. "I like you too."

"I want you to feel just how *much* I like you," she says. And then she's whisking me into my own bedroom, practically shoving me onto the bed. But oh, I fall willingly as she sinks on top of me. Without even divesting me of my shirt, she makes her way down my body, pressing kisses over my clothes onto my breasts, my stomach, the gap of skin where my top has come untucked from my pants.

She swirls her tongue in a slow, languorous circle there, and I whimper.

"I'm supposed to be making it up to *you*," I gasp, as she kisses my skin with her open mouth.

"Fine." Keeley raises herself up on her hands so she's hovering over me, caging me in. Her voice comes out low and raw, and there's something electrifying, seeing her already desperate like this. "You must really like me or something," she murmurs.

More than like, I almost admit, but I know it's too soon. We may have alluded to deep feelings back in Montana, but now that reality has kicked in, I'm scared to rush into things and ruin it all. Still, right here, in this moment tucked away from the rest of the world, I can believe love isn't so far out of reach. And I want to be sure she knows it.

I shimmy out from under her and start unbuttoning my shirt, slow and deliberate, reveling in the way her gaze roams hungrily over each newly revealed inch of skin.

"Take off your clothes for me," I say, almost in challenge. Sometimes we battle like this, who gets to take control, but I'm not going to let her win this time.

Keeley swallows, but she doesn't protest. No, she just sinks back on her heels and peels off her tank, then her shorts, quickly followed by the slide of form-fitting boxers and her sports bra. She shoves all the clothing aside, leaving nothing but the perfect expanse of soft skin for my eyes to feast on. I lean up and press a kiss to the tattoo on her rib cage, and she shudders.

"*Oh god*, I love your mouth, Jane," she says, sighing dreamily.

My eyes spark with an idea that already makes me breathless as I sink back onto the bed. I crook a finger toward my chin. "You should sit on my face."

Keeley's eyes widen, her skin flushing with what I know is desire. But she still hesitates. "Uh, I . . ."

I prop myself up on my elbows and cock my head at her, feigning innocence. "Unless you don't want to?" My words are playful, nonchalant, because I can see the tempted look in her liquid gaze. Oh, Keeley *wants* this; she's just afraid to want it.

"It's just . . . I'll crush you."

I laugh. "You're not going to crush me, Keeley. Let me make you feel good."

"Fuck, I can't say no to that," she says. I scoot myself up so my head is resting on the pillow, close to the headboard. Keeley places a thigh on either side of my rib cage, but I can tell she's hesitant, even as the intoxicating scent of her arousal fills my lungs.

I don't want her to hesitate. I want to get her off.

So I grab her thighs and tug her up to me. Keeley gasps, gripping the headboard as I pull her closer, pressing a kiss to the inside of each thigh, then dragging my mouth across her core. And then I'm lost in the taste of her. She sighs as I find the right rhythm, and then she's relaxing into me, doing exactly what I wanted her to do. Riding my face. Taking what she needs. I give her everything I can, gripping her thighs and adjusting my movements to chase the perfect keening sounds that come out of her mouth. In my periphery, I can just make out her twisting her own nipples, edging herself closer, and I moan into her, relishing the fact that *I* made Keeley this wanton.

I grip her closer, and soon she's crying my name, over and over again as her pussy clenches over me.

With one last cry, Keeley flips over and collapses on the pillow, tugging me against her damp skin.

"*God*, you're good at eating me out," she murmurs. "You make me feel so fucking good."

I preen under her praise. It makes me a little possessive, and I know I want to be the *only* one who does this to her. Ever.

"Good. That's all I want," I say, because it's all I can manage. "Even if it didn't seem like it tonight. I'm still . . . just so, so sorry I missed our dinner."

She shrugs, chuckling. "I can assure you I'm perfectly content right now."

"It won't happen again," I say, wrapping my arms around her and pulling her closer.

Keeley groans into my shoulder. "Don't make promises you can't keep. I feel too good to argue with you."

"I can keep it," I say, and I mean it.

My current pace is unsustainable. I'm wild about this woman, and she's reminding me there's more to life than working past burnout to crisis mode where I barely eat or sleep. Everything feels so out of my control, and I know I'll have to find some balance if I want to give our relationship a real chance. We've enjoyed our stolen moments, but soon I know they won't be enough. She deserves more than that.

There are so many layers to it: the ways our personal and professional lives intersect, figuring out when and how I may want to be more public about my identity, how much we share our relationship with the rest of the world. And while I know Keeley would never rush me, I'm determined to figure this out.

Because I know she's worth it. She's worth anything.

23

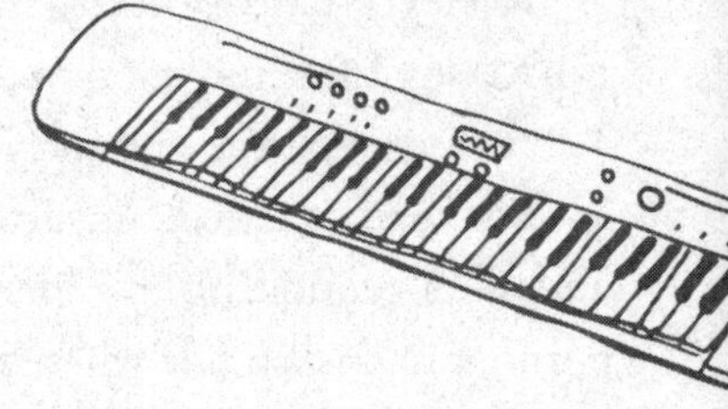

✦ Jane ✦

I'm jolted out of sleep by an urgent voice.

My room is bright with morning sunlight, and I blink groggily to try to clear my head.

"*Jane*," Keeley says. As she comes into focus, I see that she's crying, tears spilling down her cheeks in earnest. I scramble to a seat, leaning against my headboard, my head swimming as I try to figure out why she's so upset.

"Keeley? What's wrong?"

"I have to show you something. Fuck, I'm so sorry, Jane."

She hands her phone to me, and when I look at what's on the screen, I stare in heart-pounding disbelief at the words I'm reading.

Glitter Bats LESBIAN Romance Shocker!

BY RYAN TATE FOR *GOSSIP DAILY*

[cover image description: a video still shot through an open window, where Jane Mercer and Keeley Cunningham share a lip-lock]

Things are heating up between the Glitter Bats—we know you might be tired of reading that, but this time it's ***not*** the disgustingly happy CalErie. No, this is one you're going to have to sit down for, because it's almost TOO JUICY to believe. Prepare yourselves . . .

Our photographer caught an intimate moment shared between Keeley Cunningham and JANE MERCER in a charming beach house in Venice! Through a wide-open window for the entire world to see! If we hadn't gotten the money shot . . . and the steamiest video!!! I wouldn't believe it myself.

Cunningham's sapphic inclinations are no shock to fans, of course, who will never forget her longtime link to Bianca Martin that culminated in a cowritten pop hit. And even if Cunningham wasn't out, there's nothing straight about her. Cunningham could easily be a one-woman pride parade, so it's no surprise she'd fuck around with a bandmate, even acknowledging all the ways Valerie Quinn tore the Bats apart by doing the same.

But the real surprise here is Mercer. The talented pianist and songwriter has always been private about her personal life, but would you have guessed she was a secret lesbian this whole time? It certainly explains a few things. If she can keep something this sordid a secret, what else is she hiding? Is she really the angel everyone says she is?

And maybe the real reason Riker Maddox has never been linked to a bandmate has nothing to do with the fact that he's a man-child, and is simply because they're all gay.

We have been unable to reach Mercer or Cunningham for comment, but a video is worth a million words.

This is a breaking story. Keep following our Glitter Bats tag for updates!

24

✦ *Keeley* ✦

All of the color leaves Jane's cheeks as she stares in shock at the screen.

I wish I could shield her from this, that we could hide away from the late-morning sun streaming through the curtains and banish the internet forever. I wish there was something, anything I could do. But if I hadn't shown her what was on my phone, she would have discovered it through the hundreds of notifications flashing across her own where it lies face up, charging on the nightstand.

Even *I* can't bear to look at what people are saying. This is all my fault.

I should have shut the curtains. God, at least they only caught a kiss. I can't imagine what would have happened if . . . no, I won't go there. It's bad enough already.

I rise up and begin to pace the wood floor between her bed and the window. Because fortunately, this one has blinds.

"Damn it, I can't believe I was this careless!" I say.

"It's not your fault. They came to my *house*. Oh god." Jane laughs weakly, but it turns into a sob as she drops the phone onto the luxurious white duvet. "I thought I was safe here."

I race over to her, clutching her trembling hands. "You *should* be safe here. We'll figure this out."

"How?" she says weakly, gesturing at her rapidly buzzing phone. "Everyone knows."

"No. It's one video. We can explain away a kiss." My mind reels as I try to come up with some explanation to make this right. No matter how much it hurts. "We can say it was an accident. Or—oh! Tell everyone I came on to you. Kissed you without asking."

Jane gapes, a look of horror replacing the shock on her face. "Absolutely not. I'm not going to tell horrible lies about you. How could you possibly suggest that?"

I swallow back another round of tears. This wasn't supposed to happen. Jane and I were just figuring out how to be *happy*. If she wanted to come out, she was supposed to be able to do that her own way, in her own time. The world wasn't supposed to find out because of *Ryan fucking Tate* of all people.

That asshole has been targeting the band for years, and I want to fight him for doing this to Jane. The best of us. She doesn't deserve to have her private life splashed all over the internet. Especially in the vilest fucking article I've ever read.

Ryan's pieces are always salacious, but this one is just *hurtful*. Not just to Jane, but to me and Riker and even Valerie too. I've never felt so exposed in my life . . . and I dated a pop star for three years.

Usually I'm able to come up with some kind of plan, but I'm frozen. Like if I don't move, maybe I won't have to acknowledge this is actually happening, and that article will just disappear into obscurity.

For Jane's sake, though, I need to get myself the fuck together.

A knock pounds on the front door. I'm still in my sleep clothes, a thin T-shirt and some of those gender-neutral boxers that at least give more coverage than regular underwear, but I don't give a shit. I launch myself off the bed and down the stairs, nearly stumbling on the last step.

I yank the door open. "Go the fuck away!" I snap, uncaring of who it is. But when I see Caleb, Valerie, and Riker on the step, I burst into tears.

We're not alone in this. *Thank god.*

Valerie wraps me in a tight hug as the others come inside and shut the door. She's an entire head shorter than me, but her embrace is fierce, like maybe she can squeeze out all of the awful things that brought me to tears.

"It's all because of me," I gasp weakly, as Val rubs slow circles on my back.

"The fuck it is," she whispers urgently. She lets me cry for another minute, then pulls back, placing a hand on either side of my face. "Keeley Cunningham, it is not your fault that this is happening. It's that asshole at *Gossip Daily*. We sacrifice so much to be in this business, and then vultures like him swoop in to pick off anything else they can take from us. You did nothing wrong, and you don't deserve what's happening. Neither does Jane."

"Thank you," I say meekly, because of course Valerie gets it. Ryan Tate practically made a name for himself the day *Gossip Daily* posted leaked photos of her in nothing but her panties when she was only nineteen.

"What can I do? Punch Tate in the face? Go on a wild night out to distract the press from all this?" She looks me up and down. "Or I could just tell you your tits look amazing, because holy fuck I wish I looked like that without a bra on."

I laugh a little, despite the gravity of the situation, and I know that's exactly why she said it. "Keep your pants on, Valerie. I'm just as taken as you are."

"Okay, but the first two were serious suggestions." She leads me into the kitchen. Riker has disappeared, probably to check on Jane, but Caleb is busying himself at her counter, firing up the Chemex and espresso machine in tandem. There's a Tupperware container of fresh muffins sitting on the counter too, no doubt baked by Riker in a fit of insomnia.

"We didn't know what would help, but we figured breakfast was a good first step," Caleb says.

I laugh, but it comes out half a sob. "Don't you have to work today?" I ask.

He steps away from the food and coughs dramatically into his sleeve as Valerie takes over at the espresso machine. "I'm sick."

"Wow. Very professional."

He waves a dismissive hand, carefully measuring coffee out of Jane's hand grinder and scooping it into the conical filter, then pouring water over it all from the steaming kettle. "This is more important."

I roll my eyes. "Don't go getting fired for me, Sloane."

As the coffee begins to percolate, he steps over and squeezes my hand. "It's fine. How's Jane?"

Leaning against the cabinets, I shake my head. "I honestly don't know. We slept late, and by the time we woke up it had already been all over the fucking internet for hours. We literally just saw it. I think she's in shock."

"Understandable," Valerie says, pouring shots into a cup. "Nothing quite prepares you for this."

She would know better than any of us, even if Ryan lost interest now that his favorite subject is boring and married and deliriously happy. Now, he's turned his eyes to us. "God, I don't even know what to do," I say.

"Have you talked to Lacey or Wade?" Caleb asks quietly.

I blink, scrubbing a hand over my face. Of course, that's the rational thing to do. Call your agent, figure out a PR angle. "I didn't get that far yet," I say, wincing a little at the admission.

"That's okay. We can help," Valerie says. We sit in silence for a few minutes while Caleb finishes pouring the coffee, and Valerie makes up a few iced oat milk lattes using Jane's extensive collection of Mason jars and reusable straws. I accept one of the lattes from Valerie gratefully, but I don't take more than a sip. Vaguely, I recognize the pangs of morning hunger, but it's hardly more than a passing thought. The coffee alone sparks my anxiety into even higher alertness. I can't even imagine trying to hold down food right now.

Everything that's happening is making me nauseated.

Finally, Jane makes her way down the stairs with Riker in tow. When they get to the bottom, he wraps an arm around her shoulders and steers her into the kitchen. My shoulders tense a little at the casual contact between them, but I try to remind myself this isn't about me. These two have always been close.

And if he can give comfort to Jane on this awful day, it's fine.

"Oh thank god, coffee," Jane says meekly, accepting a mug from Caleb.

Caleb plants a platonic kiss on her forehead, and Jane sighs a little, leaning into his shoulder. Everything sucks, but I'm so grateful for the people in this room. Our family.

We'll figure this out together.

"You okay?" Valerie asks, as Jane and Caleb part.

"Ask me again in a few hours. I'm still processing." Jane shrugs. "I don't even know how I want to handle it. Lacey is in back-to-back meetings all morning, but her assistant is working on cancelling as many as she can so we can debrief and figure out our options."

"That's good," I say. "The agency will know what to do."

Jane lets out a shaky breath, collapsing onto one of her barstools. "I'm honestly not sure that they will. What's done is done."

While the others eat, I let Valerie cajole me up the stairs to take a shower, as if she can somehow sense I need a minute alone to process everything. By the time I'm out and towel-drying my hair, nothing can convince me I haven't colossally fucked up Jane's entire life. I change into gray sweats and a hoodie before heading back downstairs, choosing comfort over anything remotely presentable.

Just as I reach the landing, there's another knock on the door. Great.

"I'll get it!" Riker calls, but I'm already pulling it open and gritting my teeth.

My vision goes red as I take in the person in the entryway. In her signature business-casual style, Mary Kate Hampton is wearing wide-legged navy trousers with an ivory silk shirt, her long brunette hair pulled back in a sleek ponytail.

Mary Kate has been a longtime friend of the Glitter Bats. She's covered us from the start for *Buzzword*, a much less inflammatory—but still celebrity-focused—website. I like Mary Kate plenty, but the last thing I want to do is talk to the fucking press.

And how did she get Jane's address?

"What the fuck are you doing here?" I snap, using my body to block the doorframe.

Mary Kate raises her hands in surrender. "I come in peace, Keeley."

"That doesn't answer my damn question," I grit out.

"I invited her," Riker says, over my shoulder.

I whirl around to glare daggers at him. "This isn't a press day or even a fucking karaoke night, Riker! What the hell?"

I glance over to Jane, whose face has gone pale, but she nods. "It's okay. Let her in."

Clenching my jaw so hard it might crack my molars, I swing the door wide and dramatically gesture for Mary Kate to come inside.

At Jane's urging, Mary Kate settles onto the goldenrod velvet sectional in the living room. Jane sits tentatively across from her on the perpendicular couch piece, and Valerie takes the spot at Jane's other side. Riker sits next to Mary Kate—the traitor—but I just stand against the wall, crossing my arms to face our visitor. Caleb joins me, looking just as wary.

He's never trusted the press either, and for plenty of good reasons.

"Riker texted me for advice," Mary Kate says. "I'm not here for a story."

"Prove it," I say.

I expect a strong reaction, but Mary Kate simply nods. "After what you've just been through, I understand your concern." She pulls up something on her phone, then stands and hands it to me. "Here's the *Buzzword* ethical journalism policy, which prohibits us from publicly outing someone without their consent. If and when Jane decides she wants to talk about her sexuality, we would then be free to comment, but until that day comes, I would lose my job if I wrote about it, if I even wanted to . . . which I don't."

I read the policy, which seems truthful enough.

"I'm actually impressed," Valerie says. "I didn't know you did this."

"A bunch of the staff is queer including my boss, and he got really pissed when Jaxon Cole was forced out for playing his gay character on *Riverwood*. My roommate helped write the policy, so I know it inside and out."

"Okay," I say, even though my hackles haven't relaxed in the slightest. "So what are you doing here?"

Mary Kate turns to Jane. "First of all, I'm really sorry this happened to you. You deserved so much better than *Gossip Daily* taking photos and video of you in your own home. This is bad journalism, but I'm afraid the damage is done."

Riker groans, sinking back on the couch. "So there's really no making this disappear?"

Mary Kate swallows, shaking her head. "I don't think that's a viable solution. If you could appeal to *Gossip Daily*'s sense of decency—if they even have it—or maybe knew a hacker, they might be able to take it down, but there are too many reposts already. It's out there."

"So what do we do?" Jane asks helplessly.

"I'm not a publicist, so I don't know what's best for you, but I wanted to offer my platform as an open invitation."

And there it fucking is. I gape in disbelief. "So you *are* asking for a story?"

"No," Mary Kate says, her tone measured. "But if Jane wants to make any kind of statement, whether through a publicist or directly to the press, she can go through me, and *Buzzword* won't change a single word."

"I appreciate that," Jane says quietly. She grabs a pillow and hugs it tightly, and I want to be the one comforting her in this moment. We've barely had a chance to explore our relationship, and now she's already having to think about the public's reaction to it all. I just want her to be okay. "But I don't even know that I want to say anything."

"That's fine," Mary Kate says. "But I also wanted to offer something else. I'd like to ask you what your fans can do for you."

"What?" Caleb asks. "Are you finally going to admit you're secretly @GlitterbugsUnofficial?"

Mary Kate flushes, folding her hands in her lap. "I'm not going to admit to anything. I'm just saying that I have connections in the fandom. If you want us to squash this, as much as we can, I know a lot of people who will fight for you."

"Thank you, but I don't expect fans to, like, go to war at my command, or anything like that," Jane says, toying with the fringe on the pillow. "I don't want to take advantage."

Shaking her head, Mary Kate straightens. Despite my reservations, I'm begrudgingly impressed by how determined she is to help, and I *want* to trust she'll do it. "It wouldn't be like that. These first twenty-four hours will set the narrative. If you'd rather we just stay silent as a fandom, we can try that route, but we can also try to shape the public's reaction. We can call people out for enabling *Gossip Daily*'s invasion of your privacy in some shoddy attempt at journalism. Like if you two had been out at a restaurant, or something, that would be one thing. Still shitty, but unfortunately fair game. But this? Filming you in your house? That's beyond reprehensible."

Finally, Jane nods, and I can't tell if it's because she actually thinks this is a good idea, or if she's just defeated. "Okay. Whatever you think will help, I'll take it."

Mary Kate smirks, gesturing for me to give her back her phone. I'd forgotten I was even holding it. With a few clicks, she's already working away.

"Thank you, seriously." Jane reaches out a hand, and instead of shaking it, Mary Kate squeezes warmly.

"You're a real one, MK," Riker says, smiling a little sadly. For the first time all morning, the tension in the house melts a little. Nothing the fandom does will make this go away, but maybe they'll have our backs.

I'm with Jane: I don't want to use our fans, but despite my initial misgivings, I'm deeply appreciative of what Mary Kate is offering. I've seen the power of fandom. Our following isn't nearly as big as BTS's ARMY, but the way they've organized things for social issues before is goddamn impressive.

This isn't nearly the same kind of scale, but maybe our fans can pull this off.

"Look, I know I'm the press, but I think of you as friends too. I can't always use my powers for good, but I want to do this."

"As long as you make Tate squirm, you have my full support," Valerie says.

"Oh, I'm going to make him wish he became an accountant by the time I'm done," Mary Kate says, grinning.

And I can't help it; I smile at that. We have bigger things to figure out, but until Jane can work with her team, revenge is sweet enough.

[TODAY]

@GossipDaily

Glitter Bats' Jane Mercer's lesbian bombshell caught on video! More from **@RyanTaterTotz** here!

@BatsThatGlitter

@GossipDaily you should be ashamed of yourselves. Filming someone in their home is not okay, and you've basically doxed Jane Mercer. If you had any integrity left, you'd delete the article and #FireRyanTate. What a fucking horrible thing to do.

@BatsThatGlitter

Also: I'm appalled by the biphobia in the **@GossipDaily** article by **@RyanTaterTotz** today. We don't know anything about how Jane identifies—OR IF SHE EVEN WANTS HER IDENTITY TO BE PUBLIC YOU COMPLETE TOILET—and assuming she's a lesbian just because she kissed a girl is reprehensible. Not that lesbian is a bad word, but you do NOT get to just assign her a label because it sounds salacious. Fuck you.

@BitterSweetGlitterati

Beyond disgusted. Calling on all #Glitterbugs and other #GlitterBats fans not to interact with the garbage being posted about Jane and Keeley. If you're a real fan, you'll protect their privacy. #FireRyanTate

@ValerieQuinnSuperFan

@RyanTaterTotz We know you've had it out for the Glitter Bats for years but this is a whole new level of petty bullshit. What did they ever do to you? #FireRyanTate

@GlitterbugsUnofficial

Okay **@GossipDaily @RyanTaterTotz** this is enough. That article was disgusting, and it affects real people. Forget journalistic integrity—filming someone in their home is invasive and cruel. Am I surprised? No. But that doesn't make it okay. #FireRyanTate

@MakeMeMrsSloane

😐 **@GlitterbugsUnofficial** you are such a hypocrite. How can you share fic about the band and suddenly not support speculation about their personal lives?

@GlitterbugsUnofficial

@MakeMeMrsSloane because fic doesn't actually affect real people in the same way??? Whatever, I'm finally blocking you. Either help us get #FireRyanTate trending or go get a life.

@BuzzWordCeleb

Folks have been tagging us to report on recent rumors. It's our company policy not to speculate on anyone's sexuality or engage in so-called "reporting" that could out someone without their consent. This will be our only post on this topic.

@YouAreMyGhost

I am so tired of Ryan Tate treating the Glitter Bats' personal lives like his little playground. #FireRyanTate

@DragonRealmLoverrr

Wow, Gossip Daily is pretty fucking bold. Remember when Ryan tried to do this to Finn?
#DragonRealmers lets help the #Glitterbugs get #FireRyanTate trending [KristenBellLipstickGif]

@WendyTheWonder99

I HAVE RECEIPTS. I've included screenshots in the thread below of all the ways **@GossipDaily** has been blatantly biphobic about Valerie Quinn, Jaxon Cole, Finn Lewis, and now Jane Mercer. And fuck it, #FireRyanTate because he's the literal worst offender. #Wonderfans, LFG.

@RyanTaterTotz

[image description: Ryan Tate standing shirtless in a kitchen with a glass of champagne in one hand]
By #FireRyanTate, do you mean my devilishly good looks? 🔥🔥🔥 If Jane Mercer and Keeley Cunningham didn't want that sexy makeout to be all over the internet, they should have shut those curtains. Today has been fun, besties. More soon! 😘

@GossipDaily

Ten reasons we love **@RyanTaterTotz!** He's not going anywhere. Link here!

25

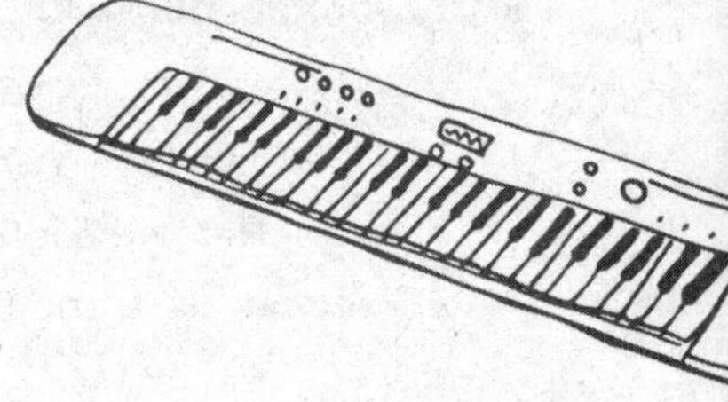

Jane

There's a reason I hadn't come out yet. I've thought about it, because of course I have, but I stuck to quiet hookups until now, because I was terrified of what a public fallout would look like. Recent events are proving I was right to protect my privacy. I don't regret anything between me and Keeley, but in the wake of everything, I just feel so incredibly helpless. Because now, well . . .

My whole family knows. Mom called me at least a dozen times, leaving voicemail after voicemail. Keeley deleted them all without letting me hear a word.

I want to believe this won't be forever, but I hardly have the desire to leave Keeley's condo. We've holed up here, even though I'm terrified journalists will somehow figure out where she lives too. Keeley only left to get a bag full of my clothes, and she's been staying close ever since.

The one silver lining is Mary Kate and the fandom. Not only did they show up, but they got the *Into the Dragon Realm*, *Shooting Stars*, and even *Epic Theme Song* fans on our side. #FireRyanTate was a trending topic, and it felt so validating to see his behavior called out. But *Gossip Daily* doubled down with a post a day later recapping all of the Glitter Bats relationship failures over the years, so I don't think there will be any real consequences for him.

I've had long meetings with Lacey and her team about strategy. Right now, we're sticking with zero comments. We cancelled all of my public engagements. I've been video-calling into the writers' room for *Into the Dragon Realm* from Keeley's couch all week, because going outside increases the chance that I'll be seen. Fortunately, no one on my team has questioned me for keeping a low profile—they've all seen the headlines.

I'm not J.Lo famous or even *Valerie Quinn* famous, but the requests for photos and interviews coming through Lacey have been overwhelming. Even if I wanted to speak out, I would be incredibly careful about who I spoke to.

True to her word, Mary Kate doesn't write a single thing about me from her professional account, and neither does *Buzzword*. Still, it's overwhelming. It's almost a good thing Label is stalling the auction for our masters, because I don't have the capacity to deal with even more press at the moment.

One day while Keeley is in the shower, I finally hear from Nora.

"I'm so sorry, Jane, this is the first chance I got to call you without Mom around. How are you doing?"

I laugh bitterly. "Not so great. Thanks for checking in."

"Of course," she says. "Shit, I hate everything they're saying about you. This never happened before."

I swallow. "Well, I didn't get caught kissing my girlfriend before. What are Mom and Dad saying?"

She sighs. "Do you want me to tell you the truth, or do you want me to make you feel better?"

My heart sinks, because I wish her lying about our parents would actually make me feel better, instead of incredibly sad. "I think that tells me enough."

She groans. "I'm sorry. You, uh . . . don't have to come to my wedding, if you don't want to. Of course I want you there, but I'm afraid it might hurt you too much to be around Mom and Dad right now."

"Thank you, Nora," I say. "I . . . I'll let you know. I'm not sure what I want to do yet." Thanksgiving is in a few days, and I doubt that this will blow over by New Year's.

I'm scared I'll ruin her special day. If I know anything about my parents, I know they'll cause a scene the moment they see me.

"This sucks," she says.

"Yeah, it does."

"Too bad that hashtag didn't work out. I'd love to see that douchebag pay for what he did to you."

I open my mouth to argue with her but close it again. Even my instinct to assume the best in people has limits. Ryan Tate *hurt* me for clicks. There's no pretending that away, not when he's forced me into hiding. Not when I can't even go out in public for fear of being accosted by the media.

"Enough about me," I say. "Distract me with wedding details. We're only a couple of months out, so what's on the docket now that your dress is all set?"

I let Nora go on about the fun things they're planning for the reception, trying to soak in even just a little bit of her joy, even as I sense she's oversharing on purpose to keep me on the phone. It pains me that she's going so far to cheer me up when she should be focusing on herself right now. I was so resistant about going to her wedding before, but now that I might miss it, I suddenly wish more than anything that I could be there for her.

That my parents could be like Keeley's. That they could take a chance on supporting me unconditionally, instead of the reaction I know is coming—using their rancid interpretation of the Bible to demand repentance for my happiness.

But I care about Keeley more than I've ever cared about anyone, and nothing could make me feel like that's wrong. If I could take the last few months together back, all these precious moments of dancing around our feelings and finally letting them win, I wouldn't dream of it. I'd choose her every time, no matter what the media has to say about it.

She has my heart.

Keeley has truly been amazing, handling not only my messages, but my emotions. I know she feels just as betrayed as I do by what happened, but she won't talk about the article or social media or any of it outside of checking if I'm okay. She doesn't ask me to consider coming out and confirm the rumors are true. Not even once. If I were in her position, I might be that selfish. Because there's nothing I want more than to be able to love the person I love loudly, wholeheartedly, for the entire world to see.

But if being Valerie's friend has taught me anything, it's that once you give something of yourself to the world, you can never take it back. Even with this undeniable video, where you can see just exactly who I've been kissing all over the internet, I've stayed quiet. My personal truth is all I have left, and I'm holding on to it because I don't know how else to move forward.

I try to focus back on Nora, saying a quick goodbye as I hear our parents return to the house in the background. More than ever, I find myself supporting this wedding, if only to get my sister out from under their influence. While I wait for Keeley to dry her hair, I start to tidy the house, throwing in a load of laundry and wiping down the kitchen.

Once that's done, I change into shorts and an oversized sweatshirt and head into the kitchen to start dinner. Keeley emerges as I'm finishing up the sauce for homemade alfredo. We finally had a chance to do some cooking together, and pasta is becoming a bit of a ritual. It doesn't get super cold here, even in late autumn, but there's something so comforting about noodles and cheese.

"Smells amazing," Keeley says, her eyes softening as she catches my gaze. Her skin is flushed and she has no makeup on, but she still takes my breath away. I set the sauce to simmer and turn to face her as she strides over to me.

"I'm starting to get used to having you here," she murmurs, pulling me into her arms as she settles onto a barstool.

"I like sharing space with you," I admit. "I know I'm staying to lay low—which I very much appreciate—but it's nice, not having to say goodbye to you every night."

I don't think I ever want to say goodbye to her, but I'm not sure how to face what that means.

"You'll get sick of me eventually," she drawls, before drawing my lips to hers. The kiss is soft, sweet, and I let myself relax into the warmth of her wrapped around me. She holds me tighter, closer, deepening the kiss until it's a tangle of lips and tongues and I want nothing more than to be consumed by her.

I draw back, leaning my forehead against hers. "Keeley?" I breathe.

"Yeah?"

"Dinner can sit for a while, right?"

I drag my lips down her jaw, to her neck, reveling in the way she reacts and softens as I press kisses on her delicate skin. All I want is to be with her, to feel *something* other than the constant ache in my soul. To be with someone who makes me feel safe.

"Are you seducing me, Jane Mercer?" she gasps, as my lips find the curve of her breast.

"That depends. Is it working?"

"*Fuck*, yes."

"Then come on."

Threading her fingers through mine, I draw her toward her bedroom, past the one window that looks out onto the street, glancing nervously to make sure the blinds are closed.

Keeley doesn't miss my check.

"Jane," she murmurs, and the worry in her tone is unmistakable. I pause, looking back at her, and the look she gives me is so *sad*, I don't know what to do about it.

"Keeley," I say, sinking one of my shoulders against the wall. "It's okay. I'm fine."

"You're not," she says. "All of this . . . it was too much. Fuck, you can't even go into work right now, and it's all because of me."

"It's not," I say, quickly pulling her closer again.

She still holds herself back. "You can't possibly be okay with everyone knowing your business."

"I mean, I did spend a sad few hours researching what it would cost to run away from it all and live on a sheep farm in Ireland for the next twenty years, but I really am fine." I laugh bitterly. "I've been dating people of different genders for years, you know. It's a miracle I've been able to go this long without getting caught."

She swallows, shaking her head as she slumps against the wall to face me. "You should want nothing to do with me."

"Well, that would be silly, because I'm wild about you."

Keeley shakes her head. "All of this, it's distracting from your incredible career, and I just can't help but think that if it weren't for me—"

I silence her with a kiss. "No, stop that. You're not holding me back, and you're not a distraction. I'm with you because you're *you*, got it?"

Keeley nods, but I'm not sure she's convinced. "Okay."

"Now, can we get to the sex? Because I desperately want to feel good, and I bet you do too."

A familiar spark of mischief lights in her eyes. "How do you feel about the stuff in your bedside table? I might have grabbed some of it when I got your clothes." She bites her lip.

My heart stutters. Keeley can make me fall apart with just her fingers or her mouth, but at this suggestion . . . my senses sharpen to high alert.

"I'm . . . open to it," I say, chuckling a little nervously. I definitely know my way around a vibrator, but I've never used one with a partner before. It's always just been for me.

But Keeley doesn't laugh. Instead, her voice lowers to a growl, and I swear I feel it in my core. "Oh we're going to have some fun."

And then she literally sweeps me off my feet, carrying me into the bedroom with ease. She sets me down on top of her comforter, and I scoot myself back so I'm leaning into a pillow. With determination etched into her jaw, Keeley yanks open *her* drawer and grabs the soft silky bag with my rabbit, along with a small bottle of lube.

Something about my toy being in her nightstand undoes me. I grin up at her, feeling a little possessive and a lot turned on.

"Strip for me?" she asks.

"Uh, yeah, I can do that," I say, desire making my mouth go dry. Without delay, I yank off my shorts and sweatshirt, and all my underthings, leaving me fully bare on the duvet while Keeley remains clothed.

"That's my girl," she says, and if I weren't already swooning, those words would make me a goner. Because I am.

Hers.

No one's ever *had* me, not like this. The idea of giving myself to someone used to terrify me. But with Keeley, I'm not afraid of giving myself to her. It just feels right even when the rest of my world is spinning out of control.

Keeley takes out the vibrator, analyzes it, then looks back at me. "Is this okay?"

Sighing, I practically writhe at the idea. I'll let her take me apart now and tell her my feelings later. "It's perfect."

"And what do you want me to do with it?" She powers it on the lowest setting, pressing it against the inside of my thigh. It's so close and yet so far, I want to cry out in protest. My eyes fall closed as she drags the toy closer to where I want it, desire burning through my veins.

"Fuck me with it," I gasp. "Please."

"Well, since you asked so nicely, I guess I can do that." Her words are equal parts seductive and tender, and I want to bask in them almost as much as I want her to just get on with it.

And without any further delay, she uncaps the lube and coats the top of the vibrator with it, then presses the toy between my legs. Even at the lowest setting, it's almost too much, the rumbling buzz against my clit, and my back arches as I let my body relax into the sensation.

"God, just look at you. You're gorgeous when you're needy like this," she murmurs. I moan as she drags the vibrator down my core, so careful not to give me too much too soon. For a few delicious minutes, she slowly rubs the toy up and down, working me up before she slides it inside.

My breath hitches as the width of the toy fills me, the external stimulator pressing at just the right spot as Keeley gives me the whole thing. My back arches in desperation.

"There you go, take it like a good girl," Keeley says, and if I weren't already so *needy*, those words would totally undo me.

"I'm not going to last long," I admit, as she draws the toy out and penetrates me again. It's too good like this, trusting Keeley with my pleasure entirely, knowing she'll take care of me.

"Good. I want to make you come."

I blink up at her. "Kiss me?" I ask.

Grinning, Keeley leans down and presses her mouth to mine. The kiss is messy, desperate, and Keeley doesn't stop in her relentless pursuit of my pleasure, multitasking efficiently.

"Fuck, you're perfect," she murmurs against my mouth. "I only ever want to do this, right here, forever."

My lust-addled mind takes that declaration at face value, even though the tiniest part of me knows this is just horny talk and it can't be trusted. But I want to believe her. I don't *want* to care what the world thinks. I just want this.

The combination of the emotion and the kiss and the perfect vibrations in my core make me fall in earnest, the orgasm sparking through my body with all the force of a lightning strike. My hands grasp at Keeley, the sheets, my own thighs, *anything* to hold on to as the current builds and takes me higher. Tears stream out of my eyes as I'm crying out her name.

I've never come this hard, and when I peak, I think I might just combust.

And then I collapse, boneless, my limbs tingling as Keeley withdraws the vibrator and sets it on a towel near the side of the bed. She pulls me into her arms, and as much as I want to take care of her too, I can barely move.

"God, that was incredible," I say.

"You're incredible," she says, pressing a kiss to my hair. "I don't ever want this to end."

"I don't either," I say. But when we eventually separate and get back to preparing dinner, I wonder if this time tucked away in her apartment has an expiration date. I can't hide forever.

What happens when I stop?

26

✦ *Keeley* ✦

I wake up in the middle of the night in pure panic. After dinner, Jane and I had lazy sex in my bed until we fell asleep, tangled up together. Everything felt okay.

But now my bed is so cold I'm shivering.

I scramble up to a sitting position, trying to make sense of what's happening. Since I'm still ass naked, I tug on some sweats and a hoodie, shove my feet into slippers, and race out into the dark living room. Part of me is terrified that she's gone, disappeared into the night with nothing but memories left behind.

But the reality might be worse.

Jane is curled up in a ball on the floor next to the couch, huddled in one of the throw blankets, face illuminated by nothing but her phone screen. The light shines on tears streaming down her face.

My chest tightens. I sprint over to her side, crouching down next to her.

"What's going on?"

Jane sniffs. "I caved and listened to the latest voicemail from my parents. They uninvited me to the wedding and . . . said a lot of other stuff."

My breath catches as my heart breaks for her. If I ever get a chance to give the Mercers a piece of my mind, I'm not holding back. How fucking *dare they* do this to her?

"Oh, baby, I'm so sorry."

When I move to wrap my arms around her, she just shoves the phone at me. "And now *Gossip Daily* is at it again, and everyone's talking about it. I can't stop reading the comments."

I take her phone, blinking my tired eyes to read an article that makes me want to vomit. It's not even Ryan Tate doing the damage this time—they've got Paige Hart in on it too. I've never liked the woman—she's the kind of fake nice that has always set my teeth on edge—and the article confirms my suspicions that she's just as bad as her colleague.

> These juicy photos PROVE Jane Mercer has been a secret lesbian this whole time! What else is she hiding? We have theories!

The worst part is, salacious captions aside, the photos aren't damning. They're just pictures of Jane and I together over the years, smiling, laughing, leaning on each other. More proof that this magic happening between us was inevitable. If I'd stumbled upon these photos out of context, I might not think anything of it, other than fondness for those memories.

But the article is, of course, vile, and the comments are vicious. And . . . oh god. A few religious people got in there. I almost lose my grip on the phone because my hands are shaking so hard, and I don't know if it's with anxiety or pure, unbridled rage. With the familiar all-caps rhetoric about hell and homosexuality, and the pasted images of bad graphic design plastered with Bible verses and

American flags, it's no wonder Jane isn't smiling. This is her worst nightmare.

She ran from people like that, and she still can't escape.

"Part of me wants to scream, *I'M BISEXUAL ACTUALLY* from the rooftops, but I don't even know where to start," she says, sniffling.

I pull her into my arms. "I'm so sorry."

"What did I do to deserve this?" Her voice trembles, and she takes her phone back from me, gingerly setting it down on the carpet before nestling into my shoulder, blanket and all. "I've always been kind to the press! What gives them the right to talk about my personal life at all? I only ever wanted to make music with the people I love and work on interesting projects."

"And you *should* get to do that," I say gently, squeezing her tighter. She shouldn't be in this position at all. We didn't know what we were getting into when we signed that first record deal, and the reality has been a lot of heartache. But, by some miracle, Jane has been able to escape it . . . until now.

She pulls out of my arms, looking at me with sad eyes, and I know she's thinking the same thing. "Do you want to know the worst part? Even when all of this was happening to Valerie, even when I saw firsthand how much it broke her, I thought I was safe! I thought if I was nice enough, was pleasant enough, no one would ever go after me. And none of that fucking mattered! They've made me scared to go outside!" She lets out a sob, and presses her hand to her mouth, and *oh*, I wish I could make all of this hurt go away.

"You deserved so much better," I say, folding my legs into a pretzel to face her properly. No one's coming-out experience is the same, but these assholes took all of Jane's choices from her. It makes me sick.

"I don't like feeling helpless and afraid," she says softly.

"I know," I say, because I don't know what else is left. "What can I do?"

Jane sniffs again, shrugging the blanket tighter around her.

"I think . . . I think I need to take some time."

"Oh." I freeze, feeling as if the floor is about to fall out from under me. "Yeah, okay, whatever you need."

Her eyes widen, and she reaches a hand out of her blanket cocoon to grab mine. "No, Keeley, I don't want to break up. I just . . . I have to clear my head."

I swallow. "And you can't . . . do that here?"

She hiccups out another sob. "I don't know. I'm so confused. This was supposed to be my choice, and those jerks stole it from me, and if I'm here . . . I'm afraid I'll let myself hide forever. Things between us just happened so fast, and I just . . . I need time to think."

It doesn't make sense, and yet, I have to respect what she wants. Jane has just gone through a ton of trauma in the worst way imaginable, and if being here isn't helping her, then I have to let her go.

Even if it feels so wrong it makes me want to scream.

"I can take you home in the morning," I say.

Jane pulls her hand from mine, and it nearly breaks me. "I can't ask you to do that. It's fine. I'll figure it out."

I hear what she's really saying, that she doesn't want *me* to take her home. She doesn't want to be seen in public with me, to fan the flames of this horrible moment any more than we already have. But she didn't bring her car in our haste to get out of her house, so she's literally stuck with me until we figure out an alternative.

"I understand. You can pack. I'll take care of the details," I say.

"Are you sure?" she asks, so softly I barely hear her. Every molecule in my body wants to pull her close, to hold her and tell her it's going to be okay, but I know that's the opposite of what she's asking for. Even if it hurts.

So instead, I jump up, putting physical distance between us. “Yeah, I’m sure.”

I want to ask if she’s coming back to bed, but we both know she’s not. If Jane is asking for time, I’ll give it to her, even if it makes me want to fucking shatter into a million pieces. When Jane doesn’t follow me, I slip into my bedroom.

Maybe *I* can’t be there for her right now, but . . . shit, I know someone who can help. It’s one a.m., but he’ll be awake. I shut my bedroom door for some privacy, trying not to look at the bed, trying to will away the memories of what Jane and I shared just hours ago as I pull up the contact.

Riker answers my call on the first ring. “Keeley? What’s wrong?”

My head spins. “Are you awake?”

“Of course I’m awake. But you’re usually zonked out by ten. So again I’m begging you: What’s wrong?” There’s an urgency in his tone I haven’t heard in a long time, and I feel bad for freaking him out. Riker has reliably been a night owl since we were kids, when he would stream video games late into the night to wind down from overhearing his parents’ screaming matches. So I expected he’d answer, but hearing his voice and knowing there’s someone else I can trust to understand the gravity of this situation almost eases my raging panic.

“It’s Jane.”

“Fuck, what happened?”

“She’s fine, physically, but she saw some more of the media and . . . she’s not okay. She said she needs time.” It breaks me even more to confide those words in someone else, and my voice wavers. “I want to give her that, but she shouldn’t be alone right now. Can you just . . .”

“Oh shit, yeah, I can be there. Give me twenty minutes?”

I blink. “I was just going to ask you to take her home in the morning, but . . . yeah, maybe you should come over now.”

Suddenly, I feel like such an asshole for being so jealous of Riker's friendship with Jane. I know that relationship is what she can lean on now.

She can have all the space she needs, but she doesn't have to be alone.

"Done. And Keeley?"

"Yeah?"

"Thanks for calling me. I know you have always felt a little weird about my friendship with Jane—"

"I don't feel weird!" I protest.

He groans. "Don't lie to me, Keels. That makes it worse. But Janey is like my sister, you know that, right?"

I relent, sinking onto my bed. Because sure, I've been jealous, but when I really look at their relationship over the years, I know it's nothing more than platonic. They both had shitty families, and they bonded over that. I can't hold that against them. "Yeah, I know."

"Good, because sometimes it seems like you're threatened by me, which is ridiculous, because Jane is so in love with you that there might as well be no one else in the entire world."

"Yeah, okay," I say, not totally convinced. *If she's so in love with me, maybe she wouldn't leave.* The tiniest part of my brain keeps telling me I'm the problem. I'm the reason Jane has to deal with any of this. If it weren't for me, she would still be happily living her life without public scrutiny.

And wanting distance, well . . . it kind of proves my point.

"Listen to me, Keeley. You're going to give Jane space right now, because I know you're respectful and all about boundaries and other well-adjusted shit, but you two can overcome this. I believe in Jeeley."

I groan, and when my voice breaks I don't know if it's a sob or a laugh. "How dare you give us a ship name that bad."

He laughs, and I can hear him in the background shuffling around his house and grabbing his keys. "No, trust me, I've been thinking about it for years, and this is the best option."

"Years?" I scoff, but the idea actually makes me smile a little, even as I feel like my world is ending. *Years* makes it feel like this fragile thing between me and Jane is less likely to fall apart.

"Obviously. I've been rooting for you since high school."

"Whatever."

"Back to the point. You two do not have names that are easy to portmanteau. I mean, nothing is as bad as CalErie, but the options for you two are, like, Kane, MercIngham, or something old-school like 'Fire and Ice.' Although I was proud of that one. You get it?"

I groan. "Yes, the hair."

"No! That's the best part. You are all fiery and she's icy cool as a cucumber most of the time, so it's actually the opposite. Maybe I should suggest that one to MK to feed to the fandom . . ."

"Don't you fucking dare," I say. "And someday we're going to talk about that whole situation."

"There's no situation, and oops, I'm about to get into the car and lose you. See you soon!"

I roll my eyes but end the call, and then the impending separation from Jane hits me, and I plunge into despair. Instead of going out into my living room to wait with her, I hide in my room like a coward until the doorbell rings. I keep it together when Riker steps inside, when he silently folds Jane into his arms, when he shoulders her bags and leads her out my door.

And then I'm faced with the reality that I'm alone. What does it mean for us if Jane needs space, but space is the absolute last thing *I* need? I just want her in my life. But she's gone.

My legs give out, and I collapse onto the floor of my now-empty living room and cry.

27

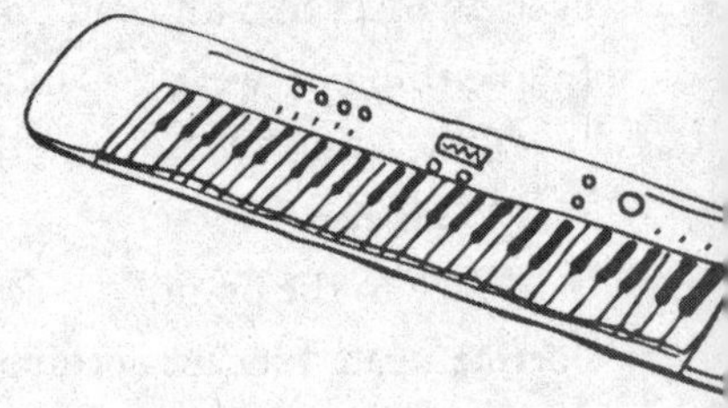

✦ *Jane* ✦

Riker and I have a tradition of spending the holidays together, so crashing at his place over the week of Thanksgiving is perfectly natural.

I truly hate going home, and he hates having to choose which parent to spend the holidays with, now that his dad is in Beaverton and his mom is in Coeur d'Alene. It's just far enough to travel for him to have to pick only *one* but upset the other parent for being in the vicinity but not actually *visiting.* Keeping the peace is impossible.

Meanwhile, I have a long history of telling my parents I'm working and can't spare the time. This year, they didn't even ask if I'm coming for the holiday.

I don't know if I should thank or curse *Gossip Daily* for that.

But since I left Keeley for the "space" I thought I wanted, I've been a shell of a person. It's . . . not pretty. *Into the Dragon Realm* has given me plenty to work on, but I've been functioning on autopilot. Wake up, drink coffee, work until I drop. Riker pushes me to call up my old therapist, and I schedule two emergency sessions to try to work through all of my feelings.

After the first, they got me in touch with a psychiatrist to get on some antidepressants, which I haven't needed in years. But it turns out self-medicating by overscheduling myself isn't working.

My friends are with me, though. Valerie and Caleb come by to work on a new Glitter Bats song they've been writing with Riker, and I jump in to help. During one of our breaks, Valerie breaks out some chocolate and volunteers to go through my DMs.

At first, I tell her no. There can't be anything good in there. But when she doesn't relent, insisting she'll find the positive ones, I reluctantly hand over my phone. And then I marvel at the fact that they're not all bad.

It's kind of incredible, actually, the solidarity.

There are kind words from fans, especially queer fans. But I've also been contacted by other people in entertainment who had similar things happen to them. Jaxon Cole, the actor from *Riverwood* who Mary Kate mentioned, sent me a message to check in and share his story about being accused of "queerbaiting" for playing a gay character until he came out on his socials. I even hear from a *New York Times* bestselling author who tried to keep her private life private, until someone uploaded photos of her with her girlfriend at an event that wasn't open to the public.

Everyone promises I don't owe the world an explanation. Still, I wonder how it might be different if I *had* decided to come out, years ago, when I first left life with my family behind. Maybe then, I wouldn't be so lonely. There's this ache deep in my soul where Keeley's warmth used to live, and the absence leaves me hollow. As much as I try to go through the motions, I know my friends can see it in my eyes.

I've picked up the phone to call her a hundred times, but I still don't know what to say. I don't know how to get to where I want to be, and until I figure that out, it's not fair to expect Keeley to walk on eggshells around me.

That's why Riker is dragging me to an instrument shop, navigating through Black Friday traffic like it's not actual hell out here. Fortunately, the cars start to move as we get closer to the shop.

"I don't want a new keyboard," I tell him as he pulls into the parking lot a little too fast, and I wince as he skips the curb with nothing but a self-deprecating chuckle. Ignoring this, I continue my protest. "I want my *old* keyboard."

"I know it's nostalgic, Janey, but you're going to need a new one eventually."

I lean against the headrest, folding my hands in my lap. "I don't know. I'm not sure I can be trusted to make any major decisions right now."

Riker raises a brow as he puts his truck into park. "You, Jane Mercer, think you can't handle decisions? Since when do you doubt yourself?"

I sigh. I doubt myself all the time lately. "We're just *looking*, Riker."

But it feels so weird to be doing this without Keeley. With how much time we've spent together over the past few months, choosing something for my house alone feels . . . wrong.

I want her to be included in it. Crap, maybe I even want us to share an address. But that's the last thing I should be thinking about, because I have a lot of choices to navigate before we can have a life together.

Riker glances at his phone. "Shit, they don't open for another ten minutes. Sorry."

"It's fine," I say. Riker begins to scroll as we wait, but I can't bring myself to open any apps. I'm still scared of what I'll find.

The media frenzy has slowed a little, but *Gossip Daily* didn't take any of the articles down. Still, when Ryan Tate and a couple of other journalists started getting called out for homophobia, they quickly changed their topics of choice for a few weeks, going back to gross old standbys like "Hot or Nots" and rehashing dirt on favorite early-aughts stars. There's even a full article dedicated to speculating whether Bianca Martin's friendship with Landon Banks's latest ex-wife is all a publicity stunt.

I feel guilty that they're still talking about other people like they're objects, but I can't deny the relief of no longer being in the hot seat.

And it wasn't because of anything I did. I have one person to thank.

"Mary Kate really white-knighted for me," I say softly, staring out the window as a couple of new cars pull into the parking lot. "I appreciate you reaching out to her that day."

Riker glances up from his phone, his cheeks turning pink. He brings a hand to his neck, sheepish. "It was nothing."

My throat tightens. "It's *not* nothing, and you know it."

He shrugs, the movement so exaggerated on his large frame that I nearly laugh. "I just sent a text. She did all the work."

"Well, I'm glad you're friends with her. She was really kind to me when it mattered."

Riker nods, a small smile tugging on his lips. "She's like that." He might be playing cool, but he goes all puppy-eyed when Mary Kate is mentioned, and it's kind of adorable.

"Can I ask you a question?" I say.

Riker raises a brow. "That was a question, but you can ask another if you must."

"Not that it's any of my business, but . . . you and Mary Kate . . . why isn't that a thing?" Every time she's around, she gravitates toward him like a magnet, and he responds to the pull. Whether it's red carpets, or fundraisers, or even just group interviews, their banter always turns any conversation into *The Riker and Mary Kate Show* and the rest of us are just guest stars.

He leans back into the driver's seat, propping up a knee and acting casual. "It's just flirting. There's nothing going on."

"Yeah, but that's not what I asked. I asked *why* it's not more. You're obviously into her."

He frowns, staring at the gear shift. "I'm into a lot of people."

"*Riker*," I say.

"I don't know, it's complicated," he says all in a rush. "I obviously really like Mary Kate, but I always figured it would be a conflict of interest, so I never went there. We're just friends."

"And that's enough for you?"

Riker's jaw sets. "It doesn't matter if it's enough for me. Mary Kate has said a hundred times that she doesn't date people in the industry. I can't tell her how I feel because anything between us would ruin her career."

I rest my elbows on the dash, looking over at him in frustration. "Isn't that up to her to decide? Why would you choose not to be together when you haven't even tried? Isn't it worth taking a chance?"

Riker raises a brow. "You tell me."

All the warmth drains from my cheeks, and I snap back up in my seat. "What?"

Riker opens his mouth. "Janey, I'm sorry. That wasn't fair of me to say. But you're kind of projecting and I know you're struggling, and . . . sorry. Never mind."

"No, tell me what you were going to say." God knows I could use perspective right now.

"It feels like you're waiting for permission to have what you want."

Oh my god.

Is this really what this is? Am I just people-pleasing myself out of my own happiness? It doesn't feel that simple, and yet, it makes so much sense.

"You might be right." I gape back at him, mind racing. Suddenly, I'm seeing my situation with so much more clarity. "When I realized I wanted to leave the church, I already knew I was bi. But I was quiet about living life on my own terms. Leaving home for LA made my parents so upset, but whenever I went back, I put my good-girl mask on in order to keep the peace. With something like this . . . I won't be able to do that anymore, and it scares the hell out of me."

He nods. "That's understandable."

"I feel like I've spent the last ten years holding my breath."

Riker softens. "I can't speak to how you feel about being out, or being *public*, now that the media has already pulled this bullshit and outed you. But you're allowed to choose Keeley, if that's what you want. We'll be right there with you to figure out the rest."

My head spins. I want that to be true, but I'm still terrified at what that would mean. Once I tell my truth to the world, I can't take it back.

But there's a part of me that just wants to be *known*. No more secrets. No more fears. I want to be my authentic self, and let people take or leave it. I don't want to let fear of my family dictate my path anymore. I've been talking to the therapist about this too, about how my identity is no one's fucking business, but they also remind me of the good I could do, if fans saw themselves in me.

I just don't know what that looks like.

I open my mouth to respond, but just then, both of our phones buzz. It's the Glitter Bats + Wade text chain:

> WADE: Sorry to bother you over the long holiday, but I just heard from Label Records. Landon is making a final decision now. Expect a press release by the end of the day. I'm sorry to not have more news than that.

"Press release? What does that even mean?" Riker groans.

"I don't know, but I'm nervous. Want to go help me pick out a keyboard?"

"Distraction it is! Let's go," Riker says.

So we enter the store just as it opens. I get sidetracked at the drum kits, imagining what they might look like in my music room, but finally I let Riker drag me over to the keyboards. Miraculously, there's the same make and model as my original Korg, and it's in perfect condition. I decide to buy it on the spot. As we check out at the register, I'm grateful that, during this awful month, at least one thing has gone my way. I have my keyboard again.

But as soon as Riker and I stop by my house to drop off the instrument, the press release hits.

Glitter Bats Masters Sold to Q Enterprises

RYAN TATE FOR *GOSSIP DAILY*

A fight for the rights to the first three Glitter Bats albums took a wild turn this week, when masters were sold to Q Enterprises. After years of bitter business dealings, the Bats took matters in their own hands and attempted to purchase their own music.

However, the sale went to auction, and another party swooped in and won the bid. Our team is still investigating the incorporation documents, but it appears Q Enterprises is owned by none other than Tonya Quinn, the Glitter Bats' first manager and Valerie Quinn's mother. Ms. Quinn has been infamous for her ruthless management of bands at the beginning of their careers, including the Glitter Bats, and it appears she decided she still wants a piece of the pie despite all ties being cut from her relationship with the Bats—both personal and professional.

Reports say Ms. Quinn was noticeably absent from Valerie and Caleb Sloane's surprise Vegas wedding earlier this year. Mother and daughter may not be close, but purchasing the masters feels like the first strike in what will likely be a long war.

Glitter Bats now have no masters and no record deal. Is this the end for the band, or will they try yet *another* comeback? But bats are not cats—they're running out of lives. There are only so many chances to stay in this industry, and honestly, watching Glitter Bats try and fail is getting kind of sad.

Maybe they should stick to their new career paths. Jane Mercer is killing it in the gaming and TV soundtrack space, and sources say her paramour Keeley Cunningham is so in demand as a studio drummer, she had to take a leave of absence. Riker Maddox is similarly busy with touring work, and even Quinn is busy promoting her television show. Sloane continues on in his ever-elusive day job. Is there really any point to keeping the band alive?

Perhaps, like Tamagotchis and Myspace pages, the Glitter Bats are best left to past nostalgia. I, for one, am curious to see how they can come back from this blow.

Keep your eyes on the *Gossip Daily* Glitter Bats tag for updates!

28

✦ *Keeley* ✦

I'm at my parents' house for the holiday, helping them chop vegetables for turkey soup when we get the news. Oliver is the one who sees it first, reading the headline on his phone from his perch at the counter.

"*Fuck*," I hiss, dropping the knife. Fortunately, it hits the cutting board and not something more precious. My mind whirls as I try to make sense of what Oliver just read. I gesture for him to hand me the phone, and I read each line with more and more disbelief.

Tonya masterminded us. Again.

My blood boils with the urge to confront her immediately. She doesn't actually *want* our masters; she just wants the revenue, and maybe some control over Valerie if she can get it. It's diabolical. Tonya's becoming cartoonishly evil at this point.

I grab my own phone, step into the dining room, and call Landon fucking Banks. Miraculously, he answers his cell, instead of passing it through an assistant.

"This is Landon," he says.

"What the fuck?" I demand, pacing behind the table.

"Happy Thanksgiving to you too, KeeKee."

My shoulders tense at the endearment. "Thanksgiving was *yesterday*."

"Yes, I know. But it's polite to say it." When I don't say anything, he continues. "I got right back to work today, of course. Had to catch up from my vacation."

"I'm aware."

"Sorry it didn't go your way. That's how this industry works—sometimes you go all in and still lose."

My vision blurs. I knew better than to ever hope this man would let us win, but I chose to hope anyway. I chose to fight.

So the entire damn thing feels like a betrayal, but not by him. I feel like I betrayed myself by sinking so much time into this fight we were destined to lose. "This industry works the way *you* decide it does."

He laughs, and it makes my skin crawl. "I'm glad we're on the same page about that."

"But how could you fucking sell our music to Tonya?"

"It's just business."

"Business, huh?" I scoff, working at a smudge on the kitchen table. But something still doesn't add up. "How did Tonya know how much to offer to win outright like that? I thought all of the bids were supposed to be private." The whole situation was weird from the start.

"Hmm," he says. "I'm not really involved in the specifics."

Like hell he's not. "I see," I say bitterly.

"KeeKee, I don't understand why you're upset with me. It's not personal."

It's been personal for years. Art is always personal.

"You know what Tonya is capable of. She's going to hold this over Valerie, over *us*, for the rest of our careers."

He cackles, so cruelly it makes me flinch. "Oh, babe, I don't give a fuck what she does with your masters. When Tonya said she was interested, I saw an opportunity, and I took it."

"It's our music!"

"The way I see it, it's Tonya's music now. Good luck with that, by the way."

"Fuck you," I say, and I hang up. God, I cannot believe him. He never planned for us to win.

Landon strung us along for months, just because his ego was hurt that we refused to sign another record contract in blood. Goddamn it, I hate this industry.

Fuming, I stride into the kitchen.

"Well, we're fucked," I say. I head over to chop more vegetables, but I can't bring myself to pick them up.

"On the bright side, you're saving a lot of money," Mom says quietly from her spot at the sink, carefully drying the wineglasses she just washed.

I whirl on her. "Are you serious right now?"

"*Sasha*," Dad warns from across the kitchen, where he's pulling turkey off the bone. "Maybe now is not the time. She's clearly upset."

"Why not? Normal families fight over holidays. Let's join in the fun!" I snap.

Mom raises up her hands placatingly. "Keeley, please, I'm not trying to fight with you."

Ollie frowns. "Come on. You're not really mad at Mom, are you?"

Shaking, I lean into the counter. "I am!" I turn to Mom. "It just really fucking hurts that we lost our music to the one person who will hold it over our heads, and there's nothing I can do. I fought so hard to do this for the band. I was willing to pour in a big chunk of my savings—and I know you thought that was a bad idea, but how can investing in the people I love be bad?"

Mom sets the glass down and hurries over to me. "It's not bad. Oh, I love that you have such a big heart. I'm so proud of you."

"Then why have you been giving me such a hard time about this?"

"I just worry about you in that industry. You were on a path with security before you said no to college for your music, and now you're nearly thirty and facing so many unknowns . . . I just want you to be okay."

My eyes fill. "I'll be okay, Mom. I made this decision with my eyes wide open, and . . ." I gasp. "Even though it didn't pan out, I don't regret fighting for the band." Now that I've said the words, I know that they're true.

I don't regret a second of fighting for our music. Even if I knew we were going to lose, I wouldn't have let that stop me from trying.

"Oh, honey," Mom says, and she pulls me into her arms.

"But what if this is it? What if we can't come back from this?"

It feels like everything is spinning wildly out of control, and I'm just holding on for dear life. I can't stand the thought of losing the Glitter Bats again. I don't think I can *survive* losing Jane. This past week apart has been torture. When she was crying on the floor of my condo, all I wanted to do was pull her close and tell her it was going to be okay. All I wanted was to kiss her and hold her and protect her.

Instead, I had to let her walk away. Because that's what she needed.

Just . . . what if she realizes she *does* want to break up? I've loved this woman since we were kids, since we barely knew what love was. Maybe it took us more than a decade to find each other, but I survived years of wanting her from afar.

I'll survive the rest of my life like this if I must. I want her safe. I want her whole. Short of making Ryan Tate erase that article from existence, doing what she asked is literally the bare minimum. It doesn't matter if I'm breaking my own heart in the process.

Everything is breaking my heart this week, though, so might as well. With a squeeze, Mom lets me go, but she doesn't leave my side.

"Have you talked to Jane recently?" Oliver asks, as if reading my mind. People joke about twintuition, but it's a thing.

"I want to know that too," Dad says out of the blue.

"Pete!" Mom protests as my cheeks heat. Oliver rolls his eyes, as if this is the silliest conversation in the world, but Dad just pours us all some wine and passes it around as we stare at him.

"What? I want to know what's going on in my baby girl's life. Girlfriends, boyfriends, nonbinary friends . . . tell me the juicy details."

I take a sip, then set the glass down. "My personal life has been all over the internet, Dad. You've seen the latest update."

His shoulders fall. "But it didn't come from you."

God, he's right, and that's the whole problem. I wanted to be able to tell my parents that I'm with this woman I really care about, and instead they found out from the fucking internet.

"I always thought you and Jane would be sweet together," Mom says quietly. "The way it all came out, though . . . I would very much like to have a conversation with that Ryan boy and give him a piece of my mind. That was . . . some bullshit."

Mom and I are polar opposites, in that swearing is part of my vocabulary while Mom uses profanity as often as, well, Jane.

So, naturally, Oliver chokes on his own wine at her comment. "Sorry, I'm fine. Just . . . yeah, it was bullshit."

"I'm sorry, but there's no other way to put it," Mom says. "How's she doing?"

My neck flushes. "I, uh, don't know. We're taking a bit of a break."

"What?" Dad asks. "Why?"

I let out a long, extended sigh, staring at the wine on the counter deliberately, avoiding all the questioning gazes of the people who love me the most. "Because us being together was hurting her, and she asked for space to figure a few things out."

"I hope you know that's not a reflection on you, sweetheart," Mom says.

I shrug. Deep down, I wonder if maybe it *is* a reflection on me. Jane wouldn't need a break from me if I was helping her. But all I've done is hurt her.

"She may just need to emotionally process what's happening," Mom continues. "Jane didn't grow up with the support system you had. And, well, being publicly outed must be very traumatizing."

"Yeah, that's the issue. I just don't see a reason she should stay with me."

"And why not?" Dad demands.

I shrug. "She has this incredibly impressive career while I'm just playing my little drum kit. And fuck, like Mom said, she got *outed* because of me. I can't be the one holding her back or causing her pain."

"Oh, Keeley, that's not how any of this works," Mom says softly. She leans on the counter beside me, wrapping an arm around my shoulders again. My eyes sting, but I blink hard, trying to force away the sadness. "We can't avoid hurting the people we love. That's part of loving someone—choosing them even when it gets hard."

"This feels different," I say, sinking into my mom's embrace as the vegetables lie forgotten. "I can hardly breathe, knowing that I hurt her. Maybe now, this will all blow over and she can keep living her life on her terms. Without me."

"Is that what she wants?" Dad asks quietly, as he dumps turkey in the stockpot.

"I don't know," I say quietly. "She said it wasn't, but . . . maybe she was just sparing my feelings."

My voice breaks, and all the despair from the last few weeks comes crashing over me like a tidal wave. I can't remember the last time I cried like this, wrapped in my mom's arms, safe in the family home that still overflows with security and warmth and love. "I just don't want to lose her."

"I can't begin to understand how she's feeling, but maybe you should give her a chance to tell you before you make assumptions," Oliver says. "And for the record, I want to go back to that part where you think you're holding her back, because that's ridiculous. First of all, your worth is not tied to your accomplishments."

I snort. "Easy for you to say, Mr. Ivy League."

He ignores me, raising his voice. "And *second* of all, your career is impressive as hell."

I lean into Mom, shaking my head. "You're just trying to make me feel better," I mumble.

"Keeley, we are so incredibly proud of you," Dad says. "And if I wasn't elbow-deep in turkey, I'd be over there too. I don't know why you don't see how extraordinary you are, but we're here to remind you of that any time."

Mom squeezes me tighter. "You didn't take the path you originally intended, but you're doing something most people only dream of—making a living with your art!" I pull back, staring at her, trying to figure out if she's just pacifying me, but there's nothing but honesty in her eyes. And I know my mom: she doesn't say stuff just to make me feel better. "I know I haven't been the most understanding of your decisions recently, but that doesn't erase how proud of you I am. And maybe you can't see it because you're the one behind that kit, but you come alive whenever you're playing. Watching you do that every time you're on a stage—it's more than any parent could hope for. I just want you to pursue the things that set your heart on fire . . . and to be safe, of course."

I laugh through a sob, blinking up at my mom, who has never put a single condition on loving me. Then I glance over at my brother, who grins at me, in that way of his that tells me everything is going to be okay. And my dad, looking over at us all from the stove with that quiet, loving concern. "Maybe," I say. Then I wipe my eyes with the sleeves of my hoodie, resettling myself in the chair. "You shouldn't be comforting me, though. I really fucked Jane's life up."

Mom hums, squeezing me again. "None of your mistakes could make me love you less, Keeley, but loving Jane isn't a mistake. Part of being in an adult relationship is knowing you can't always protect the person you love from the world—you just have to make sure you're at their side through it all."

The problem is, I want to be by Jane's side. I just wish she'd let me.

After the soup is assembled and simmering, our parents slip outside to go on a chilly walk. I top off my wine and head into the living room, curling up on the soft leather couch in front of the gas fireplace. Oliver joins me a few minutes later.

"You okay?" he asks.

"Obviously not," I drawl. Resigned, I flop against the cushions, barely avoiding the slosh of wine over my glass. "I'm sad about losing our masters, but I'm also just fucking pissed."

I'm tired of feeling like I'm losing.

All of these horrible people in this industry keep taking things from us. It's like "All My Friends Are Vampires" was a fucking prophecy, and they really did take until there was nothing left. And now, we don't have control of that angry anthem about creative freedom or any of the rest of our catalog. It makes me see red.

"You have every right to be pissed," Oliver says.

"It's just . . . Ryan Tate, Landon Banks, Tonya Quinn . . . they hurt us and exploited us and took our power away. I wish there was something I could do to retaliate." I'm not proud of it, but I want some goddamn revenge.

Anything to feel like I'm taking back control.

"What if there was?" Oliver asks, resting his chin on his fist in thought.

I bolt upright, and then some of the wine does slosh over my hoodie. Thank god it's white. "What do you mean?"

He smirks. "We're speaking in hypotheticals here, right? I can't give you legal advice, and even if I could, this isn't advisable." My brother, the ever-ethical lawyer. I'd love for him to just get to the fucking point.

"Oh my god, just tell me," I say, my pulse roaring in my ears. Even not knowing where he's going with this, I can't fight back the ember of hope glowing in the back of my mind. It's the first time I haven't felt miserable since . . . well, since Jane left.

I wait for Oliver to continue. "If studying and practicing law has taught me anything, it's that every single CEO who's rich like Landon Banks is has skeletons. They break the law, have secret addictions, utilize business assets for personal gain." He pauses, like he's waiting for me to say something.

"And?"

Oliver grins, folding his hands together. "And, if you can find proof, you can report the asshole. He just put you through months of a legal battle? Figure out if you can dish it back."

Taking a long sip of wine, I consider his words. That all sounds great, but we're missing one major piece of this puzzle. "Sure, but rich men get away with that bullshit all the time. And I'm not Veronica Mars."

"They get away with it unless the legal system can't ignore it anymore." He raises his hands. "You're in an industry where you have a fuck ton of connections."

I blink. Maybe I'm just too drained, because I still have no idea where he's going with this. "Yeah, and?"

"So start connecting! Figure out what people know. Who is close to him. Who might have dirt. If you're discreet, and you play your cards right, you won't have to retaliate at all. His own actions might take him down."

I purse my lips. "Okay, but who . . . oh shit." I gesture with my phone. "Landon Banks had another messy divorce last year, and his ex-wife hangs out with Bianca."

A lot of people wouldn't just call their ex up out of the blue, but Bianca and I are still friendly. That's why I've gigged with her off and on since our breakup. And I know she'll help me if she can.

Oliver pumps his fist. "That's exactly what I'm talking about!"

"Bianca has a way of . . . getting people to open up." She doesn't do it on purpose; she's just really easy to talk to. "And if that doesn't work, well . . . I'm pretty sure Riker *does* know a PI." He always knows a guy.

It's as good of a place as any to start. With a shit-eating grin on my face, I text my ex. Surprisingly, for a holiday weekend, she texts me back right away and offers to make the introduction.

And then we get to fucking work.

29

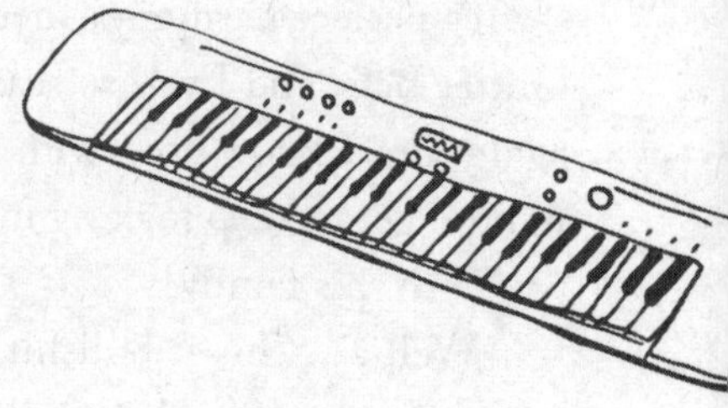

✦ *Jane* ✦

We have an emergency band meeting as soon as everyone is back in LA after the holiday. It's at my house, because I'm trying to stay there again, but . . . I'm still not completely comfortable being alone. It's nice to have the band with me.

The tension is thick where everyone huddles in the living room. Valerie is fuming, chaotic, fiddling with her rings and the fringe on the pillow she's holding in her lap. Caleb is next to her on my sectional, stoic and solemn, one hand on his partner's knee and the other clutching a mug of tea. Riker is sulking, his arms crossed from his spot across from them. And Keeley, well, leans against the wall, and I've never seen her this resigned.

She fought so hard for us to win back our masters, and now that chance is gone forever. It takes more restraint than I thought I possessed not to cross the space between us, wrap my arms around her, and tell her it's going to be okay.

The thing is, I don't know if that's true. I didn't realize how much I wanted to gain control of our masters until we lost them. All of my resistance about moving on with the band feels so inconsequential compared to what I have, in this room. These four people who I feel so alive with when we make music together, who show up for me on the best and worst days of my life, who, time and again, prove to me that I'm not alone.

It's perfect harmony. There is something so special about the Glitter Bats, and I was so scared to go all in just in case we lost it again. But I know now, with so much certainty, that I'm going to fight to get to keep making music with them.

With this family.

"Well . . . this is bullshit," Valerie says, but no one has a response for that. She shifts in her seat, folding her legs into a pretzel as we fall into silence again. No one knows what to say.

The only consolation is that we held on to the money. We pooled enough that we could make our own album *without* a label, if we wanted to be that bold.

"Have you heard from Tonya?" Riker asks, finally acknowledging the neon elephant in the room.

Valerie lets out a huff, fluffing up her bangs. "She blocked my fucking number."

"I, uh, also tried. It went to voicemail once, and then she blocked mine too," Caleb says quietly.

"I'm not giving up. I want to say she can't ignore me forever, but that's giving my dear mother too much credit. I'm pretty sure she skipped off to Europe after taking everything from us."

"I would like to fight Tonya Quinn," Keeley mutters. "Landon Banks too. He all but told me she won the bid because of information from him, so I did some digging." And then she smirks. "It turns out Landon has a bit of a gambling problem. I found that out from his ex-wife."

"What?" Caleb demands. "When?"

"Last night, actually. She was looking for a discreet PI after her last one did nothing, and Riker's contact took a surprisingly little amount of time to get the details. It turns out the company is at risk of bankruptcy, and we were one of their biggest assets. Landon needed the capital, so he not only sold our masters, but sold a huge share of Label Records a few days before the sale, while he was conveniently still overseas."

Riker beams. "I told you he could help."

"Jesus Christ," Valerie says. "Isn't that . . . illegal?"

Keeley nods. "It just fucking might be fraud. I'm not sure what we discovered is enough to take him down, but his ex is hoping it's enough to expose his shady dealings."

"And you don't think she's just helping you out with an ulterior motive?" Caleb asks.

"No." Keeley shakes her head. "He cheated her out of some family assets with a badly written prenup. This is personal for her too, and we're hoping Landon was stupid enough to leave some loose ends. Tonya is certainly not discreet."

Valerie nods. "Mom's a big spender, but I can't imagine her making this happen alone. It wouldn't be the first time she conspired with Label for her own ends."

I swallow, trying to phrase my next question carefully. "Is there any appealing to Tonya? Would she maybe let us buy the masters from her?" What I don't say is that even if she was open to it, her asking price would be astronomical. Tonya knows how much we want this. Maybe she's been planning to exploit that all along.

"I really doubt there's any chance of getting through to her." Valerie's voice breaks, and Caleb pulls her into his shoulder as she blinks back tears.

"She's been freezing us out since we didn't invite her to our wedding," Caleb says quietly.

"That makes no sense," Riker says. "She wasn't even in Vegas when you eloped."

"Yeah, well, you know Tonya."

Keeley scoffs. "Unfortunately, we do."

Tonya assumes the worst in everyone, and holds grudges for the smallest of slights, so not being present at Valerie's wedding is probably a hill she will die on for eternity.

"I really don't think she'd sell them to us even if we offered her double what she paid," Valerie says. "And we don't have that kind of money even if she'd *take* it. We already went all in and still lost. And, well . . ." She sniffs. "This is about the control she lost when we fired her. She's also still mad at me for the boundaries I set last year. I feel so helpless, but I'm truly sorry for the position I've put you all in. This is all my fault."

"It's not," Keeley says. "Valerie, your mom fucking sucks, but you're not responsible for her actions." Valerie flashes Keeley a small, grateful smile. Valerie and Keeley have not always gotten along, but they have a bond all the same. "I need you to trust me, Quinn. I don't want you to be holding all of this pressure on your shoulders alone. We can figure this out together."

"Hell yeah, we can," Riker says. "But, uh, any ideas for how to do that? I'll take anything."

"Do we rerecord?" Valerie says, just as Caleb says, "I think we should make a new album." They share a look, and Caleb just shrugs, threading his fingers through Valerie's. The room falls silent, the only sound the wick of the vanilla candles I set out on the mantle.

"I think we should rerecord. If we make the masters worthless, Tonya loses, and it makes Landon look like a fool," Keeley says.

"There's some merit to that, but I think we should make a new album," Riker says. "The best way to move on is to make something they can't touch."

Valerie groans and rolls her eyes. "Jane, you're the deciding vote."

"Are we really at that point?" Caleb asks. Valerie elbows him, but I nod. It feels like we've been dancing around the decision since that cease and desist. There are two different ways to move forward, and I agree with both sides of the argument.

If we make a new album, we get to make the music we *want* to make and have something of ours that Label Records can never touch. Landon Banks can't take credit for our success. Tonya Quinn won't see a dime. And it'll be ours. As a band, our philosophy has been to never put the notebooks down, to constantly learn and grow and get better, to always be ready for our next song. With a new album, that's what we get to do.

But . . . we worked so hard on *Wanderlust*, *Bittersweet*, and *More to Say*. Some of it may be juvenile, but our lives changed making those albums, and they're snapshots of how we felt at three distinct points in time. With *Wanderlust*, we were teenagers with big dreams, just kids who knew nothing about the music industry but desperately wanted to make music that resonated with people. With *Bittersweet*, we were in our early twenties, still basically kids getting our first taste of fame, simultaneously angry at how we were being treated like commodities but inspired that people all around the world wanted to celebrate our songs. And with *More to Say*, we were fresh off a reunion after six years apart, older and wiser, more mature and seasoned and ready to take some big risks together that paid off.

It doesn't feel right to leave those songs behind.

I know what to do.

"Let's do both," I say. Everyone stares at me, taken aback. "I know it's a lot of work, but there's no reason we can't reclaim what's ours and also look to the future."

For the first time since she got here, Keeley's eyes spark. "Are you sure? That's a big commitment."

"I'm sure," I say. "I'm ready to commit to this."

Something passes between us, and it doesn't feel like I'm talking about the band.

Riker shrugs. "Sounds like a fucking plan. I'm in."

Valerie nods. "Me too. I know schedules are tough, but this is worth it."

Caleb brings their hands to his lips, kissing the back of Valerie's. "Okay. As long as we can make it work, I'm in. We'll have to find a new label, but I'm hoping that's not too hard."

We all look to Keeley, who is still looking right at me. "Nothing could keep me away."

I really hope *she's* not just talking about the band.

For the rest of the evening, we get to work, settling down in my music room with guitars and my new keyboard. We go through all of the songs we've been writing over the past few months, and we talk about what a new album might look like. Remarkably, "Too Much," the song Valerie, Caleb, and Riker were cowriting, fits right in with "Possibilities," even though Keeley and I avoid each other's gazes while we play it for the others. Then Valerie and Caleb pull out a notebook of ideas they've been working on ever since they got back together.

And it's better than good. It's incredible.

As the night winds down, we're bleary-eyed but smiling, having retreated back to my living room. It's late. But we've got the makings of a new album, and it gives me so much hope I just might burst.

"So we're all set to meet with Wade and legal to talk about rerecording next week," Riker says, gesturing with his phone. "But this feels good, doesn't it?" He steps into his shoes and grabs his bag.

"It feels amazing," Valerie says, her eyes watering as Caleb helps her into her leather jacket.

Keeley smiles, just a little, and it makes me go weak in the knees. "I love you assholes. You know that, right?"

Valerie beams, throwing her arms around Keeley, then Riker, then me. Something about tonight feels like old times, but also so much better, because we're taking control of our own futures.

Together.

Keeley moves to reach for her sneakers, but the thought of her leaving makes panic surge through me. Before I can stop myself, I grab her wrist.

Her breath catches.

"Can you, uh, stay for a minute?" I ask.

Keeley blinks. "Uh, yeah. Of course."

Caleb smirks as he leads Valerie out the door before she can say anything. Riker salutes on his way out, and I roll my eyes.

And then we're alone in my house. For a moment, I just stare at her, speechless. I know I'm the one who put this distance between us, so I need to be the one who closes it. But all of the words fly out of my head as I look at this woman I care about so much. Keeley looks as gorgeous as ever, even this casual in baggy jeans and that green sweater that I know is incredibly soft from the last time she embraced me in it.

My pulse races. I'm terrified of what comes next, worried I've hurt her too much to even hope there's a path forward, but she makes me feel brave.

"Keeley, I . . ."

"Jane—"

We laugh as we cut each other off.

"You go," she says softly, tucking a blond lock behind her ear, twisting one of her piercings as she does it. She's *nervous*, and that alone is enough to make me want to throw my arms around her and tell her everything I've been holding in my heart.

So I do.

"I don't want space. In fact, space is the literal last thing I want." I take a steadying breath, praying to whomever is listening that I'm not too late. "I love you, and I'm sorry."

30

✦ *Keeley* ✦

I blink at Jane as her words wash over me.

Jane loves me.

Jane loves me.

Jane *loves* me.

I just . . . stare at this girl who makes my head spin. It's been such a marvel to see her so determined to fight for this band, and it has taken every ounce of restraint not to throw myself at her feet and beg her to let me back in.

And now she's done it, and I don't know how to respond, because I can't believe she beat me to those words. I'm speechless.

She blinks rapidly, her cheeks going pink. "But, if that's not enough, or it's not where your head is at and you need us to take a more permanent break, I totally get it, and—"

"Jane, stop," I say, stepping closer to her. That, at least, gets her attention. I hate that even my moment of silence made her feel anything less than what she is: worth every effort in the world. Because she's more than enough.

She's everything.

"Jane, I love you too," I say, unable to fight the smile on my face. I grip her hands in each of mine. "But are you sure this is what you want?"

She squeezes my hand. "I believe we're worth fighting for, and I hope you do too."

Tears prick the back of my eyes. "Of course I do. Whatever the future looks like, I want you there." I release one of her hands, tucking a stray curl behind her ear, dragging my fingertips down her jaw with gentle care.

She sighs at the contact, but I don't dare try to kiss her. Not until I've said everything I need to say.

"Jane Mercer, I love you." Teardrops slip down her cheeks now, and I brush them away with my thumbs, leaning my forehead against hers as my own tears return. "I am so fucking in love with you that when I wake up, you're the first thing in my thoughts, and you stay with me all day, whether we're together or apart. I'm so fucking in love with you it keeps me up at night when you're not in my bed, close enough for me to hold tight. Hell, I'm so fucking in love with you that I've filled my place with vanilla candles for years because they reminded me of your perfume. And I'm so fucking in love with you that I will get on a plane and face your family with you, if that's what you want. But I would run away to a sheep farm in *Ireland* if you thought being away from the goddamn media would keep you safe."

"I know." Jane nods. "I love you, Keeley."

A shaky breath escapes my lips. "Thank god for that." My voice breaks.

"Now will you please kiss me already? I've missed you so much."

Who am I to argue with that? Carefully, softly, I pull her mouth to mine. A tiny sob escapes her as our lips meet, and I slip my arms around her, pulling her flush against me, desperate to soothe all the ways I know she's still hurting. She tastes like rosé from the bottle we polished off an hour ago, and a bit salty from our tears, but also like coming home.

I never want to leave her again.

Jane's fingers tangle in my hair as she deepens the kiss, swiping her tongue against mine, devouring me with purpose, like she's on a mission and I'm the objective. I open to her, reveling in the delicious heat of her mouth. There's something different tonight, something desperate, and it's almost enough to undo me right in the middle of her living room.

"Fuck, I need you naked," Jane says.

I smirk, pulling her closer. "That can be arranged."

Grinning, Jane tugs me up the stairs, past that goddamn window, and into her lamplit room. It smells like vanilla and her fabric softener, and I practically swoon. She shuts the door behind us, then kisses me again, walking me back until I hit the bed and sink onto the quilt. Jane tugs off her sweater, then lets down her hair, those glorious curls cascading down her back.

My mouth goes dry, and I'm unable to do anything but stare at her as she shimmies off her jeans, then unhooks her bra, exposing those most perfect breasts to the warm light.

"You're behind," she says, gesturing at me.

"Help me then," I say, smirking at her.

Jane settles onto the bed, so she's straddling my thighs, and lowers her lips to my ear. "You're lucky I love you."

"So goddamn lucky," I whisper, grabbing her chin and capturing her mouth for a kiss. It's long and deep and sinfully sweet. Without breaking the kiss, she grabs the hem of my sweater, her fingers grazing the skin just above my jeans. I shudder at the perfectness of that careful touch, my skin pebbling. When I draw back for air, Jane tugs the sweater and my T-shirt over my head in one go.

"Better?" I ask.

"Not quite," she says. She runs her hands over my arms and rib cage, leaving more goose bumps in her wake. Her touch skates across my skin, sending a thrill down my spine as she traces my tattoo on her way around my back to unclasp my bra. "Almost there," she says.

I bite my lip as I undo the button of my jeans, tugging them down along with my underwear, then throwing them in the direction of the floor. Who fucking cares where they land.

"Now you're the one who's overdressed," I say, gesturing at the black lace of her panties.

Jane arches a brow. "Guess I am," she says, and then her weight is off of me as she rises up. Slowly, so painfully slowly, she runs her hands over her waist and hips until they find the lace. "Am I doing this right?" she asks with a wicked grin.

"You're such a tease," I say, but I've lost all cool, and it comes out in a whimper.

Finally, Jane tugs down her panties, sliding them down those perfect thighs until they've disappeared from my view. And then we're both naked, and she's climbing on top of me, and I'm so in awe of how incredible her skin feels against mine.

"You love when I'm a tease," she whispers.

"I love *you*," I say.

She grins, and it would be enough to make my knees weak if I weren't already trembling beneath her. "I love you too."

And then we're kissing and it's all a tangle of skin and heat. Her hand reaches between my thighs, sending static across my skin as her fingers find the place I want them most. Unable to restrain myself, I reach for her too, desperate to feel the slick heat of her cunt under my touch.

Even as pleasure ripples through my body, I'm overcome at just how much this moment means to me. I get to hold Jane. I get to *love* her. And I don't have to let her go.

"You're perfect like this," she murmurs after a while, as we find a rhythm. There's something so intimate about getting each other off at the same time, still being able to kiss her and hold her and press our bodies *so close* until we're breathless.

"So are you," I say, and I mean it. "*Fuck*."

I feel so much tonight it's overwhelming, and by the shining look in her eyes, I know I'm not alone.

Then we're gripping each other tighter and kissing frantically and sighing each other's names until we both fall over the edge, slick with sweat and gasping. And in this moment, I know I want nothing more than to spend my nights with this woman for the rest of my life. By the way she's smiling softly at me and whispering, "I love you," on repeat like a prayer, I think she might feel the same.

After another round in her shower, when we're lying in her sheets, sated and happy, Jane turns to me.

"Were you serious about coming with me to Nora's wedding?"

I nod. "Of course. Wherever you go, I want to be right at your side." It comes out more fiercely than I intend, but I mean every word.

"Okay," she says, nodding resolutely. "Then there's something I have to do first."

She pulls out her phone, showing me the draft of the email. My eyes widen as I read the words. I'm proud that she's come to this conclusion for herself, but it also makes me anxious.

"Are you sure this is what you want?" I ask her. "Once you do this, you can't take it back."

"I'm so sure," she says. "It's time. I don't want to hide anymore."

"I don't want you just doing this for me," I whisper.

Jane pulls me closer, and the heat of her skin against mine is a balm for my nerves. "I'm doing this for *us*, but also for me. I've spent years terrified of being known, letting people decide *for* me who I was going to be, but honestly? Fuck that. They can have all of me or leave me alone, but I'm done concealing who I am from the world."

"Okay," I say. "Then at least let me be there to hold your hand."

"I wouldn't dream of keeping you away."

EXCLUSIVE PROFILE:
Jane Mercer

BY MARY KATE HAMPTON, SENIOR STAFF WRITER, *BUZZWORD*

Jane Mercer sits in the beautiful living room of her beach house, looking chic in white jeans, an oversized navy sweater, and brown loafers, draped in a cascade of necklaces. There's tea on the end table next to her, and when I ask what she's drinking, she tells me it's the ginger-peach blend she likes to sip on when she's singing.

MKH: Thank you so much for joining me for this interview. I'm mortified that it took us so long to make it happen.
JM: That's okay. Both of our schedules have been hectic.

Mercer is being generous. I was traveling at the beginning of December, and when I did return, our calendars were almost laughably at odds.

But we were both determined to make this happen, and I'm glad we did.

Mercer's house is as warm as the woman who inhabits it. The room we're in is bright and colorful: soft green walls, wainscotting with a fresh coat of ivory paint, wood floors adorned with area rugs in peaches and yellows and blues. There are plants on bookshelves and tables and even on top of the electric fireplace, but Mercer tells me there used to be more before her house flooded earlier this fall.

JM: [smiles softly] That's what forced Keeley and I to confront our feelings—good old-fashioned forced proximity. My house was a wreck, and I needed somewhere to stay.

MKH: Confront your feelings? So this wasn't new?
JM: [laughs] Not at all. I've been in love with Keeley Cunningham since I was seventeen, when I met her at music camp. I'd already figured out I was bisexual by then, but if I hadn't, I'm positive I would have had a proper awakening during that fateful summer when we formed Glitter Bats.

I won't rehash the video that Ryan Tate and Gossip Daily *released of the two, because it was obvious our rival publication captured an intimate moment that wasn't intended for the public eye. When Mercer approached me to do this interview, I made it clear to her this would be on her terms. For that, I have promised not to edit a single word of her statements. In an effort to be transparent, I have sent the voice recording to my editor at* Buzzword *for accountability, and the transcript will be posted at the end of this article with Mercer's express permission. Mercer also approved many of my questions in writing prior to our discussion, including the following.*

MKH: When *did* you figure out you were bisexual?
JM: I, uh, had figured it out the summer before, at church camp. There was this new girl in my cabin, and something about her just . . . opened up my universe to possibilities. I'd had crushes on boys before, and I knew people *could* be bi, in theory. I just didn't realize I was. Coming from a religious upbringing . . . it was never something I even considered to be a possibility. Until we ran off from the bonfire one night

to go sit on the docks and watch the moonlight on the river, and she asked if she could kiss me. I kissed her first, because even though I was terrified, I *wanted* to, and then . . . I knew.

Mercer pauses for a moment, stuck in the memory, and I give her a second before continuing.

MKH: That sounds like a pretty great queer awakening. How do you feel about it?
JM: [laughs ruefully] It was great until our counselor caught us making out in the woods the next day.

MKH: Wow. What happened next?
JM: It was intense. We both got sent home, and they said we weren't welcome back the following summer. I told the director I would be responsible and confess to my parents what happened. The director thought I was a good kid who had been "led astray," so they didn't push it. They just sent me home with a promise, and I acted like I would keep it in sheer self-preservation. But I couldn't tell my parents. They wouldn't understand.

MKH: What did you tell your parents instead?
JM: [smirks] I told them I went home because I was getting headaches from the heat.

MKH: And how did they take that?
JM: They bought it without question, and I think it's because it never occurred to them that their perfect church girl would lie. I thought I'd feel guilty for this thing I was told was a sin, but there was something so freeing about . . . well,

understanding myself, and I couldn't wrap my head around what I was even supposed to "confess." The next summer, I knew I couldn't go back to the same camp, but I had to get out of the house. So I convinced my parents to send me to music camp instead, and that's where I met Riker, Valerie, Caleb, and Keeley. Well, Keeley and I went to the same high school, but we didn't really know each other until then.

Glitterbugs, this is one hell of a piece to break out at trivia.

MKH: So, would it be safe to say you met the Glitter Bats *because* you're queer, and no one in the band influenced you in any way?
JM: [sobers] I know people think I'm not online right now, but I definitely am. There's been a lot of talk that Keeley preyed on me, or influenced me somehow to make me want to be with her. But it's all completely untrue—and honestly, more than a little insulting to both of us. I knew I was bi before I ever met her. Believe me, I know what people are saying, but it wasn't like that at all.

MKH: What was it like, then?
JM: What happens between any people in a relationship who really care about each other? I fell head over heels in love with her. All I ever wanted was to get to be with someone who saw me for me, and that's always been Keeley.

MKH: It sounds like you two have something special. But why are you coming forward now, so many weeks after everything happened?
JM: I mean, the video certainly disrupted my plans to keep my sexuality hidden. [sighs] It's lonely, hiding pieces of

yourself away from the world. There were ways to stay quiet after what happened, and I was trying to figure out what was best for me, which is why I didn't speak out right away.

MKH: Do you feel pressure to be public about your identity now?
JM: Yes and no. It's strange, being a celebrity. I don't even consider myself all that famous, but people still think they're owed details about your personal life if you're in the public eye at all, and it's deeply violating. It's especially rampant in regards to queer identities in entertainment. But with everyone making assumptions, I wanted to set the record straight.

MKH: How are you feeling about taking your sexuality public?
JM: It's definitely intimidating. There are people in my life who don't understand, who have already distanced themselves from me. But one thing I learned growing up the way I did is that love isn't expecting someone to be something they're not. Love is embracing all parts of another person and letting them shine for who they are. I'm already out to the people who truly love me, and they all support me. The rest doesn't matter. And if me being out and proud helps even one fan feel freer to be themselves, well, then it's worth it. I spent so much time being afraid that I forgot what power I have being in this industry. I want to use it for good.

I don't usually talk about myself in interviews, because I think it's often distracting and unprofessional, but this interview was unconventional from the start. Given the subject matter, I felt it was important for me to be upfront about my own identity. There are queer people working in every industry, and representation is such an important part of progress.

MKH: **Well, I think you're brave. And as a bisexual fan, I just want to tell you how meaningful it is for you to come forward like this.**
JM: Thank you, that means a lot.

MKH: **Is there anything you want to add before we wrap up?**
JM: I just want to reiterate that while I do feel some pressure to be out, talking to you was entirely my choice, and I don't regret it. But I wish we lived in a world where it wasn't a *sensation* to see two women kissing, and it could just be accepted for what it is: a perfectly normal relationship. Until we live in that world, this is going to keep happening. I'm really lucky to have a support system around me that will never disappear just because I was honest about who I am. Because the most honest thing I can say is that I love Keeley Cunningham with my entire heart, and being with her makes me the happiest I've ever been.

MKH: **I'm rooting for you. Thank you for your time, Jane.**
JM: Thank you, Mary Kate. I appreciate you sharing your platform with me.

31

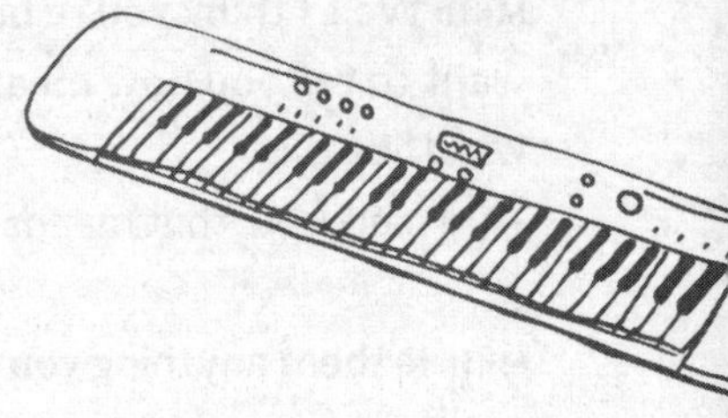

Jane

"Zip me up?" I ask, as I struggle to fasten the navy lace cocktail dress.

"I'll be right out," Keeley calls from the en suite of her parents' guest bedroom.

I meant it when I told Keeley I have no regrets. I want her, consequences be damned. But that doesn't make my anxiety feel any less pressing as we get ready at Keeley's childhood home for my sister's wedding on New Year's Eve.

After a long, tear-filled conversation over the phone, Nora and I agreed that it's best if I'm not in the bridal party, but I was determined to be there tonight however I could. My sister just made me promise that if I came to the wedding, I wouldn't show up alone. It didn't feel like that was totally up to me, but Keeley was in the moment I asked, and I knew I would be able to rely on her for strength.

I can face my parents with her by my side.

We spent Christmas with the Cunninghams and Riker, who tagged along before he had to go back to LA, and there was something so special about celebrating the holiday with people I could be my full self around.

Keeley steps out of the bathroom into the guest room, and walks over to me, her eyes slowly grazing over my figure in the mirror.

"Holy fuck, you look stunning," she murmurs, stepping up behind me. I can feel the heat of her post-shower body through the thin fabric of my dress, and all I want to do is turn around and get lost in her the way I have every night since we ended our break . . .

And again this morning, before we snuck upstairs for coffee and pastries.

Keeley tugs the zipper up slowly, her fingers tracing from my lower back all the way up my spine to my neck. I can't help it; I lean a little into that touch that leaves sparks across my skin.

"You smell amazing too," she rasps. I knew putting on my fancier vanilla perfume would pay off. Now that I know just how much she's into my favorite scent, I'm using that information. Intentionally.

I glance up at her in the mirror, and her heavily lined eyes lock on mine. "I wish we could just stay here and . . ."

She smirks. "As much as I want to make you come apart all over my face again, we really should fuck somewhere other than my parents' basement."

I laugh, rolling my eyes at her. Still, I spin around and tug on the soft collar of her ivory satin dress shirt and pull her down for a kiss. She smiles against my mouth, extricating herself before we can get too carried away.

"Come on," she says. "We can do more of this later."

"I'm holding you to that," I say, stepping back to get a good look at her. She's got the shirt tucked into midnight-blue suit pants with a matching jacket and loafers, and she looks as gorgeous like this as when she wears a gown. She's got her bob styled in a chic, smooth blowout instead of her usual unkempt tousled waves, but she still looks so much like herself.

Perfectly breathtaking in every way.

“Stop looking at me like you want to take my clothes off,” she murmurs, reaching out to thread her fingers through mine.

“The suit is definitely working for me,” I say, pressing a kiss to her hand before following her up the stairs.

“Oh my god, look at you two!” Sasha Cunningham squeals as we enter her warm, cinnamon-scented kitchen. “Jane Mercer, aren’t you just the most beautiful girl I have ever seen?”

I flush a little at the attention.

“I’d be offended if she was wrong, but she’s not,” Keeley says dryly, leaning her elbows against the counter.

“Oh, honey, you know you look fantastic too. God, I’m so happy the two of you agreed to stay with us through the holidays! This is the first time Keeley has brought a partner home in years, and I just . . .” Sasha trails off, shaking her head. “I hope we’ll be seeing a lot more of you, Jane.”

My throat tightens at the casual acceptance in this home. If it hadn’t been the Pride progress flag on the porch, there are a hundred other things that have happened over the past week that would have convinced me I was safe here. Whether it was Pete pulling me into the study to make sure I was okay after the interview dropped on Christmas Eve, or Sasha making my favorite cinnamon rolls for breakfast (with Riker’s enthusiastic help), or even Oliver cornering Keeley and me on Christmas morning and asking to talk to both of us . . . and then threatening Keeley with bodily harm if she hurts me, I know this family is full of people I can trust.

People who I think might be my family someday, if I’m lucky. That hope is a small flicker in my chest, but it burns brighter with every new moment Keeley and I share together. I can’t believe I’m here, “meeting” her parents. They already know me, sure, but this time really feels different.

And while a part of me would rather be here, safe with the Cunninghams, it's time to go face my own family.

"We should probably hit the road," I say. "I'm sorry, Sasha."

"Oh, nonsense," Sasha says, waving a dismissive hand. "You two should head out to beat the traffic. But, Jane?" She gently places a hand on my elbow. "If your parents give you grief and you want to leave, you make an escape as soon as you congratulate your sister. We'll cook up a nice vegetarian chili and open a big bottle of wine tonight instead. Do you hear me?"

"Yes, ma'am," I say.

Sasha pulls me into a hug, so careful not to touch my makeup or hair, but still so much warmer than the perfunctory embraces I'm used to from my mother that it almost breaks me all over again. This isn't the first Sasha Cunningham hug I've gotten this week, and I'm kind of addicted to them.

"Okay, enough, Mom. You're going to suffocate my girlfriend," Keeley says. I try not to preen at those words, but I can't help it. They make me happier than ever.

With a laugh, Sasha pulls back, and then Pete is shoving us out the door with reminders that the car is charged and to drive safe. And then we head to the main event. My stomach does backflips for the entire fifty-minute trip to the venue.

We find parking with an hour to spare, but I wanted to be sure to arrive early to get any awkwardness out of the way. The venue is in the basement of a beautiful historic building that has been renovated, with stone walls and exposed wooden beams and soft light filling the room from strategically placed sconces and candles. There are lush flower arrangements lining the aisle, and the altar is draped in white satin.

While Keeley heads to find our seats, I decide to go find Nora.

"You sure you don't want backup?" she asks.

I nod. "I think it's best if I try to do this alone."

She nods, her expression turning solemn. "Okay, well, just say the word and I'm there."

"I know."

With a squeeze of her hand, I slip away. A friendly staff member in all black points me down a hall and to the right, and I find a room with BRIDE on a rustic wooden sign next to the door. But before I can knock, my mom steps out, resplendent in a soft, sage-green mother-of-the-bride dress. Personally, I think it matches the bridesmaid dress I was supposed to wear a little *too* much, but I'm not about to say that.

"Jane," she says. "Nice of you to show up."

I set my jaw. Mom wants to get a rise out of me, and I'm not going to let her.

"I had a conversation with Nora, and we decided this was best."

Her nostrils flare as she steps toward me, lowering her voice. "You shouldn't be here *at all*, after that abomination of an article. I didn't raise you to live in sin." My heart hammers as she berates me, but I don't feel guilty. I feel free. "You'd better not have . . ."

"Jane, you're finally here!" Nora interrupts excitedly, from behind Mom. She's not in her dress yet, but her strawberry-blond hair is pulled back in an elegant half-updo, and her complexion glows with dewy makeup. She looks more like a forest nymph than a bride, and it's the perfect look to accompany her gown.

"Nora," I say, stepping past Mom into the room to hug my sister, careful to avoid touching her face or hair. I pull back, looking at her. "Wow, you look beautiful."

"This room is for the bridal party only," Mom snaps. "Jane made her choice."

"Well, I made a choice to invite my sister," Nora says. "Thank you for coming."

"I wouldn't miss it," I say, and I mean it. Mom can be a homophobic piece of work if she wants to be, but Nora insisted she wanted me here, and nothing could keep me away.

Nora leans past me. "Is Keeley here?"

I nod. "Yeah, she went to find our seats."

Nora beams. "I'm glad."

Mom flushes, so red I can't ignore it, even in my periphery. "This is just absurd."

Nora surprises me by striding past me, getting right in Mom's face. "This is my day, and I want my sister here. I'll never forgive you if you ruin it by being rude to her *or* her girlfriend.

Mom presses a hand to her chest dramatically. "I can't believe I raised such *willful* daughters. Maybe paying for this wedding was a mistake. Nora, you're clearly not mature enough to handle getting married if you think what Jane is doing is remotely—"

"Mom!" I snap. "I need to talk to you and Dad. Right now. Where is he?"

"Jane!" I go cold at the raised voice of my father from behind me. I turn around to see him in the hall, already dressed in his simple black suit, a white boutonniere tucked into his lapel. Since the last time I've seen him, he's gained a few more wrinkles, and he's shaved off all of his balding hair.

Mom runs over to him like she's gotten someone else on her team, but he puts up a palm. "Anne, beloved, what's going on?"

"Our oldest daughter wants to talk to us, because apparently that's more important right now than everything else going on. I'm simply too busy for this."

I clench my fists.

"That's what the wedding coordinator is for!" Nora says, too brightly. "You can talk to Jane. Nothing will fall apart for five minutes." I flash her a grateful look.

With a huff, Mom stomps off down the hall, her thick heels clacking on the stone.

Dad follows her. Unsure of what else to do, I follow them down the hall and around the corner, past a sign that says GROOM, to a small lounge set up with coffee and sandwiches.

"They set this up for the families, but we've been spending the day with the kids, helping them get ready and making last-minute preparations." He frowns. "So what did you need to talk to us about?"

I blink, stunned. "Haven't you seen . . . the article?"

Mom lets out a shriek, then sinks onto one of the chairs, holding a handkerchief to her forehead.

"We're not talking about that today; it will just upset your mother," Dad says. "Now, if you're ready to repent, that's another conversation—"

"Repent?" I ask, on a laugh. I should have expected this, but his audacity still shocks me a little. "Are you serious right now?"

Dad crosses his arms. "We never should have let you join a rock band. Of course you were led astray by that sinful lifestyle."

"Led astray?" I shake my head in disbelief. "I'm *thirty*, Dad!"

"It doesn't matter how old you are; you need to be spiritually disciplined. We raised you on biblical teachings. What you're doing, it's not a Christian way of living."

I could have guessed the talking points verbatim, but that doesn't make them sting any less. "Well it's a good thing I'm no longer a Christian, then. And by the way, your interpretation of the Bible is one of the many, many reasons for that," I say.

"Keep your voice down," Mom hisses, glancing behind me at what I'm positive is still a very empty hallway.

I swallow. My parents raised me to be quiet, compliant, and never cause a scene. They're more worried by the idea someone might overhear us than the fact that they're pushing me away with their hate. But I'm done pretending to be the good girl they so desperately wanted.

I am done making myself small just to please them.

"No," I scoff, crossing my arms. "This is who I am: a bisexual atheist who makes secular music for a living. Congratulations—you've finally met your daughter."

Dad's eyes flash. "I've known there was something wrong from the moment you joined that band, but to learn it started years before . . . the devil has a hold of you, Jane. Those band members of yours helped him gain a stronger foothold."

Wow. I knew he'd go there, but it doesn't make it any less absurd.

"My bandmates are some of the best people I know! They care about other people, and they use their influence for good. And for the record, I'd bet the Jesus depicted in your precious Bible wouldn't care if I love a woman, as long as I treat other people well."

Mom huffs. "You can't *love* a woman, Jane. It's just lust. You can be set free of this sin."

And then I laugh. I really laugh. Because I'm the happiest I've ever been, and she can't wrap her head around that without letting her worldview cast shadows upon it all. When I was younger, I might have let her gaslight me.

Now, I know how to stand tall.

"I don't want to be set free. I do *love* Keeley. She makes me so incredibly happy, and she treats me with kindness and respect. Don't *you* love me enough to be excited I've found that?"

Dad's face goes red, and he starts to splutter. Mom takes the opening.

"How could we be excited? We've truly lost you," she says.

I place my hands on my hips. "I'm really sad that you think so, because you're missing out on a relationship with your daughter. My life is so much better than it ever was when I was catering to your expectations, and you should be sad that you're not a part of it. Because I'm awesome, actually." And I can't help it, I smile, even though my parents are melting down in front of me.

Because I don't need their approval. I lost it, and I'm still standing. They don't get to dictate how I live, or who I love.

I'm enough.

"Anne, Hank, you need to back off," a voice says. We all look at the doorway to see Danny in his suit, alongside a stone-faced Keeley.

"Danny, this is a family matter," my dad begins.

Danny, to his eternal credit, isn't cowed. He just crosses his arms and raises a brow. "Yeah, and I'm about to be your family, unless that toast you gave at the rehearsal dinner was meaningless."

My dad's jaw ticks.

"And I'm Jane's," Keeley says, her eyes not leaving mine. I beam at her.

"I know Nora would back me up on this, because she called me as soon as you left the bridal suite," Danny says. "So I'm only going to say this once: you two can be welcoming to Jane and Keeley, our *guests*, or you can leave."

My parents both splutter, but Danny stands his ground. I'm starting to understand what my sister sees in this guy. But I don't want to be the person ruining her day.

"No, it's fine," I say. "Keeley and I will keep to ourselves, because we're here for *Nora*." I turn back to my parents. "But after today, I'm done with both of you unless some major things change. If you're going to keep telling me what I do is a sin, do not call me. Do not visit my home. Don't send me so much as a text message. If you want a relationship with me, you need to accept who I am with open arms. Until then, well, I guess you only have one daughter. You'd better not screw that up because she's already seeing past your bullshit."

My pulse roars in my ears, but the words don't feel bad coming out of my mouth. They feel powerful. I've been so afraid of losing their approval that I've hidden myself for far too long.

I'm done hiding. They don't get to bring me into this world, then decide to love me conditionally. I was terrified to have this conversation. Terrified, for so many years, that it would wreck me. But I'm fine. I'm more than fine.

I'm free to be exactly who I want to be.

There are members of my family who accept me for who I am. I'll have a relationship with Nora and Danny, but my real family is Valerie, Caleb, Riker, and the woman I love.

"Jane, how dare you—" Mom starts, but Dad puts up a hand.

"Fine. If this is what she wants, this is what she's going to get. We'll get along today for Nora's sake, and then you'll never have to talk to us again. But I hope you change your mind someday and repent."

I stare at him. "Well, then. I hope the same for you."

And with that, my parents leave the room.

"Are you okay?" Danny asks, striding toward me with Keeley right behind him. "I know this is the first time we've talked in, what, ten years, but I do care. Nora loves you. That means I do too. You're family." For the first time since Danny entered the room, I really look at him. He's still a little lanky for twenty-two, but it works, somehow, and he's got a bit of a Harry Styles thing going with his longish brown hair and sharp jawline. But it's something about his presence that just puts all of my last worries at ease. I can see him just *fitting* with Nora.

I smile at him, pulling him into a hug. "Thank you, Danny. Be good to my sister."

He pulls back. "I promise I will."

"Good," Keeley drawls, over my shoulder. "If you aren't, I'll break your kneecaps."

Danny laughs. "If that happens, I'll let you."

"But really, are you okay?" Keeley asks, her fingertips grazing my wrist.

"Surprisingly yes," I say, threading our fingers together. "I've been so afraid of this conversation, but standing up for myself was incredibly empowering."

"We've got your back." Danny grins. "I need to go check on a few things, but can Nora and I come visit you this spring? We're skipping the honeymoon with school starting back up in a week, but we were thinking spring break in Disneyland if we can afford it."

And now I know what I'm getting them as a late wedding present.

"Fuck yes," Keeley says. "I know where all the good food is."

"Sounds great," he says, before leaving the room.

"He's actually pretty legit," Keeley says. "Your sister told him you might be in trouble, and he came to find me immediately. Perks of being famous. I guess I'm easy to spot."

"I'm glad you came." Doing things on my own is overrated.

Keeley laughs. "But you weren't in trouble, were you? You standing up for yourself is a good look. I love it."

"I love *you*," I say, pulling her closer to me. "Thank you for coming with me today."

"I love you too," she says. "And I wouldn't miss this for the world. You're stuck with me, Jane Mercer."

As we head to our seats and the string quartet begins to play a sneaky cover of a Pitbull song that was arranged for *Bridgerton*, I don't think being stuck with Keeley sounds so bad at all. After the confrontation with my parents, I'm sad, but it would be so easy to focus on the shell of a relationship I've just lost, instead of everything I've gained by being true to myself.

I'm proud of standing my ground.

I cry during the ceremony, because of course I do. Now that I know Nora is okay, I'm able to be happy for her. I see the way Danny looks at her, like she's the most precious thing in the world, and I hope it means they're going to be okay. Even if they're not, I meant it when I said I will always have a safe place for her.

My parents hardly acknowledge us during the reception, choosing instead to stay busy and chat with everyone but our table, where Keeley and I have landed with some of my cousins and Nora's friends from high school who aren't a part of the church crowd. It stings a little, not being with my family, but I'm glad I get to be here to support my baby sister on what is hopefully the happiest day of her life. Still, she and Danny stop by while they do their lap, and I mean every word of my heartfelt congratulations.

But later, when the dancing opens up, Keeley and I don't care about where we are. We take to the floor together, wrapped in each other's arms, until the countdown to midnight brings the night to a sparkling end.

EPILOGUE

Keeley

FOUR MONTHS LATER

On a sunny Sunday in April, the entire music industry, dressed in their finest, crams themselves into the Carrington Theater for the RECORD awards.

I keep my hand on the small of Jane's back as we navigate the crowd mingling in the entry to find our seats. She's practically glowing in a gorgeous vintage piece we found at the boutique we took Nora to, a gold halter-top gown that shows off a tantalizing amount of freckled skin on her shoulders and back. After months together, even the most innocent touch to Jane's body gives me butterflies.

It's fitting that this is where we celebrated Jane's success at the *Into the Dragon Realm* premiere almost two years ago. Jane looks over at me and smiles.

"You ready?" she asks.

I laugh. "I'm not the one who's nominated!"

She shrugs. "I'm not nervous. I'm under no illusion that I'm going to win."

"Don't self-reject," Caleb says, elbowing her from her other side. Originally, Glitter Bats weren't expecting an invitation, since we've never been nominated for a RECORD as a group. I was only supposed to be here as Jane's date, not an invited guest.

But after Tonya sold "Hollow" to a new television adaptation of the hottest YA fantasy novel, *More to Say* crawled back up the charts. And with it, a bit more of the spotlight shined on Riker. He took to the attention like a flower to sunlight.

Not that we saw a dime of the royalties from that boost, but our plans are in motion to fix that. We've kept things quiet, for now, and we signed with a record label who is willing to help us make a new album and eventually rerecord our first three—legally and maintaining all of our rights.

We're waiting to make any announcements, though, because we've been in the news again. This time, because Landon Banks is under investigation by the FBI for fraud. He's poised to lose everything, just as we're on the edge of taking everything back.

Revenge is sweet.

"I'm not self-rejecting. I'm setting realistic expectations," Jane says primly. I worry, still, that she doesn't know how amazing she is.

Guess I'll just keep reminding her until she does.

Valerie weaves her way back to us from a cluster of her *Epic Theme Song* coworkers and frowns. "Where the hell is Riker?" She tosses her hair, now longer but back to its signature pink, and starts scanning the crowd.

"He got stuck at the press," I drawl suggestively.

"Oh, Mary Kate is here? I should have said hi before bolting past everyone!" Valerie says. Even though the press has cooled down since she and Caleb got married, she still gives them a wide berth these days.

Caleb leans over to us, lowering his voice. "You ever think those two will actually date, or do you think it's just going to be flirting for the next twenty years?"

I laugh. As the tallest in the group other than Maddox himself, I'm probably the only one who can spot Riker's topknot across the crowd. Mary Kate is close to the end of the press line, and he's got the pretty reporter laughing and smiling.

"Do we really want to be those couples who pressure their single friends to find someone?" Jane asks gently.

I shrug. "I don't know. Riker insists it's just flirting, but, like, just look at them when they're together and tell me you don't think there's something there."

I don't know that I've ever seen Riker light up like that without a guitar in his hands. Soft, unguarded, full of joy. And after everything Mary Kate did for Jane, I can't imagine a person I would trust more with Riker's happiness.

But they're both adults, and time will have to tell. I have no interest in meddling in Riker's affairs, even if he never extended the same courtesy to me . . . not that I'm mad about the result. I wink over my shoulder at Jane.

"We should find our seats without him. People are starting to trickle in," Valerie says.

"Eh, he's coming this way," I say. After a few minutes, Riker finally joins us, still grinning.

"How's MK?" Caleb asks.

"She's great!" Riker says; then his brows rise, and he clears his throat. "I mean, I talked to a lot of different journalists."

"Sure you did, buddy," Valerie says, patting his jacketed arm placatingly.

Riker spins to Jane, eyes theatrically wide. "So! Janey! Are you going to drop the news in your acceptance speech?"

Jane smooths her hands over her gown. "I'm not going to win, and even if I did, I won't break the rules."

"But it would be so epic if you announced it like that!"

Caleb glances around nervously. "Keep it down, dude."

I get why he's anxious. Caleb has never been comfortable with media attention, and as soon as we tell the world we're taking back our masters *and* releasing a new album, it's going to cause quite a stir.

The bigger secret is that we're already hard at work. With the help of our new label, we found a studio for rent that's an easy drive from Jane's house . . . where I'm planning to move in after the lease on my condo ends next month. We've already gotten a cat, a massive orange tabby from the local shelter who we named Navel.

I still can't believe I'm lucky enough to have found the love of my life with one of my best friends. Being partners on top of friends and collaborators was a surprisingly easy transition. And there's been a *lot* of collaborating—we've made it through a good chunk of *Wanderlust* already, and it's been so rewarding to discover all the ways our sound has matured since we recorded the album as teens.

It's an exciting time. We got interrupted by Valerie's filming schedule for season four of *Epic Theme Song*, but we're hoping to get back to work as soon as possible. After the school year ends, Caleb is taking a sabbatical from his teaching job so we can continue recording and head out on the biggest tour we've ever planned. I know the sabbatical was a difficult decision, and any kind of announcement before the school year is up might derail his plans.

"Let's just get inside before we tell the whole world," I say.

Soon enough, we find our table and the night begins with drinks all around. There are the earliest awards and musical performances and even a couple of tributes, but finally, the category for Best Album: Visual Media is announced.

Jane said she wasn't nervous, but she grips my hand tightly on top of the table. At her other side, Riker places a hand on her shoulder.

The announcer for this category reads off the names, and then the drumroll begins.

"And the winner is . . . Jane Mercer, for *Into the Dragon Realm* season two!"

I turn to Jane, who is gaping with tears streaming down her face. "No. That's not . . . what?"

Caleb whoops, Valerie jumps up and starts clapping, and Riker whistles.

I scramble out of my chair and Jane pulls me in for a quick kiss. As we part, she blinks rapidly, frozen.

Riker pats her on the shoulder. "Get down there, Janey!"

"Right. Oh my god."

Jane scrambles to weave around the tables and make it to the stage, pausing in gratitude as people congratulate her along the way. When she gets up to the microphone, I can tell it's sinking in. The smile on her face is as bright as a supernova; only the vastness of space would be large enough to contain her joy.

God, I love this woman.

Jane thanks the announcer and takes the crystal statuette as she tugs her phone out of the top of her dress. The room laughs.

"Umm, hi, everyone. I really wasn't expecting to win tonight, so you'll have to bear with me while I try to make sense of the speech I wrote in my Notes app this morning."

Everyone laughs again.

"Well, I first want to thank our showrunners and producers, Kate Taylor and Jordan Tyler, for trusting me to make the music of *Into the Dragon Realm*. This is such a special project, and I'm so lucky to get to be a part of it. Thank you to Angel Cruz, my engineer, for teaching me everything I know about soundboards and having excellent taste in coffee. Kyle Harris, Finn Lewis, Josie Ramirez, True Reynolds, the rest of the cast, and naturally, Rose

Carrington, thank you for singing my songs!" And then she groans self-deprecatingly. "Oh! And thank you to Jordan and Kyle for pushing me to finally hire another music producer for season three so I could find some work-life balance again." Laughter echoes throughout the room. "And to the rest of my team . . ."

As she continues on to thank all of the musicians and possibly the entire cast and crew, I glance around at the rest of the table. Valerie and Caleb are hand in hand, beaming at the stage. Riker is crying as much as I am.

"And to Glitter Bats, oh my gosh, I wouldn't be here if we hadn't been so determined to become a rock band when we were just kids. You are my best friends and my family and the most talented people I know. Valerie Quinn, Caleb Sloane, Riker Maddox, and of course, my love, Keeley Cunningham." She sniffs, her eyes locking on mine. "Keeley, I adore you, and I'm so grateful that you're in my life."

I can't believe the woman I love just declared herself on live TV. We've been more open about our relationship—hell, we walked the red carpet together—but it still feels unbelievably incredible that this is happening.

As I watch Jane hurry backstage as the music plays, I'm overcome with pride for my talented girlfriend. Maybe it took a while for us to be honest and find our way to each other, but that road was worth it.

I wouldn't change a thing, because it brought me to her.

Not only do we get to share our lives together, but we get to share music, this thing that is so incredibly important to the both of us. We get to fight for creative freedom together. We get to make art with our chosen family.

And we have a lot of work ahead of us, but it's going to be worth every moment.

With all the plans on the horizon for the Glitter Bats, I know I'll get to do what I love at her side, and that makes me the luckiest person in the world. We have albums to record, a world tour to plan, and hopefully, so much more music to write.

Beyond that, I can't wait to figure out what forever looks like.

Together.

ACKNOWLEDGMENTS

Everyone says writing your second published book is harder than the first, and I get it now. It's incredibly challenging to work on one project while its predecessor is launching! (Some days, I honestly couldn't remember where a conversation or event happened in the Glitter Bats time line.) But to quote an enthusiastic Elle Woods, "We did it!"—and I truly mean *we*, because I could not have done this alone.

The team at Berkley made this book a reality. To my editor, Liz Sellers, thank you for championing another Glitter Bats romance. You helped me shape a very rough draft into a story I'm proud of, and I'm incredibly grateful for your enthusiasm and insight. Thank you to my marketing and publicity team, Anika Bates and Chelsea Pascoe, for all of your effort and dedication in launching my work into the world. Carolina Fuenmayor, thank you for another romantic, dreamy cover! Erin Galloway, Jin Yu, and Craig Bunn, thank you for making my first-ever author event so special. And to everyone else on the Berkley team who has worked on my books, please know how deeply I appreciate all of your time and talent. I also want to thank the amazing team at Penguin Random House Audio and the incredible narrators for bringing my characters to life—audiobooks are so special, and I feel so lucky to get to hear other people voice my stories in such a meaningful way.

To my absolute rock star of a literary agent, Samantha Fabien, I can't even begin to thank you for everything you do for me. I'm so honored to have you in my corner! My publishing experience wouldn't be the same without your guidance, strategy, and kindness, and I'm so excited to see what stories we get to tell together next. I also want to thank the rest of the wonderful team at Root Literary for their continued support. I'm proud to be a Root author.

To my film agent, Hannah Vaughn, and the rest of the team at Gersh Books: thank you for believing my books have the potential to make it to screen. Getting to work with you is a dream come true.

Writing this book was a whirlwind, but a couple of people stepped in to give *For Our Next Song* an early read: K. M. Enright and Hailey Harlow, thank you for taking the time to review that draft and reassure me that I didn't have to rewrite the whole damn thing. You literally saved my sanity when I was careening into a full-blown panic.

For good reason, I dedicated this book to the Guillotines: Britt, Tracy, Rae, Alyssa, Koren, Sam, Jenn, Kalyn, and Ashley. Your friendship and advice (and endless pet photos) have sustained me, and I'm grateful for our writing group every day. This journey would have been so much lonelier without you.

Launching your first book into the world feels like stepping into the unknown. Without my January 2025 romance debuts—Tara Tai, Amy Buchanan, Erin Connor, Shameez Patel, Kat Mackenzie, Heather McBreen, and Emma Theriault—I'm sure I would have lost my mind. I'm so glad we are on this journey together, and I am in awe of your talent. I can't wait to read the stories you tell next!

I'm so grateful to all of the incredibly kind and talented authors who took the time to read *For One Night Only* and provide such lovely blurbs: Jennifer Hennessy, K. M. Enright, Jenna Levine, Timothy Janovsky, Jenny L. Howe, and Courtney Kae. You all rock!

Thank you to the Berkletes for continuing to be a source of support and encouragement. I'm so glad to be one of you! And many authors were part of events that launched my debut into the world. Thank you to Sarah Hawley, Ilana Long, Heather McBreen, Jo Segura, Bethany Bennett, Anita Kelly, Amy Buchanan, and Erin Connor—I'm honored that we got to talk books together!

To all of the readers, friends, and family who come to my book events, thank you for showing up! And thank you to the independent bookstores who have welcomed me as a baby author and helped me celebrate my books, including Auntie's Bookstore, Grand Gesture Books, Page 2 Books, and Third Place Books (at Emerald City Comic Con, what a dream!). I also want to extend a thank-you to the librarians who have stocked my work and recommended it to their patrons. You are such an important part of the literary community, and we need you now more than ever!

Thank you to my family for encouraging me to pursue my dreams. I won't apologize for the content of these books, but I also won't hold it against you if you never read them. (Really!)

To Andrew: thank you for always listening to me ramble about these characters in my head, and for supporting me through this long, exciting, anxious author journey. Without you, I would have given up on this dream before it ever became a reality. I'm so lucky that the love of my life is my best friend.

And to you, dear reader, thank you for spending time with Jane, Keeley, and the rest of the Glitter Bats. Rock on!